# THE HOLMES FACTOR

*Recent Titles by Brian Freemantle from Severn House*


*Sherlock and Sebastian Holmes*

THE HOLMES INHERITANCE
THE HOLMES FACTOR


*Charlie Muffin*

DEAD MEN LIVING
KINGS OF MANY CASTLES


AT ANY PRICE
BETRAYALS
DEAD END
DIRTY WHITE
GOLD
HELL'S PARADISE
ICE AGE
THE IRON CAGE
THE KREMLIN CONSPIRACY
THE MARY CELESTE
O'FARRELL'S LAW
TARGET
TWO WOMEN

# THE HOLMES
# FACTOR

# Brian Freemantle

This first world edition published in Great Britain 2005 by
SEVERN HOUSE PUBLISHERS LTD of
9–15 High Street, Sutton, Surrey SM1 1DF.
This first world edition published in the USA 2005 by
SEVERN HOUSE PUBLISHERS INC of
595 Madison Avenue, New York, N.Y. 10022.

British Library Cataloguing in Publication Data

Freemantle, Brian
    The Holmes factor
    1.  Intelligence officers - Great Britain - Fiction
    2.  Espionage, British - Russia (Federation) - Fiction
    3.  Russia - History - 1904-1914 - Fiction
    4.  Spy stories
    I.  Title
    823.9'14 [F]


    ISBN 0-7278-6207-3 (cased)
    ISBN 0-7278-9137-5 (paper)

Typeset by Palimpsest Book Production Ltd.,
Polmont, Stirlingshire, Scotland.
Printed and bound in Great Britain by
MPG Books Ltd., Bodmin, Cornwall.

To Ted and Fiona, with thanks

# Author's Note

As in the first Sebastian Holmes adventure,[*] I have used for a communicating code between him and his father, Sherlock Holmes, the secret Winchester College language known as Notions. This is not a fictional creation but an officially recognized argot evolved over the 600-year-old existence of Britain's oldest collegiate school, and is sufficiently extensive to have its own 319-page dictionary. I have also drawn upon a supplementary idiom of the school known as *ziph*, in which a word is disguised by doubling its vowels and inserting a medial 'g'.

[*] *The Holmes Inheritance*

# One

Sebastian Holmes was eagerly anticipating that evening's encounter, the arrangements already in place – the same discreet St James's club with its private entrance, doubtless the same, or matchingly similar, private dining salon, the same summoning politician. It could only be another, much-hoped-for assignment. That was certainly Sebastian's easy deduction. His still reluctant father's assessment, too.

Sebastian had hoped the resistance to his following, almost literally, in the footsteps of the legendary Sherlock Holmes would have lessened more than it appeared to have done during their shared Swiss pilgrimage to Meiringen and his mother's grave. It was a pilgrimage that had extended beyond their homage at the grave of the dedicated, doctor-qualified nurse who'd patiently restored to health his exhausted, close-to-death father after that final, fateful physical battle with the despicable Professor Moriarty on the Reichenbach Falls.

The Meiringen expedition was the longest continuous period Sebastian had spent with the man he had for little more than a year known to be his biological father, an intense period, but too brief properly to prepare for – or prevent – the strain upon his father. Both shrines had clearly and profoundly affected Sherlock Holmes to the furthest extremity of a pendulum's swing.

At the graveside, his father had stood, head bowed, un-moving, totally immune from any outside intrusion, his mind and memory in another time, a time he'd later, broken-voiced, confessed to have been the happiest of a hazardous life from which he was so determined to escape that he'd wanted the world to believe that he, as well as Moriarty, had perished in their Reichenbach confrontation. Had even had his brother,

Mycroft, transfer to Switzerland the assets of his considerable estate, intending to live there in anonymous retirement with a woman whom, after a lifetime of apparent misogyny, he'd loved to the exclusion of everything and everyone. And he'd been proud to acknowledge that devotion, as well as his parenthood of Sebastian. The inscription etched into the white marble headstone read:

> Matilde Huber, beloved companion of Sherlock Holmes
> and mother of Sebastian, cruelly taken, July 16, 1890.
> Forever missed, forever mourned, forever loved.

It was the minimal simplicity of that inscription in the river-valley cemetery that moved Sebastian close to the tears he never believed himself capable of shedding after an adolescence and short adulthood of believed abandonment, a ward of his attentive uncle. Sebastian hadn't cried though, just as wrongly imagining, because of that belief, that his hitherto dispassionate, glacially remote father would interpret his doing so as weakness, a failing he imagined, despite their brief acquaintanceship, Sherlock Holmes would despise.

That, of course, was before they'd gone to the spray-soaked ledge beside the infamous falls, upon which Sherlock Holmes had grappled for the last time in a life or death struggle with his criminal adversary. And where Sebastian had witnessed the emotional near collapse of the older man at the ingrained memory of that fateful event. Sherlock Holmes's visible distress began as they climbed the mountain path, the occasional word disjointed, his clothes and face soaked by the perspiration Sebastian at first mistook to be from the effort of the ascent on such a warm spring morning. By the time they'd reached the actual ledge, the rhetorical mumbling had become even more bewildering until Sebastian realized that his father was actually reliving the fight, even to repeating the very words they'd grunted and hissed as they'd fought. And then the movements came, Sherlock Holmes oblivious to his son's desperate pleading not to venture out again on to the slippery ledge, twisting, ducking, raising and lowering his arms against remembered blows and thrusts, coming perilously close – too close – to the very edge of the water-thundering abyss. And then there'd been the scream, an agonized cry of terror. Sebastian had still to decide – not daring to ask – whether it was the remembered echo of his father's cry, imagining himself the loser, or a mimicry of Moriarty's as the villain plunged to oblivion.

Sherlock Holmes had needed Sebastian's assistance to regain the safety of the sloping mountainside, and it took nearly thirty minutes for the tremors to subside and for him to compose himself sufficiently to communicate in anything approaching a comprehensible manner. The first of those comprehensible words, incised forever in Sebastian's mind, had been: 'That damnable man haunts me in death as he pursued me in life.'

'You were the victor,' Sebastian reminded him.

'By the merest of chances. I was close to being done for, my strength gone. Moriarty slipped . . . could not regain his footing. He snatched out at my clothing, to take me with him. Would have done if, with the last ounce of any strength I retained, I had not managed to break his hold, in doing so to send him on his way . . .'

The shaking started again and Sebastian said: 'It was a mistake to have come here . . . to have opened a box that should have forever remained sealed.' It was only at that moment, distressed himself by what he'd seen, that Sebastian's concern began, that the draining recollections might lure his father back to the confounded narcotic habit from which the dedicated Dr Watson had over recent months so successfully weaned him.

'No!' Sherlock Holmes had refused, the strength of his voice underlining his gradual recovery. 'It was right that I should have come and even more necessary that you should have witnessed with your own eyes what you have just seen; perhaps gained some insight into the perpetual burdens that have to be carried in the life and profession I have followed all these years. You have not yet, thank God, encountered a nemesis the like of Moriarty. It is to prevent you from doing so that I am so opposed to your contemplating any sort of succession.'

'Sir!' protested Sebastian. 'I am not, nor ever will be,

presumptious enough to imagine myself worthy to be your successor . . .' He let in the meaningful pause, despising himself for the hypocrisy. 'But in giving that assurance, I trust you will not take as presumption my reminder that since our coming together you have been at the greatest pains to guide me in every aspect of the art of amateur detection, in which you have attained such worldwide recognition.'

The unarguable fact momentarily silenced Sherlock Holmes, who remained stretched out, as Sebastian was, on the sun-dappled mountain grass, the roaring falls behind them no longer loud enough to smother their intimate exchanges. At last Sherlock Holmes had confessed: 'Mine is the fault . . . the belated shame. And the arrogance. I have heard from my brother, inferred from you, sir, how you believed yourself to have been so badly treated – abandoned – by me in my agony of Matilde's death at the very moment of her giving you your separate life . . .'

There was another lapse into silence, into which Sebastian had not intruded: there was no longer any physical indication, but Sebastian recognized that his father was confronting another unlaid demon.

Haltingly Sherlock Holmes resumed: 'I was bereft, cast adrift, by the loss of Matilde. I made every provision for you, denied you nothing, except that which I should not have denied you and which I now, finally, accept Matilde would have expected of me – for me to have acted properly as a father, not to have made my brother a surrogate. I am not a man accustomed to suffering mistakes, which makes it the more difficult for me to acknowledge them. My telling you in as much detail as I have of all the cases and investigations in which I have been involved, and the methods I employed to solve them, has been my ill-considered way of seeking your admiration, your forgive-ness . . .' There was a snorted, self-dismissive laugh. 'Mistake upon mistake! My misdirected clumsiness – my refusal openly to apologize, as I am apologizing now – has led you to believe I *wanted* you to be my successor, when the reality is that it is the very last vocation I wish for you.'

The open admission, on a day of unexpected admissions and revelations, had not shocked Sebastian, because there had already been sufficient indications of his father's feelings, but Sebastian was still disappointed. 'I believe I acquitted myself well on the one occasion I was called upon to perform a duty for my country.'

'Luck was in your corner, sir.'

'Has it never been in yours, sir?' Sebastian had not intended the stridency – certainly nothing verging upon a direct dispute after the obvious emotional turmoil his father had endured that very day – but an inherent legacy of an extended, self-defending education through the loneliness of Winchester and Cambridge and the Sorbonne and Heidelberg was instinctively to confront and overcome obstructive opposition rather than bend to it, even if that opposition was from someone as respected as Sherlock Holmes.

As unintended as it was, Sebastian's response had clearly jolted the older man. 'I was not minimizing what you achieved, for which you were rightly, if covertly, commended.'

'Nor did I intend any disrespect in my remark. I fear this day has included far more than was anticipated when it began.'

'Certainly more than I anticipated,' further conceded Sherlock Holmes. He'd stirred himself from the unaccustomed lounging position, agilely thrusting himself up one-handed from the ground. Standing upright, he looked in the direction of a distant Meiringen. 'I had thought to show you the apartment I'd taken for your mother and I. But I think there has been sufficient nostalgia. Perhaps another time.'

'Or perhaps not at all,' suggested Sebastian.

'Perhaps not,' agreed Sherlock Holmes. 'It doesn't take any great power of deduction to know you are anxious to get back to London to discover the reason behind Mycroft's intriguing telegram asking for your return date.'

'I would very much like to respond to it,' admitted Sebastian.

'It is your intention to follow my profession whether I agree such a course or not, isn't it?'

'I think it is one for which I am fitted.'

'I don't, not yet. There's more, much more, for you to learn.'

'I've proved myself well able to learn,' said Sebastian.

'I'm not talking of books or weary lectures from rote-reciting tutors.'

His father had never been to university, Sebastian remembered. 'Neither am I, not any longer.'

Sebastian Holmes shrugged off the unwanted recollection of that revealing day as, instinctively he hoped, he checked his murky surroundings as he stepped briskly out along Pall Mall from the Diogenes Club, in which he had established quarters after realizing it was impractical for he and his father to live together at 221b Baker Street. Despite urgings to the contrary, Sebastian believed his father had recognized as quickly and as surely as he had that, practically strangers as they were, it was impossible for them to share the same accommodation.

Sebastian's rooms at the Diogenes were slightly larger than those of his bachelor uncle, but still as spartan as Mycroft's. Sebastian's peripatetic existence had thus far only accustomed him to university and public-school lodgings, which had, perhaps surprisingly, not instilled in him any desire for the comfortable, even luxurious, accommodation he could well have afforded from the fortune bestowed upon him by his then unknown father at his coming of age two years earlier.

Domiciled in the same premises as they were, Sebastian had expected he and his uncle to have gone together to meet Winston Churchill, but the note in his pigeonhole at the so-familiar porter's lodge had warned of his uncle being delayed, as official Permanent Secretary, at a cabinet meeting at 10 Downing Street. Sebastian was to proceed ahead and present his uncle's apologies if any delay were protracted: Sebastian's admission to the venue was assured. Apologies to whom? Sebastian wondered. The purpose, as he understood it, of the forthcoming encounter was dinner – and who knew what else? – with Winston Churchill, who would surely have been present as First Lord of the Admiralty at any cabinet meeting? An unanswerable question, accepted Sebastian, who remained unfamiliar with the innermost government labyrinths in which he was, so willingly, becoming enmeshed. His father was right in some respects: there were still things he needed to learn. Of one thing, though, Sebastian was assured. From his previous encounters, Sebastian knew there would be more than adequate libation, although the Laurent Perrier champagne, Churchill's favourite, had to remain untouched until it was sampled and approved by the man himself.

Sebastian was glad of his cloak, the silk-sheened topper too: the day had been as warm, warmer maybe, as he and his father had enjoyed in Switzerland, but here in London at night the chill had settled, creating the customary, swirling, pea-souper, acrid to the throat, stinging to the eyes, in places so thick the fog enshrouded the gas-mantle lamps, rendering even this well-established thoroughfare as darkly unwelcoming as the meanest unlit side alleys, from which whispered invitations to paradise came from the loitering, indistinct dollymops. Neither the enclosing night nor the unseen loiterers and skirt-lifting habitués caused Sebastian any discomfort, although he was reassured by the swordstick that had been his father's gift, and unquestionably had saved his life in an ambush on his first – and so far only – assignment. Almost automatically he minimally withdrew the blade, satisfied with the reassuringly easy release of the fastening mechanism.

The shutter of the private entrance to the gentlemen's club withdrew at once to his summons, the nod of recognition coming from the custodian before Sebastian completed his identification.

'Third to your right, sir,' said the man, at Sebastian's entry.

The same meeting place as before, when he'd been offered the American assignment, Sebastian immediately remembered. The long corridor – so long he was unsure of its faraway ending despite the frequent gas-lamp illumination – stretched out ahead of him, the entrances to the private salons gained by separate, individual stairways. Sebastian climbed un-hurriedly, sure he was the first of his party: near the stair-top, although from some distance away, Sebastian believed he detected a female sound, possibly an easy laugh. Perhaps it wasn't such a strictly reserved gentlemen's club after all. Or rather, more strictly and privately reserved than he'd imag-ined. Perhaps one of the lingering whores outside had found reciprocal warmth for the night

The room he entered was familiar from before and, as before, the table was already prepared, the damask spotless, the crystal glittering, the decanters and bottles laid out – the Laurent Perrier in its iced cooler – a necessary warming fire flickering in the grate. Sebastian cast aside his cloak on the convenient, button-backed Chesterfield, which matched the surrounding chairs, and was studying the leather-encased menu when he detected the light, ascending footsteps, the sound of a single person.

Sebastian was confident he concealed any physical sign of his surprise at the entry of his father, although he said: 'I was not expecting you to be here tonight, sir.'

'Then you did not count the table settings,' replied Sherlock Holmes, casting his own cloak on top of his son's. 'Observe the basic rule, always look to the obvious.'

Why hadn't his uncle told him! thought Sebastian, exasperated. But why, by the same token, hadn't his father?

'Mycroft might be late. There's a meeting—'

'I know,' Sherlock Holmes cut him off, looking at the offered drinks. 'From the colour of that decanter . . .'

'It's a single malt,' said Sebastian, in attempted weak recovery, wishing at once that he hadn't attempted it.

'Why don't we see if yours is the correct deduction?' said the older man, the patronizing tone adding to Sebastian's discomfort.

Dutifully Sebastian poured whisky for both of them. As he did, his back to his father, he said: 'As you appear to be so well informed, you must already know the reason for this meeting?'

'Not its substance,' conceded Sherlock Holmes. 'But, after the American affair, I'll hazard that Churchill casts you as a useful attachment.'

'As one would an obedient dog?' said Sebastian, irritated by the disparagement.

Sherlock Holmes smiled at his son's retort. 'I think you know well enough my judgement upon Mr Churchill. The fellow is an opportunist prepared to swop parties at a whim and with the same ease to pick up and drop people who are of use to him to further his ambition.'

'Isn't opportunism a trait common to most politicians?' questioned Sebastian.

'My interest is in only one. And your possible continuing involvement with him.'

A father's long-overdue concern for a neglected son, or jealousy at having become too recognizable to be offered the assignment himself? wondered Sebastian, discomfited by the recurring doubt since Churchill's initial approach, through his uncle. 'I have some experience of caring for myself.' Once more Sebastian regretted the words the moment he uttered them, conscious of the near-wince that replaced his father's smile.

'Then let us hope it serves you better than you clearly believe I have,' said his father, stiffly.

He'd totally mishandled the exchange, Sebastian recognized. It was immature to let linger the resentment of childhood and youth. For there to be any chance of a lasting union between them, he had to reach out to the man, as his father was clearly attempting to reach out to him, not sulk in a corner and expect the approach to be entirely from one direction. 'I owe you an apology, sir, which I humbly offer. My attitude and words are petulant and you are undeserving of any of it. You have my assurance it will not be continued or repeated.'

Sherlock Holmes's lean features softened. 'Which I accept, along with your apology. There is much adjustment needed from us both.'

'And more effort on my part,' further capitulated Sebastian.

He was relieved by renewed sound from the outside stairs, the sounds of more than one person this time. Winston Churchill led the entry, the larger figure of Mycroft Holmes towering closely behind, an overpowering shadow. Neither man was dressed for dinner, clearly not having had time to change, which was immediately confirmed by Churchill's dismissive apology. 'And the hansom horse was lame, I'll wager! Some champagne will restore our spirits.'

Sebastian at once recognized the déjà vu, accepting himself the dispenser as he had at their first encounter in this very room, alert to Churchill's careless choice and dispatch of their food order via the pulley-operated dumb waiter, impatient himself to discover the objective of the meeting. Before Sebastian sat at the table, Churchill was gesturing for a second bottle of champagne to be added to the order. After which there was a momentary, silent hiatus.

Churchill filled it with attempted beguile, by saying: 'Here we are again and here I am again, seeking the expertise of the renowned Holmes family!'

This time it was an unbeguiled Sebastian who winced. His father remained expressionless, unimpressed. Mycroft said: 'How so, sir?'

Could his uncle, the convenor of the gathering, be ignorant of its purpose? wondered Sebastian.

'The forthcoming war,' announced Churchill.

'As yet undeclared,' objected Sherlock Holmes, at once.

'Little more than a formality,' declared the Admiralty supremo, with customary intolerance at being questioned. 'Has any among us discerned anything from the Balkans to suggest that Europe is not a tinderbox?'

'Volcanos sometimes rumble but remain dormant,' said Sherlock Holmes, mixing the metaphor to make a point.

'Yours is an experience to which I will unquestioningly defer,' flattered Churchill. 'But I did not accept the doubtful poetry when our blinkered prime minister first recited what you've just paraphrased. Herbert Asquith is complacent of the danger, too preoccupied by Ireland: the cabinet is too reliant upon Lord Haldane's supposed ability accurately to interpret German intentions, particularly after his most recent fact-finding visit there. I subscribe to neither and acknowledge myself an outsider because of my contrary views . . .' The portly, pink-faced man fixed Sebastian with a direct stare. 'Views considerably strengthened by your success in exposing the extensive infiltration of potentially German-favouring American industrialists by Berlin intelligence agents.'

'That success has been acknowledged and is now in the past,' dismissed Sebastian, as disinterested in blandishments as his father. 'Shall we get beyond bad poetic analogy to the purpose of our being here tonight?'

As if timed, his question ended with the sound of the summons bell for their arriving food. As Sebastian, still observing his subservient role, rose to collect and distribute it, Winston Churchill said: 'While you're up, it would be

10

convenient to open the second bottle, don't you think?' And, as Sebastian put his chosen quail in front of him, Churchill said: 'And I think a little of that decanted claret to compliment such a dish.'

Before the man could begin eating, still at the dumb waiter, Sebastian prompted: 'The purpose of our being here, sir?'

'Russia,' announced Churchill.

Mycroft Holmes sat back in his chair, wine glass between both hands, nodding in understanding. Sherlock Holmes nodded too, in acknowledgement to his brother. Unembarrassed, Sebastian said as he resumed his seat: 'I'd appreciate a more fulsome explanation than that.'

It was Mycroft who responded. 'Austro-Hungary refers to Serbia as a "hornet's nest". If it moves against Serbia – which all the speculation is that it will – Russia has a treaty obligation to come in on the side of the Serbs . . .'

'Which will mean Russia mobilizing along the borders of Germany and Austria, which will give Berlin the territorial excuse it seeks to declare war, into which we will be drawn by *our* treaty obligations, one of which binds us to Russia,' took up Churchill. 'If Russia remains firm in the East, our undivided concentration can be upon a Western front. At the moment, unable as we are accurately to count our allies, we need to be assured of Russia's strength and commitment.'

'This is all hypothetical!' protested Sherlock Holmes.

'It's necessary defensive forethought,' rejected Churchill, helping himself to more claret before offering the decanter around the table.

'We have an embassy in St Petersburg,' said Sherlock Holmes. 'It's surely their function to assess the Russian strength?'

'I have no confidence in the assessments of an embassy which singularly failed to predict the attempted revolution against the Tsar in 1905 or the concessions that Nicholas II has been forced by civil unrest to concede since,' dismissed Churchill. 'I have the gravest doubts about the Russian empire. It was defeated in the Crimea and again in 1905 by the Japanese, losing too large a proportion of its naval fleet in the process and paving the way for that failed revolution of the same year.'

11

'What, precisely, are we considering?' pressed Sebastian. 'Russia's ability to conduct a European war or the very stability of the Romanov dynasty?'

'Possibly both,' answered Churchill. 'In my judgement they're intertwined, which brings forth a further complication.'

'Which is?' queried Sherlock Holmes.

'Tsarina Alexandra was the favourite granddaughter of our late and beloved Queen Victoria,' reminded Churchill. 'A personal, physical threat to the Romanov family, with a blood link to our own royal family, would be something greatly to occupy the British government. Maybe, even, affect its course of action in many ways.'

There was another silence around the table, all the plates set aside, food no longer of any interest.

Sherlock Holmes said: 'In this very room you entrusted my son with a mission, one he completed with great success against considerable odds. The remit then was comparatively simple; discover if indeed the Germans were deeply embedded and seeking further bedfellows among those in America who foresaw immense profit from a European conflict. This enterprise, which requires much clearer explanation still, for my satisfaction, is an altogether different set of conflicting circumstances. What – precisely – do you require?'

Churchill returned to his Laurent Perrier. 'A totally unbiased, independent assessment of the strengths and weaknesses of the Russian imperial family, balanced against the probability of Tsar Nicholas II successfully leading his armies to long-awaited victory in an international conflagration . . .' He paused. 'And an indication of German infiltration in the country would assist, too.'

'For the American episode, you were able to provide Sebastian with useful introductions,' persisted Sherlock Holmes. 'I, for my part, was able to recommend a very worthy New York policeman whose assistance proved lifesaving, for my son. What local assistance is there at hand on this occasion, should he even be minded to undertake such a mission?'

'A trusted acquaintance at the British embassy, from whom I am aware of its inadequacies,' responded Churchill, kindling the sizeable Havana cigar he'd habitually favoured since

12

his military involvement in Cuba during the Spanish-American war.

'In America, Sebastian, amply although unofficially funded from government coffers, posed as a potential investment banker to gain access to those industrialists and entrepreneurs dallying with the idea of supporting Germany in any conflict,' reminded Sherlock Holmes. 'What is to be his excuse and way of penetrating similar levels in Russia?'

There was an uncomfortable silence at a clearly unconsidered question. Mycroft said: 'What chances, Winston, of your gaining Sebastian accreditation to the *Morning Post*, through which you've earned well in the past?'

Churchill's face cleared. 'A capital idea. Easily achieved, I'm confident. And maybe there will be information which I could, anonymously of course, turn into something approaching a public warning!'

He was overdue intervening on his own behalf, Sebastian recognized. 'I was seriously endangered – a brave British military intelligence officer lost his life – through conflicting enterprises mounted by separate ministries here. What likelihood is there of other interested British parties carrying out the same enquiries you seek from me?'

The question visibly disconcerted the politician. 'I do not know: can give no guarantee against your encountering such a situation again.'

'You are presenting a wide and uncertain remit,' accused Mycroft.

'Which I would not propose if I did not consider the urgency of the situation required it,' assured Churchill. 'I do not seek an immediate response. My only urging is that you carry with you in your consideration the awareness that you are being asked to perform a possibly invaluable service for your country.'

The same moral blackmail as before, Sebastian recognized, isolating the final déjà vu.

# Two

Although he had virtually decided upon accepting Churchill's unknown proposal prior to having it put before him by the politician, Sebastian Holmes acknowledged, as they talked in such power-backed and influential surroundings, that the task this time was far more formidable than that with which he had been entrusted in America, an awareness that quickly strengthened upon even closer examination and more forceful objection from his father. The dispute came to its head the very next evening at 221b Baker Street, which enabled gathering the additional and valued contribution from Dr John Watson, Sherlock Holmes's long-time chronicler. A further anticipation was that their meal would be prepared by Mrs Hudson, Sherlock Holmes's dedicated housekeeper.

Sebastian was already dispensing cocktails when Mycroft entered, almost an hour late. Sherlock Holmes had clearly rehearsed for such tardiness, poised for the moment his brother accepted his whisky, to declare: 'I am most vigorously against this enterprise and the dangers inherent in it. Sebastian is being asked to go, virtually without any introductions or assistance, into a situation which, if we are to accept Churchill's word, our own diplomatic mission is incapable of interpreting. How can Sebastian conceivably do any better than our established diplomats, with the access open to them?'

'Are you forgetting the shipboard acquaintances I made during my outward voyage to America aboard the *Lusitania*?' demanded Sebastian, hopefully as prepared as his objecting father.

'The Imperial Russian Grand Duke Alexei Orlov,' acknowledged Sherlock Holmes. 'Whom I identified to you then to be the head of the Okhrana, the Tsar's secret police. Is that

14

your ploy, to knock on the man's door and ask to be shown all the police files?'

'His was a social outing, showing his daughter America,' said Sebastian. The enigmatically beautiful Princess Olga, he remembered. How different his mission might have been had it been she with whom he'd become romantically involved, rather than another princess.

'Don't disappoint me with that belief!' rejected Sherlock Holmes. 'The daughter provided an excuse for the journey. The man was obviously there on some official business.'

'He relaxed sufficiently in my presence indiscreetly to complain about the influence within the Russian court of some mystic . . .'

'Rasputin,' Mycroft supplied. 'Gregory Rasputin. 'I, too, have been busy today. I fear Winston overstretched his denigration last night. Our embassy in St Petersburg does not to my reading appear as indolent or as inefficient as he contended. There have been several telegrams about this man. The Tsarevich Alexei suffers a blood condition: it will not clot, if he suffers a break in the skin. If there is a contusion, there is painful internal haemorrhaging. This mystic appears to have gained considerable sway within the court because of his ability to quieten the child and ease his discomfort.'

'More gossip and tittle tattle,' dismissed Sherlock Holmes. 'A mad monk is going to contribute little to any understanding of the political situation in the Russian court. And what hope have you of re-establishing an aquaintanceship with your Grand Duke – that he'll even be minded to acknowledge you?'

'I won't know that until I try to re-establish such an acquaintanceship, will I?' responded Sebastian, curtly.

'The Tsar is wholly reliant upon the army, as he was in 1905,' offered Dr Watson, whose own career as a military surgeon in Afghanistan had been cut short by injury. 'Then they obeyed his Bloody Sunday order to open fire on a protesting procession. But no army favours shooting its own people. And there was serious discontent in the decimated navy, with the mutiny, on the *Potemkin*, of the Black Sea fleet.'

'And we must not forget the palace connection,' urged Mycroft. The discussion was interrupted by Mrs Hudson's summons, which the men promptly obeyed. Sherlock Holmes carved the beef, which Sebastian judged better than that he had eaten the previous night. He decided his father's Margaux was the better claret, too.

After Mrs Hudson, dutifully complimented, quit the room, Sherlock Holmes said: 'Is it a factor as important as Churchill indicated?'

'I'm repeating well-informed gossip,' admitted the Cabinet Secretary. 'There's been no formal discussion, but the situation is complicated by the Tsarina's German birth, which allows questions of loyalties and allegiances.' He looked between father and son. 'Here our embassy has been lacking. I am not betraying any confidences in telling you that both the government and the palace would benefit from guidance upon the imperial family's personal safety.'

'Are you talking sanctuary?' demanded Sherlock Holmes, presciently.

'It could become a consideration,' disclosed Mycroft.

'I ask again, what possibility is there of Sebastian gaining access to that sort of echelon from which he might obtain any reliable insight?' said Sherlock Holmes.

'To which I make the same reply as before,' said Sebastian, directing the decanter around the table. 'We won't know until I go there and try.'

'According to what Holmes has told me of last night's gathering, reference was made to service to one's country,' recalled Dr Watson. 'The interest of the King surely qualifies as that, does it not?'

Sherlock Holmes directed a sharp look of annoyance at the man from whom he always expected unquestioned support. 'Embassies provide services for their countries: that is their function,' he insisted. He'd done little more than rearrange the food upon his plate.

Sebastian had eaten only sufficient to avoid Mrs Hudson's wrath. Pushing his plate away, he said, flatly: 'I wish to undertake this assignment.'

'As you always intended,' challenged his father.

'As I always intended,' agreed Sebastian. 'Which renders pointless any further discussion.'

'No it does not,' refused the partially resigned Sherlock Holmes, although looking at his brother. 'Sebastian must be assured the protection and assistance of the embassy. Methods of communication must be decided upon . . .' Apparently reminded of his being briefly excluded from American exchanges between Mycroft and Sebastian, he added: 'Communication to which I am admitted. And not conducted in the code of that arcane secret language of Winchester College. Matters of such import should not be discussed in schoolboy slang.'

'All British subjects are assured the protection and assistance of their embassy . . .' began Mycroft, to be almost immediately silenced by his brother.

'Don't patronize me, sir! You know damned well what I am saying – know the sort of protection and assistance I have in mind!'

Everyone around the table was surprised at the sudden vehemence.

Mycroft said: 'I do not seek to patronize. I'll ask you to bear in mind that this enterprise is unofficial: Sebastian will again be working as Winston's emissary, not that of the British government. I'll discover from Winston the identity of his promised embassy introduction. Perhaps some method of exchange could be established through him?'

'I would have expected you to have had a name already,' criticized Sherlock Holmes.

'We have only just received Sebastian's agreement,' Mycroft pointed out. 'By this time tomorrow I shall have a name.'

'And what of remuneration?' persisted the detective. 'The labourer is worthy of his hire. Or is it Churchill's expectation that the Holmes family, whose expertise he claims so fervently to admire, perform services to their country from its own purse?'

'There are many who do,' retorted Mycroft.

'And a lot of them are reduced to penury by so doing, I've little doubt,' came back the other man. 'If Sebastian is to be employed, he should be financially rewarded. That's the principle by which I've always worked.'

Sebastian's concentration was not primarily upon the

exchange but upon Dr Watson, whose concentration, in turn, was entirely upon Sherlock Holmes. Bringing himself back to the dispute, Sebastian said: 'I always understood you to be satisfied by an honorarium reflecting the success of your endeavours, a procedure I'd be content to continue.'

'We'll need Churchill's assurance on that. And upon the reimbursement of expenditure,' insisted Sherlock Holmes.

'Winston is not personally a wealthy man,' warned Mycroft. 'And this is, as I've already made clear, a private matter.'

'I see no cause for Churchill's difficulties to become ours,' said Sherlock Holmes.

'I will pass on your feelings,' promised Mycroft.

The near acrimony of the dinner-table discussion created an uncertain atmosphere they carried with them when they withdrew for port, brandy and cigars. Sebastian immediately began manoeuvring around the room with his passing of decanters and humidors, and without difficulty succeeded in isolating Dr Watson from his father and uncle.

'It's not good,' announced the doctor, responding to the unasked question before Sebastian spoke.

'You think he's relapsed?' asked Sebastian.

'There's every indication of his having done so,' confirmed the older man. 'Unrestrained, irrational belligerence was always an early indication.'

'He's certainly displaying an abundance of that,' agreed Sebastian. He looked around the room. 'I would have expected some evidence of his use . . . a hypodermic . . . ?'

'If your father does not want his going back to his old ways to be discovered, a pack of bloodhounds and the combined resources of Scotland Yard would not uncover a grain of evidence,' said Dr Watson. 'I truly thought I – and he – had the situation tightly in check.'

'I know the cause,' revealed Sebastian, succinctly recounting the experience at Meiringen.

Dr Watson listened, head bowed, nodding in agreement. 'An ill-chosen expedition.'

'A fact I did not realize until too late. How long before you can reverse the setback?'

The doctor shrugged. 'Impossible to say. He first has to

acknowledge his mistake, which is always a difficult task for your father. Everyone of his inclination insists it is not a dependency but a relaxation easily controlled.'

'Would it help if I refused this Russian enterprise after all?'

'Absolutely not!' refused the other man, at once. 'Your father knows *why* he is behaving thus. Your wanting to undertake the mission is merely his excuse to vent his discomfort and ill humour. He would interpret your withdrawal as pity, an unthinkable condescension for someone like Sherlock Holmes to bear. It would most likely drive him deeper into his method of attempted escape than help him out of it. Far better, far more likely to help him, to go to Russia and involve him from afar as much as possible.'

'Then that's what I'll do,' agreed Sebastian.

'I have known your father for many years now,' said Dr Watson. 'I believe his concerns for your safety to be completely genuine and paramount in his thinking. It's the manner in which he is expressing that concern that is ill chosen.'

'You don't have to apologize for him, sir.'

'It was not an apology,' corrected Dr Watson. 'It was an attempt to remove a regrettable doubt I believe I have detected in some of your exchanges with your father.'

'You are sometimes an unsettling observer, Dr Watson.'

'My intention is to be an honest one. My understanding of its recent history is that Russia is a most volatile place of conflicting passions and persuasions. Take every care, Sebastian. One thing of which I am totally sure is that your father could not endure harm befalling you. There would be no recovery for him then.'

'Then I have additional cause to succeed as well as to be careful.'

'God's speed and protection.'

They rejoined the brothers before their separation could arouse suspicion. The cigars and the port decanter were almost exhausted, and the desultory conversation also, with little left for any of them to say. Sebastian thought there was further indication of his father's relapse in the older man's visible fatigue.

In the hansom on their way back to Pall Mall, Sebastian

said: 'I do not wish to impose financial demands upon Churchill in advance of my going to Russia. You are well enough aware of my means to know that I do not need any agreed terms of remuneration. It is something well left until my return.'

'I had no intention of troubling Winston upon the matter at this stage,' disclosed Mycroft. 'There'll be an accounting when the circumstances are right.'

In his renewed anticipation, Sebastian was anxious to get to St Petersburg as soon as possible, but observed one of the many edicts of his father, that no case should be embarked upon without the maximum possible preparation. To that end, he immersed himself for a day and a half in the magnificent reading room of the British Library in the British Museum, acquainting himself with the so recently celebrated 300-year rule of the Romanov dynasty. He was disappointed there was not more of its immediate past and the quelled unrest of 1905 because of the initial refusal of Tsar Nicholas II to risk eroding his absolute autocracy by considering a constitutional government. The Tsar's capitulation and establishment of a Duma, with a prime minister, appeared only to have partially restored political stability, although the accounts of those celebration ceremonies did not record any protests.

Mycroft Holmes kept the undertaking to supply, within twenty-four hours, the identity of Winston Churchill's embassy contact. Captain Lionel Black was the military attaché and had been a contemporary of Churchill's at Sandhurst. Sebastian went personally to the First Lord's preferred working eyrie atop Admiralty Arch, with its uninterrupted view of Buckingham Palace, to receive Churchill's handwritten letter of introduction and the verbal assurance that Black was someone who could be implicitly relied upon. He also received Churchill's promise, before his departure, of accreditation as a researcher and journalist for the *Morning Post*, for which Churchill had with distinction and fame reported the Boer War. Mycroft accompanied Sebastian and, during the discussion, a secure method of communication was agreed, sealed letters and packages addressed to Mycroft in the diplomatic bag that was carried to London in the custody of the King's Messenger. Sherlock Holmes's despised Winchester College code could be invoked in emergencies: Mycroft maintained in his Diogenes apartment the telegraph he'd installed for the American affair, bemoaning the fact that no telephone contact was possible between the two capitals.

'My father will believe himself isolated if he is not privy to our exchanges,' warned Sebastian, mindful of his conversation with Dr Watson.

'He will share sufficient for him not to think that,' promised Mycroft. 'As with America, there'll doubtless be a considerable contribution from him.'

Did Mycroft's reluctance reflect the man's unspoken concern about his brother, matching that of he and Watson? wondered Sebastian, uncomfortable at plotting against his father. He'd been surprised there'd been no reference in the back of the hansom to Sherlock Holmes's bewildering aggressiveness the night it had emerged at 221b Baker Street. 'I have little doubt that I will have need of his wisdom and experience during the course of events, which would make it unwise to exclude him.'

'You have my word that Sherlock will not be excluded,' promised Mycroft. 'Were he not so well known, by appearance as well as reputation, it would be with him that we would be making these preparations. As it is, I am concerned at your remarkable similarity of appearance.'

That same day Sebastian withdrew £5,000 from his Coutts bank account in the Strand and established a further £5,000 in letters of credit and occupied the afternoon deciding the quickest route to St Petersburg. Uncertain what he should prepare for, he packed almost as many trunks as he'd considered necessary for America but, after studying maps and comparing sea and rail schedules he determined that, although so much luggage would be an inconvenience, it would be quicker by at least two days to cross the North Sea by packet and continue by train than to make the entire journey by ship. A further hour's consultation of schedules found him a ferry crossing from Harwich that connected at the Hook of Holland with a companion service to the trans-Siberian express, upon which he reserved a first-class sleeper and day-room accommodation capable of holding all his baggage. When he returned to the Diogenes from making his travel arrangements, there was a telegraph awaiting him, confirming his suite at the Grand Hotel in St Petersburg, as well as the delivery of his *Morning Post* accreditation cards.

The last requirement was that Sebastian should bid farewell to his father, which he journeyed to Baker Street to do on the morning of his departure. He found Sherlock Holmes subdued, totally without aggression.

Sherlock Holmes said: 'You're fully prepared?'

'As fully as I can anticipate.'

'You can't be more.'

'It will be inadequate, I know. As I know that I will need your assistance, as I always will.'

'And which will always be available.' From the pocket of his smoking jacket, Sherlock Holmes took a slip of paper. 'Upon which matter I hope you'll benefit from this.'

'What is it?'

'I made enquiries among émigré Russians here in London after your encounter with the Grand Duke Orlov aboard the *Lusitania*,' reminded Sherlock Holmes. 'Yesterday I rekindled associations I made then. This is the location of the Duke's palace in St Petersburg. I don't share your confidence in his acknowledging your approach, but as you so forcefully made clear to me, you won't know unless you try.'

'I am in your debt before I begin,' thanked Sebastian. 'I will not fail you.'

'Be more concerned not to fail yourself,' advised Sherlock Holmes.

# Three

Sebastian Holmes had grown increasingly discomfited, although not immediately able to identify the cause, during his journey northwards on the St Petersburg express.

Initially it had been the journey he imagined – the contemplative recovery he sought – after the steam-billowing confusion of personally ensuring that each piece of his extensive baggage was safely accounted for and loaded, after the similar endeavour successfully to get on and off the Harwich ferry. His compartment was well appointed and his personal steward attentive, although the accommodation lacked the total, even extravagant, luxury of the personalized railway carriages of the American millionaire industrialists he'd come to know and travel with during his American mission. The landscape of northern Europe had been predominantly flat, the blurred townships and villages neatly set out in agreeable patterns and arrangements, bystanders occasionally smiling and waving, never-to-meet people acknowledging never-to-meet people.

By Sebastian's estimation they would have been many miles north following a comfortable night's rest after snipping off the extremity of Germany to enter the northern regions of a Russian empire spanning half the world, when the unformed impression first came to Sebastian. His four-course luncheon was already ordered from his personal steward, his midmorning champagne aperitif still foaming in his glass, when the speed slowed. It wasn't a proper stopping point, not even a halt, maybe an awkwardness of the track that required the reduction to a walking pace. The unashamedly naked, dirt-grimed child had been a girl, perhaps three years old, perhaps even younger. It was not until the train stopped completely that Sebatian saw she was tethered by a rope around her left ankle, insufficient to have prevented her straying to her death on to the line, but knotted tightly enough to stop her wandering from where she had to stand. And then he saw that she was not completely naked but had a roughly scrawled, single-worded and numbered sign around her neck which he could not read, because Russian was not one of his languages, nor would he need it here. It was clearly a sales sign, complete with a demanded price, for prospective buyers on slower, stopping trains. She stared sullenly at Sebastian and Sebastian gazed back in shocked disbelief until the train jerked into motion. She did not move her head to follow his departure. He strained to keep her in sight until a curve in the track took her from view. Within minutes, outlined on a commanding promontory, there appeared a turreted and castellated mansion reminiscent of the more elaborate castles with which Sebastian was familiar from living in Germany. And then, within a slightly longer period, more children, a group this time and not entirely naked, nor tethered with sales notices, but unshod and as begrimed as the first, and who, like the first, stood sullenly to regard the passing of a conveyance the name of which they would probably never know and only ever see from the outside. Hopefully but without apparent noise, they stood with begging hands outstretched. Sebastian jerked to his feet, scrambling for money, but every time he got it to hand – even when he waited in readiness – they were gone before he could open the narrow ventilation window. He consoled his conscience by recognizing that they would have had no knowledge – nor opportunity – to convert the money he carried into useful, necessary currency. There were adults, too, bow-shouldered gangs of them working the fields, some, Sebastian saw, between the shafts of roughly hewn ploughing and tilling contraptions there were no animals to haul. And, frequently enough to be noticeable, more grand houses in distant, grass-carpeted estates, or closer when the train slowed to pass through townships and cities.

Sebastian was pitched back into the steam-filled maelstrom upon his arrival in St Petersburg early the following morning, wisely over-tipping his expectant steward for the man's help, along with two porters whom he also generously rewarded, whose help was invaluable in obtaining the two horse-drawn carriages necessary to convey him and his belongings to the Grand Hotel. The premises proved worthy of their title, but once ensconced in an agreeable although overly Victoriana-cluttered apartment, it took him a further hour to unpack his various trunks and valises. Keeping his American experiences in mind, Sebastian had carried with him the revolver he'd necessarily purchased there, as well as his swordstick, and both were the first out of their case, the gun initially installed in the bedside stand, the swordstick closely at hand upon the living-room day bed. To the suite safe, within the largest of the closets, Sebastian consigned, in their money belts and pouches, all the letters of credit and his cash, less £200 he at once converted into roubles, keeping in gold a few sovereigns and half sovereigns.

Sebastian at once moved to obey another edict of his father's, the necessity thoroughly to acquaint himself with his immediate surroundings. He surveyed on foot the waterside Hermitage and the fateful Winter Palace approach of Dvortsovaya Square upon which the Tsar's army had carried out their Bloody Sunday massacre. He was awed by the scale and grandeur of the buildings designed by European architects to fulfil the determination of Peter the Great to create from a mosquito-infested swamp a city comparable if not superior to any Western capital. It was as he retraced his steps, confident enough of the city's most essential layout to take a round-about route, that Sebastian strayed from the major thorough-fares, initially into minor roads, and then into unpaved, rutted and puddled back alleys. Almost at once he encountered the reverse, dark side of the polished St Petersburg mirror, and the badgering, unidentified feeling that had lurked within him since crossing the border into Russia. The urchins and scavengers scurrying in packs through the refuse of the ostentatious city palaces and straggling, block-long mansions weren't the blank-eyed, begging railway-track waifs, but guttersnipes of the same family, here, though, sharp-eyed survivors of unimaginable deprivations and poverty, nevertheless determined to exist, if not ever properly to live as other human beings live. Or were entitled to live. Twice, in the deepest

25

and darkest of the back streets, packs grouped and watched his hurried progress, debating more by instinctive thought than in word, like rats undecided whether to attack in force a weaker prey. Both times Sebastian unclipped his swordstick in readiness, although sure he could never permit himself to inflict injury upon a child, even a child prepared to inflict injury upon him. On both occasions the predators slunk away into the fetid labyrinth in which they existed, and after the second, Sebastian, assured of his direction, struck out for the expansive, safer boulevards.

Back at the hotel, Sebastian rationalized that it had been an unsettling experience, although nothing more, something capable of happening among the rookeries of London or the sewers of the Les Halles area of Paris. It was expediency, certainly not apprehension, that decided him upon fulfilling the afternoon's tasks by carriage, not on foot. He lunched lightly, without any conscious appetite, his moves mentally planned before entering the hotel's writing room. He wrote on the Grand Hotel's letterhead his own note of introduction to Captain Lionel Black at the British embassy, attaching to it his personal card and Winston Churchill's handwritten letter. He took more time over the second communication, using a hotel letterhead again, briefly to write to the Grand Duke Alexei Orlov on the recollection of their shared *Lusitania* voyage to America. Again he attached his personal card before wax-sealing both envelopes.

Sebastian needed the translation of the doorman to direct his carriage to its destinations, using French himself to set them out. He stipulated the Grand Duke's palace first, ahead of the British embassy, leaving Tsarskoye Selo until last.

'Tsarskoye Selo means the Tsar's village,' responded the man at once. 'It is many kilometres from St Petersburg. The imperial palaces are there.'

'I know,' said Sebastian, who also knew from his London research that Tsar Nicholas and Tsarina Alexandra preferred the seclusion of the Alexander Palace there to the city-located Anichkov Palace, disdaining St Petersburg as too modern.

'It is forbidden to ordinary people: sealed off by soldiers,' said the man.

'How close can I get?'

'I do not know,' said the man, uncomfortably. 'It is more than twenty kilometres away to the south. People know it is forbidden to approach.'

'Is it possible to see any palaces from the highway?'

'I told you, I do not know.'

Nodding to the expectantly waiting coachman, Sebastian said: 'Will you ask him to take me as close as he can?'

The coach driver's smile to the initial address was followed by an immediate head-shaking refusal at the mention of the Tsar's park-enclosed residence.

Sebastian extended two gold sovereigns in a cupped hand before the driver and said to the doorman: 'Tell him these are his if he'll undertake the journey.'

Greed competed with nervousness on the coachman's face. There was a babble of Russian before the doorman turned back to Sebastian. 'He says he will take you as far as is safe for him. If he is identified by soldiers or police, he will be arrested and jailed. He could even be exiled.'

'As far as it is safe for him,' agreed Sebastian, tipping the grateful doorman a half sovereign for the interpretation. It would probably be a wasted expedition, but Sebastian wanted to orientate himself as completely as possible. The fact that the safety of the Tsar and his family was so closely guarded was an interesting discovery in itself.

The city palace of the Imperial Grand Duke Alexei Orlov occupied virtually an entire block of the boulevard running parallel to the river Neva. Its outer wall was exactly that, a protective surround with only one huge, metal-studded and banded main gate, with the actual building quite separate inside, beyond a wide-open parkland divided by what Sebastian decided, from his brief view through the soldier-guarded gate-house, to be a ditch or maybe even a moat. Sebastian managed a language bridge with the gateman in uneven French and was assured that the letter would be delivered immediately. He got the same undertaking, in English, from the custodian at the porter's lodge at the British embassy.

The well-paved road the coachman took out of the city was lined with imposing mansions. Directly beyond, when they cleared the city outskirts, Sebastian pressed forward against

27

the glass, identifying at once a distant railway line running roughly parallel to the road, unthinkingly expecting similar scenes to those he'd seen from his train carriage window or the St Petersburg back lanes. But here there was nothing of the squalor. The occasional house was brick-built, the gardens neatly arranged. Even the sporadic tree clumps or coppices had an order about them. Tsar Nicholas wouldn't know – perhaps because he didn't choose to know – the condition in which some of his people lived. One cynicism led to another. The neatly tended houses could act as guard posts, he guessed, providing warnings of any approach along the empty, single-tracked road. Sebastian wondered if the possibility had occurred to his nervous driver.

Sebastian calculated they had travelled approximately 15km, at once recalling the hotel doorman's estimation of Tsarskoye Selo being more than 20km from the city, when, as if in answer to Sebastian's reflection, the coachman reined in at a convenient turning point in the road and began to manoeuvre his carriage around. Sebastian at once shouted in protest, using sign language to urge the driver further on, but the man responded with head-shaking refusal. Sebastian actually leaned through the window when the coach was sideways on across the road, straining in the direction of the palace enclave. There was the glint of water and grey, twilight mounds on the horizon that could not be distinguished as buildings, and then even that view was gone and the coach began to rock with sudden speed in the driver's anxiety to get quickly away from the scene. He'd been cheated, Sebastian accepted, unperturbed. But could he have expected a man to risk his liberty – even deportation, although he found such punishment difficult to believe – for two gold sovereigns?

It was at that moment that Sebastian finally resolved the uncertainty that had troubled him since his entry into Russia. It was, he accepted, a premature impression predicated upon no more evidence than what he'd seen with his own eyes, and could still be open to correction. But what he had witnessed so far were the two furthermost extremes of human existence, incalculable wealth and incalculable, animal-survival poverty. Which represented the perfect breeding ground for discontent and civil unrest, by which the country had already once been threatened – and to quell which the Tsar had been forced to make concessions – eight short years earlier.

So eager was the coachman to depart after their return to the hotel that he practically snatched his money from Sebastian's outstretched hand and whipped his horse forward. Sebastian objectively accepted that it was unrealistic to have expected otherwise, but he was disappointed there were no messages awaiting him at the reception desk. There should be a response – an acknowledgement at least – from Captain Black the following day. Sebastian believed he had started well and didn't want the momentum to slow.

'Experience, Watson!' declared Sherlock Holmes, striding triumphantly into the Baker Street lodgings. 'Experience, the foundation rock upon which success can be built!'

'How so, Holmes?' asked Dr Watson. He was intently alert, more interested in worrying ulterior signs than in Sherlock Holmes's obvious exuberance, which in itself compounded the worrying indications.

'Gave Sebastian a test.'

Watson recognized the familiar to-and-fro exchange and was encouraged by it, at the same time recognizing it could present a wrong diagnosis. 'And?'

'He failed.'

'Failed!' echoed Watson, believing, if it were true, that there was cause for a different concern.

'Didn't fully follow the golden rule – look, look and look again. And beyond that, look still further.'

'I wasn't aware we already had a mystery here,' protested the doctor, encouraging the other man hopefully to offer less obtuse indications.

'Sebastian did the obvious. He went to the reading room, studied the most accessible: I went there today on a ruse, to give myself access to the withdrawal register. Which he'd utilized with great diligence. But it's the least obvious that's always the most productive.'

'Which you pursued?' anticipated Watson.

'Which I pursued,' confirmed Sherlock Holmes. 'With the

assistance of the excellent library and the journalistic coverage of that acknowledged organ of record, the London *Times*. To discover something truly ironic.'

'Which was?' duly prompted the doctor.

'London is, or was, the very hotbed – the comfortably warm dormitory at least – of those whom Sebastian has journeyed so far to uncover, and to expose their evil intent . . . And guess the irony.'

'I'm not sure I'm able,' confessed the neatly moustached man.

'Many of them are known by name and choose this very city to which to flee and prepare their venal schemes to over-throw authority. They've even publicly held their conference here, in London!'

'You surely jest!' accused Watson.

'Were it that I felt so able,' said Sherlock Holmes. He tossed an attaché case upon a side table and said: 'They're damnably devious, to boot. They cower behind pseudonyms and false identities so much and so often that I'll wager they end scarcely knowing who they truly are.'

'You have such disguises?'

Sherlock Holmes tapped the discarded case. 'More ficti-tious names than have graced the London stage since Shakespeare was at his height. Which have to be communi-cated to Sebastian at once. I've shared my findings with Inspector Lestrade, at the Yard. He's got many a match and believes many more have returned to Russia to stir up unrest and discord.'

Professionally observing his friend as closely as he was, Watson decided that Holmes's enthusiasm was genuine, not artificially or damnably induced. 'You've done well, Holmes.'

'Would you have expected less?' demanded the detective.

Watson hesitated at the inadvertently offered opening. 'I had some fears.'

'I don't understand that remark, sir!'

'I fear you do,' directly challenged the doctor. 'And I am glad that, at the moment, I detect no evidence for my concern.'

'There never has been cause for concern.'

Watson saw another beckoning opening. 'There would most

definitely be cause were your regrettable failing to endanger Sebastian's safety.'

The lean, sharp-featured man was stilled by the remark, immobilized in the middle of the room, with his entire, intense concentration upon the smaller-statured man. When he finally spoke, Sherlock Holmes's voice was strained, held tight against the emotion. 'Are you seriously suggesting that I would let anything endanger Sebastian's safety?'

'I am *telling* you that such a risk could be beyond your control.'

'You are most seriously threatening our friendship!'

'To lose which would cast me into the deepest despair,' said Watson. 'But which I would surrender as a worthwhile sacrifice to save you from a veritable devil and Sebastian from losing respect for a father he has only so very recently become acquainted with.'

There was a protracted silence, the two men confronting each other, no retreat possible, no escaping word for either. It was Sherlock Holmes who finally spoke, his voice now so strained as to be unrecognizable as his. 'I must ask you to excuse me. I have work to do.'

'Of course,' accepted Watson.

'Excuse me for the foreseeable future.'

'Of course,' further accepted the distraught Watson.

It was not until Sebastian returned to his suite that he realized how fatigued he was from the crowded activities of the day, a tiredness compounded by what he calculated for the first time to be a journey that had well to exceed a thousand miles, maybe more. Sebastian bathed, long and gratefully, and at one stage, briefly, considered eating in his rooms, if eating at all. But then grew irritated at himself at such easy capitulation, formally dressing to descend to the dining room and his already reserved table.

Sebastian was halfway across the expansive foyer when the ambush was expertly triggered, the enclosing men behind him unnoticed until his way was blocked by a slight and diminutive man who abruptly presented himself directly in Sebastian's path.

'We would like you to accompany us,' announced the small man, in perfect French. Light reflected off his owlishly round spectacles, making him appear sightless.

'Who the devil are you?' demanded Sebastian.

'Police,' said the man. 'We have every authority and power. If you attempt the slightest resistance, the man immediately behind you will shoot you in the back, shattering your spine.'

Sebastian felt the hardness of a weapon pressing against him. 'I want proof of your official identity.'

'You're not in a position to make any demands,' said the man, mildly. 'We're all now going to turn around and leave. Don't worry about your table reservation. It's already been cancelled.'

Sebastian was turned towards the exit by the very movement of the men around him, like a set manoeuvre in a military tattoo. Unwittingly in step, Sebastian saw that the small man now directly in front of him was doing his best to conceal a bald patch on the crown of his head by greasing across it hair that wouldn't conform but instead stuck up like a bantam cock's tail.

# Four

Sebastian Holmes felt no fear. Instead he was held by a combination of fury and shame at his own crass stupidity. Of course the coach driver, maybe the doorman too, would have reported their bizarre discussion with a foreigner on the hotel steps to the police. Sacrificing his offered gold – if indeed it had been sacrificed – was surely preferable to incarceration or exile. His father would not have made such a basic, infantile error. Examining it now – trying to prepare for whatever lay ahead – the attempted visit to Tsarskoye Selo had been pointless from its inception. He'd *known* of the Tsar's protective retreat, in such obvious contrast to the central palaces of King George V or Kaiser Wilhelm! Should have known also – realized also – after the country's immediately preceding history, the extent of the informant-based protective screen that would enclose it.

It was easy, although scourging, to reflect. They were in a horse-drawn but unwindowed metal detention wagon. Sebastian was separated from his captors by a metal grill, both ankles painfully shackled – which instantly conjured memories of the child tethered beside the railway track – to his bench supports, through which the handcuff restraints were threaded. Directly facing him in the uncertain, flickering internal lantern light of the wagon was the bantam-tailed arresting officer, flanked on either side by two cohorts. Four more were alertly positioned behind.

In French Sebastian said: 'Are all these chains necessary? I see little chance of escape.' Was it conceivable that he had been seized by the Okhrana, headed by the very aristocrat through whom he'd hoped to be guided in the direction to fulfil his assignment!

The diminutive man looked back at him expressionless, wordless, as did the rest of his squad.

Sebastian said: 'This is a serious mistake. There will be serious consequences.'

They continued to stare, saying nothing. For him to protest further would indicate an apprehension he didn't feel, Sebastian decided. The ankle restraints as well as the wrist bands were too tight, cutting into his skin. Sebastian stopped trying to make them more comfortable, guessing they would interpret that as nervousness, too. Painful though they were, they held him firm against the unexpected lurching and turning of the enclosed carriage. He became conscious for the first time of the smell – from the terrified release of prisoners who had preceded him – and realized he was sitting – stinking – in their mess. Which was, he recognized, a further attempt at disorientation.

The sealed carriage abruptly stopped, to the sound of heavy doors opening, then closing the moment the van passed through. It was so dark in the outside courtyard that virtually no light penetrated when the rear doors opened. Everyone, including the man in charge, got out, continuing to ignore him. Sebastian suddenly felt the need for a lavatory himself, and understood better why the van smelled so badly. His anger at himself still burned but Sebastian was forcing the rationalization, assessing his predicament, confronting himself with the accusations he imagined himself shortly to be facing. A competent, convincing liar tells as few lies as possible, Sebastian recalled his father lecturing: the fewer the falsehoods, the fewer to be recalled and upon which to be caught out. Another axiom was never to underestimate the resources of an opponent, no matter how ineffectual he might appear: his father's analogy was that the weakling David slew the unsuspecting Goliath with a thumbnail-sized pebble.

There was shuffled movement from outside the van, inside which he would be visible in the vague lantern light. It was difficult to remain unmoving, the more so with the need to relieve himself, but Sebastian determined not to submit to such minimal torture.

He guessed at a further fifteen minutes, stretching the wait

34

to almost an hour, before the general movement resolved itself into a definite approach, and men clambered heavily back into the arrest wagon, unlocked the mesh separation and finally released Sebastian from his restraints. His wrists were bleeding, he saw, and from the renewed discomfort, he guessed his ankles were, too. Bantam tail, with his impeccable French, was not among them, so Sebastian obeyed the grunted gestures finally to get out. Weak though it had been, there had been faint light within the van and Sebastian was totally disorientated in the abrupt blackness of the outside yard. He stumbled into the unseen men around him, striving to retain his balance and remain upright when he was roughly – intentionally – pushed back from every collision. The unexpectedness of the full electric light the moment a door opened ahead of him blinded Sebastian further and he almost went down to a further, intentional shove, managing to thrust his elbow just as intentionally into the ribs of his assailant, winding him, in a flailing effort to keep his feet. He tensed against a retaliatory blow but none came.

It was a narrow and low corridor, the ceiling dripping, the walls stained brown by what could have been blood, the passageway slimed and wet underfoot. The combined stench of excreta and urine was much stronger than in the van. Inexplicably Sebastian's lavatorial need had abated, for which he was grateful. He became aware that the walkway was sloping downwards, which could only mean they were descending below ground. Small corridors suddenly began splitting off from that they were following, and from some came the sounds of movement, of people: occasionally there were cries, of despair or pain, or both.

An open door to his right cast a brighter beacon light. Two men stood shoulder to shoulder just beyond it, blocking his path. Sebastian hesitated at its entrance, instantly encompassing everything. It was not a cell, as such. It was a windowless rectangle totally bare except for a table and, beyond, a single chair upon which already sat the diminutive, jut-haired arresting officer. On the table between them were Sebastian's revolver, swordstick and money belts. Sebastian was conscious of several people crowding in behind him and then of the door thudding shut.

The man opened his mouth to speak, but before he could Sebastian said, continuing in French: 'I demand at once an explanation for my detention! And immediate communication with the British embassy. I also wish to know the authority you represent.' He very consciously splayed his feet, at ease, his hands looped casually behind his back.

'What are those?' said the man, gesturing to the gun and swordstick.

'Personal protection, to which I am entitled and by possessing which I am breaking no law,' insisted Sebastian. 'Law which you and your cohorts have broken by intruding into premises legally mine by contracted rental, for which I demand a further explanation.' He stopped, breathless. Recovering, he said: 'I am awaiting answers to my questions!'

'What do you intend purchasing with so much money?' persisted the man, patting the money belt and the pouch in which Sebastian had put the sovereigns.

'I want answers to my questions,' insisted Sebastian.

'I want answers to mine,' came back the interrogator.

How would his father have conducted this confrontation? wondered Sebastian, belatedly. Most probably by not making the mistakes that he had, or having permitted it to occur in the first place, came the immediate answer. 'I am prepared to forgive your misunderstanding. I am a British subject, recently finished university, embarking upon a traditional Grand Tour of Europe. I decided to extend such a tour by including Russia and its capital, which I seek to explore to its fullest, maybe even to write newspaper articles on its attractiveness. This afternoon I attempted to see Tsarskoye Selo, not truly appreciating the restrictions despite warnings from both the doorman at the Grand Hotel and the coach handler. Quite wrongly, impetuously, I tempted the coachman with gold. Briefly he gave way to that temptation, until we were still some way from the Tsar's village. From which he at once turned back. If fault there is in what I have done, then it is innocent fault which I regret and for which I apologize – and for which neither man whom I inveigled are in any way responsible or to blame.'

'You are a foreign anarchist and revolutionary, preparing an outrage.'

'And you are a fool for so thinking,' said Sebastian. He tensed for a reaction from behind, before remembering those at his back did not have the language. There was a response though, for the first time, from his interrogator. The man flushed, the anger pricking out on both cheeks.

The man said: 'I have the power to have you shot, without trial.'

'I doubt that, but for you to do so would create an international incident and doubtless result in your own execution before another firing squad.'

'What is your interest in the Imperial Grand Duke Alexei Orlov?' suddenly pounced the man, believing it an off-balancing ploy.

'Ask him,' responded Sebastian, at once. Seizing the opening, he said: 'I am acquainted with the Grand Duke. Get into contact with him at once, as I demand.'

'I'm asking you.'

'And I've replied to your question.'

'I wonder if a period of solitary confinement will lessen your arrogance?'

'I wonder if yours would be lessened by the repercussions that would follow.'

'I will make things easier for you if you give me the names of your fellow conspirators.'

'I have no fellow conspirators. There is no conspiracy. I want this nonsense ended, now!'

Almost imperceptibly the questioner's demeanour faltered and there was shuffling behind Sebastian, from men who didn't need the language to understand that the interrogation was not proceeding as it was intended to, and Sebastian decided he had adopted the right attitude. He was unsure if it was sufficient to gain his release, though.

'I will hold you in custody until I get a satisfactory explanation,' announced the man.

'I want the British embassy immediately informed of my detention,' insisted Sebastian. 'There will be an official protest at my unfounded arrest and the strongest censure lodged against you, personally.'

The man confronting him coloured again. There was a burst

of Russian and Sebastian was roughly jerked around and thrust through the quickly opened door. There was a cell directly opposite and he was even more roughly shoved into it by the man whose ribs he had elbowed, getting eventual revenge. It was virtually as bare as the interrogation room, different only in the uncovered concrete ledge Sebastian presumed served as a bed. Beside it was an excreta-ringed bucket, which Sebastian used, gratefully, before moving it as far away as possible from the resting place, which wasn't far enough.

He was, Sebastian acknowledged, in a sorry state. Objectively his arrest was not unfounded, although eventually it would be easily resolved. He had no fear of the man who could not exercise his interrogation threats any more effectively than he could control his diminishing hairline; no apprehension, even, at being incarcerated in this stinking hellhole in which he currently found himself deservedly to be. And in which, with relief matching that of his use of the bucket, Sebastian stretched out aching limbs on the concrete ledge. His dismay was at the inevitable identification his release would require, within a British embassy whose doubtful effectiveness he was in St Petersburg to question. All of which uncertainties were compounded by his not knowing – but fearing – who his captors were. He'd failed, Sebastian decided: failed himself and failed his father in whose footsteps he had no inherited right nor justification to tread. His was going to be a deserved ignominious return to England.

Sebastian didn't properly sleep. The earlier hotel-suite fatigue engulfed him, lessening the awfulness of his surroundings but never fully taking away his awareness of it, and he was alert to the grate of the key in the cell door before it fully opened.

The fresh-faced intruder was not Russian. The suit was Savile Row, the burnished brogues unquestionably Lobb, the tie regimental. He said, in perfectly modulated English, 'Good heavens, sir, what a pretty mess this is!'

Sebastian said: 'A mess, indeed. Nothing of it pretty.'

It was a succinct explanation, Captain Lionel Black talking in staccato spurts, which Sebastian inevitably, mentally likened to machine-gun bursts. Black had been alerted to his arrival by a message from Churchill, and responded to it as soon as possible after receiving Sebastian's note, calling personally at the Grand Hotel. He must have arrived within minutes of Sebastian's seizure, of which he'd been informed by another doorman. It had taken him three full hours to discover in which prison Sebastian had been incarcerated, and at least one hour further to persuade the authorities that Sebastian was not an anarchist or a plotting revolutionary, but an upright, responsible British citizen with influential connections in London.

'The misconception that you were a revolutionary was easily arrived at,' completed the attaché. His hair was cut short in a military fashion and his stature ramrod straight, although he was still several inches shorter than Sebastian. The man disdainfully avoided contact with anything in the odorous cell, his nose permanently wrinkled in disgust.

'Am I to be released?'

'After an apology.'

'Which I have already made.'

'They require it to be made again. Formally. As a statement.' There was a hesitation. 'Got the impression you upset them. Some disrespect.'

'Let's get the confounded business over with,' said Sebastian, impatiently. 'Who knows about it, at the embassy?'

'No one,' assured Black. 'I told you the circumstances of my discovery.'

'I demanded that the embassy be told of my arrest.'

Black nodded. 'So I've been told, in turn. Part of your complained of disrespect. They weren't going to do anything about it.'

'Then I am truly fortunate.' More than he'd imagined possible, Sebastian accepted.

The group were waiting in the opposite interrogation room, the small inquisitor back behind his desk. Sebastian repeated his apology, his attitude contrite this time. The man laboriously translated from French to Russian and even more slowly wrote down the agreed words, stretching Sebastian's humiliation. As a further accuracy check, Black read the Cyrillic script and confirmed the apology truthfully to be what

Sebastian had said. As Sebastian was signing it, the small man retrieved Sebastian's money belt, coin pouch and weapons from some storage place beneath the desk.

Quietly, in English, Black said: 'The belt and pouch will be a little lighter than when you arrived. I would not advise protest.'

A coach and driver were awaiting them outside. The attaché stood back to allow Sebastian to enter and, as he followed, said: 'I trust you won't take offence, sir, but something rather unpleasant appears to have occurred to the clothing you are wearing.'

'Of which I am extremely anxious to divest myself,' said Sebastian, the apology this time more sincere than that in the prison.

'I'll organize some caviar and a little vodka, while you're doing so,' undertook the captain.

While his bath was running, Sebastian bundled his filthy clothing – even his shoes – into a laundry basket and ordered their disposal by his floor concierge. Wincing at the instant stinging discomfort to his chafed wrists and ankles, he submerged himself completely beneath the water to rid himself of the arrest wagon and prison smell, which seemed to cling even after he'd added to the pain by scrubbing his hands and face close to rawness. Sebastian dressed in the first lounge suit he came to in his closet and, on impulse, just as he was quitting his rooms, he checked the money belt and pouch and ruefully decided the loss could have been greater.

Captain Lionel Black occupied a discreet corner of the lounge, a carafe of vodka already opened and sampled, Beluga in a silver bowl, black bread beside. 'As the Russians eat it,' he recommended, as Sebastian sat.

Sebastian said: 'My punishment was ten gold sovereigns and a five pound note.'

'I would have expected it to have been more.'

'So would I.' There were several matters immediately to be cleared, Sebastian decided. 'I am deeply in your debt.'

Black indicated the caviar and vodka. 'Slightly mitigated. I've charged our overly late supper to your chambers.'

Sebastian smiled, allowing the man his joke. 'Mine was not a good beginning for someone supposed to be travelling as incognito as possible: certainly not to impose a burden on the embassy.' Despite his father's insistence otherwise, Sebastian thought.

Black answered Sebastian's smile, isolating the concern. 'I've already told you no official approach was made. There is no record of my need to intercede. Nor will there be.'

'I am profoundly obliged.' His escape from any London embarrassment was complete, Sebastian recognized.

'You come preceded by high credentials.'

'Scarce credit to the family name on today's showing.'

'It might have been better for us to have talked first.'

Moving to another isolated concern, Sebastian said: 'Who were those who arrested me?'

'Specialists,' identified the soldier. 'The Okhrana, the Tsar's secret police and intelligence organization.'

His fear confirmed, Sebastian wondered where that left his approach to Grand Duke Alexei Orlov. Not a consideration to be quickly addressed, but one needing balanced reflection. Needing a pause, Sebastian tasted the Beluga with the black bread for the first time. It was superb with the biting coldness of the vodka, taken neat. 'They seem very efficient.'

'And ruthless,' said the other man. 'Their vengeance upon those who tried to overthrow the Tsar in 1905, and the revolutionary groups who have tried to establish themselves since, has been total. No one will ever know how many have been indifferently killed, executed on false evidence in illegal trials or deported and exiled to the four winds.'

'My inquisitor said he could have had me shot, out of hand.'

'Which he could,' confirmed Black. He put aside his vodka and caviar. 'Which brings us to other things. Winston urges me to give you every help: recommends you highly from a recent excursion in the United States. But his letter provides little guidance upon your actual mission here.'

'To have the eyes and ears of a stranger,' improvised Sebastian. 'Churchill is uncertain of the Tsar's military support, which could become a crucial question in the coming months. As could the civil unrest against the Tsar's authority, which is no secret in London. There's also the question to be answered of German influence within the country.'

41

'I think you have isolated a problem with your remit,' said the attaché.

'Sir?'

'To observe and listen as a stranger . . . dooms your role of a stranger. I fear you have little chance of seeing or hearing anything from the distance at which you will be kept, unless you have many more introductions in a considerably higher circle than a second-level diplomat like myself.'

'To whom I repeat I am profoundly obliged,' said Sebastian. 'But I accept the point you're making.'

'Have you?' demanded the attaché, directly, in his machine-gun style of speaking.

'Sir?' questioned Sebastian again.

'Many more introductions?'

He had much, too much, upon which to reflect before disclosing any knowledge or brief association with the man who controlled the Okhrana, so it would not be a positive deception at this precise moment to avoid an answer. He was, however, much beholden to the captain, which required sparing an accredited British diplomat any professional difficulties, quite apart from embarrassment. 'I fear I find myself lacking.'

'Then I am afraid your mission will end similarly lacking.'

'I'd appreciate, beyond my already expressed appreciation, your assessment.' Which was an exaggeration, Sebastian conceded.

The military attaché toyed with a stray piece of black bread on his discarded plate. 'I believe there will be further civil unrest: conceivably, at the very extreme, another attempted revolt against the Tsar. But I also believe the Tsar and his most intimate advisors have learned . . .' The man extended an open palm, closing his fingers around it. 'This is how I believe – and your recently distressing experience should vouch for it – the Okhrana have the dangers enclosed. So complete has been their pogrom since 1905 that those revolutionaries whom they haven't killed or exiled, under permanent police surveillance, are fragmented, squabbling their philosophies among themselves, lacking any sort of organization or focus.'

'What about military allegiance in the event of war?' asked Sebastian, moving on.

'Not at risk, by my measure. Certainly the army and the navy have been shown wanting, the navy badly mauled by Japan. But they will stay loyal to their Tsar.'

The resident diplomat's reading of what Churchill supposed to be an uncertain situation appeared cast in stone, allowing no doubts, thought Sebastian. 'Your opinions are encouraging for the stability of the Romanov dynasty.'

'Still measured, although by a long straw,' qualified Black.

'Which I appreciate your sharing with me.'

'I do so only because of the recommendation of Winston. And by so doing put myself at your mercy, through my indiscretion.'

'By the same token – and my indebtedness – it is unthinkable that from my lips there would ever be the slightest hint of what's passed between us.'

'I am as grateful for that assurance from you, as a gentleman, as you were by mine about your recent misfortune.'

'Worded, sir, in the manner of a true diplomat.'

'I think, Sebastian, that we are well met.'

Thus far most certainly, thought Sebastian.


'It's a complete irony, with many implications!' insisted Sherlock Holmes. 'And brings up many failings within this very city.'

His brother was harping on something he saw to be his total involvement – even his supervision – in the Russian enterprise, Mycroft at once recognized. 'As always, I suspect I shall need guidance in such a role.'

'All the more pity that those whose function it is to protect the government and the palace against difficulties are so inept,' criticized Sherlock Holmes.

They'd dined at the Diogenes Club, the meal dismissed by Sherlock Holmes as disgraceful, matched by similarly disappointingly laid-down claret and undrinkable port, and Mycroft was resigned to a fractious conclusion. 'As I indicated, I'd appreciate your guidance.'

'Does Churchill know more – fear more – than he's conveying to us?'

'That's not guidance,' protested Mycroft.

'It's an apposite question I require answering.'

'An answer I don't have. It's my belief that he has been open with us.'

'As open as any politician – particularly Churchill – allows himself to be.'

'Don't permit your animosity towards the man to influence your judgement.'

'Don't allow your contrary allegiance to mislead you into imagining that I would. My view, as it always is, is objective. Yours, my dear brother, is subjectively misdirected, which I fear dangerous, from there being so many different directions.'

'I did not foresee this evening to be staged for a personal disagreement,' objected Mycroft.

'Neither did I. But if that is the way the play has gone, then let us for a moment follow it,' said Sherlock Holmes. 'I fear you are endangering what should be your total impartiality as Cabinet Secretary by tying yourself far too closely to Churchill's coat tails. You are *not* a politician. You are a permanent civil servant, supposedly aloof from any political faction.'

'A civil servant whose function it is permanently to serve his country.'

'Not in the way that you are choosing to serve, not your country, but one opportunist.'

Mycroft could not recall an occasion upon which there had been such a dispute between he and his brother: certainly no more than could be counted, with fingers to spare, upon one hand. 'We chose our different paths a long time ago, Sherlock. I am content with mine. I admire, as so many others do, that which you chose to follow. And from which I still await your promised guidance, which I thought to be the purpose of this meeting.'

'It certainly could not have been for the excellence of the dinner,' said Sherlock Holmes, irascibly.

'Which was not with the suggestion of irony with which you began this conversation, and which I seek to be explained,' accused Mycroft.

'Do you genuinely expect me to believe that the British government was totally unaware that the overthrow of the Russian Tsar – the very destruction of imperial Russia – was actually plotted here, in this very city of London?'

Mycroft Holmes sat regarding his brother for several moments in speechless astonishment. Eventually he said: 'I had no idea of what you say. But want to, immediately!'

'The failed coup of 1905 – and the continuing civil unrest in Russia since that time – was initiated by a revolutionary group known as the Russian Social Democratic Labour Party,' declared Sherlock Holmes. 'Which held congresses here in London – gatherings fully reported in *The Times* – in 1902, 1903 and 1907. It is composed mainly of two conflicting parties, the Mensheviks and the Bolsheviks, who appear to be burying their differences to achieve their common revolutionary aim. There are even Bolshevik representatives within the Duma the Tsar has been forced to concede as a parliament, but which he is currently trying to neuter. Also well reported in *The Times*. But about which no mention was made when Sebastian was given his mission. Reference was made then, I recall, to the Balkans being a hornets' nest. I fear my son, your ward, has been thrust unsuspecting into a matching if not more dangerous hornets' nest . . .'

'Sherlock!' broke in Mycroft. 'Upon the honour and trust that has always existed between us, I ask you to believe that I had no knowledge whatsoever of this until this very moment!'

'Why is there no intelligence-gathering mechanism!' demanded Sherlock Holmes. 'The leaders of these groups are scattered but openly active throughout the capitals of Europe, in each of which we have embassies, as we have in St Petersburg. Is there no one – no system – within the British Foreign Office of bringing together what is reported from our various legations, as there clearly is in our leading newspaper!'

'No!' admitted Mycroft, simply. 'There is no such system because no such system has ever been considered necessary.'

'Put your mind to circumstance,' urged Sherlock Holmes. 'There was discussion, in Sebastian's presence, of blood ties between our own royal family and the Romanovs. How would it reflect throughout the royal households and chancelleries of Europe if the Romanovs were overthrown by revolution-aries so freely able to hold their worldwide conferences in London?'

'Winston is the only man through whom I can introduce such awareness.'

'Then use the damned man as he is so eager to use us.'

'What of Sebastian?'

Sherlock Holmes patted the attaché case he had carried with him to Mycroft's lodgings. 'It is all here. And more. I want the government diplomatic facilities to carry it to him.'

'I'll ensure they're made available.'

'I also want the assurance that I am privy to all communications between yourself and Sebastian. He's been despatched woefully unprepared.'

'You will not be left out.'

'I do not intend to be,' warned Sherlock Holmes.

# Five

Winston Churchill stood at his favourite vantage spot atop Admiralty Arch, gazing down the Mall at Buckingham Palace, the smoke from his Havana cigar ascending in an unwavering straight line. Without turning to Mycroft Holmes, he said: 'Here in London, for all to see and know! Reported in our own newspapers! Holmes is right. It's a scandal and would be seen as such, were there to be a successful revolution.'

'We remain in the realm of hypotheses,' reminded Mycroft.

'Stop sounding like an echo from the confounded cabinet meetings, and men who fail to see the noses on their own faces!' Churchill turned back into the room. 'It would seem that we are in need of both father and son. Have you heard anything of Sebastian?'

'A message communicating his safe arrival, through Captain Black. To whom I've had dispatched all Sherlock's material, to be passed on.'

'There is written material? Proof?'

'Yes.'

'What does it say?' demanded the politician at once. 'Do we have our own copy: something I can study?'

'It was sealed, of course.'

'I asked if we had our own copy.'

'I'm not in the habit of opening another gentleman's mail,' protested Mycroft.

Churchill held the other man in an unbroken look for several moments. 'Honour far too frequently interferes with practicality. What of Sherlock himself?'

'He plays his cards close to his chest. We can but wait for him to tell me of anything further he might uncover, as and when.'

'Scotland Yard should be alerted. Investigations should be

initiated to establish if any of these blackguards remain here in London.'

'I discussed that course with Sherlock,' said Mycroft. 'He rightly points out that it is not against English law for extreme political parties to gather on English soil: even to espouse revolution. Karl Marx wrote *Das Kapital* in the British Museum reading room, don't forget. But to launch a hue and cry might drive any who are here underground. He told me to let matters remain in his hands, for him to work through his sources at the Yard.'

'We have an entire police force at our disposal!' argued Churchill

'Which often calls upon Sherlock Holmes for guidance and advice, and the inadequacies of which he even more often has to correct,' reminded Mycroft. 'It also appears to be a police force unaware of what it took Sherlock only a day or two to discover. I think we should give Sherlock his head.'

'But closely monitor his success,' insisted Churchill. 'A hue and cry might do more than drive them underground. It might drive them abroad to be some other country's burden.'

Mycroft gave no reaction to the political cynicism. 'What of the King?'

Churchill examined the civil servant closely. 'What is your question?'

'I say again that we are indulging in hypotheses,' said Mycroft. 'But do we have any clear indication of the King's feelings about sanctuary, if the Tsar were to be overthrown?'

'It's something to be pursued,' agreed Churchill. 'The problem is that the ineffectual Asquith will have to be the conduit. The damned man has trouble enough dealing with actualities. Conceivable eventualities are beyond his mental capacity.'

'I fear that's extreme,' protested Mycroft.

'The only worthwhile outcome of the forthcoming conflict will be that Asquith will have to accept a coalition government with himself no longer at its head.'

Mycroft gestured beyond Churchill, to the distant palace. 'We're diverging from the subject concerning us. What other route is open?'

'The Lord Chamberlain, perhaps?' suggested Churchill. 'A trusted confidant of the King himself?'

48

'Who would have to be a trusted confidant of the proposer of the question,' cautioned Mycroft. 'Do you have such a mutually linked person?'

'It needs consideration.'

It didn't, thought Mycroft: there either was or was not such a mutual intermediary. 'It could become a matter of the most extreme political importance.'

'An unnecessary reminder,' rejoined Churchill. 'I think there needs to be an exchange between Black and myself.'

'Sherlock lacks trust that he will be included in every communication.'

'A point he has already forcibly made.'

'And which he just as forcibly reiterated at supper. My brother is too astute – and too necessarily an ally, which he has proved himself to be with this discovery – to be partially excluded upon grounds as fragile as government business to which he has no right of access. And, as his brother, I would protest such exclusion.'

'I believed you to be my man, Mycroft.'

'I have allied myself to you, sir, because I believe there are too many in the government too complacent of dangers ahead, dangers I most sincerely hope will never come to pass. In doing so, I knowingly risk my integrity and supposed impartiality: open myself, even, to criminal prosecution and justifiable imprisonment. I do so because I seek to serve my country, not to intrigue. Which I will not. I am not your man, Winston. I am my own man, someone who has embarked upon a course I fear I might have every reason to regret . . .' Mycroft hesitated, aware that he had spoken far more than he'd intended, but at that moment not regretting it. The die cast, he continued: 'I do not wish – nor intend – to continue in this enterprise without Sherlock's full inclusion.'

'This is a belated turn of events,' complained Churchill, expressing his anger with the strength with which he stubbed out his cigar.

'I intend no offence nor difficulty between us,' said Mycroft. 'I followed your cause because I believe it the right one, for the country. And exceeded my position and oath in so doing.

I don't think we can afford – certainly don't think that I, personally, can afford – to be without Sherlock.'

'Then, if you don't, I don't,' mollified Winston Churchill.
'It's good that the air has been cleared.'

'I hope it is,' said Mycroft.

Sebastian Holmes was in low spirits, his only anticipation the
arrival of a promised package from his father, which in itself
did little to lift his depression, because it illustrated his reliance
upon his father, which he sought to avoid if he were ever to be
recognized in his own right. Underlying every reflection and
consideration was Sebastian's continued embarrassment at his
arrest by the Okhrana, which went, upon that reflection, beyond
the very fact of the arrest itself. Despite their apparent acceptance of his innocence and the ridiculous apology, Sebastian
recognized that he had marked himself. No organization half
as dedicated as that which Captain Black had described would
dismiss such an incident as simply as it appeared to have been.

The following day Sebastian tried to establish the extent of
the surveillance under which he was sure to be, walking the
streets of St Petersburg and utilizing all the ruses his father
had instilled – or hoped to have instilled – to identify his
pursuers. And he had grown more despondent at his complete
failure to do so, a failure that did nothing to dissuade him
from the impression that he was being watched.

Paramount in his dejection was, of course, the likely bar he
had himself erected against there being any response from the
Grand Duke Alexei Orlov. Objectively he had to accept that his
father had been right in insisting there had been little likelihood
in the first place of the man responding to what had been nothing
more than an acquaintanceship forced upon him by their proximity during the *Lusitania*'s passage to America. But it had been
a chance to be explored, now ruined if the man learned personally of the Tsarskoye Selo incident. Was it futile to hope that
the supreme head of the Okhrana was too elevated a figure to
be acquainted of it? At once came a balancing conjecture. Could
it help rather than impede his case if it did come to the Grand
Duke's attention, arousing the man's curiosity as to his reason
for being in St Petersburg? Poor efforts at reassurance from

either direction, accepted Sebastian. So with what was he left? Whatever was en route to him from his father. But could that be sufficient to lift him to the echelon Captain Black insisted it was necessary to attempt, quite separately from fulfilling his remit? Hardly, acknowledged Sebastian, reluctantly maintaining the objectivity. Which brought the so far avoided, further acknowledgement. He was allowing himself to be sucked down into a swamp of miserable self-pity, an unthinkable collapse. Which was totally unacceptable.

The train bringing the courier with his sealed diplomatic pouch was scheduled to arrive at St Petersburg at five that evening, the cocktail gathering with Captain Black discreetly established by telephone for seven o'clock in the familiar lounge corner of the Grand Hotel. Sebastian was impatiently early, the vodka and Beluga in readiness, once more intent upon his watchful surroundings, but yet again unable to isolate his anticipated observers.

Black strode militarily into the hotel precisely on time, a wax-sealed package tightly under his left arm, extending his right as he approached. Offering the manila-wrapped bundle to Sebastian, the attaché said: 'It feels of some bulk.'

'Let's hope its contents match its weight,' said Sebastian, putting it quickly into a document case brought in readiness. Indicating the already ordered provisions, he said: 'Would you prefer something other than vodka?'

'When in Rome!' said the man, slumping into the opposite chair and smiling his thanks when Sebastian proffered a frosted glass.

'Any belated repercussions from my misdemeanour?' enquired Sebastian.

Black shook his head. 'I told you, it's a closed matter.'

'I don't believe it can be so easily dismissed. I'm sure I remain under surveillance, which by our continued association endangers you as an accredited diplomat here.'

'You've detected surveillance?'

'I'm following the law of logic.'

Black sipped his drink reflectively. 'I came to the prison as a British diplomat and was accepted as such, upon the presentation of my credentials: if I hadn't been able to prove myself, you would still be in that stinking cell. They have no way of knowing the embassy has not been fully informed. I don't see how I can be endangered by our meeting like this. Or in any other circumstance.'

'Is there not the likelihood of their suspecting some English conspiracy and making further official enquiries?'

Black's reflection this time was longer. Finally, doubtfully, he said: 'I'll allow that's a possibility.'

'Against which you should safeguard yourself.'

'I appreciate your forethought.' The man nodded acceptance to his glass being replenished.

'How wide are the powers of the Okhrana?'

'Limitless. Theirs is the authority of the Tsar.'

'After my arrest they searched my rooms. Took my money from the safe there.' Sebastian hefted the case. 'This will not leave me this evening. But I am worried about its further safe keeping, after I have fully absorbed it.'

'You're considering the embassy?' anticipated Black, immediately.

'But with the same reservation,' said Sebastian. 'It further involves the embassy. And by inference, yourself. A caveat to my mission is not to attract any attention or embarrassment to the legation.'

Black remained silent for several moments. 'I've been reflecting upon your need for contact with some level of St Petersburg society.'

Sebastian frowned. 'I'm not following your direction.'

'It's a Foreign Office recommendation for English visitors to report their presence to the embassy of any country in which they find themselves,' said the attaché. 'Were you to do so, it qualifies you for embassy facilities. Which satisfactorily settles your safe-keeping request. It would also qualify you for invitations to embassy social functions.'

Sebastian smiled at the resolve. 'Am I required to give a reason for my being here?'

Black shook his head. 'Winston indicated you came with some journalistic accreditation. That should suffice if you are asked, which I doubt you will be. I shall arrange the formalities of your embassy registration.'

52

'Then that is how I shall deliver this package, by calling at the embassy tomorrow to register my being here.' Sebastian was impatient to see the contents of the package wedged beside him on his seat, but courtesy required that he spend a further thirty minutes entertaining the attaché. Sebastian tried to steer the conversation productively, probing on the German embassy staffing for indications of additional German presence in the Russian capital, to Black's insistence that he'd discovered no evidence of any increase.

Sebastian was manoeuvring towards an escape when the military diplomat announced his departure with the expectation of seeing Sebastian the following day. Overriding his anxiety at once to return to his rooms, Sebastian unhurriedly added to his vodka glass, intent on any abrupt movement in the lounge to pursue Black. There was none. He still remained in his seat for a further fifteen minutes, the impatience building within him, before finally quitting the room, pausing at a display case in the outside lobby, but once more detected no obvious follower.

Finally secured behind the locked door of his suite, the package removed from the document case, Sebastian hesitated at the moment of unfastening it, recalling his father's assertion that he could accurately judge the character – even the age – of a person from his handwriting. And realizing for the first time that he had never read anything in his father's own hand. Would there be, here? And if there were, what additional, unintended lesson could there be from the script of someone whose character he believed he knew well – albeit anecdotally through the diligent Dr Watson? The wax splintered in his sudden hurry, and the topmost, handwritten pages tore in the haste with which he extracted them.

The package was predominantly made up of neatly clipped and annotated newspaper cuttings, separately secured and named under individual identifications and cross-references.

Sebastian did not immediately attempt to read the handwritten words, but instead studied their shape and formation, and only after that their grouping and composition. He was surprised. It was an oddly – totally unanticipated – childish hand, the letters rounded, every *i* dotted, every *t* crossed, every possible punctuation inserted. Sebastian instantly dismissed the impression as

53

quickly as it came. It was not a childish hand, devoid of character. The contrary. It perfectly represented his father, uncaring of pretence or artifice in circumstances that required neither, the essential need being total clarity and immediate comprehension.

Finally Sebastian read, his first unsettling awareness that, had he better prepared himself before leaving London, he would personally have discovered what his father was making available to him. England and its capital had been, in the past – and potentially remained – a focus for international revolutionary groups and those seeking to lead them. In London there had openly been held three congresses of an encompassing revolutionary movement known as the Russian Social Democratic Labour Party, which embraced both the Bolshevik and Menshevik factions. From the enclosed newspaper accounts, Sebastian quickly understood that proper identification was difficult, because every Russian delegate appeared under a pseudonym, having been arrested and exiled to Siberia, imprisonment from which many had escaped. His father particularly drew Sebastian's attention to the newspaper references to a person described as a leading intellectual and foremost theorist of Marxism, variously named but most often as Vladimir Ilyich Ulyanov or Vladimir Lenin. A prominent Menshevik, again the user of several aliases, chose Lev Trotsky in preference to what Sherlock Holmes understood to be his true identity of Lev Davidovich Bronstein. Both had atteneded the London conferences and others in Paris and Prague. So, too, had a delegate to whom Sherlock Holmes particularly drew Sebastian's attention, in two articles in *The Times* suggesting that he moved under as many as twenty false names, some as bizarre as Koba or Soso. His real name appeared to be Josef Vissarionovich Djugashvili, although in the most recent enclosed cuttings the surname was Stalin.

Sherlock Holmes judged this man particularly worthy of Sebastian's attention, for one very obvious reason. From enquiries he had made beyond the newspaper archives, Sherlock Holmes had discovered that, in the past year, in St Petersburg, publication had begun of a Bolshevik-orientated newspaper entitled *Pravda,* for which Stalin was a writer and commentator, which indicated that the man was resident in the very city in which Sebastian found himself. The premises would most obviously occupy the attention of the Tsar's secret police, but if great care were taken to achieve it, personal contact with such a revolutionary figure could provide a substantial amount of the information Sebastian had been asked to find.

Sebastian read and reread his father's advisory letter before turning to the carefully annotated newspaper material, which he absorbed just as avidly, making his own assessment notes and eventually – inevitably – concluding that the men suggested by his father were those who appeared to be the motivating forces within the Russian revolutionary groups. He added Yakov Sverdlov and Felix Dzerzhinsky. After reflection, he additionally listed Alexander Kerensky to his personal list.

Sebastian was surprised to discover it was past midnight when he finally straightened from the bureau at which he had sat for all that time, eyes blurred with fatigue, his stomach rumbling with the futile reminder that he had long since missed dinner. He had a direction to follow, Sebastian accepted. Having already come to the notice of the Okhrana, and convinced as he was of being under permanent observation, it was a path of the greatest danger, and precisely that which his father had warned him to avoid. But which he couldn't.

'I confess myself astonished,' said Mycroft Holmes.

'I'm in despair,' admitted Watson. 'We've had our disagreements in the past but always of a professional nature, involving a case. This is altogether different.'

'You've no doubt of it's cause?'

'You must have noticed it yourself. Sebastian certainly has.' The doctor shook his head against more port.

'I was refusing to acknowledge what I was seeing,' confessed Mycroft. 'Can you help him, medically?'

'I was succeeding, before this relapse. And am sure I could succeed again. But I can do nothing now, banished as I am. Which is why I am appealing to you.'

'I shall of course do everything in my power to affect a reconciliation. But you of all people need no telling of my brother's stubbornness.'

'Is he involving himself deeply in this latest affair?'

'Very much so.'

'That will help, until I can be with him again. Boredom is a dangerous worm. So is his unshakeable belief that the damned stuff sharpens his intellect.'

'I know of no other person with a sharper natural intellect. He is certainly not in need of artificial stimulants.'

'Join me in convincing him of that if you can.'

'What discussions have you had with Sebastian?'

'He is deeply worried. He talked to me of refusing the Russian assignment, in the hope of it having some effect. I advised strongly against such a course, arguing that it would have the opposite result.' Watson changed his mind, taking up the port decanters. He snorted a laugh. 'Here we criticize stimulants and at the same time indulge ourselves in what we believe to be the same.'

'I would not have Sebastian's worry distracting him from the enterprise at hand.'

'There's possibly something to reflect upon there,' identified Watson.

'How so?' demanded Mycroft.

'Holmes's personal devotion to his son is absolute,' Watson said. 'Any risk to Sebastian's safety is unthinkable . . .'

'Which Sherlock's renewed and continuing transgressions might create,' picked up Mycroft.

'It could be a desperate ploy.'

'In what some – myself at their head – would consider a desperate situation,' said Watson.

'In these most recent days and weeks, I find myself regretting this latest episode,' said Mycroft, his latest conversation with Winston Churchill foremost in his mind. 'Were I able to reflect upon events.'

'Were any of us able to reflect upon the outcome of our first decision, it would more often than not be revoked, most likely for the best,' said Watson. 'At this moment I have only one priority, reconciliation with Sherlock Holmes.'

'How do you plan to achieve that if I cannot find a way?' asked Mycroft.

'That's the scourge,' said Watson. 'I do not know. And that's why I am putting myself in your hands.'

# Six

Sebastian Holmes identified his observers the moment he stepped out from the Grand Hotel, and his depression lifted with his spirits at his at last proving himself *to* himself. There were two of them, both men, one – despite the summer warmth – overcoated and hatted, the other neither. In hailing distance close behind, in case he took a horse-drawn carriage, was a coach in readiness, its driver upon his box. The apparent engrossing conversation of the two men broke too quickly, the hatted one hurrying to the opposite side of the road to enclose him in the classic – but again too obvious – surveillance pincer, the moment they realized that he intended to remain on foot. Sebastian loitered between them, someone in no hurry, once drawing them behind him to confirm the pursuit by cutting down a side street. It was a ploy with a double purpose, ensuring that there were no others he hadn't identified. During a hesitation by a reflecting window back on the main thoroughfare, he saw that their precautionary carriage was about twenty yards behind the two men. How was it, he wondered, that the previous day the surveillance had been so discreet against today's virtual amateurishness?

The necessary exercise delayed his scheduled arrival at the embassy, but Captain Black was, as promised during their telephone conversation, within a minute's summons of the gatehouse. It was sufficient for Sebastian to establish that his pursuers were re-engaged in intense discussion in an alley providing an uninterrupted view of both entrance and exit from the legation's metal-fenced perimeter. Their carriage was once more reined in just behind them.

Sebastian's interest switched as soon as the military attaché escorted him beyond the checkpoint into the inner precincts, at once relieved at seeing various drives and courtyards invisible from the outer road.

'I've confirmed that I'm being watched,' he told the soldier, as they walked.

'You've no doubt?' queried Black.

'None.'

'That will be restrictive for you.'

'An enemy you know is less dangerous than one of whom you are ignorant,' said Sebastian, surprised how easily one of his father's axioms came to mind. 'It does mean, however, that I need to impose upon you a little more.'

'I am, as you know, readily at your disposal,' assured Black, standing back for Sebastian to enter the indicated office in an embassy annex.

The diplomat kept his promise by having the formalities already prepared and awaiting Sebastian's arrival. Sebastian completed the registration forms, alert for a hoped-against reaction to his name, but none came from a perfunctorily operating clerk whose only comment was that his ambition before leaving St Petersburg was just once to visit the Grand Hotel. Following Black's prior guidance, Sebastian did not seek deposit facilities then, but followed the man deeper into the embassy, to Black's own office.

Once more out of anyone's hearing, Black said as they walked: 'There's a fortunate coincidence, which should have occurred to me last night. I apologize for the oversight.'

'Which is?' questioned Sebastian, his interest more upon the man's assistance in another direction.

'Your acceptance now within the British community here in St Petersburg. I can now ensure your name is upon the invitation to the embassy garden party which inaugurates the celebration of the King's official birthday.'

How easily déjà vu reappeared, like pop-up figures in a children's illustrated book, reflected Sebastian: his initial entry into American society had been at a German embassy reception, similarly to honour Kaiser Wilhelm II. His mind so directed, Sebastian said: 'Who is likely to attend?'

'Few, if any, of the echelon you seek. But something of society.'

'Any Russians?' persisted Sebastian.

The other man shrugged. 'I don't receive the acceptances.'

'What of Germans?'

'There, I think, there's a guarantee. They're the most frequent attenders of embassy soirées,' said the military diplomat. 'They have the most avid interest in the affairs of other legations . . .' He smiled. 'That should be something to report back to Winston, to harden his suspicions.'

Sebastian frowned once more. 'I understood you to tell me there was no evidence of German spying?'

'I understood you to be asking me if there had been any increase in the German embassy *staffing*. Of which I've seen no evidence.'

Why the need to be so pedantic? wondered Sebastian. To be accurate and avoid misleading or misinterpretation, he supposed. 'So, Germany *is* active in intelligence-gathering!'

'The function of an embassy is to keep its government as aware as possible of events and feelings within its host country,' lectured Black.

An activity in which, according to Winston Churchill, the St Petersburg legation was proving itself singularly inept. 'I look forward to the occasion.'

'I can guarantee nothing more than entertainment: nothing to contribute to your enterprise here,' said the man. They entered the main embassy building and Black said: 'I thought my personal safe preferable to the normal embassy facilities. I'm sure you'd prefer that.'

'I'd have thought the normal security facilities inside the embassy would have been sufficient.'

'As you have so often anticipated since your arrival, embassies have to protect themselves against embarrassment. Material deposited in the public section is required to be identified, in a written form.'

'And as you have so often anticipated since my arrival here in Russia, I think that would be best avoided.'

The attaché frowned down at the package that Sebastian handed him. 'You've heavily resealed it?'

'It surely would not have been accepted unsealed?'

'No, surely not,' agreed the man, his back to Sebastian as

he twirled the combination of the safe, which revealed a surprising emptiness when its door opened. Black stood, turning to face Sebastian, but jerked his head back in the direction of the safe. 'Is there anything there with which I should be acquainted?'

'Suggestions of who might be among the foremost fomenting unrest here,' generalized Sebastian. 'An unsettling suggestion that they could have plotted that unrest in London itself.'

'What?' exclaimed Black.

'There have been gatherings in London of the Bolsheviks and Mensheviks.'

'I should alert Winston to that,' said Black, at once.

'He's already been told,' said Sebastian. If Black were a trusted confidante of Churchill's, why had he himself been recruited? wondered Sebastian.

'It stands repetition,' insisted the man.

'As you wish,' said Sebastian.

'You spoke of an imposition?' prompted the attaché. 'I really had anticipated participating in a more active manner.'

'You've already performed a service for which I remain eternally grateful,' reminded Sebastian, taking the chair the attaché indicated. 'The subterfuge I propose is simply your summoning a carriage in which I might secrete myself and escape the attention of those waiting outside for my re-emergence.'

Black gestured for the second time towards the relocked safe. 'To begin at once upon the information there?'

'To orientate myself to something of possible interest, which as you know I was attempting by approaching Tsarskoye Selo.'

Black remained silent for several moments before saying accusingly: 'You are concerned at avoiding embarrassment to the embassy. Do you not feel there is a risk of your doing exactly that, arriving here the subject of Okhrana surveillance, to at once disappear but then reappear at the Grand Hotel with the apparent magic of Houdini himself? Quite apart from the danger to which you have already once fallen victim.'

'Which is?' demanded Sebastian.

'Public coachmen are informants of the Okhrana. Their licensing numbers are automatically taken by the permanently assigned observers of every foreign legation, quite separate from those paying you particular attention: the embassy has its own carriage fleet, which makes the summoning of public conveyance something to record. By nightfall, you'd be back in the Okhrana's prison, and this time I doubt I could achieve your release or prevent your mission being very publicly exposed.'

'It was my intention to hold the same carriage for my return and to re-emerge from here,' lured Sebastian.

It appeared difficult for the attaché to avoid openly smiling. 'A public coach would arrive empty, depart seemingly still empty, return still seemingly unoccupied and leave yet again without an occupant. Tell me, sir, do you not think that might arouse the curiosity of our embassy observers, quite separate from the requirement of every coachman in the city to report upon the movements of foreigners?'

'It would appear my intended evasion was ill conceived,' further encouraged Sebastian.

'An easy mistake in unaccustomed circumstances,' soothed Black.

'I have to devise a different strategy.'

'Not necessarily so,' said the soldier, at once. 'You employed the word *orientate*? Is that all you seek to do, further acquaint yourself with certain parts and places in the city?'

'Yes . . . ?' questioned Sebastian, curiously. 'It is a method –' he stopped, reluctant to introduce his father and the man's operating advice into the conversation – 'the manner in which I choose to work.'

'You have no intention of seeking a meeting . . . any encounter with someone who might be considered a revolutionary?' pressed Black.

That had been precisely Sebastian's intention in going to the newspaper office and chancing there'd be a language bridge. 'Absolutely not.'

'Then we can use a coach from the embassy pool,' declared Black.

'You jest!' *We*, isolated Sebastian.

'We'd even have a degree of diplomatic immunity,' smiled the man. 'At least, I and my coach would. What's our destination?'

61

'The offices of *Pravda*.'

Black at once shook his head. 'I've reported fully to the War Office – as well as to Winston himself – on the existence and subversive content of that publication.'

'Have you spoken to any of its writers? It's editor?'

Black snorted a laugh. 'A newspaper with such views is obviously too much of a focus for the Okhrana for me to have attempted open contact.' He shrugged. 'It makes your excursion pointless: I can describe its position in a particularly insalubrious section of the city . . . how ill it looks . . .'

'I would like to see for myself,' insisted Sebastian.

There was an almost imperceptible sigh. 'Winston charged me with providing every assistance. I have your assurance you won't attempt any open approach?'

'My assurance,' promised Sebastian.

It took only minutes for a coach to be summoned from the embassy stables and for the two men to enter, Black to sit very visibly next to the window that would be seen from the side street in which Sebastian had described his watchers to be skulking, Sebastian crouched – with some difficulty because of his height – out of sight in the footwell between the seats. Black sat with his face resting on his hands, shielding his mouth, able to mutter: 'They're still in residence,' as they passed the alley.

Sebastian allowed a further five minutes before gratefully straightening to take the opposite seat, instantly alert to his outside surroundings, at once using the river and the broad Dvortsovaya Square, opposite the Winter Palace, as his location markers to the direction in which they were going. Very soon after passing the square, the coach plunged into the narrow back streets of the guttersnipes, in which Sebastian had grown unsettled during his first reconnaissance. Twice, careless of the casual whip swipes of the coachman, groups of threadbare urchins swarmed the coach, hammering its side panels for coin. When Sebastian reached to his pocket, Black said urgently: 'No! If you show compassion they'll pursue us all the way back to the embassy, attracting precisely the attention you seek to avoid. Never proffer money on the street to beggars: they'll engulf you and strip you bare by sheer weight of numbers. In fact, don't ever contemplate walking unaccompanied in areas such as this.'

It was something he would most likely have to contemplate, Sebastian thought. But he found it difficult to believe it was as hazardous as Black purported: urchins made noise, not injurious mayhem. And now, unrewarded, there was no longer noise.

'We're getting close,' warned Black. 'To your right.'

It was a long, low building, all its windows covered from any outside scrutiny, the single Cyrillic word, which Sebastian guessed to read *Pravda*, painted black against a white background. Sebastian counted six ill-dressed men, divided into two groups, standing listlessly in front of the property.

The attaché said: '*Pravda* means truth.'

'From the shades and guards in attendance they don't welcome outside interest,' judged Sebastian. 'I wouldn't imagine the door to be unlocked for casual entry, even if I attempted such a direct approach.'

'Which you've sworn against!' said Black, quickly.

'I need no reminder,' said Sebastian.

There was one more attempted urchin ambush before they regained a major highway, which Sebastian recognized sufficiently to know they were picking up the route back to the embassy.

Accusingly, Black said: 'This seems to have been a pointless exercise.'

'As you inferred, the newspaper and its location were listed in the material I received from my father.'

'To what purpose?'

'He suggested it as a possible Bolshevik outlet.'

'Which I could have told you.'

'But which you didn't,' said Sebastian, pointedly.

'Has this been in the nature of a test?' retorted the man, just as pointedly.

'Not at all,' lied Sebastian. 'My need was to escape the attention of those I identified to you outside the embassy. Do you judge the newspaper office to be of sufficient interest?'

'It has a proletarian readership, for those of them able to read.'

'Those who can't read can listen to what is read to them,' suggested Sebastian. 'Is it subversive?'

'It could be considered so by some.'

'It was your opinion I sought.'

'It supports the democratic Duma.'

'Is the Duma democratic? Or a meaningless gesture by the Tsar?'

'It's the best those striving for change are going to achieve.'

'You say that after 1905!' challenged Sebastian.

'I say that *because* of 1905,' responded Black, instantly. 'The attempted revolution was quelled by the Tsar's firmness. Which is how he remains, firmly in control of his country, with the support of his subjects.'

The outing was proving more productive about Churchill's source than he'd anticipated, Sebastian realized. 'You – your embassy – do not expect there to be another uprising?'

The other man smiled. 'I have advised Winston so, more than once. I am at your assistance because of my Sandhurst association with the man, but I fear your mission here is ill founded. I advised him of that, too.'

'You must have resented my coming here – Churchill's very approach to me – in the light of that advice?'

The attaché shrugged. 'Winston does what Winston does, once he becomes fixated upon something. Yours is a fresh face in the insular society in which I currently find myself: I welcome the chance of new companionship, most certainly I do not resent it.'

'But dismiss my mission as pointless?'

'And impossible to boot, were your mission even well founded.'

'Did you so advise Churchill?'

'On two separate occasions, as forcibly as I felt able.'

'And were ignored?'

'Winston does what Winston does,' repeated his school friend.

Sebastian became aware of their closeness to the embassy, easing himself from his seat into the footwell again. As they passed the alley, Black said: 'Your patient followers are still waiting.'

'Not for much longer,' promised Sebastian.

The coach lurched to its right, turning into the embassy grounds, and Black said: 'You're out of their view. You can raise yourself now.'

Sebastian did, disembarking into an inner courtyard. He said: 'I am obliged to you yet again.'

'What further can I do to assist?'

'I need to give matters consideration,' avoided Sebastian. 'And communicate with London.'

'My personal telegraph is at your disposal,' offered Black.

Sebastian was sure it would be. 'I need to compose my thoughts.'

Sebastian quit the embassy – picking up his dutiful followers and their escorting coach – intending to do just that, mentally composing his reservations about the views and attitudes of Captain Lionel Black as he walked. He'd scarcely travelled more than two hundred yards, however, before he was mentally stopped by an abrupt but balancing thought as he reviewed his conversation with the attaché. If Churchill had trusted the opinion of the man who'd made no secret of being the politician's informant – or of more than once opposing Sebastian's coming to Russia as Churchill's emissary – then his mission would not have been mounted. The morning had been useful for bringing him to the conclusion not to attach any credence to Black's arrogant dismissals of any risk to the Tsar's rule. But there were more pressing matters at hand than a confirmation of what Churchill must already suspect, if not positively know. To confirm which there was no immediate urgency.

The necessary mind change brought Sebastian's concentration back to his original intention of the day. In another reflecting window, Sebastian identified the continued inept pursuit and thought again of his earlier judgement. It *was* amateur, in the extreme. Which he, considering himself a trained opposite, could surely evade in the manner of his father's instruction! If he did not succeed, there would be no difficulty in isolating those behind him and abandoning the attempt to get into the *Pravda* building.

Sebastian quickened his pace, avoiding the turn that would

have taken him back to his hotel. Totally sure of his surroundings, Sebastian cut short his crossing of Dvortsovaya Square, hurriedly deviating into one of the Winter Palace's bordering roads. It was a manoeuvre that unintentionally restricted him, limiting him to a straight, unbroken highway running along the east of the palace's outermost wall. Sebastian chanced a backward glance at the eventual turn, taking him deeper into the warren, to see the now bustling pursuit had been taken up by the clattering coach. It was a convenient side road, wide enough in itself but bisected by further alleys and lanes. Sebastian darted into the first, to his right, and then just as quickly into the first opening to his left, which kept him in the direction of his objective. As Sebastian zigzagged, he more obviously checked for pursuit, his confidence growing at the continued absence behind him of either the coach or its occupants. He was in the urchin jungle, he recognized, at first isolating only the odd guttersnipe, but then more, grouped in increasing packs, hovering like the hyenas they were, each gang waiting for the boldest scavenger to attack before joining the assault for their own scrap of flesh. It had been unthinkable that morning to go to the British embassy armed with his revolver, but how much he needed it now, not to kill, but to disperse them with a warning shot over their heads if they did attack.

Outwardly tense, his swordstick released in readiness, Sebastian's mind still calculated. How truly amateur were those supposed professionals behind him? Twisting and turning though he was, he was providing a general lead to his destination which could, by deduction, become increasingly obvious, not needing his visible hare to the Tsar's baying hounds. And what about when he got to the *Pravda* office? Would he be able to get beyond the loitering unkempt guardians, only to find himself facing a barred, bolted and impassable door? For once his own clichés came to mind – I won't know until I try. So he would try. The intervening ruffians would be a formidable obstacle, but if he could bluster his way past them, his claim to be a journalist – from a city and country in which the revolutionaries felt it safe to conduct their scheming congresses – might just get him beyond the door. To what? I won't know until I try, he told himself again.

VISIT US AT
nymag.com

**BUSINESS REPLY MAIL**

FIRST-CLASS MAIL    PERMIT NO 104    FLAGLER BEACH FL

POSTAGE WILL BE PAID BY ADDRESSEE

*NewYork*

PO BOX 420212
PALM COAST FL 32142-7456

NO POSTAGE
NECESSARY
IF MAILED
IN THE
UNITED STATES

Sebastian knew he was close now. Knew, too, that the packs were closing in. He could actually hear their scuffling, see the occasional adult hurrying from a scene and a situation of which they were determined to be no part. To reach his destination, he needed to go to his right, Sebastian calculated: two, maybe three bisections would bring him back to the wider road along which the guttersnipes had nevertheless pursued his coach a few short hours before. But this current road was too wide to fend off attacks from more than one direction, too deserted now to expect – even to seek – any assistance. Sebastian tensed further, relying on the sound, and the moment it came, the first concerted rush from his right, he darted to the left into what was even less than an alley, a passageway scarcely sufficient for a single person, reducing attack from four to two directions, front and back. And in the brief moment before turning to confront the pygmy mob, Sebastian saw that, initially at least, there was none behind him.

They came at him like a pack of dogs, well-trained dogs, three or four going for his ankles to trip and bring him to the ground, others swarming above them to distract and unbalance him. Sebastian kicked out against those grabbing for his ankles and legs, at the same time trying to retreat – to run – backwards as best he could to avoid being caught between another pack doubtless doubling around to attack from the rear. Sebastian was thrashing out with his stick, the sword still sheathed, despite his danger, remaining reluctant to draw steel upon children, until he saw that the leaders of the pack were not children at all but youths, young adults even. And that one actually had a drawn knife held low in readiness, alert for an opening.

The assault wavered momentarily at the flourish with which he finally drew his weapon, the pause enough for him to direct the first slashing cut at the youth with the knife. Sebastian was later to concede to himself that it was more luck than judgement that brought his blade down across the knife-holding hand. The youth screamed in surprise and pain, his blood splattering over those closed tight around him. Sebastian at once altered his fighting stance to lessen the chance of his sword being warded off, not slashing full-bladed but jabbing, point

67

first, using the expertise he'd learned in the fencing salons of Heidelberg. He felt a hit, another scream, then another. The pack did not pull back. Sebastian created the distance between them and himself by continuing to retreat, and maintained it by thrusting continuously out, arm fully extended.

Sebastian guessed himself to be almost at the exit from the passageway when he heard the scrabbling feet and then the war cries of those who had come around to block his retreat. His frontal attackers answered the shouts, surging forward. He'd go down, Sebastian knew. Engulfed by sheer numbers, as Black had warned. And those he'd injured – certainly the knifeman who had withdrawn from the fray nursing his blood-gushing hand – would show him no mercy. So he could show no mercy, no quarter, himself. Sebastian turned, his back to the passage wall, jabbing left and right, left and right, but they were closing now on both sides, those trying to trip him sliding in on their bellies, like writhing snakes. So near! he thought. The rectangle of brighter daylight that could have been his escape could not be more than a yard distant, two at the most. Desperately Sebastian gouged and jabbed on either side at the encroaching gangs. His left leg was clamped, a body wrapped around it, too tight to be shaken off. He slashed downwards, knew he'd cut someone from the scream, but the hold didn't slacken. His right leg was seized, lost as he kicked out but seized again immediately. His cheek stung and Sebastian guessed he'd been caught by a knife. They had him then, his legs locked, bringing him down. Sebastian was careless now, stabbing wildly, his only hope to hurt anyone – young adult, youth, guttersnipe, anyone or anything – about to inflict the worst hurt they could upon him.

The explosion was devastating.

Sebastian was later to realize that he never heard – or couldn't remember hearing – the actual noise. His recollection, incredibly, was of a sudden, seconds-only silence before the shockwaves that scattered the very attackers blocking his escape like dust in the wind. It scorched, too, down the passageway, its narrowness creating a funnel that accentuated its force. From which, standing sideways as he was, Sebastian was less thrown than his would-be murderers, although he was smashed back against the passage wall. Most of what he did at that moment was instinctive, kicking himself free from the stunned anchors around his legs, stepping over – treading on – others and bursting free from what only seconds earlier he'd accepted to be his grave-maker.

There was carnage on the street upon which he emerged. The very exit from the passageway was clotted with the unconscious and wounded quivering bodies of his ambushers. There were a lot of other bodies and staggering people all around. Two carriages, maybe even three, appeared locked together, reduced to frames by the explosion and fire destroying them further: a fire-atrophied figure of one coachman still sat upon his smouldering box, hands positioned to hold reins already burned away. He was deaf, Sebastian realized. A lot of staggering people had their mouths open, their lips moving, but he couldn't hear their cries, their bloodied pleas for help. Too dazed properly to be aware of what he was doing, Sebastian actually trod on unconscious or maimed bodies beyond the passage. In what he believed to be a run, but which was little more than an unsteady stagger, Sebastian tried to get away, colliding with other stumbling figures who pushed at him to get past as he pushed at them.

Sebastian's first conscious awareness was that he was closer to the newspaper offices than he'd imagined: that they were at the left-handed spur of this very road. It was the waving, surrender-like fluttering of the curtains that made Sebastian realize all the windows had been blown out, which made him look down further to see that the unevenness of his awkward path was virtually a lumped carpet of glass and that no window or shop front for as far as he could see remained intact. He began to hear, distantly, not intelligible words but sounds: the crackle of glass underfoot, wood ablaze, the screaming whinnying of a disembowelled carriage horse, thrashing in its doomed effort to stand. None of the previous guards remained in front of the newspaper building: two of what could have been their number lay unmoving in the gutter. Just beyond was the smoking crater marking the detonation point of what had to have been a substantial bomb.

Sebastian forced himself on, reaching the premises at the

very moment that the door opened from inside, to release crying, shaking women and men, whose cries he could more easily hear. He thrust against them, past them, through the still-open door.

And was in.


'So Watson scuttled to you?'

'Watson did not *scuttle* to me,' refused Mycroft. 'He *came* to me distressed at a most unlikely contretemps between you. Because he is concerned for your well-being. As we all are.'

'All are?' picked out Sherlock Holmes, rising angrily from his chair, the Persian slippers scuffing the carpet at 221b Baker Street in his anger.

'Watson. Myself. Sebastian.'

'Sebastian!'

'It ill suits you to play the surprised man, Sherlock. You have a problem as obvious to those who know and love you as Nelson's monument.'

'I have no problem!'

'Nor need of artificial stimulants which dull rather than aid a mind and a brain that has never required stimulation.'

'You come to my lodgings to insult me!'

'I come to impress upon you the concern shared by us all.'

'Then all of you can go to damnation.'

'Which is where we will have to follow you, if needs be.'

'I am not interested in playing word games with you, sir!'

'Nor I with you, sir,' retorted Mycroft. 'This is too serious a matter to be dismissed as a game.'

'I fear this discussion is taking the same course as that with Watson.'

'With whom you have severed contact.'

'With whom I have severed contact,' confirmed Sherlock Holmes.

'Then fear it well and deeply,' said Mycroft.

Sherlock Holmes turned hurriedly from the window overlooking Baker Street. 'What, pray, is the substance of that remark?'

'Your son – someone of whom you made me guardian, which I legally remain – is currently engaged in circumstances and business of great importance to this country, at possible great personal risk to himself. I will do nothing to endanger either, most certainly not Sebastian, whom I love as if he were my own son, by continuing to act as a conduit for information or advice in which I can no longer have confidence.'

Sherlock Holmes remained motionless, looking down in ill-concealed astonishment at his brother. His voice shaking with fury, he said at last: 'Are you telling me that you would stand between me and my son?'

'For the safety and well-being of your son, yes, that is exactly what I am telling you. Your reasoning in the condition to which you are increasingly reducing yourself cannot be trusted. I will not have Sebastian misled or misdirected because of it. Sebastian needs your help, not your hindrance.'

'I wish you out of my house!'

'In which I no longer wish to remain, confronted by your current attitude. But think deeply upon what I have said.' Mycroft rose, scooping up his light overcoat as he did so. 'I look forward to contact from you, dear brother, when you have considered what I've said.'

# Seven

Sebastian Holmes drew back, hiding himself in the chaos that surrounded him, needing as much time as he could gain for his hearing to clear sufficiently for him to detect the pitch and sound of his own voice, unsure what he was going to say when the time came to speak. The screaming and name-calling, people trying to find people who might be hurt, was subsiding. The fine, mist-like dust that had been falling from everywhere was easing, although it gave everyone – including Sebastian – a grey, spectral appearance. It was probably that, everyone appearing the same during the gradual moments of recovery, that delayed the discovery of Sebastian as an intruding stranger among them. By the time that happened, Sebastian had his environment established. Getting past the front door was a small victory. The room in which he found himself was cut from wall to wall at its centre by a wooden divide heavy and thick enough to be the revetment for the metal-meshed separation that topped it. In the mesh there were two minuscule openings, behind which Sebastian assumed reception clerks normally sat. Between the two windows, although the mesh was unbroken, was a door, at the moment so widely – or perhaps wildly – swung open that he could easily see on its inside the security of two heavy individual locks with at least a five-inch-thick metal slide-bar, for which there had to be receiving sockets on either side of the formidable counter.

It was a grime-covered man, possibly one of the original outside guardians, now uniformly grey and blackened like them all, who recognized Sebastian as an intruder when he turned from securing the outer door. There was a shocked moment of astonishment before he began groping into his clothing, shouting a warning as he did so.

First in English, then French and finally German, Sebastian shouted even louder: 'I am an English journalist. I seek Josef Vissarionovich Djugashvili.' Sebastian hoped that, with his now hearing-restored linguist's ear, he managed a sufficiently close approximation of the Russian pronunciation of the name. By the time he completed the German rendering, he was facing three separately held revolvers. Each hand that held them was shaking. For the first time he realized that he still carried the swordstick, the blade fortunately sheathed. He couldn't remember returning it to its scabbard or clutching it still as he'd staggered through the carnage. They'd consider him armed, he knew. Striving to keep the anxiety from his voice, Sebastian repeated himself, in all three languages, more heavily stressing his nationality this time.

There was a sudden babble, none of it in a language Sebastian knew nor needed to. All the responses were angry, threatening demands. All three gunman moved closer, too close for any of them to miss if they fired. Slowly Sebastian raised his arms. The babble continued, louder, angrier. Pointlessly, except to hurt, one of the three jabbed his revolver into Sebastian's ribs. Sebastian only just managed to stiffen himself against being winded. For the third time, detecting the first tinge of desperation in his own voice, he shouted his trilingual appeal to a fresh, uncomprehending opposing wall of sound.

'Who are you? What do you want?' The German was bad, ungrammatical, but sufficient to be understood.

Sebastian guessed he would only have one opportunity. He said: 'My name is Sebastian Holmes. I am a British journalist, representing the *Morning Post*. I am researching an article, more than one perhaps, upon the Russian Social-Democratic movement, which held congresses in London which were also reported in the *Morning Post*. In those articles, Josef Vissarionovich Djugashvili was listed as a delegate, although as Josef Stalin. I know that Josef Stalin is a contributing writer to this publication. I seek his guidance, for what I intend to write.'

'What do you intend to write?'

The mesh was too fine, those behind it too many, for Sebastian to isolate the German-speaker. 'Honestly. I have already seen the squalor and deprivation behind the impressive facades. I want to provide a balanced account of the lives of ordinary people in Russia.'

There were isolated bursts of Russian.

The voice said: 'They think you had something to do with the explosion.'

The derisive snigger was not difficult for Sebastian, although it released just a little of his anxiety, too. 'An English-speaking bomber who immediately after the explosion enters his intended target, identifies himself, and asks to speak to someone who might well have been injured or killed!'

There was hurried, coded knocking upon the street door and a shouted exchange. The German-speaker said: 'The authorities are close. They will go through the building. Identify everyone.'

His identification to the Okhrana was inevitable, Sebastian recognized at once. Into his mind came the perfect recall of Captain Black's warning. *By nightfall you'd be back in the Okhrana prison, and this time I doubt I could achieve your release or prevent your mission being very publicly exposed.* He said: 'I don't wish my being here to become known to the authorities.'

The recognizable voice spoke in Russian, to what was clearly a fresh babble of protest and objection, and then in German again: 'Come through.'

'I am at gunpoint.'

The order was curt and the reluctance obvious from the three men confronting him as they lowered their weapons. One kept his ready in his hand, only finally holstering it to fresh warnings from the outside street. Sebastian went through the opening in the counter, alert for the German-speaker, although no one initially greeted his entry. Almost as one, people began to retreat further into the building. Deference was being shown to a burly, heavily moustached man around whom an inner coterie of four men protectively grouped themselves; one gestured impatiently for Sebastian to follow, which he did. The formation put the large man at the head of their line, with three others separating him from Sebastian, who in turn had another man behind him. They went through a littered

74

newsroom and then down two flights of stairs at the bottom of which were silent printing presses, none of which at that moment appeared to be manned. All the workers' activity was in a paper storage room to the right. The huge reels were being manhandled, in what was clearly a rehearsed exercise, on to wheeled pallets to clear a route through to what appeared to be a steel-pillared and sheeted wall. As they reached it, one of the steel panels was unbolted to provide an opening just sufficient for a man to pass through. As he went by one of the printers, the burly man accepted an already lighted lantern. The man immediately in front of Sebastian was handed another. Sebastian reached out expectantly but was ignored, the final illumination going to the man behind him.

It was a roughly cut passage supported by wooden struts, slippery underfoot and constantly dripping from above. The wall against which Sebastian put out a steadying hand was slimey. He tried to calculate how far they were from the river but couldn't. He did, however, estimate that they had travelled almost twenty yards before a door became visible. The leader rapped against it in the prearranged code employed on the outer door of the building they had just left. There was the sound of scraping bolts and the door opened immediately into what was briefly a dazzling, electrically lighted basement in which three men already waited. There was an instant burst of questioning at Sebastian's entry into the room, cut off by the leader's sharp retort.

The moustachioed man frowned at Sebastian's dirt-caked appearance, then down at his own. 'We look as if we dug the tunnel ourselves.'

'I feel as if I had,' said Sebastian.

The man said: 'I am Josef Stalin.'

They could only shake or brush their clothes with their hands, which did little to clean off the dust or mud from the escape channel, but a communal bucket of water and cloths was produced for them to wash. By the time they finished, there were vodka and glasses on the table. One of the original four now grouped protectively behind Stalin poured for them all, but ignored Sebastian until a sharp order from the man.

Stalin raised his glass in a toast and said: 'To truth.'

'Which I know to be the title of your newspaper.' Sebastian copied the gesture, finishing the drink in one tossed-back movement. Putting his glass aside, he extracted the *Morning Post* accreditation card from a waistcoat pocket and offered it across the table.

'And hopefully what you will learn,' said Stalin, as the other glasses were refilled. He glanced at the card before slipping it carefully into his own pocket.

'Perhaps with your help,' said Sebastian. The other man did not look like an intellectual. His face was heavily pockmarked – Sebastian wondered if the moustache was to conceal some particularly bad indentation – and, since they had sat, he'd often fingered his jaw, as if in pain.

'Bursting in as you did was foolhardy, to the point of madness,' said Stalin. 'Had you been seen doing so, you almost certainly would have been shot, as one of our attackers.'

'Then I was indeed lucky,' said Sebastian. 'Who were your attackers?'

The other man shrugged. 'It will be dismissed by the authorities as internal, factional feuding, but it was doubtless inspired by the police, to give them a reason to search the building in the hope of finding something they can use to close us down.'

'Is there factional feuding?'

The other man's smile seemed difficult, strengthening Sebastian's impression of some facial discomfort. 'An astute question! If you are to write accurately you must understand the differences between the various wings of the Social Democratic Party. At the second congress in London there was a divisive, party-splitting vote upon the editorial composition of the party newspaper, *Iskra*. It went in favour of a group—'

'Headed by Vladimir Lenin,' risked Sebastian, anxious to support his assumed role.

Stalin nodded. 'You're already well researched. That vote and that success gained them their name, *Bolsheviki*, members of the majority. Those of us who opposed, and in fact won the greater proportion of votes on other matters, are *Mensheviki*. The split between the two was repaired at a later congress, in

76

1906, the year after the first revolution. But widened again last year . . .' He gestured to the door leading back into the tunnel. 'Which gives the Tsar's people the excuse to stage today's sort of attack and blame others.'

'What's the difference in ideology?'

'There are many shades of grey. The most obvious is that the Bolsheviks advocate violent reforms, the Mensheviks a constitutional approach.'

There was much to be learned if he could guide the discussion properly, Sebastian decided. 'You talked about "us" in referring to the Mensheviks. So you, presumably, are in favour of the Duma?'

The other man abandoned a second attempted smile. 'Don't try a British comparison with your constitutional monarchy. There are both Bolsheviks and Mensheviks in the Duma, a supposed parliament which is nothing of the sort and which the Tsar dismisses with contempt.'

'The Duma was a concession forced upon the Tsar?' ventured Sebastian, carefully.

'Not a concession, a charade,' insisted Stalin.

'Which will not bring about reforms and improvements constitutionally?'

More vodka was added to all the glasses: the heads of those grouped around Stalin on the other side of the bare table were shifting back and forth with the conversation, trying to infer the exchange from the tones of voice. Stalin's attitude became wary at the question. 'No democracy in the world was achieved overnight.'

Not an answer, Sebastian decided. 'How long will it take in Russia?'

'Who knows?' said the man.

He was losing the direction in which he wanted to take the discussion, Sebastian thought. 'How long will the people wait?'

'Who knows?' repeated the man. He managed a smile this time. It brought a whiff of bad-toothed halitosis across the table.

'I have spoken to people who believe the Tsar has re-established his autocracy.'

'Russian people? Or supposed Western observers?'

77

He was edging back on course, thought Sebastian hopefully. 'Westerners. Who point out that the army is the Tsar's strength and that the Tsar has the army's loyalty.'

'Has he?' asked Stalin, rhetorically.

'He had in 1905.'

'It's now 1913, a long time since. Much has changed.'

'I sought your guidance on truth and accuracy. And am grateful for what I believe to be that guidance. Do you genuinely believe the civilian unrest has spread to influence the Russian military?'

'The navy mutinied in 1905.'

'Just one vessel, the *Potemkin*,' argued Sebastian.

'How many more will there be next time?'

He *was* getting his guidance, Sebastian acknowledged. Not in positive statements of fact – nor, thank goodness, in a diatribe of political polemics – but in and by inference that could hardly be misunderstood. 'Will the split between your two factions heal yet again?'

'Politics is compromise.'

'I understood from your definition that *Bolsheviki* means strength of the majority?'

'I was educated, until my expulsion for inciting unrest, in a seminary, difficult though it is for me now to imagine myself an orthodox priest. I still remember the catechisms, though. It's a whimsical hope that the meek shall inherit the earth.'

He was being misdirected again, Sebastian accepted. Or was he? 'There was little whimsy out there in the street a few short hours ago.'

'Nor will there be in the coming future.'

It would be a mistake to attempt a time limit again, Sebastian judged. 'I have introductions, enquiries to pursue. I would, however, welcome an opportunity for us to meet again.'

'You believe you've heard enough?'

'I believe I've begun to hear what I came here to learn.'

'Those around me think I have made a mistake already in trusting you as I have.'

'Why did you?'

'The *Morning Post* reported our congress meetings fairly. We need people in the West properly to understand our philosophies . . . the true situation here . . . And despite those around me, I scarcely felt myself in any danger, even from that inadequate swordstick.'

Sebastian was conscious that he was colouring. 'Why didn't you demand its surrender?'

'Why, with three pistols at your head?'

'I asked if we could meet again,' reminded Sebastian.

'These have been circumstances in your unexpected favour,' said the burly man. 'I cannot imagine such arising similarly.'

'Nor would I wish them similar in any circumstance,' said Sebastian, with feeling. 'Were such a possibility to arise, could I approach you again?'

'It could be at your own peril from the Tsar's people.'

'Which it was today,' Sebastian pointed out.

'Where do you stay?'

'The Grand Hotel.'

'Grand indeed!' The mocking turn of the word sounded a more derisive sneer in German than in English.

'Can I anticipate contact there?'

'I don't know. There has not been such an attack upon our premises before. We must be causing too much concern.'

'Does the Tsar need an excuse to close you down?'

'That could prove to be too forceful a move, creating too much of a reaction. For the moment they'll risk no more than intimidation.'

A nugget when he'd believed there was no more inference to sift, Sebastian recognized. Persistently he said: 'I would greatly appreciate our meeting again.'

'Don't attempt to come to the *Pravda* office,' ordered Stalin, abrupt authority in his voice. 'If I choose another meeting, there will be contact . . .' There was a burst of Russian. 'You'll be escorted back to where it will be safe for you to make your own way.'

'I am in your debt,' Sebastian thanked him.

'Be careful of being in anyone's debt,' said Stalin, turning the cliché as he'd earlier turned the name of Sebastian's residence. 'Debts have to be repaid.'

The house connected to the tunnel was only two streets

from the river, and Sebastian would have been able to find his own way, but he was escorted as far as the recognizable approach to the Hermitage by two unspeaking men who, without even a grunting farewell in their own language, abruptly turned and left him. The half-light prevented too much curiosity in his bedraggled appearance until he reached the hotel, from which the doorman who had translated for him initially attempted to bar his entry.

'What happened?' the man demanded upon recognition, remembering to speak in French.

'An accident,' dismissed Sebastian.

'Do you require a doctor?'

'No. I am not injured.'

'Your face . . . ?'

Sebastian had forgotten the stinging blow got in the melee with the urchins. 'It is nothing.'

When Sebastian regained his suite to wash away the congealed blood, he found the cut to be a little over an inch long and too deep to be described as nothing, although the bleeding had ceased. The mirror surround of the bathroom, before which he twisted, showed the beginnings of a large bruise that would doubtless grow larger across his back, where the shockwaves from the bomb had driven him against the wall. As he discarded yet more clothes for disposal, Sebastian reflected that this latest enterprise was taking a heavy toll on his wardrobe. He lowered himself into a hopefully ache-easing bath, satisfied he had learned sufficient that day for a considerable memorandum to Winston Churchill and his uncle. And to his father, Sebastian quickly added, regretting the brief omission.

Mycroft was the host and chose Rules, to Winston Churchill's approval, although the food and the favoured champagne did little to improve the politician's mood. He said: 'Asquith has infected the King's brain with Ireland!'

'How do you know?' asked Mycroft.

'Chesterfield,' identified Churchill. 'He attended the Privy Council meeting at the palace yesterday. Ireland was the only subject of discussion. His majesty is fearful of civil war.'

'With some justification,' Mycroft pointed out. Curiously he said: 'I was unaware of the earl being an ally.'

Churchill shook his head dismissively. 'I'm not convinced he is. I've had to show my hand more than I wished.'

Mycroft frowned. 'How?'

'I've pressed Chesterfield to raise the sanctuary of the Romanovs at the next gathering of the council.'

'Is he minded to do so?'

'He went as far as saying he'd consider it, if the circumstances arose. My difficulty is that he's a Haldane disciple who doesn't believe the threat of war with Germany as I do: it flies against his opinion.'

Why then consider using the Earl of Chesterfield? wondered Mycroft. 'That doesn't augur well.'

'Nothing augurs well,' complained Churchill. 'Heed my judgement, Mycroft, there'll be war in Europe before there's war in Ireland.'

'Were there to be neither,' said Mycroft, who at that juncture was not interested in Churchill's judgement.

'Reality, sir!' insisted Churchill. 'Face reality.'

'Something that is being forced upon me,' said Mycroft, more to himself than the other man.

'I did not catch that,' protested Churchill.

'I seek your help,' admitted Mycroft.

Churchill waited, expectantly, adding claret to both their glasses before the sommelier could reach their table.

'I wish you specifically to invite Sherlock to our next gathering at the club. But as if it were just the two of you; no one else.'

Churchill sat with the glass suspended before him. 'What is this?'

'A personal matter.'

'Involving Sebastian?'

'He is unaware of circumstances.'

'Could it – this personal matter – affect the outcome of what Sebastian is engaged upon?'

'It is possible,' allowed Mycroft.

'Who else will be at this next meeting?'

'Myself.'

'No one else?'

'No.' Should he consider Dr Watson? wondered Mycroft. There was time to reflect upon it.

'It's no secret to me that your brother is not one of my most fervent admirers. What if he declines my invitation?'

'He won't,' insisted Mycroft. Churchill was his brother's only possible link to Sebastian: there couldn't be any doubt of his acceptance.

'Is this all you ask of me?' queried Churchill, solicitously.

Mycroft hesitated, considering the offer. 'For the moment.'

'Don't let your brother's antipathy to me influence you. My response won't be influenced by it.'

'Your generosity embarrasses me.'

'I haven't been called upon to perform any act of generosity beyond that which you've already extended to me.'

It was past three before Sebastian finished his account of the meeting with Stalin and was able gratefully to haul himself into bed and immediate, exhausted sleep. He'd described the bomb attack but mentioned nothing of his closeness to it, nor of his street fracas with the guttersnipe gang.

# Eight

Sebastian was more familiar with al fresco celebrations in Europe than in his own country, but decided, upon his exit from the embassy building into its grounds, that an English summer scene had been transferred to Russia. A complete bandstand had been erected for the occasion and seats set out for an audience. There were groups genteelly playing croquet, which Sebastian knew to be a game anything but genteel, and on the faraway lake, boats were being rowed, or steered and manned by attendant boatmen. Groups formed and disbanded, a lot of the men wearing boaters, most of the women warding off the summer sun beneath fringed parasols. There were two tea tents, tables and chairs laid out in front of each, and throughout the park, retinues of uniformed waiters circulated with trays of champagne and fruit cup.

Captain Black, who'd again met Sebastian at the gate to receive and secure that night's shipment to London before escorting him out on to the lawns, said: 'These are occasions when I feel homesick.'

'Only a temporary absence,' dismissed Sebastian, who found nostalgia for garden parties curious from a serving soldier.

Black indicated the nearest group. 'The ambassador and his lady and their chosen ones. Do I introduce you as the journalist that Winston described you to be?'

'Best to remain as consistent as possible,' said Sebastian.

Sir Nigel Pearlman was a lean, tall man – easily matching Sebastian's six foot four inches – with a shock of pure-white hair. Sebastian guessed the man's wife to be at least twenty years her husband's junior. At their moment of introduction she managed to shake Sebastian's hand practically at the same time as deftly exchanging an empty champagne glass for a full one. Lieutenant Roger Jefferson, the immaculately uniformed naval attaché, was clearly someone who believed manliness was proved by the crushing strength of a handshake. By grateful comparison, the greeting from John Berringer, the portly *chef du protocol*, was practically effete: that of his wife, Ludmilla, was firmer. Sebastian, a visitor from home, was corralled by them, prodded from all sides by questions about what he intended to write, which Sebastian evaded by saying he was too recently in the capital to have decided upon his subject. That reply prompted an offer from the eager-to-volunteer Ludmilla Berringer personally to escort Sebastian to all the historic sites of her native city. To an immediate although light rebuke from his wife, Sir Roger asked if Irish unrest were still the political preoccupation in London, to which Sebastian was easily able to respond, from so much contact with Churchill, but was cut short by Lady Pearlman, still juggling glasses, asking how long Sebastian thought it might take for the suffragette demonstrations to end, through lack of commitment. Sebastian said that, from his reading of English newspapers – at the last moment adding his own, most obviously of all – he hadn't detected any lessening of determination. With unwitting prescience, the naval attaché said he hoped Sebastian had not received his facial injury from a street attack, which Sebastian laughed off with an account of a stumbled encounter with a bathroom-cabinet door.

It took almost thirty minutes for the socially adept military attaché to extricate Sebastian. The moment they were alone, Black said: 'You're managing to provide Churchill with a lot of material?'

'Just the impressions he asked me to form.' In what he had just entrusted to the attaché, Sebastian predicted further and increasing civil unrest, with the Tsar's support by the army and navy more uncertain than it had been in 1905. He guessed that the ideological divisions within the Social Democrat movement would be moderated in the face of the Tsar's contempt for the Duma – actually quoting Stalin that compromise was the basic element of politics – and illustrated as the Tsar's political weakness the man's apparent uncertainty as to public reaction if he moved to close down the anti-government newspaper.

'Winston might choose the telegraph to respond,' suggested Black.

'There was nothing of urgency,' insisted Sebastian.

'I've been at the telegraph a lot myself earlier today,' volunteered the attaché. 'There's been an official statement from the government that the attack upon *Pravda* was mounted by divisive factions within the reformist movement.'

'I'd not heard that explanation,' said Sebastian. Apart from Stalin's accurate prediction, he thought.

'There are more Russians here than I expected,' said Black, surveying the crowded lawns.

'What about Germans?'

'Surprisingly absent,' said Black. 'Ah!' he abruptly exclaimed. 'Now there's someone you might benefit from meeting. Alexander Kerensky. Elected to the Duma last year. It's rumoured that he has links with some revolutionary groups. He's a Social Democrat and a leading lawyer here. Regarded as a rising political star.'

The man whom Black indicated was a prominent-nosed, close-cropped man more formally dressed than most people around him, in a wing collar and dark jacket. Sebastian said: 'Do you know him sufficiently to introduce me?'

'As a journalist?' queried Black.

'Collecting material for an article upon the social conditions in the country,' confirmed Sebastian, wondering why the man had repeated his earlier question.

There was something almost Germanic in the heel-clicking formality with which Kerensky responded to the introduction. In heavily accented English he said: 'You pick an interesting time to be here on such an assignment.'

'I hope so,' said Sebastian.

'What are your impressions so far?'

'Unformed, as yet,' avoided Sebastian, easily. 'I am interested in the parliamentary developments of which I understand you're a part.'

'Very early developments,' qualified Kerensky.

The same reservations as Stalin, gauged Sebastian. 'But developments, surely?'

'Time may well be the judge of that,' said the lawyer, with equal evasion.

'A Duma has been established.'

'And needs to have the authority to act on its own behalf, not by permission.'

Another echo of Stalin, Sebastian identified. 'I was recently reminded that democracy is rarely achieved overnight.'

'There are many in Russia who are impatient.' He shook his head against an offered tray of drinks.

Sebastian and Black both took champagne. Black said: 'Then patience will have to be learned.'

Sebastian thought there was an irritation in the way Kerensky looked at the attaché. 'Often more easily said than achieved,' remarked the Russian.

'If it is achieved, do you foresee a constitutional monarchy?' asked Sebastian, challenging the man on the point Stalin had dismissed.

'There are many different views,' further avoided Kerensky, looking beyond Sebastian as if seeking an escape.

'Perhaps I might call upon you to continue our conversation in more convenient surroundings?' said Sebastian.

'I find myself very occupied at the moment,' refused the politician, moving away. 'You must excuse me . . .'

Sebastian and Black remained side by side, watching the Russian approach a group which the attaché identified to be French. Black said: 'He thought your question impertinent.'

'I wonder if his refusal to answer wasn't in itself an answer,' said Sebastian.

Black frowned. 'I'm not sure I understand that remark.'

'Do you think Russia can be governed by a parliament *and* a Tsar?'

'No,' said Black at once. 'Russia has been ruled by a Romanov for three hundred years. And will continue to be so ruled.'

'Don't you find easy similarities between Russia now and France of the 1790s?'

'Good heavens, no!' rejected Black. 'No one's going to lose their heads here. That's the stuff of a hundred years ago.'

Sebastian looked impatiently away from the man and the opinions recited almost by rote. And at once saw Princess

Olga Orlov, with whom he'd sat for five nights as the captain's guest aboard the *Lusitania*, where Sebastian had easily employed French, which she and her father spoke fluently, as a conversational bridge with others at the favoured table. Today she was dressed entirely in white, the expansively brimmed hat in the same appliqué design as her full, ankle-length skirt and tassle-fringed parasol. Her two attendant companions were dressed in matching designs, one in fawn, the other in a floral pattern against pale rose-red.

Sebastian looked anxiously around, seeking her father, and when he looked back realized at once that the princess had seen him. For the first time he realized that, as well as her two female companions, the princess had two lounge-suited men close at hand. There was a momentary frown, of recall, from the princess before her face cleared. Sebastian couldn't decide if the slightest tilt of her protective parasol was an acknowledgement or not.

Beside him Black said: 'I have duties to perform: more arrivals. Shall you come with me for further introductions?'

'Leave me,' said Sebastian at once. 'I shall not dominate your time.' Sebastian was less than a yard away, still undecided how to approach her, when the princess finally smiled in open greeting. In French she said: 'A most unexpected reacquaintance!'

'Which I consider myself most fortunate to make,' said Sebastian. He was conscious of the two men moving closer, and of an almost imperceptible gesture from the princess, halting them. The two female companions held back, too, but Sebastian didn't anticipate a long conversation, which meant it couldn't be wasted. 'Did you enjoy your visit to America?'

'Very much. And you?'

'It was eventful,' understated Sebastian. Would the imperially linked princess have still been in America to read the newspaper hysteria that erupted at President Woodrow Wilson's decision to expel the German spy ring he'd exposed to the authorities? His participation had not been identified, so there was no way she could have associated him with the furore.

'It seems a very distant memory now.'

'I trust your father is well?' He'd forgotten the virtual blackness of her eyes and the way – total confidence, he supposed

– in which she held the gaze of anyone she was addressing, as she was holding his now.

'Extremely so.'

He had to force the pace, Sebastian told himself. 'I took the liberty of leaving my card.'

'I know.'

Sebastian waited hopefully for her to continue but she didn't. 'Will your father be here today?'

'I doubt it. He finds himself extremely busy.'

'I'd hoped to renew his acquaintance.'

'He has little time for socializing.'

'Would it be considered impertinent for me to call upon you?'

'Probably,' she said, smiling.

'I would not wish to offend.'

'You were extremely courteous to my father and I, aboard the liner, in the way in which you interpreted.'

How, in turn, should he interpret that remark? 'It was an easy service.'

She indicated the hovering attendants. 'We were making our way to our carriage.'

The opportunity was slipping away from him, Sebastian realized, desperately. 'Then I must delay you no longer. But I—'

'I have no engagements tomorrow afternoon,' interrupted the princess. 'I would be pleased to receive you.'

Sebastian bowed, very slightly. 'It will be my continued pleasure.'

The parasol flicked its indeterminate flick, revolving, and she led her personal procession further across the barbered lawns towards the ambassador to bid their farewells.

Captain Black gained Sebastian's side as Princess Olga reached the ambassador. Black said: 'You know the princess!' For the first time the edge of condescension was absent from the man's voice.

'A chance encounter, on an ocean liner,' dismissed Sebastian.

'Her father is a member of the Tsar's court. Someone of great influence. Her being here today will be judged extremely important by other foreign legations who witnessed it.'

And by me most of all, thought Sebastian. Surely he could

now manoeuvre an encounter with the Grand Duke! 'Indicating what?'

'I'll need advice to answer that,' said the indecisive attaché. 'This has proved to be a most useful and intriguing day!'

For him also, thought Sebastian. It would be premature to allow too much hope, but after what he considered his success with Stalin and what he believed he had inferred from the Duma politician, Sebastian's spirits were buoyant. 'I'd be interested in hearing what that advice might be.'

'Of course, of course,' said Black impatiently. Looking beyond Sebastian he said: 'Damnation! The Germans have arrived too late to have witnessed her presence.'

Sebastian turned at the identification. To put himself less than twenty yards from a German diplomat he had last confronted, manacled, in a New York police precinct house, and whom he now identified as Hans Vogel, a legal attaché at the Washington DC embassy, from which he'd led Berlin's spy apparatus.

Sebastian jerked instantly away, unsure if there had been any recognition from the aloof, flaxen-haired man. Sebastian said: 'I need your shielding escort to leave. Immediately!' How shielding? he thought. He was several inches taller than the military attaché, who'd provide little barrier at all.

'What is it?' demanded Black.

'I'm known by one of the arriving Germans. And don't wish to be identified.'

Sebastian guided their departure route, as widely circula- tory as possible, on the far side of the bandstand from the German contingent, in whose direction he did not risk looking. Black did, however, and as they approached the concealment of the embassy said: 'We seem to be of no particular interest.'

'Let's hope you're right.'

'Who is the man?'

'In New York and Washington I knew him as Hans Vogel, a legal attaché at the German embassy. In reality his function was cultivating pro-German American industrialists and men of influence in the event of a European conflict. He was expelled.'

'As a result of your endeavours?'

'I was influential in it,' allowed Sebastian, modestly.

'I have your permission to bring this to the attention of people who should be told, here and in London?'

He had no alternative, Sebastian recognized. Perhaps his agreement would result in more worthwhile intelligence reaching London from the embassy in the future. He said: 'Remind your people of the episode. It created a great deal of newspaper attention.'

'We're clear!' declared Black, as they entered the confines of the embassy.

Was he? wondered Sebastian. He said: 'I need immediate use of your telegraph.'

'I did not wish you to become a victim like myself,' apologized Dr Watson.

'It was not of your making,' assured Mycroft Holmes. They were strolling in Green Park, away from the attention of any Whitehall eyes or ears.

'It's evidence of the extremity of the situation.'

'I'm manoeuvring a situation hopefully to bring about some element of reconciliation.'

'If you can achieve that with your brother, then you must abandon my difficulty,' insisted the doctor.

'Please don't be offended, Watson, by my telling you that it's my brother's difficulties that are my greater concern, not yours.'

'Absolutely no offence taken,' assured Watson. 'What was your assessment at your last meeting? Had he deteriorated further?'

'He was extremely irascible, taking every exception.' They reached the furthest edge of the lake and turned back towards Buckingham Palace.

'When is this manoeuvre to come about?'

'When there's good enough excuse. There is a shipment on its way from Sebastian, which should be sufficient.'

'You're going to need all your diplomatic skills,' judged Watson.

'And more to boot,' agreed Mycroft.

# Nine

M ycroft Holmes carefully timed his arrival to be thirty
minutes after Churchill's summons to his Admiralty Arch
eyrie, his admission prearranged by the First Lord. He smiled
in uncertain anticipation at seeing his brother's signature
directly above his own on the visitors' register. Mycroft
was glad, upon reflection, that Churchill had changed the
suggested venue to somewhere more official, hoping it would
convey the impression of Sherlock Holmes's deeper involvement. Mycroft considered the overnight telegram alert from
the St Petersburg embassy, which even Churchill had not yet
seen, to be a further although at the same time ambivalent
advantage.

The slowness of the creaking elevator ascent to the top of
the arch was, as always, compensated once he got there by
the view, which Mycroft paused to admire while recovering
his breath, still unsuccessfully trying at even this late stage to
prepare himself for what was to come in the next short while.
He'd become increasingly uncomfortable at involving Winston
Churchill in what was the most delicate of personal matters,
and had greeted each intervening day with the hope of his
brother responding to the two letters of attempted reconciliation he'd personally delivered to 221b Baker Street. The fact
that there had been no reaction whatsoever had surely to indicate Sherlock's continued unpredictability, from which there
was potential embarrassment in front of the politician. And if
Sherlock considered himself tricked into such a confronta-
tional situation, the risk was of widening the rift between them
even further. Which frightened him, Mycroft conceded: frightened and distressed and worried him, a conflict of emotions
to which he was unaccustomed.

Mycroft was recognized by Churchill's outer-office staff and gestured through without prior announcement, which was also prearranged. Mycroft still entered discreetly, no approach rehearsed, and remained just inside the door, surveying the scene before him. Churchill was at his familiar window spot – far superior to that which had greeted Mycroft at his emergence from the lift – the cigar well alight, his back to the room. Sherlock Holmes was on a leather couch, the material that had earlier arrived from Sebastian spread out on a low table before him, his concentration so absolute that momentarily he was unaware of anyone entering. It was Churchill's turning back into the room which disturbed Sherlock Holmes's absorption, but it was still several moments before he became fully aware of Mycroft's presence.

The reaction was as Mycroft had feared. Sherlock Holmes reared up to his full commanding height, still clutching the papers he had been reading, his initial words coming disconnectedly. 'What's this . . . ? I consider myself deceived . . . This was not my understanding . . .'

'It's most certainly mine,' halted Churchill, thick-throated. He moved back to his desk, waving generally to the Russian material. 'And what you've got in front of you, sir, is something further to understand. The opinions and judgements of your son match mine and regrettably fulfil all my worst fears. I wanted Mycroft to be with us tonight, which is why he is here. Moreover, why you are here. When this enterprise began, you demanded to be kept fully informed of every part of it. Which you are being. What you have before you is Sebastian's first dispatch.'

Mycroft had rarely, until now, been present during any of his brother's investigatory sessions – which he regarded this to be – and never, at any time, had he witnessed his brother confronted so forcefully. Mycroft was intently studying Sherlock Holmes during the exchange, concerned at the sharpness of his brother's face and hand movements. Quickly Mycroft said: 'And I have the second dispatch . . .' He produced the overnight telegraph from St Petersburg, and with intentional theatricality read aloud: 'Encountered Hans Vogel, German spy exposed in America. Unsure his recognition of me. Reassigned

92

German embassy here. My judgement infiltrating revolutionaries. Captain Black aware. Grateful inform father.'

'May I see that message?' asked Sherlock Holmes.

His suspicious brother did not believe the concluding request, Mycroft guessed, advancing further into the room. Unhesitatingly he offered the transmission slip, at which Sherlock Holmes no more than glanced, for confirmation.

Churchill said: 'Once more your son is discharging his task in an exemplary manner, Holmes.'

'But in a very short time appears to have been exposed to great danger,' said Mycroft, seizing the opening. 'There's unexpected pressure upon Sebastian now, due to the presence in the city of a German spy by whom he is known. And who would, I've not the slightest doubt, reciprocate physically for the damage Sebastian inflicted upon their activities in America. Sebastian is going to need all the support and guidance he can receive from us . . .' The pause was staged. 'From you in particular, Sherlock.'

'Sebastian has indeed done well, confirming many of the doubts you charged him to resolve,' agreed Sherlock Holmes, talking to Churchill but ignoring his brother. 'The danger you talk about is very real. I propose his immediate recall.'

'It's unthinkable to recall him, after so much success,' protested Churchill.

'Sebastian could already be uncovered. In mortal danger,' protested Sherlock Holmes in return.

No longer so strident, assessed Mycroft: the body movements were less jerky, too. 'It's surely our purpose to provide as much support as we are able.'

'I believe myself to have become sufficiently acquainted with Sebastian to know that he would not return upon demand,' said Churchill. 'Nor do I seek to make such demands. He still has much valuable work to complete.'

Sherlock Holmes indicated the discarded dispatches from Russia. 'There's little indication there that Sebastian has any confidence in our embassy in St Petersburg. Not even in the very man to whom you provided an introduction!'

'I made no secret of my complaint against the embassy,' reminded Churchill. 'Black was expedient.'

'Nor I of my demands that he be given the maximum protection by it, which I doubt, from what I've read, they have the ability – the inclination even – to provide, despite his officially registering his presence,' argued Sherlock Holmes.

'Sebastian cannot be identified as someone on a covert mission at the behest of a minister of an unaware British government,' Mycroft set out, formally. 'That's been well enough understood from the outset.'

'We are ineffectual to provide any support from this distance,' insisted Sherlock Holmes. 'Sebastian is being left too exposed.'

His brother's attitude was very different from what he'd feared it might be, Mycroft decided. In fact, so far there had been virtually nothing argumentative to cause personal family embarrassment at all. 'Everything lying on that table before you stems from information you personally provided from here.'

'But to which I have been unable to add,' confessed the detective.

'What of the information Sebastian has provided in return?' questioned Churchill. 'It satisfies my concern, as far as it goes. Do you assess it similarly?'

'I need to study it more fully than I've so far had the opportunity to do.'

'I'd respect your confirmation of Sebastian's views,' said Churchill, with rare humility. 'Deeper study might open a further avenue to explore.'

'I'll devote myself to it, of course,' said Sherlock Holmes. 'Crucial, I think, is Sebastian's assessment that to achieve their purpose the Bolsheviks and Mensheviks will come together to agree a common purpose.'

'That's how I read Stalin's remark that compromise is a tenet of politics,' agreed Churchill.

An art in which Churchill needed little career instruction, thought Mycroft, objectively. 'What's our way forward?' he asked, talking directly to his brother.

'The strongest urging to Sebastian to take every physical care,' replied Sherlock Holmes at once. 'Praise, for what he's so far achieved in remarkably short time. A note in my personal hand that I'm closely studying the material and will advise him of my assessment within twenty-four hours.'

His brother had been anxious for the reconciliation but looked for it less directly than by responding to his open approaches, Mycroft guessed. Which left the ostracism of Dr Watson unresolved. And also, he reminded himself belatedly, the cause of the quarrel. But tonight was at least progress.

'Personal congratulations from me, also, for what's been achieved,' echoed Churchill.

'I shall need to take all this with me,' said Sherlock Holmes, gathering up what lay on the table. 'I'll be in contact with you tomorrow.'

'I'm dining with Dr Watson,' chanced Mycroft. 'Would it be convenient for you to join us?'

There was a minimal hesitation. 'Not at that wretched Diogenes Club.'

'A restaurant of your choice,' offered Mycroft, at once.

'I'll put a mind to it,' said Sherlock Holmes, unwilling to concede further.

After Sherlock Holmes had left them, Winston Churchill said: 'Am I to be told the underlying reason for this performance?'

'A difficulty that I hope has been settled far more easily than I dared expect. I apologize for involving you.'

'I have enough intrigues of my own for one more to be a burden,' said Churchill. 'But were it to arise again, I'd object to being kept in ignorance.'

'It's my hope that it won't.' said Mycroft. Hope was still all that he could do, he thought.

Once more Sebastian identified his pursuers hurriedly entering their coach as the hotel doorman hailed him a cab, not bothering to confirm the pursuit through the convenient rear hatchway, idly wondering about their reaction at the discovery of his destination. He had, of course, omitted any mention of his being under Okhrana scrutiny in his account to London: to have disclosed it would have required an admission of his naive approach to Tsarskoye Selo, and Sebastian had no intention whatsoever of confessing naivety. Was it

95

not equally naive for him to expect somehow to reach the Grand Duke through his daughter? Perhaps. But, as he had so quickly decided at the garden party, the encounter, which she appeared to welcome, was an opportunity that he had to seize, no matter how ungallant. Unbidden into his mind came the cliché that all was fair in love and war: love didn't enter into his calculations, but the possibility of war was an absolving consideration.

Two men in militarily coloured but civilian-cut frock coats came sharply to attention in the guardhouse beside the studded door, in front of which stood more identifiably dressed soldiers – their uniforms of matching colours – as Sebastian's coach pulled up. He slowed his disembarkation sufficiently to see the following coach rein in, and he toyed, for a few seconds, with the idea of a mocking gesture of awareness, dismissing it at once, not wanting a return of the first-day professionalism. Sebastian studied both frock-coated men intently, trying to recognize their features as those of the two dark-suited bodyguards of the previous day – which annoyingly he couldn't – but which they had to be, from their instant recognition of him. Both slightly inclined towards him and immediately turned to escort him deeper into the palace. Sebastian dutifully fell in step just behind them.

His earlier, brief impression was right. There was a moat completely encircling the building he was approaching and, as he crossed the main, vehicle-wide drawbridge, Sebastian saw protruding for maybe two feet above the now placid water a criss-cross of spikes and blades that would make the ditch impassable when it was frozen solid during the winter. More spikes and blades were embedded into the moat walls, unevenly, to prevent their becoming footholds after an unlikely successful crossing. There was a second gatehouse inside the main entrance, at which Sebastian was studied by more soldiers during a muttered conversation with his escorts, before being gestured on across another, smaller open area.

The building into which he was led truly was a palace, its enormity hidden behind the matching enormity of its surrounding walls. Its frontage was Doric-columned below huge, storey-high windows, topped as far as Sebastian could see in his quick entry by the first-floor surround of a wide balcony. The entrance hall was vast, a marbled cathedral of a room dominated by a two-sided circular stairway upon which at least five people, side by side, could have mounted and descended without inconveniencing each other. Ancestral military portraits which Sebastian did not have to examine closely to recognize as the work of masters adorned the surrounding walls, above marble statues and busts Sebastian guessed to be more of the Grand Duke Orlov's predecessors.

They did not mount the stairs to what were obviously the major reception rooms, but continued on through an enormous, two-balconied library and along a linking corridor into what opened out to be a garden room, all the far windows of which were already opened on to grounds so extensive that it was difficult to locate the continuation of the inner encircling wall. Princess Olga Orlov was close to one of the exit doors into the garden, seated in profile, yesterday's concealed deeply black hair today pinned into a tightly combed chignon by two diamond clips that matched the diamond-clustered brooch close to her left shoulder. Her dress was the palest of periwinkle blue. Attracted by an intentional movement, Sebastian saw that one of the princess's earlier companions was working on a frame-stretched embroidery. She did not look towards him but the princess did, lowering her head in initial greeting until he crossed the room. As he got nearer she said: 'It is good of you to call.'

'And of you to allow my attending,' said Sebastian. Aboard the New York-bound *Lusitania*, the necessary etiquette had not been called upon – and his interest had been occupied by another princess, who had proven to be both unconventional and dangerous – but Sebastian was uncertain in such impressive surroundings, anxious to guard against an oversight that might jeopardize his unexpected opportunity to have at least got beyond the door of the Grand Duke's palace.

He remained standing until she gestured to a high-backed chair on the other side of her window view and said: 'Please.'

She'd spoken first, which according to English protocol enabled him to make the conversation. Which opportunity, as the previous day, couldn't be wasted. 'I found the embassy garden party pleasant. Did you have an opportunity of anything similar in the United States?'

'Nothing on yesterday's scale. You?'

'By coincidence there was the celebration of the Kaiser's birth. It was very elaborate and formal.' And his first encounter with Hans Vogel, he reminded himself.

'The Germans often are,' she said, enigmatically. She tugged at a summons cord within reach without her having to stand and said: 'We'll take tea.'

For the first time Sebastian saw an ornate silver samovar, with cups already set out. Almost immediately three liveried maids entered with covered silver serving trolleys they lifted to display cakes and pastries. The princess said: 'In Russia we take our tea black but there is milk or cream, if you wish. And sugar.'

Sebastian said: 'I must follow custom,' and thought of Captain Black's *when in Rome* cliché.

'And I recommend the sugar cake.'

The tea was too strong and too bitter and the cake too sweet and too difficult to eat without showering debris. He looked up in time to catch the end of a fleeting smile and decided he didn't need overly to concern himself any longer with protocol: if she'd chosen him for the afternoon's passing entertainment he would have to play the jester. But more for his benefit than for her amusement. He found it curious that the embroidering companion was not included in the tea ceremony.

'Did you tell your father of our chance meeting?'

'I have not seen him since the party.'

'He is away?'

'Often.'

So there was no possibility of his meeting the man! Sebastian felt a surge of frustration, quickly dismissed. 'Perhaps when he returns he'll consider my card.'

'What's your purpose in being in St Petersburg, Mr Holmes?' she demanded with surprising directness.

Had he spoken aboard ship of being a financial investor, which had been his subterfuge during the American investigation? 'Seeing Russia and its capital.'

'You intend travelling extensively?' she picked up at once.

'I haven't decided yet,' avoided Sebastian. 'How widely did you travel in America?'

'We saw New York and Boston.'

'I understood from our conversations aboard ship that Washington was also on your itinerary.'

'I don't recall my telling you that.'

There was almost a rebuke in the reply. 'It may have been in conversation with your father.'

'We were briefly there,' she agreed.

Why the prevarication? wondered Sebastian. 'I found it an interesting city.'

'Preferable to St Petersburg?' she challenged at once.

'No,' said Sebastian, just as quickly. 'Both are very different. And Washington is a very new city, in comparison to St Petersburg.' And as far as I am aware doesn't have packs of attacking guttersnipes, he thought.

'You've received an injury?' she said, with fresh abruptness.

Sebastian instinctively brought his hand up to the healing cut. 'My own clumsiness. I stumbled and caught a cabinet-door edge.'

'Did you have it treated?'

'I didn't consider it necessary.'

'It will scar.'

'A reminder of my own awkwardness.' He was curious both at the conversation and the princess. Illogically he had the impression of being tested in some way.

'Shall we walk in the park?' she said, rising before Sebastian had the chance of replying.

He hurried to his feet as the princess picked up an obviously positioned parasol and walked ahead of him through the open verandah doors. To his right Sebastian saw the companion rise, to follow. The princess stood waiting outside.

She smiled over his shoulder at her approaching companion and said: 'My father is very strict about chaperones. I find it very old-fashioned.'

The conversation was taking another unexpected turn, this time to the flirtatious. Responding, he said: 'I promise to remain gallant at all times.'

'If I had doubted otherwise I would not have agreed to your calling upon me.'

The grounds immediately beyond reminded Sebastian of Capability Brown landscaping, boxed hedges marking out a myriad of colours and flowers and plants which would obviously need an army of gardeners to tend, and probably separate battalions to repair and replace those frozen to death every winter. The princess easily supported her parasol with one hand and placed the other on Sebastian's offered arm, guiding their path through the perfumed arbours. Beyond the formal layout, the land dipped into a rolling, coppice-studded park, interspersed with ornate stream-fed fountains full of carved animals and fish, which brought Sebastian a further recollection, of the Versailles palace in which the French King Louis XIV lived with Marie Antoinette, unsuspecting of their impending fate. Beside three of them were resting, shading pagodas. Princess Olga directed them towards the largest, sufficient for the chaperone to occupy it with them.

Sebastian said: 'It's very beautiful.'

'It was begun by some of the original designers of Tsarskoye Selo. And developed by others since.'

'Do you know Tsarskoye Selo?' asked Sebastian, quickly.

'Very well. It's my father's boast that the Tsar's eldest daughter, the Grand Duchess Olga, was named after me, although I don't believe it. I am only five years her senior. We played together as children. See each other quite frequently still.'

How could he be this close but yet so far away? thought Sebastian, agonized. 'I believe there are several palaces, including that of Catherine the Great, which contains what one British ambassador judged to be one of the wonders of the world.'

'The Amber Room,' the princess identified at once. 'It is unbelievably exquisite. The amber panelling is jewelled and glows yellow in the candlelight. When I was younger I used to think that being in it was like being in the very centre of a honeycomb. We had a bee game, Olga and I. I was allowed to be the Queen Bee because Olga said she would be a real queen one day, married to a real king, but that I never would.'

100

'She may be proved wrong,' flattered Sebastian.

'I'd insist on a white charger.'

They were back to flirtation, Sebastian recognized. 'Nothing less. And a castle twice the size of this.'

Her smile widened into a surprising grin, at her enjoyment of the game. 'Not twice the size! It becomes dreadfully cold in the winter.'

'A sun king.'

'The sun is said never to set upon the British Empire. And your king already has a wife.'

'But with eligible princes.' Having been told the Grand Duke was not in residence, Sebastian was anxious to get back to the hotel for any response from Josef Stalin or Alexander Kerensky, to whom he had earlier that day had delivered a *Morning Post* accreditation card, as well as a personal one, by hotel messenger, despite the politician's peremptory dismissal. But although there was no longer awkward formality between them, his departure had to be at the princess's indication.

'I have visited London. It rained and there was fog which made me cough. And unpleasant smells.'

'I'll complain to the King.'

'Do you have access to the King?'

It was a definite questioning, the lightness going as with the flick of a finger. 'I do not have personal access,' admitted Sebastian, cautiously. In which direction were they going now?

'Are you acquainted with people at court?'

'Yes,' openly lied Sebastian, to maintain the conversation.

'How close is your King to his people?'

'He is greatly loved. He makes himself as publicly available as is fitting, often driving around the city by carriage. He is an enthusiastic sailor, enjoying regattas in which he competes and is seen and applauded. As he is at race meetings: he has an active stable.'

'Are you a monarchist or a republican, Mr Holmes?'

There was only one answer in such surroundings with such a person, Sebastian realized. 'A monarchist.'

'I think—' began the princess, but stopped at the most

101

unobtrusive of coughs, nothing more than a discreet clearing of the throat by the chaperone. 'I have fallen unaware of the hour,' she finished.

Sebastian rose ahead of her this time. 'And I have occupied too much of it, for which I ask you to forgive me.'

'There is nothing to forgive,' said the princess, rising.

They made their way back towards the palace as they had left, the princess again easily managing her parasol with one hand, the other on Sebastian's arm. He waited until they entered the hedged avenues of the formal garden before daring to say, 'Perhaps it is his absence that has prevented your father responding to my card? Maybe I could be allowed to re-present it upon his return?'

Princess Olga did not reply, gaining the door through which they had left, and Sebastian decided he had overstepped his opportunity. The inner shade against the outside brightness momentarily clouded his vision as he followed, and in the first few seconds he was unaware of the commanding, full-bearded figure waiting in the centre of the room.

A deep voice said: 'It is good to see you again, Mr Holmes,' and Sebastian at last focused on the Grand Duke Alexei Orlov.

Dr John Watson listened, hunched forward, without interruption until Mycroft had obviously finished his account of the meeting with Sherlock Holmes. Then he exclaimed: 'Capital! Absolutely capital!'

'I hope so,' said Mycroft. 'And by nightfall I received his dining choice in preference to the kitchens here at the club.'

'Which is?' asked Watson.

'221b Baker Street,' smiled Mycroft.

Watson smiled in return. 'We're being accepted back!'

# Ten

Sebastian recognized that he was caught up in a contrivance – believing now that he had been practically from the moment of his arrival – but was content to be ensnared, imagining there was more to be gained than lost, his achieving his audience with the Grand Duke the most obvious benefit. The greeting was effusive. There was an immediate insistence that he stay to dine with them, with quarters immediately made available to refresh himself, and the suggestion of returning to the hotel to dress for dinner dismissed as unnecessary. Everything was conducted at such a pace that it was not until he gained his suite that Sebastian was able to rationalize – or try to rationalize – what was happening.

The princess could not have known in advance of his being at the embassy garden party. So her agreeing to his calling upon her had to have been impromptu. The Grand Duke awaiting him in the garden room had to have been staged, so there must have been prior discussion and arrangement between the princess and her father. But she had said there hadn't been: that she had not seen her father. Which was a lie too easily exposed by the man being there when they returned from their stroll in the park. Which didn't make the contrivance a clever one, despite the fact that he could never accuse either of them of falsehood. The leapfrogging conversation with the princess had been clumsy, too. Could that be explained by her having to work in certain prompting suggested by the Grand Duke? Possibly. Isolating him in the opulent suite that overlooked the park in which he had so recently walked was clearly an artifice for father and daughter to discuss the afternoon's conversation, which Sebastian recalled in detail, as he guessed the princess was reporting it, satisfied that he had not said or implied anything that could be turned back awkwardly upon him.

Having had the facilities made available, Sebastian bathed leisurely, slightly discomfited at having to dress again in linen that had already been worn, reflecting as he did so upon another thought that came to him. Why *had* there been the insistence that he stay within the palace? It would have taken a little over an hour to journey to and from the hotel, with only an intervening thirty minutes to bathe and dress as he was doing now. Which would have caused no delay whatsoever to dinner. Another inconsistency, to add to all the others. What preparations could he make to match theirs? None, Sebastian told himself. His only course was to follow the Grand Duke's lead, alert to every nuance behind every word, and not end the evening with more uncertainties than he'd already isolated.

Sebastian descended the curved marble staircase precisely at the appointed time, to find a footman waiting to escort him along a different corridor to what appeared a combination between a study and a trophy room. The dark panelling was adorned with the heads of animals whose kills were recorded on brass plates, guarded by four different sets of full medieval armour. There was also a decorative display of weaponry: swords and daggers and pikes and early flintlock pistols and rifles. There was a huge desk, the inlaid leather matching that of the burnished leather furniture, and above a now dead fireplace there were portraits of the princess and a woman so similarly featured as to be unmistakably the Grand Duchess. The huge, bearded man was standing full-height in front of the fireplace, which dwarfed him, still considerably wearing the suit in which he had greeted Sebastian, glass already in hand. Behind an extensive array of bottles, a liveried butler stood in readiness. Sebastian accepted champagne poured from an unusual cristal bottle and the fireplace-bordering leather chair, the cushion of which sighed under his weight when he sat.

From the depths of an opposite chair, the now seated Russian said: 'It's women's prerogative to keep men waiting.'

'And men's duty to be patient,' dutifully responded Sebastian. How patient was he going to be, tiptoeing through the pleasantries before they got to the point of this intriguing situation?

'Today is a most fortunate coincidence, although I was of course going to respond to your card.'

'I hoped you would not consider it presumptuous.'

'How could that possibly be? Had you advised me in advance of your arrival, I would have welcomed you as a guest.'

'That *would* have been presumptuous,' insisted Sebastian.

'How did you discover where I lived?' There was a sudden edge to the question.

His father had not told him how he'd come upon it, remembered Sebastian, anxiously. 'I contacted the Cunard Steamship Company.'

'Of course! It was an enjoyable voyage.'

'I thought so, too.'

'How long did you stay in the country?'

No danger in the truth, Sebastian decided. 'A little over two months. You?'

'Just slightly shorter,' said the Russian.

'The Princess Olga told me you visited Boston, New York and Washington?'

'Interesting cities, all different. You?'

It was tentative chess, pawn to pawn, thought Sebastian. 'New York and Washington.'

'Successfully?'

Had he talked of his supposed purpose in travelling to America? wondered Sebastian yet again. He was being self-taught a necessary lesson, never to be off guard: nor to forget his father's axiom about the minimum of lies. 'It was an exploratory mission, seeking investment possibilities in a rapidly expanding industrializing country. But I found nothing to interest me.'

'A disappointment then?'

'It left me uncertain if I am equipped for the dangers of business.'

'You seem to have suffered a misadventure?' said Orlov pointedly, looking at Sebastian's face.

'I stumbled clumsily in my hotel bathroom,' said Sebastian, maintaining his earlier excuse. 'It is nothing.'

'So here in Russia you content yourself to sightsee and enjoy our history?'

'That's my intention.'

'What have you enjoyed thus far?'

'I have scarcely orientated myself to the city,' avoided Sebastian. 'I seek guidance from yourself and the princess.'

'It would be—' began the Grand Duke, but was interrupted by the arrival of his daughter. Princess Olga wore a high-necked, tight-bodiced black evening gown, the jewellery limited to pearls at her throat and wrist. Her hair had been redressed but was still tightly coiffeured. The pins were pearl-topped, too. They stood, to greet her, and remained standing when their champagne was replenished. As the butler poured, the Grand Duke explained that the wine, Roederer, was the court favourite and was always supplied from France in exclusively made clear cristal bottles.

Seizing the opening, Sebastian said: 'Strictly limited to the court, of course?'

'To particular members of the court,' further qualified the other man.

A boast or another opening? wondered Sebastian. 'It's superb.' Far better than Churchill's favourite, he thought.

There was more served with the caviar, but flat wine with the following sturgeon, and after the fish the wild duck. The main topic of conversation was their respective American trips. Sebastian had fortunately socialized sufficiently to be able to contribute the necessary anecdotes and was alert for the diplomatic reception that the princess had inferred that afternoon but there was no mention of it. By the desert the conversation had switched to places and events Sebastian should see and enjoy during his visit to St Petersburg, culminating in the suggestion that he should consider a river voyage as far south as Moscow. It was during that conversation that the Grand Duke was briefly called from the table, returning after a few minutes with repeated apologies but no explanation, leaving Sebastian wondering about the likelihood of another bomb attack. After dinner they retired to a music room, where the princess gave an excellent but short piano recital, excusing herself directly afterwards pleading tiredness, which Sebastian judged as staged as the Grand Duke awaiting him in the garden room that afternoon. At the bearded man's insistence they returned to the study, now empty of any servants, for brandy. Sebastian declined a cigar.

Gesturing towards the matching portraits above the fireplace, Sebastian said: 'The likeness is very marked.'

'I mourn her loss still,' said Orlov.

'I am sorry,' said Sebastian, hurriedly, annoyed with himself. 'I did not intend to arouse memories.'

'Memories are always with me,' said the other man, gazing up at the portrait, momentarily lapsing into silence. Abruptly he said: 'I should have been with her, but I had court duties. I had not provided protection. She was alone in the coach, which was recognized by the mob, at the height of the 1905 unrest. They stormed it. Turned it over. She was crushed. Before they ran, the mob took all her jewellery and left her half-clothed. They killed the coachman, too, so that he could not identify them.'

Sebastian was hot with embarrassment, convinced he was responsible for the reverie. 'I feel, sir, that I have overstayed my welcome. I believe I should bid you goodnight, with the hope of our meeting again.'

'No!' positively refused the man, turning away from the portrait. 'There are things for us to talk about. Refresh your glass and let us sit.'

Sebastian did, with no intention of drinking: his intake throughout the entire evening had only been four glasses, the last left half-full. He occupied his previous chair, facing the Grand Duke.

The man said: 'I think we've played sufficient games, don't you?'

'Games?' questioned Sebastian. Was this yet another? Or an explanation of one of those that preceded it?

The Grand Duke smiled across the cavernously empty hearth. 'I know who you are, Mr Holmes. And to whom you are related. Which is why you are here in my house, being given my hospitality, and why we are about to have a conversation of great importance.'

He had to match like with like, Sebastian decided. 'And I

know who you are. And the organization you head. Which is why I sought this encounter.'

'Touché.'

This had ceased being a tentative chess game but it was very much his next move, Sebastian recognized. Snatching at the fencing analogy – and hoping to switch control of the exchanges as well as metaphors – Sebastian said: 'Do we need to take guard again?'

'We always need to be on guard,' said the Russian. 'Although I hope not against one another.'

'My hope too,' said Sebastian. Parry, half-thrust and check, he thought, the terms easily at hand from the fencing he'd practised at Heidelberg.

'I also know – because it is my business to know – what your purpose was and how successfully you achieved it in America,' announced the man.

The Russian could be bluffing, Sebastian thought. 'How do you judge that success?'

The Grand Duke lowered his head as if in acknowledgement of Sebastian's caution. 'By the expulsion of a twenty-strong German spy cell, eight of them diplomats, and in prompting it proving to the American government the extent of Berlin espionage in expectation of war.'

Orlov *did* know, accepted Sebastian. Cautious still, he said: 'How did what happened in New York cause you to investigate me?'

'It's my business to investigate people. And it became my business to enquire further into the German expulsions.' The man sipped his brandy. 'Do you doubt there will be conflict in Europe?'

'More a question for you to answer than me,' hedged Sebastian.

'It's a likelihood that has to be guarded against,' said the Russian, throwing Sebastian's word back at him.

Should he reveal the presence in St Petersburg of Hans Vogel? wondered Sebastian. Not yet: it had to be kept for maximum benefit. 'Great Britain has treaty obligations.'

The bull-chested man came forward in his chair. 'But will she honour them?'

108

'You must surely accept that I am not in a position to answer such a question!'

'I believe you have access to people who can.'

'The government of Great Britain has an embassy here in St Petersburg, to which such a question should be put.'

The Grand Duke sighed heavily. 'I'd sincerely hoped the game-playing was over.'

'If you ask me a direct question that it is within my power to answer then I will honestly answer it.'

'What's your purpose here in St Petersburg?' demanded the man, almost irritably. 'Why did you attempt to reach Tsarskoye Selo? Where were you during the time my men lost you, three days ago? What caused your dishevelment when you returned to your hotel? How did you receive the wound scarcely healed upon your cheek? What was in the package you returned to the embassy after its delivery to you by Captain Black? What did you have delivered upon Alexander Kerensky by hotel messenger?'

It was an impressive litany intended for his maximum discomfort, Sebastian recognized. But none of the questions unsettled him. Nor should answering them cause any difficulty. It was time at last for honesty. Or at least as much honesty as could be allowed. 'My reason for being here is very similar to that of my being in America. I was naive approaching the Tsar's village: my sole reason for attempting to do so was to look at it, as one can without hindrance look upon Buckingham Palace in London or the White House in Washington. When your followers and I became separated, I was seeking to reach the offices of *Pravda*. I received the cut to my face in the explosion there. The package contained advice from my father, in England, which I thought more safely stored in the embassy than in my hotel room, which your people searched and had the safe opened after my seizure.'

'You've omitted Kerensky.'

'My card. I briefly encountered him at the British embassy party, which I am sure your daughter has already told you.'

'Did you succeed in speaking to anyone in the *Pravda* offices?'

He wasn't going to become a tethered bait if Stalin or

Kerensky responded to his approaches, Sebastian decided. 'The confusion was too great. I admit to having been concussed: not sure of what I was doing or where I was for some time afterwards.' Sebastian allowed the pause. 'You have just tested me, as I believe I have been under test for much of today, most of which I have still to understand. Just as I still fail to understand the direction of this conversation. What do you want of me?'

'A conduit, for informed advice,' replied the Grand Duke, at once. 'I need accurately to advise His Imperial Majesty of the strengths and weaknesses of both his enemies and his allies. I do not doubt Russia will declare war upon Austria if Austria moves against the Serbs. Which will bring in Berlin. I need to know if Great Britain will honour its treaty agreements or abandon Russia . . .' The man looked briefly up to the portrait of his murdered wife. 'And I need to know the degree of friendship that might be extended in the event of further anarchy within this country. I lost a wife. I will not lose a daughter. It was I who carried the Tsar's orders to the troops on Dvortsovaya Square, to open fire on the mob approaching the Winter Palace . . . it's my hope that some of those who died were those who killed her . . .'

Sebastian was grateful for the head-slumped reverie into which the older man again lapsed, needing to quantify what he had just been told. Russia, racked by internal dissent after its defeats in the Crimea and by the Japanese, would be taken into war again by the present Tsar if war broke out in the Balkans. And Grand Duke Alexei Orlov, who commanded the Tsar's secret police, responsible for crushing that internal insurrection, personally doubted his capability to do so and was using his concern for the safety of his daughter to hint at the question of royal exile. Realization came upon the back of awareness. He was being asked to perform a service for Orlov very similar to that he was conducting for Churchill. And with the same caveat: if he were discovered or exposed, he was officially deniable, easily discarded to the wolves. 'Haven't these questions been broached through the embassy?'

'How could they be?' demanded the Grand Duke, irritation again close. 'I am not a diplomat. The Tsar and the Duma are at arm's length. The Tsar could not make the enquiry, even if he were minded to, which he is not. And for me to consider discussing with anyone in the Duma anything of what I am discussing with you could easily spark another uprising.'

He was being inundated with information, Sebastian realized. In addition to which, the Grand Duke was disclosing some desperation. 'You place great trust in me.'

'Your recommendation is the known integrity of your father. And the trust that others placed in you to do what you did in America.'

'What if you came to doubt me?'

'You would be disposed of,' answered the secret police chief, at once.

The immediacy briefly stalled Sebastian, before he managed: 'I suppose I must appreciate your honesty.'

'It's *my* integrity.'

'I believe I could explore your questions, to get some guidance,' granted Sebastian, guardedly.

Orlov smiled. 'The answer I hoped to hear.'

'I do not like my every move being monitored.' How many concessions could he manoeuvre?

'Surveillance will be lifted.'

'I would like access to the court circle.'

'The Tsar and his family are reclusive, choosing to live in Tsarskoye Selo. That's not an easy demand to meet.'

'You spoke aboard the *Lusitania* of the monk, Rasputin, and his undue hold upon the imperial family.'

'An indiscretion that now embarrasses me.'

'I would like to be in a situation to encounter him.'

'You have your choice of bawdy house or drinking hovel,' sneered the Grand Duke.

'You despise the man?'

'Utterly.'

'Consider him a danger?'

'I believe his influence unacceptable.'

'Your function is to protect the Tsar. Why not remove Rasputin?'

The Grand Duke splashed more brandy into his goblet. 'The Tsarina is besotted by the man and how he helps the Tsarevich

111

with his recurring blood illness, for which no cure has been found. You must understand a Russian dichotomy. The Russian people – the Tsar and his family particularly – are deeply religious. But parallel to that religiousness is a belief, an acceptance of a conflicting mysticism. They believe in shamen, in miracle makers, as so many Russians do.'

'Tsarina Alexandra is German, not Russian,' reminded Sebastian.

'Such is her devotion to – and concern for – the Tsarevich that, as most mothers would, she seeks help from any quarter. The Tsarevich is sometimes a wilful child, acting without thought or concern for himself and his condition. A simple tumble or knock, which to any other child might result in a moment's tears, reduces him to agony. I have seen it happen too many times. As I have seen how quickly Rasputin can ease his suffering.'

'I don't choose to search bawdy houses or drinking dens. I am sure there are few moments when you are unaware of his every move.'

'I will arrange an encounter,' undertook the Grand Duke. 'What was your mission in America?'

The other man hesitated. 'Seeking the same answers as I am seeking from you.'

'How?'

'The embassy was my only approach.'

'And the response?'

'That the administration of President Wilson was neutralist. Which was, of course, before your exposure of the Germany spy ring, run from their very embassy!'

'You spoke of the expulsion from America of that ring necessarily becoming something of interest to you?'

The Grand Duke was momentarily silent. 'There have been suggestions – information – that Berlin is seeking to infiltrate and influence the revolutionary groups here in Russia, as they try to infiltrate themselves among American industrialists.'

Churchill's concern, isolated Sebastian. The thinking of the two men was remarkably similar. 'Among a German contingent at yesterday's garden party, there was a man named Hans Vogel, one of the leaders of the cell expelled from America.'

The Russian had been increasingly slumped in his enclosing chair. He came up and forward now, intent upon Sebastian. 'I have the names of everyone at the German embassy. Vogel is not one of them.'

'Would it be, his having already been exposed elsewhere? Alternative identity is not difficult to arrange for someone representing his country, is it?'

'You have no doubt?'

'None. I left immediately, to avoid being recognized myself.'

'Did you succeed?' demanded the Russian, at once.

'I believe so.'

'But you can't be sure?'

'No, I cannot be sure.'

'Were you with Olga?'

'No. The military attaché, Captain Black.'

'Would Vogel recognize you, if he caught sight of you?'

'Unquestionably.'

'I must have the man identified!'

'In Washington his accreditation attached him to the embassy's legal department.'

The other man finally put aside his empty brandy snifter. 'We've talked of many things. You haven't positively committed yourself.'

'As you haven't, upon all the requests I have made,' bargained Sebastian.

'I will do everything in my power to get you where you seek to be.'

'I will do everything I am able to answer the questions you've posed,' matched Sebastian.

'You have already answered one, without being asked it,' said the Russian. 'But if Vogel did recognize you, you are compromised.'

'Or he is,' Sebastian pointed out, seeing an opportunity to rid himself of the potential problem. 'If you were able positively to identify him as who I say he is, wouldn't that be reason enough to declare him persona non grata?'

'There's much to consider from tonight,' avoided the older man.

'How shall we communicate?'

113

'I will have contact made with you.'

'I'll be awaiting it.' How much truth and trust could he take from this bizarre encounter? Sebastian asked himself, on his journey, in a monogrammed coach, back to his hotel. It was going to take hours of concentrated recall properly to answer that among all the other questions. Certainly, on what he had already analyzed, he had another large and important memorandum for London: sufficient, almost, to consider his mission achieved. But now he had another opportunity, he thought. One from which he might learn far, far more.

Sebastian brought himself from reflection to the present as he entered his suite, remaining initially just inside the door, examining the first room before moving cautiously through the apartment, checking his traps. His seemingly carelessly discarded gloves on the bureau top had been moved from the way he had carefully placed them and a drawer he had left slightly protruding had been fully closed. The lining of an inner pocket of one suit in the closet he had left disarranged was now in place, and again the closet door was firmly shut where he had left it slightly ajar. The safe containing his pocket book holding the letters of credit, and the money belt and pouch appeared untouched, with no cash missing this time.

It came as no surprise, but Sebastian knew now why he had been kept at the palace and not allowed to return to the hotel to change. And possibly the reason for the dinner-table interruption. He felt no offence. It didn't quite qualify as *the enemy you know is safer than the enemy you don't* but it told Sebastian how much trust to expect from Grand Duke Alexei Orlov. But he'd scarcely needed to be warned of that, either.

There was a palpable uncertainty in the room, which the diplomatically attuned Mycroft moved quickly to quash, although initially keeping the conversation general, engaging the two other men in a general discussion of an article in that day's *Times* setting out the competing nationalistic ambitions of the Balkan states. As he orchestrated the debate, Mycroft was conscious of Dr Watson's professional concentration upon Sherlock Holmes, in whom he could not detect any indication

114

of his brother's recent worrying behaviour. There was no irritability when he was confronted by a contrary argument, and his in turn were balanced and well made.

'I believe I've taken things forward,' Sherlock Holmes announced simply, waiting for an exchange between the doctor and Mycroft to wither and die.

'How so?' demanded Mycroft, who was concerned that what he had to offer might overwhelm Sherlock Holmes's account, widening the gap between them once more.

'I believe Sebastian correctly read the man Stalin, momentarily claiming to be a Menshevik,' said Sherlock Holmes. 'He certainly stayed true to his group at the London congress which brought about the schism. But I've delved even deeper into the records of the conferences here. And those in Paris and Prague. Stalin emerges as a pragmatist, changing sides as the benefits present themselves. He's currently regarded as the heir apparent to Julius Cedarbaum, the leader of the Menshevik faction within the Social Democrat Party. It's my judgement – as it is Sebastian's – that he's a wind-sniffer: if he believed himself – his grouping – about to be beaten by Lenin's Bolsheviks, Josef Vissarionovich Djugashvili, or Stalin, or whatever other of his numerous aliases he chose to adopt for the day, would switch allegiance like that . . .' He snapped his fingers, dismissively.

'Which makes him what?' demanded Dr Watson.

'Someone to be taken very seriously into account, if there was a successful coup,' declared Sherlock Holmes. 'Let's not overlook Sebastian's other assessment, with which I also agree: indeed, which I believe shows the revolutionary's true colours. There's nothing in anything that Sebastian recounted to suggest a constitutional transition. If the Tsar is overthrown, Stalin will support his demise, to remove someone who could remain a dangerously rallying figurehead.'

'That's a frightening prediction, Holmes,' protested Dr Watson.

'Reached from the evidence available, circumstantial though it is,' insisted the detective.

Mycroft had removed himself from the discussion, anxious for as much uninterrupted time and opportunity as possible to

115

restore the long-established relationship between the two other men. To Mycroft's eye it was as if there had never been a falling out. And he judged Sherlock's visible enthusiasm nothing more than satisfaction at carrying a task forward. Having reassured himself, Mycroft only just prevented a facial reaction to Dr Watson's next remark.

'It would appear Sebastian is once more acquitting himself well.'

The choleric reaction Mycroft feared did not materialize. Instead, actually smiling, Sherlock Holmes said: 'Indeed he is, Watson. And I find it most gratifying.'

So surprised was Mycroft that it was several moments before he could pick up the conversation. Finally he said: 'There's cause for another meeting with Winston, beyond your analysis.'

'Why?' demanded Sherlock Holmes.

'Sebastian warned us in his telegram of his recognizing the German spy from the American mission,' reminded Mycroft. 'The Foreign Secretary produced it at Cabinet today.'

'To what reaction?' asked Dr Watson.

'Muted, because of Ireland,' said Mycroft. 'He was told to seek further information. But it was Sir Edward Grey who concluded the Anglo-Russian Entente that would bring Great Britain into any conflict. It gives him a very personal and vested interest.'

'But will he express it?' pressed Sherlock Holmes.

'Now that the matter has attained cabinet discussion, I think he will,' guessed Mycroft.

'Which should make Churchill happy,' remarked Dr Watson.

'I think Winston might have preferred to be more centrally, more personally, involved in bringing about the belated interest,' disagreed Mycroft.

They rose, obedient as always to Mrs Hudson's summons. Sherlock Holmes carved the venison and Mycroft dispensed the claret. The dinner-table conversation continued to revolve around what they had already talked about, but without any further or better-clarified conclusions. It was towards the end of the meal that Sherlock Holmes talked of he and Dr Watson meeting the following day, for further discussion and analysis, and charged Mycroft with arranging another meeting with Winston Churchill, although suggesting he allowed sufficient time for a possible response from the St Petersburg embassy to the Foreign Secretary's demands.

'And possibly for some further communication from Sebastian,' he added.

The moment they were in their shared hansom, Mycroft said: 'Well?'

Dr Watson shook his head, decidedly. 'Absolutely not. Tonight we talked and dined with the old Holmes, without need for anything other than a case to get his teeth into.'

'Your remark upon Sebastian's continued success alarmed me.'

'Not a casual remark,' corrected the burly, moustachioed man. 'Holmes has got to accept the situation with Sebastian without rancour. His reaction to what I said gave me every confidence that he is doing so.'

'And you are reunited,' reminded Mycroft.

'Gratefully so,' agreed the doctor.

# Eleven

Sebastian had worked late into what remained of the previous night, compiling notes of everything he'd discussed with Orlov, rising twice from his bed to add sudden, awakening recollections, and resumed early the following day, further expanding his impressions and inferences before setting out to create a comprehensive account of the entire day, including the afternoon's encounter with Princess Olga prior to the clearly engineered confrontation with the Grand Duke. Sebastian was on his third draft, the bureau strewn with papers overflowing or discarded on to the floor, when the urgent knock came at his door, so unexpected Sebastian physically jumped. The summons came again before Sebastian had time to respond to it.

Stepping uninvited in from the corridor, Captain Lionel Black said: 'I'm greatly relieved to find you in!'

Sebastian had little alternative but to move further aside for the attaché to enter, but led him away from the bureau. 'It was my intention to call upon you later today, after telephoning . . .'

Black looked over Sebastian's shoulder, to the bureau. 'We could travel together.'

'I've much more work left to assemble and complete. I might not even finish in time for today's diplomatic pouch.'

'I've created a furore in London with the news of the German presence here,' announced the man, unable to contain himself any further. 'There's been a telegram from the Foreign Secretary himself! It's been declared my responsibility.'

Welcomed with open arms, guessed Sebastian. Black would milk the opportunity for every last droplet of career advancement. But then, thought Sebastian, why shouldn't he? Sebastian wondered by how much the man had exaggerated his access to information. What began as a casual, unconsidered reflection abruptly hardened into concern. Sebastian said: 'Did you cite me as your source?'

The attaché made an uneasy, shoulder-humping movement. 'Not in as many words. I referred—'

'Good,' Sebastian cut him off, uninterested in the other man's excuse. 'Have you said anything to London of my presence here?'

Black gave another shrug. 'I thought you didn't wish that . . . that your being here was unofficial.'

'It is, very much so . . .' Unembarrassed by the inherent threat, Sebastian said: 'As your help to me is unofficial. And as I made clear upon your securing my release from jail, I do not wish in any way or manner for you to be caused professional inconvenience. The knowledge of Hans Vogel's presence here must remain your discovery.'

Black gave a relieved smile, quickly gone. 'London want more.'

'I've no doubt they do. I have no more than the identification of the man.'

'How can you be so positive it is the same man?'

'Because a very few months ago he stood not a yard away, training a pistol upon me. Those are circumstances in which you very clearly remember the man about to kill you.'

The reply briefly silenced the other man. 'What were those circumstances?'

Under the merest pressure, Black would reveal his presence, Sebastian decided: the man's arrival and questioning actually provided an addendum to his still incomplete dossier. 'I cannot divulge that.'

'I have offered you every help and assistance,' reminded the attaché.

'For which I have expressed my gratitude. And reciprocated by alerting you to Hans Vogel being here in St Petersburg.'

'To what purpose?'

Sebastian suppressed the sigh, deciding yet again that Churchill's doubt about the embassy was well founded. 'What other purpose could there be?'

119

'If your reasoning is right, it alters completely the guidance I and others have been giving London for several months.'

'Don't accept my reasoning!' said Sebastian, exasperated. 'Make your own assessment.'

Black nodded beyond Sebastian, to the bureau again. 'Am I to be allowed to read what is there?'

'No,' refused Sebastian, instantly. 'For me to allow that would compromise you and Churchill. Both of you could be ruined, you perhaps more than he.' A half-thought began pricking at Sebastian's mind.

'Does it bear upon Vogel's presence here?'

Only as confirmation of Churchill's concern at German intentions, thought Sebastian. An awareness now open to Black and the Foreign Secretary. 'There is nothing there additional to what I have already told you. It is a matter of interpretation.'

'I have to respond,' pleaded the man.

Sebastian's mind cleared, the idea as clear as a burning candle. 'Your need is positively to confirm that Hans Vogel is the man who was expelled from New York?'

'Absolutely.'

'Germany's humiliation was in its public exposure, in the New York media. Every member of the spy ring was photographed, in a barred holding cage of a precinct house,' recalled Sebastian. 'Have London get from New York – from newspapers or from the police – copies of every photograph to pass on to you here. You will then possess the entire gallery for comparison with the German embassy staff here.' It was a demand he would make in another addition to what he was preparing for London. And use further to ingratiate himself with Orlov if some of the men in the photographs were proven by simple surveillance also to have been transferred to St Petersburg.

'That's a brilliant idea!' enthused Black.

It wasn't, conceded Sebastian. It was logical and should have come to him sooner. He was curious if it had occurred to his father. 'It gives you your reply to London. And time to consider.'

'Consider what?'

'If your advice to London has been sufficiently comprehensive,' said Sebastian, diplomatically.

'You're right!' accepted Black, eagerly.

He shouldn't allow the moment to go unexplored, Sebastian decided. 'Has there already been a re-evaluation?'

'Not yet. Too soon,' said the other man. 'Because the telegram came in the name of Sir Edward Grey, it's got priority, though.' The man hesitated. 'Can I look upon you to alert me of anything more of significance?'

No, thought Sebastian. 'Of course, providing there is no danger to you or Churchill.' Or to his uncle, he mentally added. Mycroft was probably more open to ruin than any of them.

Black looked yet again at the disordered bureau. 'I'll expect you at the embassy.'

'What time is the pouch dispatched?'

'Four.'

'Prior to four then.'

Sebastian composed his two addendums and went carefully through the entire document, comparing its contents against every reminder he had made. It took a further hour before he was satisfied. He was actually reaching for the heavy manila envelope when the doubt came and he sat back in his chair, remembering Black's covetous examination of the bureau. Sighing, Sebastian decided there was a necessary precaution he had to take, reaching out for fresh paper. It took him a further two hours to transcribe what he had originally written in open script into Notions, the unique and abstruse 'secret language' that evolved over its 500-year history for pupils and dons to communicate at Winchester, Britain's oldest public school, from which Sebastian went up to King's College, Cambridge.

Sebastian finally put his account into the waiting reinforced envelope, lit his taper and used it to melt the wax into two separate sealing blobs, heavily imprinting into each the head of the signet ring that had been his father's gift to him at their first reconciliation.

Sebastian was at the embassy easily by three thirty. As promised, an ebullient, telephone-alerted Captain Black was within hailing distance of the gatehouse.

121

Sebastian said: 'I'd also welcome a moment at your telegraph.' As they walked to Black's quarters the attaché said: 'I've already responded to London. And got their reply.'

'They've accepted your suggestion?'

'Enthusiastically.'

They reached Black's office. The attaché stood away for Sebastian to get to the machine. Sebastian dialled his uncle's connection at the Diogenes Club, not needing to consult what he had written on a reminder slip. The message read:

QUILL PRIXLESS PAX TASK SCALDINGS SCONCE
UNDERCONSTUMBLE DOCK CROPPLE CRUX ENTRY

'What's this?' exclaimed Black, from behind him.

'A message, intended to be private, to someone in England,' said Sebastian. He hardly needed confirmation of the need for his precaution, he decided.

'But it's a code!'

'To prevent it being read and understood by those for whom it is not intended.'

'In England?' qualified Black.

'There is a possibility of it being intercepted,' said Sebastian, not wanting positively to antagonize the man.

Black smiled. 'So what does it mean?'

'I repeat yet again, I do not wish to involve you any further than you already are, to the risk of your career.'

'The risk is mine and I am prepared to take it,' insisted the officer.

'I'm not,' Sebastian continued to refuse. 'As I've already assured you, I will give you every assistance with the German business. My other affairs must remain my own, for your protection.'

'I've just told you I don't give a fig for that.'

'And I've told you I can't allow such risk.'

The man moved to speak but appeared to change his mind. 'So be it,' he said.

We'll see, thought Sebastian.

Sebastian went hopefully to the enquiry desk upon his return to the Grand Hotel. There were no messages. He hadn't spotted Orlov's men, either, but he was sure they had been with him to and from the embassy. Just as he now believed it had been intentional for him to identify those who had made themselves so obvious.

Winston Churchill had remained overnight in Kent, where he was searching for a country retreat, and continued on the following morning to Sherlock Holmes's house in Sussex, which gave Mycroft the excuse to drive from London in his open-topped Rolls Royce Silver Ghost, which he cherished with the pride of a lioness for its cub, and which he drove, too fast, in leather travelling coat, leather gauntlet gloves and protective goggles. Sherlock Holmes and Dr Watson declined the offered transport, preferring the train to Brighton. Mycroft made a race of it and lost by thirty minutes, which he blamed on slow-moving carriages creating congestion on the roads. To Mycroft's visible satisfaction, Churchill gave the same reason for his delayed arrival.

'And I must return to London soon after luncheon,' said Churchill, continuing the apology. 'I've had word from Chesterfield, which surely refers to the King's attitude towards the Romanovs.'

'Let's talk outside,' invited Sherlock Holmes, leading the way out into the gazebo in the rose garden that it had become his hobby to cultivate since buying the weekend home. The Pol Roger was already in its cooler, glasses alongside.

'I've heard from Sebastian,' announced Mycroft, after the wine was poured. To his brother he said: 'I know you've made yourself familiar with the vernacular, so I've made you a copy . . . copies for all of us, in fact . . .'

Sherlock Holmes did not immediately look at his son's message. Instead he said: 'What of my assessment, of what he's already sent?'

'Dispatched yesterday, under the Holmes seal,' assured Mycroft, indicating his crested signet ring.

Frowning down at what he'd been handed, Churchill read: '*Quill prixless pax task scaldings sconce underconstumble dock cropple crux entry . . .*' The frown remained when he looked up. 'Is this—?'

'Confounded Winchester patois!' completed Sherlock Holmes. 'He's using the telegraph of Captain Black, your trusted friend. Why does he need to descend into gibberish . . . !' The pause was immediate, reflective.

Mycroft pointedly filled the hesitation. 'I think that's the question that needs to occupy us before we even attempt to unravel the message itself. The telegraph at my club is exclusively mine: it has no other reader and is therefore totally secure.'

Churchill, whose head had been slumped in contemplation, reared up. 'Captain Lionel Black is an officer!'

'Which does not automatically extend to being a gentleman,' pointed out Watson, the former military surgeon.

Churchill came even further forward over the rustic table. 'I resent that slur upon a fellow officer.'

'There was no slur,' insisted the doctor. 'It was an observation predicated upon my own observations, as an officer, of other officers.'

'Sebastian would not have felt the need without just cause,' insisted Sherlock Holmes. 'I think Mycroft is right. Sebastian is not confident of the security at his end.'

'Shall we examine the message?' suggested Churchill, impatiently, refilling their glasses. 'I have things to talk about beyond it.'

'There's a greater need for accuracy than speed,' insisted Sherlock Holmes.

'Perhaps the content might enlighten us,' came back Churchill.

'I'd welcome a translation better than my own,' confessed Mycroft.

'*Quill?*' demanded Churchill.

'To curry favour with someone,' interpreted Mycroft, at once. 'It's not the commencement that causes me difficulty. Let's move along. *Prixless* means priceless . . .'

'And *pax* has the meaning of an intimate or particular friend,' intruded Sherlock Holmes, who'd travelled to Winchester to discover the language in which Sebastian chose to communicate during his American assignment. 'My reading is that Sebastian has, after all, succeeded in establishing contact with the Grand Duke Alexei Orlov.'

124

'I'll go with that translation,' accepted Mycroft. 'The strict Notions definition of *task* is a composition, either in prose or verse. I'm taking that to be advice that there is new information on its way to us . . .'

'From a priceless source like the head of the Okhrana!' picked up Sherlock Holmes. 'That's surely beyond any expectation!'

'Let that be your interpretation, as it is mine,' said Mycroft. 'It fits what follows. *Scaldings* is a cry of warning. There are several uses for the word *sconce*. That which I am choosing is an indication of an obstruction or interference.'

'*Underconstumble* is – or was – a little-used word,' volunteered Dr Watson, smarting still from the trickery of a Winchester College-employed yokel who'd extracted money and drink on the pretext of providing a complete Notions lexicon available at the Winchester College bookshop for a few guineas. 'It means to understand.'

'And now begins my difficulty,' admitted Mycroft. '*Cropple* has no contextual connection whatsoever. Its translation is an imposition upon a pupil for not sufficiently preparing a lesson. It even has a definition beyond the Winchester College language. In Hampshire dialect it means to cripple or to disable a person. *Dock* has no place, either. It has at least five different Notions meanings, all revolving around a definition of to rip out or to curtail. I spent every mile of my journey here today trying to fit every definition into this conundrum. And failed . . .'

Sherlock Holmes appeared to be indifferent to the to-and-fro conversation, hunched over a writing block scribbling hurriedly, equally quickly crossing out, then writing again.

'Let's get to the end,' urged Churchill. 'What in heaven's name is the definition of *crux*, beyond that which we all know?'

'That which we all know,' echoed Mycroft. 'At Winchester a crux is a problem or a difficult situation.'

'Which further compounds my difficulty in understanding what Sebastian is trying to convey,' protested the politician.

'And an *entry* is an unseen translation,' finally provided the determined Dr Watson.

Sherlock Holmes went back to his much-scribbled-upon and corrected paper, groping slowly through the other various suggestions. 'Sebastian has established contact with a priceless source, which unquestionably has to be the Grand Duke,' he insisted, head bent over his notes. 'There is an account en route to us. We have to understand he's trying to convey a warning, about another translation – another situation – which is a totally separate problem.'

'This gets us nowhere,' protested Churchill. 'I want words I can comprehend, creating sentences I can understand.'

'You will because I will,' promised Sherlock Holmes, without conceit.

'Why not send him a telegram in return, asking for clarification?' demanded Churchill.

'And make everything easier for whoever it is whom Sebastian does not wish to read his exchanges!' sneered Sherlock Holmes, openly contemptuous of the politician. 'Why, sir, do you imagine my son made his communication as difficult as he did?'

'If just one part of your various interpretations is correct – that there is further information on its way to us based on intelligence from the Grand Duke – then this is surely a meaningless puzzle?' retorted Churchill. 'We simply have to wait for its arrival.'

'If it was as simple as that, Sebastian would not have bothered us *with* a puzzle,' rejected Sherlock Holmes. 'It has a purpose and we have to discover it. And if we don't – if I don't – then we're failing Sebastian. Which I will not do.'

'We none of us will,' returned Churchill at once. He fluttered his paper. 'If we have its dictionary we surely have its key!'

'I am defeated,' confessed Mycroft.

'As am I,' said the hunched Sherlock Holmes, reluctantly.

'Then we must return to Sebastian,' said Churchill.

'We shall do nothing of the sort,' refused Sherlock Holmes. 'We will wait, unlike panicked chickens in a hen house at the entry of a fox, until I have deduced Sebastian's meaning.'

'I seem to have taken a considerable detour for little purpose,' protested Churchill.

126

'From what we can comprehend, my son has taken an even greater detour to important effect, of which you will very shortly be the lucky beneficiary,' retorted Sherlock Holmes. 'You spoke upon your arrival of having other things to discuss?'

'Black's alert to the presence in St Petersburg of a German spy whom Sebastian encountered in America has caused pandemonium within the cabinet,' disclosed Churchill. 'It's for a cabinet committee meeting that I have to return to London today.'

'So your desires are satisfied?' suggested Sherlock Holmes, pointedly. 'At last the government is refocused upon a problem beyond Ireland?'

'It's not being presented with full authority or clarity,' said Churchill. 'Grey vacillates, interested more in becoming the longest-serving Foreign Secretary in history than proving himself worthy of such a doubtful record, under Haldane's insistence that the presence of the man Vogel – if indeed it *is* Vogel, which he questions – is no indication of German interference in the politics of Russia.'

'I'm not aware of it being dismissed as lightly as that!' protested Mycroft.

'I'm talking of the committee, before which I am being pilloried for returning the Mediterranean Fleet for exercises in the North Sea, to show the Kaiser what his warships will be confronted with,' disclosed Churchill.

'I didn't know such an order had been issued,' said Mycroft.

'You do now,' said Churchill, in ill-tempered petulance.

Such a movement should have been discussed in full cabinet: been a cabinet decision, thought Mycroft. He could not openly challenge Churchill, in front of the others in the room: could not have challenged him, in fact, if he and Churchill had been alone. How endangered had Churchill made himself, by the arrogance of such an arbitrary decision? And by connection how endangered were he and Sebastian? The fact that Churchill had clearly been summoned back to London was worrying. It certainly didn't allow him to remain overnight in Sussex, which had been his original intention. He had to be back in the corridors of power, hearing the whispers and their echoes.

Luncheon was a desultory intervention. Churchill relaxed

sufficiently to extol the beauty of Kent and of a property called Chartwell that he was bringing his wife Clementine to consider, and Mycroft tried with little success to interest the table in motoring anecdotes, despite Dr Watson's efforts to express interest. Sherlock Holmes made no effort whatsoever to contribute, his mind occupied by the enigma by which they were confronted. There was patent relief upon everyone's part at Churchill's insistence on departing immediately the meal was over.

'Has the opportunist finally overstepped himself?' demanded Sherlock Holmes, emerging from his self-imposed isolation before Churchill's chauffeured car cleared the driveway.

'I don't know,' admitted Mycroft.

'I *need* to know,' insisted Sherlock Holmes. 'Sebastian's safety depends upon my knowing.'

'I'm returning to London at once,' said Mycroft. 'I'll be able to answer the uncertainties by tomorrow.'

'If uncertainties remain, then Sebastian must return at once,' said Sherlock Holmes. 'I'll not have Sebastian entangled in a failure not of his own making.'

'I think we are moving ahead of ourselves,' cautioned Watson. 'There's no way Sebastian can become entangled in the political difficulties that Churchill has intimated, although I agree that if the man were removed from office, there would be no purpose in Sebastian any longer remaining in Russia.'

'This isn't how the day was intended,' said Mycroft. 'Shall you return to London with me?'

'No,' refused Sherlock Holmes, at once. 'There's no immediate contribution I can make there. And Watson and I have a conundrum to solve.'

Mycroft almost missed the smiled nod of satisfaction that Dr Watson directed towards him.


'I'll concede these damned Notions have a usefulness, Watson, in their being insoluble to anyone without a knowledge of their various definitions, but they have their limitations,' lectured Sherlock Holmes. They were at the dining-room table, the largest available in the house, its surface cleared of everything but paper and pen. 'Their drawback is their lack of *precise* meaning, to fit Sebastian's needs. He is reliant upon our becoming attuned to his extensions of their Winchester definitions.'

'What's our way then, Holmes?'

'We work separately,' decided Sherlock Holmes. 'We create encryption graphs of every conceivable use of every possible definition. Which we then exchange between us and eliminate after every test we can devise to make intelligible what remains a mystery to us.'

'And if we fail?'

'We exchange again, each to go through the other's work to find the misdirection.'

'And if—?' started Watson.

'We devise another approach,' said Sherlock Holmes.

They worked concentratedly, without any interruption or respite, throughout the remainder of the afternoon and slightly into the evening before Watson pushed his sheets away and sighed: 'It's no good, Holmes. It has me beaten.'

'I'm in no better condition,' admitted the detective. 'Let's exchange, as agreed, to find the other's error.'

It was Sherlock Holmes who spoke, after a further two hours. 'We've trod the same path, each in the other's footsteps.'

'What now then?' asked the doctor, wearily.

'Fresh graphs,' declared Sherlock Holmes. 'List the definitions, of each and every word in the given translations. And then enumerate every possible variation of each and every word, to see if we can make any possible sense from any of them.'

They refused Mrs Hudson's offered dinner and continued on until just before midnight. It was then that Watson said: 'It's no good, Holmes. I'm done for.'

Sherlock Holmes angrily banged his fist against the table, staring down at sheet after sheet of paper. 'It's here, somewhere! In front of our eyes and we can't see it.'

'I can no longer see even what's in front of my eyes,' protested Watson.

'My son has a difficulty and I need to discover what it is,' declared Sherlock Holmes.

# Twelve

There'd been no prior alert but the coach was drawn up to one side of the hotel's main entrance as discreetly as a highly polished, monogrammed coach can be discreet. Several pedestrians were lingering, examining it curiously: one man was actually tracing his fingers along the filigreed initials, trying to decipher the lettering interwoven around and between the eagle-dominated Orlov crest, when a sharp bark of rebuke from inside sent him scuttling. Sebastian accepted that he had to approach, but as he did so felt a spurt of annoyance. He was still at least three yards away when a footman whose features he now recognized – not in livery but wearing the dark lounge suit of the garden party – emerged from the inside of the vehicle and stood with the door open for Sebastian to enter. Which Sebastian did, further annoyed at the man's head-bent gesture of what to any observer would have appeared matching recognition or even servitude. There was the scrabbled sound of the man ascending the box to sit beside the driver as the vehicle lurched into motion.

Sebastian twisted on the plush seat, easing the holstered revolver to a more comfortable position, intent upon their route through the shutter-slanted windows. He'd emerged from the hotel without real purpose or direction, once again checking the desk for non-existent messages on his way, the only positive wish to escape the increasingly claustrophobic surroundings of his suite. He should, Sebastian supposed, be grateful for the unexpected development. His immediate expectation was to be taken in the direction of the Grand Duke's Neva-bordering palace but, although they were travelling roughly parallel to the river, Sebastian quickly realized that was not their destination, and came closer to the window, opening the slats wide for a clearer view of their route. On impulse he swivelled and more fully adjusted the rear hatchway. There was an escorting, similarly marked, coach about ten yards behind. It was, strangely, the rear view that first alerted Sebastian to their direction, quickly confirmed when he came back to the wider panorama of the side window, isolating first the parallel exclusive railway line, then the occasional sentinel house and the dotted coppices on the forbidden road to Tsarskoye Selo. Was he gaining more than he feared he might be losing? It was unthinkable that without warning or protocol – and certainly without a personal search that would have discovered the now encumbering pistol – he was going to be allowed any close proximity to the imperial family. What then? All he could imagine – believed he could expect – was the earlier interrupted orientation to the Tsar's village that had led to his brief imprisonment. Which, balanced against what he could conceivably be losing, did not seem as important now as it had done on the first day of his arrival. There was little, nothing in fact, that he could do to change his circumstances. He could only use whatever he was about to encounter to its maximum advantage, at the same time hoping that his fears would eventually prove unfounded.

Sebastian easily isolated the ballooned area in the road in which his Okhrana-informing coachman had turned his vehicle, and then, more quickly than he anticipated, the glint of water he'd detected the first time, although still too far distant to establish precisely as a river or sea or something man-made. He lost sight of it completely in an unexpected dip in the road and it remained hidden behind sharp hills that created a valley. When the coach eventually climbed from it, Sebastian couldn't detect any glint at all. There were more trees, though, suffi- cient almost to be considered a forest, but which ended as suddenly as they had begun, clearly cultivated to provide a barrier or protection. And then buildings at last came in sight, not the high baroque of gilded palaces, but low structures, some no higher than a single storey and many further submerged in a depression too orderly to be a natural valley like the one from which he had just emerged. Closer, Sebastian made out the soldiers and realized the buildings were barracks – and newly constructed – and that an effort had been made to conceal them as much as possible in the artificial cleft in the ground.

The coach passed through a total of three checkpoints, at each of which the coach door was opened and its interior scrutinized, but Sebastian was never searched. There was only one palace in view, and that too distant to distinguish any particular features, when the coach came to a final stop by an isolated house substantial enough to be considered a mansion, but far short of the grandeur Sebastian had anticipated. By the time the carriage door was opened, Grand Duke Alexei Orlov was at the mansion entrance.

'Welcome to Tsarskoye Selo,' greeted the bearded man. 'I hope you won't consider it a wasted excursion. This is as far as I can permit you to enter at the moment.' He gestured vaguely in the direction of the only palace visible. 'That is the Catherine Palace, the most opulent of them all, a veritable treasure house. Alexander Palace, occupied by the Tsar, is beyond. There are others.'

'And this?' asked Sebastian, as he was led inside the mansion.

'My humble working quarters,' smiled Orlov.

Sebastian supposed they were humble compared to the St Petersburg palace, but they were magnificent by most other criteria, marble once more the preferred stone, the panelled room into which Orlov led him again a combination of study and trophy room, complete with ancient weaponry and armour. Illogically, Sebastian's impression was of everything being too established and comfortable, beyond any concept of violent upheaval or change. 'You live here, as well as in St Petersburg?'

'When it is required,' said Orlov, gesturing to predictable leather-crafted chairs. 'What can I offer you?'

'Nothing, for the moment,' declined Sebastian. 'I was beginning to wonder if there would be any further contact between us.'

'There has to be a purpose,' said the Russian.

'Which is?'

'What of you?' avoided Orlov.

He'd delay his complaint, Sebastian decided: offer something, even. 'I've sent a lengthy account to London.'

'About what we discussed?'

'Of course.'

'Identifying me?'

There'd been no restriction against that, remembered Sebastian. 'It was necessary, to provide authority for what I said and asked. But that communication was coded, against interception. Which is impossible anyway.'

'Your recipients are discreet?'

'Totally.' It was too late for the man to concern himself now, Sebastian thought.

'Nothing has been discussed here, at the embassy?'

'Absolutely not,' assured Sebastian, surprised at the belated caution and deciding to make his further revelation now. 'The only thing of which the military attaché is aware is the presence of the German spy expelled from America, which I had no alternative but to disclose, as you already know. And I've tried to take that further. I've asked London to obtain photographs of all those expelled, which I shall make available to you when I receive them.'

Orlov smiled. 'You'll naturally expect to be told the results of any further identification, beyond Hans Vogel?'

'Naturally,' smiled Sebastian in return. It was always going to be necessary to deal professionally with this man as an equal, not to adopt a subordinate position, Sebastian decided.

'What's your impression of that much of Tsarskoye Selo as you've been permitted to see?' asked Orlov, unexpectedly.

He'd continue the honesty for as long as it suited him, Sebastian determined. 'As possible revolution is a matter on our minds, I think it is vulnerable.'

Orlov frowned, affronted. 'The barracks you saw are my innovation. There are others, at strategic positions throughout the park, which is too vast to wall or satisfactorily to enclose.'

'If it's too vast to wall, it's too vast to defend by soldiers alone, no matter how well armed or provided they are. And you remain dependent upon their loyalty.'

The frown had gone but Orlov remained serious, considering Sebastian's point. 'The troop is the Imperial Guard, individually sworn to loyalty to the Tsar. Their weaponry is the latest and extensive. And we have the private railway line to resupply men and equipment.'

'In my opinion Tsarskoye Selo is too remote to be properly defended against a consistent and sustained attack by superior numbers. The simplest of bombs would blow your railway line and cut you off from reinforcements or provisioning.'

'You were schooled in soldiering?' demanded the other man.

Had the Grand Duke been? wondered Sebastian. Or in secret police work, for that matter? Or had he gained his role through trustworthiness and the elevation of his birth, like so many private armies, British and Russian, in the Crimea conflict? If he were an amateur attempting a professional function, it would explain some of what remained unexplained from that first day at the St Petersburg palace. Sebastian said: 'I was fortunate to have a very wide and varied education, through a variety of European universities. At Heidelberg I studied the history of warfare. It's a subject upon which the Germans consider themselves experts, particularly since Bismark's unification.'

'How would your studies guide you here?'

'Transfer of the Tsar and his family to their much more easily defended Anichkov palace in St Petersburg at the beginning of any serious unrest,' replied Sebastian, at once. 'It would additionally serve a political message that the Tsar, the ruler of All the Russias, was back in his capital, confronting events.'

Orlov relaxed slightly, briefly smiling. 'Perhaps an astute proposal.'

Sebastian recognized the opportunity to take the conversation beyond the ambiguity of the discussion in the other trophy room, of which this study was a copy. 'It would also place the imperial family in convenient proximity to the sanctuary of the British embassy if events went against you.'

Orlov fixed Sebastian with another of his expressionless stares, which stretched into a long silence. Breaking it, Orlov said: 'You listen and understand well, Mr Holmes.'

It was another opening, acknowledged Sebastian. 'I hope we both do.'

Orlov's frown returned. 'Your doubt confuses me.'

'When you taxed me, I spoke immediately of my encountering Alexander Kerensky at the British embassy,' reminded Sebastian. 'And of leaving my card upon him in the hope of response, which has been unforthcoming.'

'I remain confused,' complained Orlov.

'What likelihood do you imagine of Kerensky responding to my approach with a monogrammed coach clearly identifying you stationed outside my hotel!' And it was even more unlikely that Josef Stalin would make contact, Sebastian thought, with a fresh surge of irritation.

Briefly Orlov's expression remained, before clearing. 'It is the coach of a member of the court circle.'

'It is the coach of the head of the Okhrana secret police!' insisted Sebastian.

'You know that,' acknowledged Orlov. 'The mob do not. To them it identifies nothing more than a member of the aristocracy.'

'I hesitate to ask this question,' apologized Sebastian in advance. 'But why do you imagine your coach was attacked by the mob in 1905?'

'*Because* it represented privilege and wealth and authority.'

'So be it,' accepted Sebastian. 'But I am not talking of keeping a rabble from my door. I am talking about socialist members of the Duma – Kerensky was identified to me as a rising figure, politically – and even revolutionaries. Do you sincerely believe your position is not known among them? It only took my father a matter of days to discover your function, from among the ranks of exiles and émigrés in London. Exiles and émigrés with whom those identified to me as potential leaders of further uprisings have contact and exchange during their periods of banishment after easy escape from Siberia!'

The statement visibly unsettled the huge man. 'I do not believe my position is so easily known. It is equal to that of a State secret.'

'I don't believe you should be so sanguine. If we are to continue our contact, I believe there needs to be a more circumspect method of communication,' insisted Sebastian. He did not consider he was the only one against whom the accusation of naivety could be brought. Unless, that is, Orlov was intentionally barring him contact with any other source than himself. There had that morning been the additional precaution of an escorting coach, he reminded himself.

'I have an ear on the streets,' insisted Orlov, in return. 'I would have heard an echo.'

'There's no guarantee of that,' refused Sebastian. 'I don't benefit from such public association with you.'

'I understand your objection,' assured the man. 'Some alternative will be devised.'

Most probably after it's too late, thought Sebastian. '"This is as far as I can permit you to enter *at the moment*,"' quoted Sebastian, with added emphasis.

'You lose me again!' protested Orlov.

'Your welcome, upon my arrival here,' reminded Sebastian. 'My inference is that I might be allowed further, at another time?'

Orlov shook his head. 'Then I owe you an apology.'

'There is no further purpose for my being brought here?'

'You seek some entry into royal circles?'

'I've made that clear enough.'

'Prince Felix Yusupov is married to the Tsar's niece, Princess Irina Alexandrovna. There is a grand ball being staged, a continuing part of the celebrations marking the three hundred years of Romanov rule. It would please me if you would be the Princess Olga's escort.'

Sebastian hesitated, astonished at the suggestion. 'I would be honoured. But would she?'

'She hasn't objected to this approach,' assured Orlov. 'Although I don't imagine she'd welcome your carrying the pistol that is disarranging your clothes.'

'Why wasn't I asked to surrender it?' Sebastian was disconcerted at it being so easily identified, as the swordstick had been so dismissively isolated by Stalin.

Orlov shrugged. 'I know you not to be an assassin, Mr Holmes. But on the night of the ball at least, allow me to guarantee your security.'

He had no alternative but to accept the mockery, Sebastian acknowledged. It could have still been achieved by seizing the weapon with which he should not have been allowed to enter even the remotest outskirts of the Tsar's village. Increasingly Sebastian wondered at the Grand Duke's competence. But then perhaps he should question his own, as well. Sebastian said: 'Will the Tsar and his family be at the celebration?'

'They have accepted, obviously, as part of the anniversary celebrations. But that does not automatically guarantee their attendance. Their movements are much dependent, as always, upon the well-being of the Tsarevich.'

'Is he currently unwell?'

'No,' said Orlov at once. 'If he were, Rasputin would be in attendance, which he is not. I know the identity of everyone within Tsarskoye Selo, as I have to know the names of everyone attending Prince Yusupov's grand ball.'

'Is Rasputin to be there?'

Orlov sighed. 'The influence of the man upon the Tsarina is a cause of great concern to everyone within the court, myself particularly. And increasingly outside. There are the most salacious rumours, some even openly appearing in St Petersburg newspapers, suggested an inappropriate relationship between the Tsarina and the priest. I succeeded in suppressing one such publication a month ago. It puts public opinion against the imperial family.'

Had that been reported to London by the embassy? wondered Sebastian. He said: 'It would only be by a slight margin, but perhaps more discreet communication could continue through my calling again upon the princess?'

'Something to explore,' agreed Orlov. 'I'd hoped there might have been some communication from London we could have discussed today.'

That remark betrayed unexpected anxiety, Sebastian decided. 'Too soon. Perhaps I may call tomorrow?'

'Olga and I will both look forward to it.'

Sebastian returned to the city oblivious of the journey, hunched in the carriage with its window slats open only sufficiently to admit the minimum of light, once again more nonplussed than enlightened by the encounter, although believing there was more to relay to London. His greatest confusion was the apparent willingness with which the man was prepared to involve his daughter in his machinations, no matter how discreetly and well she was protected, particularly after the manner in which the Grand Duchess perished. So engrossed in his uncertainty was Sebastian that the halt far short of the Grand Hotel, which he had insisted upon at his moment of departure from Tsarskoye Selo, came as a surprise. He walked in the general direction of the hotel for almost fifteen minutes, the embarrassing revolver feeling heavy at his hip, before managing to hail a public cab to complete his journey.

Captain Lionel Black rose at once to greet him from a foyer seat, a wax-sealed package in hand. 'I hope it's some progress,' said the attaché, inanely.

'So do I,' said Sebastian. What? he wondered.

Sebastian's full account of his once doubted meeting with the Grand Duke was entirely in Notions and occupied three closely written pages of translation that took Mycroft a full day and some of the early evening to complete. The delay, which co-incided with yet another cabinet committee meeting, prevented Churchill's initial attendance, providing Sherlock Holmes, his brother and Dr Watson with the opportunity for a preliminary discussion at the Diogenes Club.

Mycroft said: 'Sebastian's telegram alerted us to his gaining access to Orlov, as well as to the danger of the German presence. And I am confident that I have fully translated as he intended his impressions of that meeting. Which only leaves unresolved the full explanation of that confounded telegram itself!'

'Which remains unresolved, despite every effort to decipher his full meaning,' said Watson, to whom the admission of failure had been delegated.

'The full account will throw Churchill into a paroxysm, quite apart from our already knowing of the German presence,' said Sherlock Holmes, distractedly. 'All Churchill's fears appear to chime with Orlov's.'

'The most worrying of which is Orlov's apparent underlying doubt of stability,' judged Watson.

'You're both too well aware of my concern about Sebastian's safety in such circumstances to need my repeating it,' said Holmes.

'On a broader level, it makes of the utmost importance whatever exchange Churchill had with the Earl of Chesterfield after the most recent Privy Council meeting,' insisted Watson.

'How is Churchill, without challenge, going to be able to introduce into an acceptable cabinet presentation what Sebastian is discovering?' queried Mycroft, as engrossed in inner thoughts as his brother.

'He can't, not without disclosing a source and a covert enterprise, both of which are impossible,' replied Watson. 'We're becoming men restricted by our own knowledge.'

Becoming even more deeply reflective, Sherlock Holmes said: 'Sebastian's entire account was in Notions?'

'Which is why I have had to labour so long to understand it all,' protested Mycroft.

From the case beside him Sherlock Holmes produced the graphs and encryptions of the previous day, spreading them with difficulty upon a table smaller than that which had been available in Sussex. At its top he put Sebastian's alerting message. 'Why!' Sherlock Holmes suddenly exclaimed.

Both men started back, in surprise. Watson said: 'Holmes . . . ! What . . . ?'

'What's the purpose of a code?' demanded Sherlock Holmes.

'Secret communication,' responded Watson, accustomed to their partnership.

'How did Sebastian's communication reach us?'

'By diplomatic bag.'

'Secure from interference, intrusion or obstruction?'

'Yes,' agreed Watson, although doubtfully.

'Sealed?'

'Yes,' said Mycroft.

'So why encode it in this Winchester jargon that has taken you lost hours to interpret, if it was beyond any interference, intrusion or obstruction? And would never be read by any other than its designated recipient, yourself?' Sherlock Holmes was anxiously shuffling through the sheets now, sometimes in inaudible conversation with himself, making up yet another crib on a separate piece of paper.

The other two men remained unspeaking, both aware there was no contribution they could make. Silence enclosed the room apart from Sherlock Holmes's mumbling.

'The diplomatically sealed package in Notions and the telegram in the same is what doesn't fit,' declared Sherlock

139

Holmes, loud enough for them to hear but not looking up from his calculations. 'Why do that . . . ?' Now he did look up. 'The package . . . the envelope . . . do you have it?'

'Of course,' frowned Mycroft. 'It was the easiest way to carry it within my briefcase.'

'Please!' said Sherlock Holmes, urgently, extending his hand.

His brother retrieved it from a side table, offering it.

'A glass!' demanded the detective. 'I need a magnifying glass!'

'Have mine, Holmes,' said Watson, hurrying forward.

For several minutes Sherlock Holmes hunched over the empty, twine-reinforced envelope before sitting back, satisfied, in his chair. He extended his left hand, palm down, towards his brother and said: 'Under the Holmes seal!'

'Talk further,' demanded Mycroft.

'Your reply when I asked you if you'd responded to Sebastian's first message,' reminded Sherlock Holmes.

'Yes?' frowned Mycroft.

'You broke the seal on this package?'

'It was addressed to me,' said Mycroft.

Sherlock Holmes pushed the envelope across the table to the other man, together with Watson's magnifying glass. 'Delivered to you under British embassy seal?'

'Of course.'

'The "His" of what would have continued "His Imperial Majesty" is clearly visible,' pointed out Sherlock Holmes, indicating the splintered wax. 'But look closer, under the glass, at the "s". And then look the slightest degree to the left, where it failed to over-register the underlying "s" of the Holmes crest, to which you so recently referred . . .' He searched among his papers, coming up with the most recently scribbled assortment. '"*Cropple*" was our clue, which we missed, Watson, by ignoring the one essential alternative definition of the word "imposition". Sebastian is imposing – impressing – his own signet-ring seal into the sealing wax. The seal is being broken, by the inquisitive Captain Black, in an attempt to read everything that Sebastian is sending back to us. And then resealed with the embassy emblem. Which is why Sebastian encoded what took you so very long to translate. I think, Mycroft, that you should immediately send a telegram to Sebastian. One word will suffice. *Underconstumble.*'

'Understood,' translated Watson, unnecessarily. 'Yes, it's important that Sebastian knows that we understood his warning.'

Winston Churchill burst into Mycroft's chambers in his usual haste as the Cabinet Secretary turned from his transmission, in the side room. Seeing the man, through the open door, still at the machine, Churchill said: 'Something important!'

'A great deal,' said Mycroft. 'Perhaps this the most immediate.' Succinctly he recounted Sherlock Holmes's deduction of the meaning of the coded messages, producing the broken-seal packaging for Churchill personally to examine under the magnifying glass, and the three-page Notions original.

'The blackguard!' accused Churchill at once.

'A strong temptation for someone knowingly attracting attention in London for identifying a dangerous German presence in a city he's charged with monitoring,' remarked Sherlock Holmes, philosophically. 'We can be confident Black will not be able to read Sebastian's latest and most revealing message, so we have lost nothing and gained the knowledge that the man is prying into Sebastian's affairs . . . knowledge that might even be turned to our advantage in some as yet undetermined fashion.'

'It's still not the behaviour of a gentleman,' insisted Churchill, to Mycroft's recollection of the man's expectation at an Admiralty Arch meeting that he should have broken the seal of Sherlock's first message to his son.

'The man is necessary to our purpose,' reminded Sherlock Holmes. 'And that is scarcely the attitude of the gentlemen we consider ourselves to be, either, but rather that of practicality. I do not think the episode should detract any further from our considerations of what Sebastian has discovered.'

Without argument Mycroft handed Churchill his personal copy of Sebastian's translated account of his encounter with the Grand Duke, which Churchill first scanned, then read again intently. He looked up from the paper, appearing distracted, obviously still assimilating it all. His voice distant – but far

141

from suffering the predicted paroxysm – Churchill finally said: 'Now here's a situation that's going to require a lot of handling.'

'By whom? And how?' questioned Sherlock Holmes, at once. 'We know there's a German spy presence in St Petersburg. We've got doubt about the Tsar's safety, from the very man entrusted with ensuring it, confirming my impression – and Sebastian's – that the Tsar and his family could be in genuine physical danger if there is another uprising more successful than the first. And a clearly implied question of sanctuary. But all upon Orlov's initiative, nothing of it official. Nor can it be presented as such, through any acceptable channel.'

'Hamstrung by the very knowledge we sought to acquire,' repeated Watson.

'It must be presented in some way.'

'What news from Chesterfield, upon sanctuary?' demanded Mycroft.

'He thinks the King would be minded to offer it,' said Churchill, guardedly.

'*Thinks!*' qualified Sherlock Holmes, immediately. 'Does that mean safe passage, under British protection? A positive assurance that can be given to Orlov?'

'I don't know,' admitted Churchill, a rare admission.

'Is Chesterfield passing on the King's word, having raised the question at Privy Council? Or surmising?' persisted Sherlock Holmes.

'I believe it's the thinking of others on the council, not anything direct from the King himself,' conceded Churchill.

'Then it's hardly sufficient to communicate to Orlov,' decided Mycroft. 'I fear you chose an inadequate emissary.'

'I fear so, too,' said the politician.

'Then we must find another, more reliable conduit,' insisted Sherlock Holmes. 'Great trust has been bestowed upon Sebastian. He must not be exposed to doubt or misinterpretation in responding to it.'

'What's the outcome of your ordering the North Sea exercises of the Mediterranean fleet?' Mycroft asked Churchill, directly.

Churchill smiled, wryly. 'Begrudging acceptance, which

there might not have been without Black's German warning. Which, in turn, there might not have been without Sebastian sounding the alarm.'

Sebastian had, inadvertently, saved Churchill's position and decision, accepted Mycroft.

'Is the fleet on passage?' asked Sherlock Holmes, reflectively.

Churchill gave another smile. 'It was the fact that they are, as much as the other matter, that brought about the agreement. It has already passed through the Strait of Gibraltar, so the Germans must unquestionably know of the movement. To have turned it around would have conveyed entirely the wrong impression to Berlin, of our being in fear of their superiority in any confrontation, when the reverse is the intention.'

Churchill had gambled upon his fleet withdrawal to home waters being accepted, without the St Petersburg information, guessed Mycroft. The cavalier manner with which the man took risks was sometimes frightening.

Sherlock Holmes said: 'I'll not dispute the German's awareness, but I doubt it's yet come to the awareness of St Petersburg. Sebastian might gain Orlov's confidence a little more if he passed it on as an indication of Great Britain's preparation.'

'A titbit instead of the answers that Sebastian seeks, on Orlov's behalf,' said Watson.

'Orlov was not to know of our anticipation,' Sherlock Holmes reminded. 'He cannot expect an immediate response: an indication, even. We have time enough for a further approach to the palace, however that might be achieved.'

'And to get from America the photographs Sebastian seeks,' said Sherlock Holmes.

Sebastian was without any doubt that, with the exception of the last and most informative dispatch, Captain Black had opened and read every communication between him and London, and theirs to him in return. It meant that Black knew of his encounter with Josef Stalin, the identities of others he'd been recommended to seek out if they were in Russia, and his father's discoveries of the revolutionary conferences in London.

In the security of his suite, Sebastian looked down now at

143

the most recently delivered package from Black, the seal, impressed by his uncle's crested ring, unbroken, smiling in understanding at Black's easy acceptance of his returning alone to his suite to read its contents. The arrangement was that he once more deliver a package for diplomatic dispatch to London. Clearly Black expected this latest shipment from London to be assigned at the same time to the security of his safe, from which it could be retrieved, the reseal broken for its contents to be read at leisure.

It was a slim package and Sebastian opened it taking every care to disturb the seal as little as possible. It was hardly more than an acknowledgement of his earlier reports, with congratulations in the personal hand of Churchill and his father, with his father's additional warnings to take every personal and physical care. He also asked of any success Sebastian might have had in tracing the other revolutionaries named in his earlier advice.

It was unnecessary to keep what amounted to an acknowledgement, Sebastian realized at once. And he'd already decided that Black would have read all his preceding messages. The consideration began simply to burn the three single sheets, to prevent their being recovered by any Okhrana burglar, but stopped halfway. Instead Sebastian laboriously printed out a two-block section of meaningless, unconnected words that would make nonsense of any believed or attempted decoding of Notions, remote though that might have been, except for a former Wykehamist, who in turn would have been baffled.

Sebastian replaced London's open-script message with the counterfeit code, added more wax to the seal and imprinting from his signet ring the Holmes crest, with its distinctive curlicues, alongside the earlier impression made by his uncle's ring. In the fireplace of the suite living room he lit the London message from a taper, watched it burn and then scattered the black debris into ash.

# Thirteen

The knife snick, just healed, stood out pink against the surviving tan of his Swiss sojourn with his father. Sebastian leaned closer to the bathroom mirror, tracing his finger along it, frowning. His distaste was not vanity, from which he didn't suffer, but disappointment that the minimal scar, which would fade into nothing in time, had not diminished more with the close approach of his finally ascending a royal echelon with Olga at his side. Or was there vanity? he challenged himself. Not in any narcissistic way, but with a reluctance to accompany such a flawless woman at the very height of society looking like someone who had . . . Who had what? Been involved in a street brawl, he supposed. At least, he tried to reassure himself, he didn't bear the permanent scars of the Heidelberg sabre contests with which he could so easily have been marked. He still wished it wasn't there, like a misplaced badge.

Sebastian was in no hurry. In fact he was unsure how further to fill his time, apart from delivering his latest account to Captain Black at the embassy, for that afternoon's shipment to London. He'd occupied the remainder of the previous evening, after concocting the supposed Notions message from his uncle, composing in genuine code his previous day's visit to Tsarskoye Selo. Although it had already been discussed, he'd recounted Orlov's diatribe against Gregory Rasputin, stressing the concern at the man's excessive influence upon the Tsarina, which extended beyond the intimate court circle to become a matter of public disquiet and comment in St Petersburg newspapers. He'd written that he hoped to encounter the religious mystic – omitting how or when – and be able to convey some personal impressions. Orlov, he'd said, appeared eager for responses to questions posed earlier – as was

Sebastian – but all communications should from now on be encoded.

Sebastian emerged from his bedroom into the drawing room of his suite still in his dressing gown, his only thought at that precise moment whether to bother with a late breakfast, to fill as much of the remaining morning as possible, before an empty afternoon until his visit to the embassy, timed for the delivery of the diplomatic bag from London. And at once he saw the white slip of paper so fully beneath his door it could not have been visible from the outside corridor. Sebastian's strict instructions to the reception staff had been to be immediately notified, night or day, of any messages or approach. So the envelope at his feet had been slipped surreptitiously and so far beneath his door as to leave no outside indication of it being there.

Obeying his father's credo that nothing, not even a hair wisp, is insignificant in an investigation, Sebastian lifted the envelope by a furthest extremity, twisting it back and forth and even holding it to the light, in the hope of establishing anything unexpected within, which he didn't. The outside was plain, unaddressed, and there was nothing handwritten inside, just three words cut from an English newspaper – DUMA. NOON. KERENSKY.

Sebastian's hopes lifted, his day no longer empty. With no way of knowing how full it was now likely to be, it made good sense to bring forward the embassy delivery, clearing himself of that encumbrance for whatever lay ahead. And there was time, before noon. Sebastian was dressed – his two sealed packages in the document case, and the succinct summons secure in his pocket – within fifteen minutes, and at the British embassy, Black forewarned by telephone, in a further thirty. The attaché was waiting at the gatehouse.

Their overnight arrangement had been for Sebastian's visit to coincide with the afternoon delivery from London, and as they set off across the now familiar courtyard, Black said: 'Why the change of time?'

'Something's arisen that could delay my getting here in time for the four o'clock arrival and dispatch of the diplomatic bag.'

'What?' demanded Black, shortly.

146

For the first time, previously too preoccupied by what appeared to be an approach from the Russian politician, Sebastian became aware of a tightness about the other man. 'A response, to an approach. And no, before you ask. It has no bearing upon any German activity here.'

'It never appears to,' complained the military diplomat.

He hadn't come to argue, Sebastian reminded himself. 'You have my undertaking, if it does.'

'And in the meantime I am kept in total ignorance of what is going on.'

Only since I came to suspect your integrity, thought Sebastian. 'For reasons already too much and too long discussed.'

'I don't consider myself being treated well here, Holmes!' openly objected the man. 'I've allowed myself to be drawn into this affair and believe I should be permitted greater knowledge of it.'

Only since the Notions code had closed the door upon him, thought Sebastian. 'Make the plea to Churchill,' proposed Sebastian. 'I'm his emissary. It's his decision to make.'

Black lapsed into uncertain silence for several moments before announcing: 'There is a telegram for you. I intended bringing it to the hotel later.'

'You're saved the journey.'

'There was nothing of Germany in yesterday's package?' persisted the man.

'I've already assured you of that,' said Sebastian, curbing the irritation. 'I have it with me, for safe deposit.'

'I am unsure how much longer this convenience can continue,' declared the man, suddenly.

A different tack, Sebastian recognized. 'How so?'

'From Winston's initial approach, I did not expect such volume, practically a daily shipment. Curiosity is being aroused.'

An element of truth or petulant bluff? wondered Sebastian. 'As I have always made clear, I don't wish to cause you inconvenience.'

'It might assist if I were able to answer possible questions,' said the attaché.

'Which, specifically?' encouraged Sebastian. The man was bluffing: bluffing very badly.

'A general indication of the content of what's being passed to and fro. The diplomatic bag is not a private postal facility.'

He didn't have either the time or patience for this, Sebastian decided. 'If you'll allow me a brief further use of your telegraph, I'll make that clear to Churchill and come to alternative arrangements. Which will relieve you of the need even to talk to Churchill yourself.' If he continued the Notions code, he supposed he could use the hotel's telegraph, although he had to expect the omnipotent Orlov's quick curiosity. It could, even, establish just how tightly he was still under the suspected Okhrana surveillance.

'The situation has not yet reached that pass,' hurriedly retreated Black. 'I was just indicating what might become a situation.'

'Why don't we anticipate it, before it does become one?' bullied Sebastian, allowing himself further irritation. Just as quickly he retreated, although not so obviously as the attaché. He was using the convenience of the man as much as Black was trying to take advantage of him. It was quid pro quo.

'It's not necessary, not yet,' pleaded Black, again. 'Let's talk no more about it, until it becomes necessary.'

'Communicate with Churchill,' urged Sebastian, as they entered the attaché's personal section. He handed over the two wax-sealed packages, one for safekeeping, the other for that day's pouch, and glanced down at the telegraph slip that Black handed him, smiling in satisfaction at the single word, *underconstumble*.

'What does it mean?' asked Black, with continued persistence.

'Just acknowledgement, at the safe receipt of everything in London,' said Sebastian. It would have been his father who deciphered the warning of interference, he guessed.

'It's a curious code,' suggested the attaché.

'And an effective one.' He guessed Black would have already tried letter and number associations and would resume his efforts comparing *underconstumble* and *acknowledgement*, literally taking one to be the letter by letter translation of the other.

148

'Apart fom the garden party, we've socialized little,' said Black. 'Perhaps you'd allow me to show you some interesting parts of St Petersburg? Some particularly good restaurants.'

A similar offer to that from the *chef du protocol*'s wife, recalled Sebastian. 'I'd enjoy that. We'll make a date.'

'How much longer do you anticipate being in St Petersburg?'

It was a question he needed to confront, accepted Sebastian, recalling his earlier speculation that he'd achieved virtually everything he'd been sent to the Russian capital to discover. 'A few more days, certainly. I'm in no great haste to return to London.'

'We have time then?'

'More than sufficient.'

'What of this afternoon's incoming pouch? Would you have me bring to the hotel anything addressed to you?'

'I've caused you enough inconvenience,' apologized Sebastian. 'If I become delayed, tomorrow will be soon enough.'

'I'll call, on the off chance,' announced the man.

The desperation was almost pitiful, thought Sebastian, although without pity, recalling the as yet unproven suspicion of the man's tampering with the exchanges. 'If I am not at the hotel, don't delay. Ensure, of course, the safekeeping of anything entrusted to you.'

'You'll need a carriage to take you back into the city,' Black insisted. 'I'll put an embassy vehicle at your disposal.'

With a driver carefully instructed to report his destination, Sebastian knew. 'Let's not impose further to cause more curiosity within the embassy. I have time enough before my next appointment.'

Black made two further equally resisted attempts to provide embassy transport as they walked back towards the main gate, where they parted with Black's hope of Sebastian being at the hotel that evening if there was any dispatch for him. Sebastian strode out towards his hotel, not bothering to attempt to locate Orlov's observers even through the rear hatch of the cab he succeeded in hailing within ten minutes. It brought him to the white-fronted Duma building virtually on time, and as he made his final approach on foot, Sebastian saw Alexander Kerensky in the forecourt, in conversation with two other men, but positioned to look towards the outside road. As soon as he saw Sebastian, Kerensky detached himself to reach the entrance in greeting.

'I am glad you were able to keep the meeting,' said the Russian.

'I am glad of the opportunity to have it,' said Sebastian. Over the other man's shoulder he had a fleeting image of someone he was sure was Josef Stalin.

Kerensky's office was a single room, the only door opening on to an outside corridor, bare but for a desk and chair and one further chair for visitors. There was a passing similarity to the Okhrana interrogation cell. The heavily featured man wore the familiar wing-collared, striped-trousered uniform of an attorney, and Sebastian guessed the books in the three-shelved bureau were legal references.

Sebastian said: 'I appreciate your seeing me. I feared you would not, after our brief encounter at the British embassy.'

'A courtesy from one journalist to another, which I did not know you were until I received your card,' smiled the man, holding up the *Morning Post* accreditation. 'Soon after I joined the Socialist Revolutionary Party, I became editor of *Burevestik*, its newspaper. And of course was exiled . . .' There was a further smile. 'It's difficult to find anyone in the Duma who has not spent some time as the Tsar's guest in Siberia.'

'Whom did you think I might have been?'

'Are you familiar with the Okhrana?'

'I have heard of it – know what it is,' said Sebastian, confident he had shown no surprised hesitation at the totally unexpected question.

'Their network of agents is very widespread.'

'Surely not among foreign nationals, in foreign legations!' Was this man insinuating a spy presence within the British embassy!

'What better place to have informants, with eyes and ears beyond our borders, where so many of those who would see change within Russia are banished?'

He had to pursue this conversation as far as he could,

Sebastian decided. 'What convinced you I was not an Okhrana spy?'

'I telegraphed the *Morning Post* and established your credentials.'

Churchill had been unexpectedly thorough, thought Sebastian, gratefully. 'You feel it's necessary to go to such lengths?'

'Siberian prison camps are not places to visit more than once,' said Kerensky.

'Would you not be in danger if I reported that? Reported, in fact, everything you tell me?'

'There is sometimes protection in becoming known outside of Russia: the Tsar's court is nervous of adverse foreign opinion. And I am now a politician, not a newspaper editor. The Tsar might treat the Duma with contempt but I doubt he'd let his secret police move directly against one of its members.'

They were moving away from what he wanted to concentrate upon, Sebastian realized. 'You would not object to my writing of Okhrana informants within foreign embassies then?'

There was another smile from the lugubrious man. 'It might even bring about an interesting reaction.'

'Which embassies do you consider the most likely?' risked Sebastian.

'Those of the Triple Entente and the Triple Alliance are surely the most obvious targets?'

A lawyer's answer, a question to a question, judged Sebastian. He had to appear naive, he accepted. 'But Britain is a partner with Russia in the Triple Entente! Why spy on one's allies?'

'To determine, as accurately as possible, that allies remain allies,' said Kerensky, simply.

'You believe the Tsar doubts Britain? Or its other partner, France, for that matter?' Kerensky's remark practically echoed Orlov's. But for different reasons, guessed Sebastian.

'I have no idea whom the Tsar trusts or distrusts. I don't believe the Okhrana trusts anyone, which is the philosophy to which I subscribe. And why I initially behaved as I did towards you.'

151

'If the Okhrana is so all-pervasive – which I suppose it has to be if it is to fulfil its function – the Tsar's position is secure?'

Kerensky shook his heavy head. 'The people's appetite for democracy has been whetted. To ignore it, as the Tsar is trying to ignore it, will lead to his downfall.'

'The Okhrana would regard that remark as treasonable,' insisted Sebastian.

'They probably would,' agreed the lawyer.

Sebastian hesitated. 'Mr Kerensky, are you setting a challenge, *trying* to create a situation through what might appear in an English newspaper?'

'I am not afraid of my views becoming widely known.'

'Despite Siberian prison camps not being places to visit more than once?'

The familiar, humourless smile came again. 'My views are already well enough known within the country, particularly among the industrial workers who are my supporters and whom I believe myself to represent.'

An opportunistic politician, anxious to establish an international reputation? wondered Sebastian. 'You've referred to treaties. What are your views upon Balkans nationalism?'

'Obvious, I would have thought.'

'The major problem with the Balkans is that nothing is obvious,' countered Sebastian.

'You know your subject,' praised Kerensky.

Learned at the feet of others, thought Sebastian. At which he'd also learned not to be deflected by flattery. 'Balkan nationalism?' he insisted.

'There will be conflict.'

'War?'

'Almost inevitably.'

'Supported by the Russian people?'

The smile now was no longer empty. It was of admiration, the reply again that of a lawyer. 'What do you think?'

On this occasion Sebastian chose to answer. 'I think a European war would be welcomed by those who seek political change in Russia – those who would seek the maximum advantage from it.'

'Is that what you intend to write?'

'Is that what you're hoping I will write?'

'I'm hoping you will be honest.'

'I'm hoping the guidance I am getting will be honest.'

'So do I.'

The man was trying to escape again. 'Why did your invitation come to me in the way it did?'

'It was deniably from me, if it were intercepted.'

'A weak defence.'

'It would have been proof of Okhrana surveillance.'

'Okhrana surveillance of the Duma is surely not in doubt?'

'You press me, Mr Holmes.'

'I do, sir. I seek to discover how I am being used.'

'Willingly used, surely?'

'Willingly used, certainly. But to what purpose?'

'The Okhrana are not the only people with informants.'

He could not afford to lose this momentum, Sebastian knew. What was his next move, his next knowing question? And then he knew, and felt a brief, hollow uncertainty. 'How many knew?'

'Those who had to.'

'A very few?'

'Those who had to,' repeated the Russian, dogmatically.

'Will I be told?'

'It is of no interest to you.'

'I've been your unwitting bait!' protested Sebastian. 'Of course it is of interest to me!'

'In exchange for my manipulation, you have sufficient for more than one article.'

'I have a right to know.'

'You have a right to nothing.'

'I could print what you've done.'

'By which time the purpose will have been served. We will have found the traitor within our own ranks.'

'I want mine,' insisted Sebastian. 'Who's the spy within the British embassy?'

'I do not know that there is one.'

'I think you do.'

'That's an outrageous accusation!'

'You're not sufficiently outraged,' dismissed Sebastian.

'You are asking too much.'

'I ask what I need to know.'

'You have sufficient, for you to discover it.'

'So there *is* a spy – and informer – within the British legation!'

Alexander Kerensky remained silent.

'Reporting to whom?' persisted Sebastian.

Still Alexander Kerensky did not speak.

'I consider myself ill used,' objected Sebastian, who didn't but was anxious to keep doors and avenues open with this enigmatically unsettling man.

'Are you truly a journalist?' challenged Kerensky.

'You established my credentials.' The man was weaving away again.

'That's not an answer to my question.'

'It was sufficient for you to accept me today.'

'You debate well, Mr Holmes.'

'Debate is not my object here.'

'Which curves the circle. What *is* your object here?'

'Discovering – perhaps analyzing against other factors – the true political reality here in St Petersburg.'

'The reality is that at the end of it all, however tortuous that end might be to reach, there will be a democracy in Russia.'

'Are you sure?'

'I did not say that I – or anyone else in this insecure experiment of a Tsarist independent parliament – would be the person to attain it.'

'But the Tsar will fall?'

'The rule in Russia will change.'

'For the better?'

'That is an astute question.'

'Will you answer it?'

'I am not sure that I can.'

'Which, of all the factions, is the strongest?'

'The Bolsheviks, I suppose.'

'Sufficiently organized?'

'Astute again. That is the problem throughout every reform group or party, an ignorance of the way, the structure, with which democratic government is conducted. There will be internecine conflicts, a lot of mistakes.'

'What about outward conflict? Has any consideration been given to the possibility of a civil war?'

'I'll concede the possibility. I cannot speak for other factions.'

'Isn't that your problem, too many factions, each with differing priorities, none working with the others?'

'I've spoken of internal difficulties,' reminded Kerensky.

And of a great deal more, decided Sebastian. He didn't think he could expect much more, certainly not at this meeting. Sebastian felt himself almost overwhelmed as it was. 'I bear no ill will, for the deception.'

'There was no deception,' insisted Kerensky. 'You sought an interview, which I granted. And was totally honest in our exchanges.'

'I have your word?'

'Would I not expose myself to international ridicule, in print, if everything we've talked about were nonsense?'

The man *did* see an international platform from the encounter, quite separately from whatever else he sought to achieve. 'You will see me again?' demanded Sebastian, sure of his bargaining strength.

'I'll send word.'

'Will you know by then?'

'I don't know. It's possible.'

'I believe I have the right to be told,' reiterated Sebastian.

'It might take longer.'

'I still think I have the right to know.'

'We have to see if it will work.'

'You could provide me now with more from the embassy,' insisted Sebastian.

Kerensky shook his head. 'I do not have an identity.'

'I want to hear from you,' demanded Sebastian.

'You will,' promised Kerensky.

Sebastian guessed he would be fobbed off, unless he could convince the man of some personal benefit.

Sebastian remained alert to the swirl of people as Kerensky escorted him from the fledgling Russian parliament building, but he did not see anyone resembling Josef Stalin. Sebastian made no attempt to locate a carriage, not risking any back

155

streets and welcoming the walk to analyze what he believed he had discovered. Unquestionably the most important was the virtual confirmation that within the British embassy – and possibly other foreign legations – there was an Okhrana spy. Which Alexander Kerensky and a limited number of people within his party knew, from themselves having a reciprocal informant within the Tsar's secret police. Whom that day was being tested to identify a further, as yet unknown, Okhrana source within the Duma, reporting the encounter between himself and Kerensky.

His situation with Orlov – whatever that might be – was unendangered, Sebastian determined. He'd openly talked of Kerensky and his wish to meet the politician. Was there proof of an embassy informant *from* the garden party? He'd believed his encountering Princess Olga had been entirely by chance. But it would not have been chance if the Okhrana source had alerted Orlov to his being on the invitation list. And he'd already wondered at Orlov's willingness to employ his daughter without exposing her to danger. Uncovering the embassy informant had to be his absolute, single-minded priority, Sebastian determined. And to achieve that he had to repair as many damaged bridges as possible between himself and Captain Lionel Black, and no longer keep the man at arm's length. The ground was already prepared. Sebastian accepted he had to associate with more members of the embassy. Which in itself would be insufficient. If someone – more than one person even – was an Orlov spy, the association would be too deeply concealed for him to uncover from casual, outside acquaintance. The word *outside* sounded like a bell in Sebstian's mind. His need was for his own source *inside* the embassy. Or the Okhrana. Despite the confusion of Orlov's occasional apparent indiscretions or inconsistencies, it was beyond comprehension that he could manoeuvre the slightest indication, indiscreet or otherwise, from the Grand Duke. And his only contact within the embassy was a man whose acumen he judged to be strictly limited. What other route was there for him to take? Alerting London on the basis of the single conversation he had just concluded with Alexander Kerensky, without anything approaching another source, let alone proof, was as unthinkable as everything else that was coming to mind. And, in a further warning to himself, Sebastian decided he should not overlook the possibility that there was not, nor ever had been, a spy within the British or any other embassy, and that the entire story was a fantasy invented to serve some end known only to Kerensky.

So deep in contemplation was he, that Sebastian was unaware of the time it took him to complete, wholly on foot, his journey back to the hotel. That realization only came as he entered, immediately to see Black in his customary foyer chair, package clutched before him. As the man rose, Sebastian thought that the scene was becoming virtually a nightly ritual.

# Fourteen

His priorities adjusted and without any burden of hypocrisy, Sebastian did not hurry to escape the waiting military attaché, despite the tantalizing thickness of the latest consignment from London. Instead he insisted upon drinks, the package quickly secured out of sight in the much-used document case, and let the conversation drift to Black's choosing, which predictably circled around the attaché's German preoccupation. There had been nothing in the London delivery for him, Black at once volunteered, except the reassurance that photographs were being obtained from New York, but that there would be the minimum of at least a five-day delay bringing them across the Atlantic by even the fastest Cunard mail ship. Sebastian volunteered in return that he had asked for photographs as well – sure the man would already know from his package-meddling – but that he would be victim of the same delay. Sebastian agreed that his being recognizable by Hans Vogel precluded his attempting any too obvious observation of the German legation, and accepted Black's offer to share the other man's comparisons when the pictures did finally arrive, unwilling to rely upon Orlov keeping his word and glad of the double opportunity.

Sebastian was very rapidly coming to realize that he couldn't rely upon anyone to keep their word, which freed him in return from giving an assurance he didn't intend either. Sebastian edged the conversation towards the few diplomats he had met at the embassy, bemused how quickly Black responded to the invitation to gossip. Russia was to be the last ambassadorial appointment for Sir Nigel Pearlman, whose wife drank too much – which Sebastian might have noticed from the garden party – and whose drunken indiscretions were increasingly becoming difficult on the embassy circuit. Pearlman hoped for some advisory post within the Foreign Office in London, where Lady Pearlman would be less of a public embarrassment. With a self-satisfied smile, Black said that, from the reaction it had created it had obviously become common knowledge within the insular legation that he was the source of the German spy warning, which had created jealousy between himself and Roger Jefferson, the naval attaché, with whom relations had not been good from the moment of their respective appointments. They were now scarcely on speaking terms, which was to Jefferson's disadvantage more than his. John Berringer was the most fluent Russian speaker at the embassy and considered himself an authority on the country and its history. As he was sure Sebastian had fully realized from their garden-party encounter, Ludmilla Berringer was Russian, born in St Petersburg and an acknowledged historian of the city. Berringer was due for ambassadorial promotion and it was no secret that the man saw himself as Pearlman's logical successor, unusual though such internal elevation would be. It was not, in Black's opinion, a happy embassy, although this was his first posting, so he didn't have a criterion from which to judge. He'd heard a lot of other people with more experience than his make the same complaint, though. He saw it as a necessary career tour of duty for an automatic job in the War Office, the chances of which had increased considerably because of the German business.

'What about contact with Russians?' asked Sebastian, choosing his moment.

'Not encouraged,' said Black.

The immediate reply surprised Sebastian. 'Doesn't that negate the purpose of having an embassy here at all?'

'Sir Nigel insists on very strict guidelines being adhered to,' said the attaché.

'What about politicians in the Duma?'

'Forbidden,' declared Black at once. 'On both Sir Nigel and Berringer's explicit instructions. They don't want any embarrassments from associations with radical, anti-Tsarist groups.'

Sebastian found the ostrich-like attitude numbing, which was an apposite word to describe the mentality of the embassy diplomats – the embassy itself, even, numbed into self-imposed, ineffectual ostracism. How could he possibly hope to isolate an Okhrana informant in such an ossified environment! 'Despite such isolation you're still confident of showing me some interesting places?'

'There is an approved list of places and restaurants,' said Black. 'This hotel is one of them.' Black smiled. 'Fortunate, in view of the difficulty of your arrival.'

Which the other man had handled with great speed and diplomacy, right into the very heart of an Okhrana prison, Sebastian suddenly remembered. Was it likely that, from a single encounter with an hotel doorman, Black could have discovered so quickly where to find such a jail and gained access to the very men who'd seized him? Surely this ramrod-straight army officer wasn't . . . ? No, it was unthinkable. *Why?* Sebastian at once challenged himself. One of his father's many philosophies was that coincidence should never be ignored, because coincidences occurred. So he wouldn't ignore his introduction being to the very man who could be the Okhrana spy within the British embassy. Neither would he take an ill-fitting circumstance to be anything more than that, an occurrence that could, upon examination, appear at odds with Black's account of how the embassy confined itself.

Sebastian heard the sound of a distant clock, although he wasn't able to discern the time it struck: whatever, he had to be dangerously close to his appointment with Orlov. With repeated assurances to discuss with Black anything relevant in the package from London, Sebastian finally excused himself from the attaché, hurrying up to his suite.

The bulk of the latest delivery was caused by a complete, enlarged set of photographs of each of the German spies expelled from America, including Hans Vogel. A note in his father's hand, although encoded in Notions, explained that, to avoid the shipment delay from New York, they had been obtained from *The Times* and the *Morning Post*, each of which had obtained the pictures at the time of the episode to illustrate their coverage. Another coded note, also from his father, confirmed the tampering with his seal with the assurance that in future no communication would be in open script. Churchill had been prevailed upon not to challenge or reproach the military attaché. Mycroft wrote separately that there were indications that the King would look favourably upon receiving the Romanov family in exile, but that Sebastian should not offer it as a positive assurance until stronger guidance came from the palace. Churchill passed on his congratulations for what Sebastian was achieving, as did they all.

Sebastian quickly changed, with less than an hour to reach the Grand Duke's palace. He began returning everything to the document case he intended carrying with him, but then hesitated, deciding that, with every written message encoded, there was no longer any risk of their being understood by an intruder. He kept only the photographs in his document case, returning everything else to the envelope and putting it into the safe, setting a trap with its slightly off-centre positioning and a cotton wisp, on the edge of the flap.

He had a lot to offer Orlov, Sebastian decided, as he hurried into a conveniently waiting coach at the hotel entrance. What was he likely to be offered in return?

There was pretence – fantasy even – at the Neva-bordering palace, complete with its liveried, white-gloved attendants at every corner, and expectantly behind every door. Sebastian and Orlov gathered again in the trophy-room study and Orlov once more recited his tattered explanation for women's lateness thirty minutes before the entrance of the exquisitely white-gowned, diamond-bejewelled and coiffeured princess. And there was the expected Roederer Cristal champagne in its unique bottle. They continued into what Sebastian now accepted to be the smallest of the small family dining salons, perfect for such an intimate gathering. Sebastian thought the ice-carved long-necked bird to be a simple table decoration until swan was served as the meal's main course. It was Olga who introduced into the conversation the impending commemorative ball, which Sebastian immediately insisted he would look forward to, and there was a brief, even flirtatious, exchange between them on her inability to dance the dances of Western society, to which she was sure he was accustomed – and his apology at not being able to perform those of the Russian

161

court, ending with the hope that there might at least be a few waltzes they would recognize. That night the retirement of Orlov and Sebastian for port and cigars was perfunctory, neither did Princess Olga give another piano recital, but sat at her father's side as he disclosed the Tsarevich Alexei's indisposition that day, after an overexuberant chase-and-catch game with Grand Duchess Anastasia Nikolaievna, the youngest of the imperial daughters. 'Fortunately the steps upon which he stumbled were an elevation between corridors, three or four at the most. There is a swelling bruise but the skin was not broken.'

'Does that preclude the presence at the ball of the Tsar and Tsarina?' asked Sebastian, at once.

'That depends entirely upon the Tsarevich's improvement. The child, as always, is in great pain.'

'So, Rasputin . . . ?'

'Is at Tsarskoye Selo, weaving his doubtful magic,' anticipated Orlov, cynically.

'With his presence just as dependent?' anticipated Sebastian, in return.

'Correctly guessed,' said Orlov. 'But he quite rightly sees opposition behind every rock and tree, and a gathering of the court, which this is to be, will concentrate that court. Rasputin will move aside every obstacle to be there.'

'My namesake, the Imperial Grand Duchess, expects to attend,' announced Olga. 'Perhaps together with the Imperial Grand Duchess Tatiana Nikolaievna.'

That would bring at least two members of the imperial court into the uncertain streets of St Petersburg, thought Sebastian. The security – Orlov's responsibility – would be immense, even if the Tsar and Tsarina did not attend. 'It will be an occasion to remember.'

'For the right reasons,' insisted Orlov. Briskly he said, 'I am a devotee of the English game of snooker, Mr Holmes. Do you play?'

'Badly,' lied Sebastian. Orlov had not greeted him at the door but by now would have been told of his arriving with a document case, and Sebastian was curious how long it would be before the man referred to it.

'Exactly the opponent I try to choose.'

In the way of the seemingly stage-managed household, Olga excused herself and Sebastian followed Orlov along yet another corridor into a heavily panelled room, adorned with more trophies, with a green-baize table at its centre, the balls already on their spots. More brandy, port and a humidor were already set out on a side table, to which Orlov gestured an invitation. Declining it, Sebastian went to the racked cues, trailing his hand along the selection before extracting one at random and automatically testing its balance.

Orlov said, although lightly: 'You seek to cheat me, sir! No one who plays badly tests his stick thus.'

'Something I've seen others more capable do,' smiled Sebastian.

'I'll recognize intentional poor play,' warned the bearded man.

'I wouldn't insult you so,' insisted Sebastian, remembering his determination always to treat the Grand Duke as an equal.

'The host defers to the guest to break.'

In the hope of getting an advantage from the spread of reds, thought Sebastian, trying to gauge the speed of the table by the touch of the cloth, which felt high and resistant. Sebastian's opening shot was perfectly judged, barely disturbing the red triangle but with sufficient strength to return the cue ball to the baulk cushion. Orlov's initial attempt was much heavier, spreading the reds and exposing the black, and Sebastian scored twenty-four before returning the white ball to baulk. From which the game relapsed into safety play.

Rising from a baulk return, Orlov said: 'I am worried about Olga.'

Sebastian extended his examination of the table position, and then his address to it, to consider the remark. And then to prevaricate. 'What is your worry?'

Orlov did not immediately bend for his shot. 'Her vulnerability. I am her only family. Without me, she has no protection.' His shot skewed badly, missing the intended red to strike the black, awarding Sebastian a penalty seven.

Sebastian made no immediate attempt to play. He said: 'You embarrass me.'

'That's not my intention.'

'What is your intention?'

'Her well-being; her safety.' Orlov bent, to play a wild shot that hit the blue and gave Sebastian a penalty five.

'Encourage her to go elsewhere.' What revelation was this! 'I have a fully staffed property in Paris. Resources established there.'

'Send her there.' As my father sent me, thought Sebastian. His shot was as wild as the Russian's, although just whispering against a red to avoid his losing a point.

'She refuses, arguing in return that, without her, I have no one.' Orlov saw an opportunity Sebastian had not covered, putting himself ideally upon a black after sinking a red, and after that putting away five more in quick succession, moving himself convincingly ahead.

Why was the man choosing to expose himself like this! 'You have an impasse.' Sebastian recovered, lessening the distance between their scores to five and snookering Orlov behind the pink.

Orlov made a three-cushion escape, not only striking a red but snookering Sebastian behind a wall of three colours. 'I posed you a question, about sanctuary?

What new tangent was this! 'I have a response, along with other things . . . a response although not a definitive answer.'

'Which is?' Orlov cleared the reds, giving himself two blacks and a pink and going ahead again by thirty-two points.

The Grand Duke was winning but not playing as an equal, Sebastian abruptly decided. And needed the distraction of this unnecessary game, during which they had not once looked directly, eye to eye, at each other. 'That there would be a sympathetic response.'

'I'd hoped for more.'

'You might receive more.'

Orlov at last abandoned the game, looking fully at Sebastian. 'I have told Olga with what I charged you. Tell her the response from King George is positive; that the English are preparing for the Tsar's overthrow.'

'That is not the truth of the matter!' protested Sebastian.

'I am not interested in the truth of the matter!' dismissed

164

Orlov. 'I am only interested in convincing Olga that she should move from this troublesome country until the unrest is quelled.'

What manoeuvre was this! Grand Duke Alexei Orlov, head of the organization responsible for maintaining the Romanov's autocratic rule, was exposing himself, as if he were naked, to a stranger whose unproven integrity was assumed from inheritance. Which was the most inconceivable thing of so much else that was inconceivable. There had to be a machination, a puppetry in which he was the manipulated marionette for whatever deviousness this man was orchestrating. 'You expect her to believe me, above her own father?'

'She knows who you are. I have told her your purpose for being here.' The cues were abandoned, like the game.

From everything he had learned – every impression he had formed since arriving in St Petersburg – there was every reason for Orlov's fear, Sebastian acknowledged. So he would not be deceiving the princess by telling her what her father was demanding of him. Sebastian's difficulty was in what he saw as his own resented, mysterious exploitation. But which he was powerless to confront or oppose if he were to maintain whatever advantage he could expect from a man through whom he appeared to have gained access to the highest in the land. 'I will do as you ask, because I believe the uncertainty here is far more dire than most believe it to be.'

The Grand Duke smiled, although sadly, and wordlessly extended his hand, which Sebastian took, his discomfort increasing when the man covered the gesture with his other hand in a fulsome expression of gratitude. The awkwardness hung between them for several moments before Orlov abruptly broke it, in a surprising transformation, and said: 'All's said that needs to be said. Our game seems to have fallen by the wayside but, unfinished, I'll not claim victory.'

'All is not said,' corrected Sebastian. 'Have someone fetch the case I brought with me tonight.'

An immediately responding footman returned with the document case within minutes and, as he handed the photographs to Orlov, Sebastian realized that, by comparing the Russian's identification against that promised by Captain Black, he would have a test of the respective co-operation of the two men.

Sebastian said: 'The name on the back of each print is that by which they were known in America.'

'I'll have their current identities within days,' predicted Orlov. 'And their purpose for being here shortly after that.'

'I understood us to have an agreement?' suggested Sebastian.

'You will know when I know,' promised Orlov. 'I'll allow no spy ring to be established here, taking advantage of the unrest.'

'The effectiveness of their seizure in New York was the publicity it generated, making public in America for the first time the German preparation for war,' reminded Sebastian.

'I'll not waste an opportunity, if one presents itself,' said Orlov.

It was important that he appear to be honest with the Russian, even if it meant telling the man what he doubtlessly already knew, Sebastian remembered. 'I visited the Duma today. Met with Alexander Kerensky.'

'There are many prepared to put their trust in the man,' said the Okhrana chief. 'And others prepared to make use of him.'

'Use of him as what?' questioned Sebastian.

'A figurehead behind whom they can skulk and plot.'

'I got the impression that he was aware of such man-oeuvrings.'

'He has every need to be.' Orlov hefted the photographs he still held in his hand. 'I thank you, for making these available.'

'From which I hope to benefit,' reiterated Sebastian.

'I fulfil the undertakings I give,' insisted Orlov.

The hand-delivered envelope awaited Sebastian at the reception desk of the hotel upon his return, his name made out in awkward, uneven lettering. So preoccupied was he by the invitation, in the same uneven writing, that Sebastian almost forgot to check his safe, which he did before immediately writing an acceptance. The envelope that had contained the photographs was still slightly off centre, as he'd left it, the cotton wisp undisturbed.

'And here, Watson, is the example of why *The Times* justly deserves the accolade of being the newspaper of record,'

166

announced Sherlock Holmes from behind the barrier of the broadsheet itself.

'How's that, Holmes?' asked the doctor, not so engrossed in the *Morning Post*.

'I quote,' declared Sherlock Holmes. '"Several evenings past, Vladimir Ilyich Ulyanov, who prefers his revolutionary name of Lenin, addressed an overflow meeting of social democrats here, at which he predicted sweeping revolutionary, democratic changes throughout Europe . . ."' Sherlock Holmes looked over the top of his newspaper. 'One of the very men with whom I advised Sebastian to make contact.'

'I am at a loss, Holmes,' protested Watson.

'According to the dateline, Lenin is in Geneva.'

'Far beyond Sebastian's attention,' said Watson, uncomfortably, although for several days, practically a fortnight, he'd had no cause to suspect Sherlock Holmes of a relapse.

'But not mine,' insisted the sleekly thin man.

'You very recently returned, considerably out of sorts, from Switzerland,' said Watson.

'I won't this time,' determined Sherlock Holmes. 'This time there's work to be done. And I'm the person to do it.'

'Alone?' asked the doctor, nervously.

'Of course not, Watson. I need your companionship and advice.'

# Fifteen

Had he not constantly been in the man's company for the preceding thirty-six hours, Dr Watson would have been suspicious of Sherlock Holmes's high spirits, which emerged during the train journey through the Kent countryside and persisted during the packet's crossing of the Channel. Their Swiss-bound French express awaited in Calais, and the two men made for the first-class dining salon immediately after stowing their luggage in their reserved carriage. Sherlock Holmes at once insisted upon their reservation being switched from the right to the left of the salon, which he argued enjoyed the better views, particularly during the final ascent into Switzerland.

'Which you must surely recall,' demanded Sherlock Holmes.

'I was choosing not to remember,' confessed Watson. He knew from Sebastian that this was the route that he and his father had taken for their recent pilgrimage to Meiringen, a retracing of the earlier journey that had ended in the fateful confrontation with Moriarty on the Reichenbach Falls.

'It set me back before,' admitted Sherlock Holmes. 'It won't this time. For one thing, we'll not be going anywhere near the place of so many memories.'

'I sincerely hope you're right,' said the doctor. He was going to have to remain extremely vigilant, a task that was not going to be professionally easy if Holmes's current ebullience remained.

Sherlock Holmes ordered champagne for their luncheon aperitif and said: 'I think Churchill's taste in champagne is one of the few things I admire about the man.'

'What's our strategy to be here?' enquired Watson.

'Lestrade, at the Yard, has proved useful with an introduction

168

to Geneva's detective chief superintendent, whom I've already telegraphed to inform him of our arrival,' said Sherlock Holmes. 'I'm hoping that, as a foreigner, Lenin will have been required to register with the local authorities. He's been attracting publicity, so his whereabouts should be known to local newspapers, if there's not an official registration.'

'And what do we do when we learn the address of his lodgings?'

'Stay discreet. Wait. And watch.'

The train was in the open countryside now, as flat as Kent had been a few hours earlier, the fields seemingly bigger, although the activity on those being worked looked haphazard. Quite often there was no activity at all, the labourers at ease with glasses and jugs in hand, resting on hay clumps for their midday break. Watson was brought back inside the salon by the arrival of the waiter, realizing that his companion had already ordered and tasted the wine and chosen his meal. Watson ordered beef, laboriously insisting in stilted French that it be well done, and demanding an assurance that the waiter understood the request.

Sherlock Holmes said: 'They'll label you a Philistine in the kitchen.'

'I'm surprised the French bother with the flame of a kitchen, so prepared are they to eat their meat in its own blood.' Watson tasted the burgundy, nodding approvingly.

'Simpsons serve it thus.'

'Not if you ask them to cook it properly,' denied Watson. Anxious to resume their earlier discussion, he went on: 'For what are we waiting and watching?'

'For sight of the man. Assessing the strength of his following, if that's possible. There seems a confidence in his preparedness to hold public meetings and exhort revolution, in Switzerland of all countries.'

'Shall we confront him?'

Sherlock Holmes pursed his lips, uncertainly. 'It's difficult to imagine anything to confront him *with*. We don't carry a *Morning Post* accreditation, which Sebastian appears to be using quite effectively. And which might have gained us an audience from someone who appears to court publicity;

169

certainly he doesn't seem averse to it. I think we might have to chart our course as it unfolds before us.'

A waiter cleared their entrée plates, followed by another with their main course. Sherlock Holmes watched expectantly as Watson cut into the steak. Waving his arms to retrieve their waiter, Watson said: 'It resembles the massacre victims I treated on the north-west frontier!'

'You'll forgive me for starting at once, to prevent my own choice being spoiled?'

The waiter did not, of course, protest but there was a sullenness in the manner in which he returned the meal to the kitchens. Looking at Sherlock Holmes's cutlets, Watson said: 'I admire your bravery!'

'Cooked to perfection,' disputed the detective.

Dr Watson gave up with a shrug of his shoulders. 'How long do you propose we watch and wait?'

Now it was Sherlock Holmes who shrugged. 'Until we see something of interest, perhaps.'

Dr Watson tried two mouthfuls of his returned steak before abandoning it for the vegetables, which he also condemned as being undercooked. As they reached Geneva in mid-afternoon he was in ill humour, which only begrudgingly lifted at their final arrival at the Beau Rivage Hotel on the quai du Mont Blanc, and the allocation of his suite overlooking Lac Leman. Sherlock Holmes allowed his companion fifteen minutes to unpack before knocking sharply upon the communicating door to announce that they were awaited at the police headquarters by Detective Chief Superintendent Hugo Kuranda.

'Who sounded a most excellent fellow during our telephone conversation,' Holmes added. 'As Lestrade has proven himself to be. We arrive well recommended. And Kuranda had heard of me in advance anyway.'

'I would have been surprised if he hadn't,' said Watson.

As they entered a waiting carriage on the quai, Sherlock Holmes said: 'What a benefit it would be if I were able to speak to Sebastian in St Petersburg by telephone, instead of being reliant upon the telegraph. Mark my words, Watson. One day it will be possible.'

'Possibly before the French learn how to cook their meat properly,' remarked the still disgruntled doctor.

The police headquarters were back from the lake, but the office into which they were shown was on the top floor, from which it was just possible, over the intervening roof-tops, to see the sun sparkling off the water. Kuranda was a stocky, full-stomached man totally without hair who, with apparent effortlessness, maintained a gold-framed monocle in his left eye. He greeted the two men expansively, with tea and pastries, and with the assurance that every facility of the Geneva police authority was at the disposal of Sherlock Holmes, whose considerable reputation had preceded him.

'I am particularly interested in one man and perhaps any companions he might have,' said Sherlock Holmes, accepting the tea but declining pastries. 'His true name is Vladimir Ilyich Ulyanov. He has several aliases but his current choice is Lenin.'

'Ah!' exclaimed Kuranda, the exuberance faltering. 'Hardly a surprise.'

'You are familiar with the name?' Sherlock Holmes was aware of Watson taking a second pastry.

'And the man, although I have refrained so far from any personal encounter.'

'I'd appreciate any guidance or help you find yourself able to give me,' said Sherlock Holmes.

Kuranda left his desk for a filing cabinet against the far wall, rummaged through some drawers and turned triumphantly with a bound file held aloft. 'The labours of several police authorities from several European countries . . .' There was a hesitation. 'Although, surprisingly, little from your own country . . .'

'An oversight belatedly being rectified by our mutual friend at Scotland Yard,' promised Sherlock Holmes.

Kuranda bent over his documentation, talking without looking up. 'A very active political agitator who travels with a group of like-minded radicals. There are records here of their being in France, the Czech Republic, Slovakia and Austria, apart from London and now here. He is almost always accompanied by his wife, Nadezhda Krupskaya, whom he married

171

during internal exile in Siberia. One of his intermittent European travelling companions is Jules Martov, who heads the Menshevik splinter party.'

'There have been press reports in England of meetings here.'

'And even longer accounts in our own newspapers,' nodded Kuranda, looking up. 'We've very closely monitored the events. He and his cohorts are very clever and very circumspect. Here in Switzerland they preach nothing that could legally be construed as sedition under Swiss law. Neither have they in any of their other countries of temporary residence.'

'Yet you watch them closely?' queried Watson, wiping his fingers upon a napkin.

'For other activities that are suspected – but so far unproven – particularly as concerns Lenin,' smiled Kuranda. 'These men are self-proclaimed revolutionaries who follow no gainful employment. But need funds to support themselves and their newspapers and to finance their meetings and their congresses . . .' The policeman went back to his file, flicking through several pages to find what he wanted. 'Lenin personally obtained a substantial donation from the Russian author Maxim Gorky. And also from Sava Morozov, whom the Tsar's police describe as a millionaire. But there is suspicion in Russia that a considerable part of their income is from bank robbery. Specifically quoted is an armed raid upon Tiflis post office where the haul was two hundred and fifty thousand roubles: several people were killed when a bomb was thrown. That affair led to further alienation between the Bolsheviks and the Mensheviks . . .' The man looked up again. 'My interest in Lenin and his followers is criminal, not political. I'll not have them put Swiss lives at risk trying to plunder banks or financial institutions here. My surveillance is no secret to them. My wish is to be on a station platform, bidding them a permanent farewell.'

'You referred to the Tsar's police,' picked up Watson. 'Does your information come from the Okhrana or the more recognized State police?'

Kuranda made an uncertain gesture. 'As I've pointed out, there's co-operation between several European forces. That specific information was passed on to us from Prague, along with other things.'

'Such as?' demanded Sherlock Holmes, at once.

'The possibility that Lenin has a personal as well as an ideological motivation,' disclosed the Swiss detective. 'When Lenin was seventeen, his brother, Alexander, who belonged to the Narodniks or People's Will Party, was arrested for involvement in a plot to assassinate Tsar Alexander III. He was executed.'

'Personal motivation indeed,' agreed Sherlock Holmes.

'And there's a coincidence, which Lenin might well be utilizing to his advantage,' continued Kuranda.

'How so?' asked Watson.

'Lenin was born in Simbirsk, on the Volga. His early education was at the gymnasium there. His headmaster was the father of Alexander Kerensky . . .'

'Now a prominent member of the Duma in St Petersburg,' completed Sherlock Holmes.

'I have made available most of what I know about Vladimir Lenin and his people,' said Kuranda. 'I'm content to make the entire file available to you, for translation into English. I would, not unnaturally, appreciate knowing about the interest of the renowned Sherlock Holmes.'

Sherlock Holmes's reply was well prepared, taking only minutes. He did not identify Winston Churchill, or his brother, or disclose Sebastian's presence in St Petersburg.

'So, Lenin is achieving political importance in London?' pressed Kuranda.

'Precautionary interest,' qualified Sherlock Holmes.

'He would be flattered to learn of it.'

'He won't, not from my lips,' said Sherlock Holmes. 'The composite file you are so kindly making available to me – I presume it contains Lenin's address, here in Geneva?'

'Of course,' confirmed Kuranda. 'The only thing missing is the date and location of the next meeting he is scheduled to address. It's tomorrow night, at a hall on the Rue de Canoule. Your timing is most opportune.'

'Most opportune, Watson!' said Sherlock Holmes, in the carriage taking them back to the Beau Rivage. 'Things are

173

moving along at a pretty pace. There's much to advise Sebastian of.'

'But little for Churchill.'

'Sufficient, if he has the intellect to analyze it.'

'I don't think you can doubt him on that score.'

Sherlock Holmes made an impatiently dismissive gesture with his hand, as if disturbing an irritating insect. 'Of more importance, Watson, is the experience you are going to enjoy tonight. A feature of this excellent hotel and its even more excellent restaurant is its fondue, a French dish perfected by the Swiss. You are provided with a spirit flame and a cooking pot, in which to prepare your own meal. Melting cheese, to eat upon bread, is a favourite. So, too, is cooking your own meat in hot oil. You can incinerate your beef as black as you choose.'

The British embassy carriage arrived at the Grand Hotel at the promised time and carried, in addition to the *chef du protocol* and his wife, Captain Black and his wife Mary, a fey, blonde girl who stammered when she spoke, which she rarely did unless addressed directly, and then reluctantly. Ludmilla Berringer was very much the hostess in charge, setting out an itinerary upon which she had already decided, and would accept no alternative. Because *Das Rheingold* was such a long opera, there was to be a light supper first. She didn't doubt that Sebastian would be a devotee of Wagner: the German was the favoured composer of St Petersburg opera lovers, most particularly because of the German background of the Tsarina Alexandra. It was possible, even, that the Tsar and Tsarina might attend tonight's performance. It was a sell-out: she'd had to impose every diplomatic pressure, through her husband, to obtain their box. Sebastian would certainly appreciate the Mariinsky Theatre: it was an artistic masterpiece, as was everything created by Catherine the Great.

Sebastian *was* an opera enthusiast, and had been since the Heidelberg period of his education, despite the travelling distance to Bayreuth. There he'd savoured the very best of European productions and performances in the German in which they had been composed, and as he was carried into the promised light supper in Ludmilla's wake, Sebastian couldn't avoid the imagery of being a footman in Brunhilde's entourage. The chosen restaurant was on one of the Neva canals, fully glass-sided and partially glass-roofed to put everyone in a glittering diadem of bounced-back light from a multi-chandelier waterfall. In her native Russian, Ludmilla assembled a real-life entourage of restaurant attendants, refusing their reserved table with an insistence upon one on the spur of the dining room that actually extended over the water. She was just as insistent upon accepting the food, refusing to allow anyone to taste the oysters or blinis and caviar or cold fish selection until she had first approved them. She deferred only to her husband in agreeing the wines – including champagne, although not Cristal – and even the vodka, which did come in specific decanters.

Ludmilla's table arrangement put Sebastian between Berringer and Mary Black, who mumbled into silence whenever there was any cross-talk, despite Sebastian's considerable effort to bring her into any conversation. To Sebastian's seemingly casual but specifically directed approaches, Berringer said there was no way of predicting the presence of the imperial royal family; their movements were never disclosed, often not even after an event, and most definitely never announced beforehand. From what he'd been told by Orlov of the Tsarevich's accident, Sebastian suspected that Ludmilla was exaggerating the possibility of seeing them that evening.

Vaguely disconcerted at so constantly being talked at by the *chef du protocol*'s wife, Sebastian said: 'Don't you find the repertoire slightly ill chosen?'

'Ill chosen? How can that be?' at once challenged Ludmilla Berringer, to matching curiosity around the table.

'*Art and Revolution*,' quoted Sebastian. '*The Artwork of the Future.*'

'You do indeed know your Wagner,' conceded John Berringer.

'Youthful foibles,' dismissed Ludmilla, contemptuously. 'Wagner was no more a revolutionary when he wrote such pieces than any of us around this table.'

175

'He associated with anarchists,' reminded Sebastian, intent upon the response around the table. 'Mikhail Bakunin was an acknowledged friend.'

'Who spent all his life disowning his birthright, fomented and took part in revolution wherever he could find it, and achieved what?'

'An iconic place in the history of socialism,' retorted Sebastian. He was abrogating every rule of social etiquette, he acknowledged, conscious of Black's shift of discomfort from across the table. But once again he could not let an opportunity pass, and the choice of composer and Wagner's known history provided the slimmest of excuses.

'Why should the repertoire and its composer be ill chosen?' demanded Berringer, taking up the debate.

'I was reflecting upon Russia's recent history.'

'I'm reflecting on genius, which Wagner unquestionably had,' intruded Ludmilla, tartly. 'Wagner's revolutionary dalliance was a youthful foible, which he freely conceded and dismissed in adulthood. But tell us, Mr Holmes, are you proposing a rabble-rousing polemic from your researches here?'

'Most definitely not,' denied Sebastian, feeling the conversation slipping away from him.

'Consider another view,' invited Berringer. 'Doesn't the choice of Wagner show confidence in the stability of the country?'

'It is an alternative consideration,' conceded Sebastian. He'd arrived at the familiar mantra, he recognized. There was little purpose in furthering the etiquette breach.

'Look elsewhere for your revolutions,' insisted Ludmilla. 'Another will not occur here.'

'We should allow for the congestion of arrival at the Mariinsky,' came in Black, diplomatically.

He'd achieved nothing, accepted Sebastian, in the jolting coach ride away from the river, although neither of the Berringers had betrayed irritation at his introducing the conversation, merely at his intentionally controversial point of view.

The Mariinsky was unquestionably an architectural masterpiece, an opulent cavern of sweeping marble and glass reflecting the chandeliers, and giant and elaborate flower displays, the seats of their velvet-plush box yellowed by genuine gold leaf. Ludmilla Berringer dictated the seating arrangements with military authority, unnecessarily pointing out to Sebastian the very obvious royal box, which was almost directly in their eye line.

'That's where the Tsar and Tsarina will sit, possibly with one or more of their daughters, if they attend,' she promised, even more unnecessarily.

They didn't, but who did caused a greater immediate social stir than if it had been the imperial party. The auditorium and all the other boxes were already filled when the entry into the royal preserve of liveried attendants heralded a special arrival. The hubbub stilled and from where he sat Sebastian saw every head straining up, the conductor most intent of all, although Sebastian supposed he would have been one of the few people to know of the Tsar's presence, so he could initiate the anthem that would have brought everyone respectfully to their feet. Also from where Sebastian sat, level with the royal box, he was able to see the intended occupants the moment the rear door was opened. Framed in it was a startlingly attractive, blonde woman whom Sebastian guessed to be about thirty years old. Diamonds from a treble-stranded necklace, matching those of a tiered tiara, flashed against the blackness of an otherwise unadorned silk dress, the sheen of which reflected its own light.

From beside him Ludmilla muttered something in her native Russian, and then, in English, said: 'Princess Irina Yusupov!'

Sebastian instantly recognized the name as that of the hostess of the commemorative ball to which he was escorting Princess Olga Orlov, and only just held back from coming forward, the better to see her. Prince Felix Felixovich Yusupov followed directly behind, a diamond-encrusted royal order on the left breast of his tailed opera coat. The person behind also wore black, although it was a cassock, not a coat. There was a discernible communal sound, intakes of breath just short of gasps.

Berringer said: 'Unbelievable.'

His wife said: 'Rasputin!'

Sebastian ignored the others in the party who followed. The monk was tall, perhaps six foot, and heavily bearded in the required observance of the orthodox Russian priesthood. His hair, centrally parted, was long, too, merging into the unkempt and uncombed beard at the nape of his neck. The immaculate, buttoned cassock swept the floor. A black cross hung almost to his waist from a single gold chain.

Ludmilla said: 'This is preposterous! Too much!'

Her husband said: 'This is the Tsarina, determined upon his public acceptance and recognition.'

Would the diplomat pass on the episode to London, as he should, or dismiss it as the embassy appeared to have dismissed so much else? wondered Sebastian. He was conscious of an unnatural silence in such a vast theatre filled with so many people. Virtually every head was turned towards the royal box. Without any apparent uncertainty, Rasputin sat to the princess's left, her husband to her right, leaving everyone else to arrange themselves behind.

'Thank God she didn't insist upon any of the imperial princesses taking part in the charade,' said Ludmilla.

'This is not a charade,' said Berringer.

So engrossed were they in what was unfolding before them that the *chef du protocol* and his wife appeared oblivious to the others in the box around them. On the far side of the auditorium, Rasputin was leaning familiarly towards the princess, his face too close to hers. She laughed with him at whatever he whispered in her ear. Rasputin moved practically at once, coming forward to the rail of the box, better to make himself visible to those in the seats below, sweeping his eyes defiantly throughout the crowd. Sebastian saw a surprising number of women sharply avoiding his gaze, as if afraid of allowing their eyes to encounter his.

The lights dimmed and the orchestra went into the prelude. Sebastian kept his eyes on the royal box and the auditorium below it, estimating that a good third of the audience were looking up and to their right, not at the stage. So, too, were John and Ludmilla Berringer and Captain Black. Sebastian estimated it was almost thirty minutes before the attention finally switched to the stage. It was an excellent production, falling just short of performances Sebastian had seen at Bayreuth, which he forgave because of the understandable

178

difficulty of singers performing in Russian a libretto originally written in German. There was more champagne but the conversation was subdued, both in the Mariinsky – all eyes immediately reverting to the royal box and the gesturing Rasputin during any raising of the lights – and in the carriage back to the hotel. There his offer of late refreshment was declined by them all. As he wrote his letter of thanks in his suite, Sebastian wondered if Rasputin's presence so far from the Tsarevich's bedside at Tsarskoye Selo meant there'd been a recovery sufficient for the Tsar and Tsarina to attend Prince Yusupov's celebration ball after all.

The Geneva political meeting was raucous, the speeches strident, in German – which neither Sherlock Holmes nor Dr Watson spoke – for the predominantly Swiss-Deutsch-speaking audience. Sherlock Holmes insisted they dress as inconspicuously as their travelling wardrobe allowed, in their darkest overcoats and hats pulled low, and kept themselves at the rear of the hall where the lighting was weakest, and from where they could slip out the moment the meeting concluded.

Once outside, however, Sherlock Holmes led his companion into the shadowed concealment of a darkened shop awning, actually pulling them into its doorway. 'Well?' he demanded.

'This man Lenin is a compelling orator,' judged the bewildered Watson. 'I would have liked to have understood his argument.'

'But what of our fortunate discovery?'

'Discovery?' questioned the doctor.

'You disappoint me, Watson, after our many conversations upon the importance always of observation.'

'Observation?' Watson continued to question.

'As now,' prompted Sherlock Holmes, concentrating upon the departing crowd.

Dr Watson was silent for several moments, his direction guided by the detective's look, before suddenly saying: 'Good God! Otto von Hagel. What do we do now, Holmes?'

'What I already decided. Watch and wait. But watch very carefully.'

# Sixteen

The excursion gave Mycroft Holmes an excuse to drive his Rolls Royce to Southampton and the perfect weather provided the opportunity to do so with the hood down, although he still needed his leather coat and helmet against the wind created by the speed at which he drove, on straight stretches reaching 80mph and occasionally startling the horses of carriages he overtook. Being on the King's business strengthened the position he'd already capitalized upon as the Cabinet Secretary, and the promised police presence – a sergeant and two constables – was waiting, a space cordoned off for him in the waterside car park, with the assurance that the vehicle would be protectively watched during his absence on the Isle of Wight.

Mycroft exchanged his heavy travelling clothes for the cabinet box and his overnight luggage in the boot and boarded the island-bound steamer minutes before it departed to Cowes, choosing to remain on deck during the hour-long voyage, in preference to an inside lounge. The wind was stronger offshore, whipping up furrowed waves and sometimes lifting the bow spray above the rail against which he leant, although not sufficiently to force him under cover. Mycroft, a stranger to yachts, supposed it was what the experts would call good sailing weather. It was fifteen minutes before he was proven right by the first sight of the regatta competitors, their multicoloured spinnakers ballooned like pigeons' breasts ahead of them, their crews, uniform in dress as well as in rehearsed movement, scurrying ant-like between winches and lines and raised and lowered sails. They appeared to be large boats and Mycroft wondered if the King were racing in *Britannia*. Sail had the right of way over steam, and the ferry conceded, reducing its approach speed and no longer creating a bow flume, edging through the mooring trots to the landing stage. Mycroft, a reserved man who found it difficult to comprehend how easily his brother endured public recognition, was self-consciously aware of the attention of other ferry passengers as he entered the waiting, royal-monogrammed coach, grateful for its immediate concealing inner darkness. The route to Osborne House took him along the seafront, its protective wall crowded with regatta spectators eager for sight of the King, and on past the Royal Yacht Squadron. The horses shied slightly, as they began to ascend the hill, at the sudden cannon shot signalling the start of another race.

The sea was always in view as they wove along country lanes that in many places could not have accommodated his beloved car, the fields patchworked on either side, and he found it easy to understand why Osborne House had been the favourite palace of Queen Victoria and its redesigner Prince Albert – and, after his death, the sanctuary to which she retreated and was finally to die.

The word, the reason for his undertaking this journey, stayed with Mycroft and he felt a stir of unease at his uncertain enterprise. It had been Mycroft's idea, eagerly endorsed by Churchill, when he'd read in *The Times* of the King attending the annual Cowes Regatta, and it had been an easy matter to arrange for himself to be the King's messenger, delivering the weekly cabinet dispatches. Mycroft's doubt centred upon Lord Stamfordham. The King's private secretary was a person of considerable reputation, the words rectitude and integrity the most frequently used to describe a man considered one of the King's closest confidants. He, perhaps more than anyone else, would know the King's attitude towards offering sanctuary to the Romanovs. Mycroft recognized his danger of appearing to someone of unquestionable rectitude and integrity an untrustworthy gossip-monger, ill equipped for his position as Cabinet Secretary, in his efforts to gain the guidance he sought.

Mycroft lost sight of the sea on the last half-mile before the country palace, with a short turn inland that brought his carriage to the rear of the building. A footman was already waiting to lead Mycroft through a labyrinth of ground-floor passages that finished at Lord Stamfordham's study, which adjoined that of the King. The yacht-speckled Solent was perfectly visible again from the front of the palace and, when Mycroft entered, Stamfordham was at the overlooking window, a tall, aesthetically featured man who passingly reminded Mycroft of his brother. On the drive to Southampton, Mycroft had calculated that he'd been in the other man's company on perhaps five previous occasions, always at crowded official functions where they'd merely exchanged clichéd social pleasantries, giving him no opportunity to form his own judgement upon the man.

'I'm unaccustomed to receiving government business from such capable hands,' greeted the courtier, accepting the dispatch box from Mycroft before offering his hand. The shake was firm and brief, the hand physically dry and cold. 'You'll take sherry?'

'Thank you,' accepted Mycroft. 'I'm spending the weekend with Lord Carnarvon. I'm as interested as is my brother in Egyptology, and Carnarvon's support of the man Carter and his search for pharaohs' tombs. And I've acquired a car which I enjoy driving. To bring the cabinet material seemed a convenience all round.'

'You'll stay overnight here, though?' said Stamfordham, handing Mycroft his drink. 'I thought it was already agreed?'

'It is,' assured Mycroft. 'I appreciate the invitation.'

'It'll be a dull affair, I'm afraid,' apologized the other man. 'Just the two of us at dinner. Grouse, from Balmoral. The King is attending a function at the Squadron.'

Exactly what he'd hoped, thought Mycroft, following the taller man to leather armchairs bordering an empty fireplace. It would be wrong to hurry his mission, betraying the ulterior reason for his being there. Dinner would be the moment, after there'd been time to build a rapport. 'Has it been a good regatta for the King?'

'Three firsts, so far. Our sailor monarch is determined to break records with *Britannia* and is well on the way to achieving his ambition.'

Mycroft's admission that he did not sail prompted a similar disclosure from Stamfordham, who added that on several occasions he'd come close to seasickness crossing to the island from the mainland. He hoped the sea would become calmer for their return from the regatta.

'I suppose I should cast my eye over the contents of your box,' said the King's secretary, nodding towards where it lay on the desk. 'And no doubt you'd like to settle in. Cocktails at seven? I'm looking forward to hearing of the exploits of your esteemed brother.'

Mycroft was happy to accept his dismissal, unsure if he could manoeuvre Stamfordham's parting remark into a discussion of the Russian situation. It was Mycroft's responsibility to decide the contents of the King's box and he'd been careful to include the identification in Moscow of Hans Vogel. Mycroft was suddenly confident he didn't need the three hours until he met Stamfordham again to prepare his anecdotes about Sherlock Holmes. There were, after all, the excellent chronicles of Dr Watson.

Lord Stamfordham, a solicitous host, awaited Mycroft in the study when he descended upon the stroke of seven. The distant Solent was still littered with returning yachts, and the courtier said: 'Another first, to end the day. It'll be a convivial evening at the Squadron tonight.'

The repeated sherry warned Mycroft that Lord Stamfordham's table, despite reflecting that of the King himself, was more austere than he was accustomed to as Winston Churchill's dining companion. His reminiscences prepared, and to Stamfordham's quick urging, Mycroft unhurriedly recounted two of his brother's most recent exploits with which he was most familiar, which Watson had recorded as 'The Tiger of San Pedro' and 'The Disappearance of Lady Frances Carfax' unashamedly embroidering upon Watson's accounts, even more unashamedly to create an ambience of shared confidence between himself and the courtier. Mycroft was only halfway through the Carfax case when they were called to dinner, and didn't conclude until the grouse had been served, accompanied by a Margaux that lifted Mycroft's fears from the sherry aperitif.

'What of his current endeavour?' prompted Stamfordham.

Mycroft smiled at the perfect invitation. 'An odd coincidence.'

'How's that?'

'You've gone through this week's box?'

'Of course.'

'He'd be extremely curious if he knew of the military attaché's telegram on the presence in St Petersburg of the German spy expelled from America,' easily improvised Mycroft. 'He took great interest in the episode: began a file upon it, which he frequently does about situations in which he is tempted to involve himself.'

'Unfortunate, perhaps, that because of your position you are precluded from alerting him.'

'That would be unthinkable,' said Mycroft, knowingly damning himself if everything ever became public.

'I'd put that telegram aside, for discussion between us,' disclosed Stamfordham.

For the first time, but only momentarily, Mycroft was silenced by the remark. Could it be that, despite the admiration for rectitude and integrity, the King's trusted courtier was amenable to corridor conversations behind shielding hands? Mycroft said: 'I think it could be of some significance.'

'We have received little warning of it,' complained Stamfordham.

By 'we' the other man meant the King, Mycroft knew. 'It is no secret that the King is greatly occupied by events in Ireland.'

'He is preoccupied by the prospect of civil war there.'

'You must understand that I am expressing a personal view, in no way reflecting upon the attitude to which I am privy in cabinet, but I believe thought should be extended to the possibility of conflict in Europe.'

The older man gestured for their plates to be cleared. 'War in Russia?'

'In the Balkans, into which Russia would be drawn by treaty obligations, as would Germany. And as would Great Britain. Germany would be greatly aided by a civil war or internal unrest in Russia that would divert from its eastern border the largest army in Europe.'

184

'You are drawing an unsettling picture,' said Stamfordham.

'A personal view,' repeated Mycroft.

'A convincing one.'

'Which Sir Edward Grey might be encouraged to explore further as the result of our military attaché's warning,' prodded Mycroft.

'Encouraged he might well be,' agreed the man with the closest access to the King's ear. 'There's the too recent history of civil unrest, which shouldn't be ignored.'

He was confronting the biggest gap – prone to the greatest misunderstanding – he'd so far tried to cross, Mycroft recognized. And having got this far he had no alternative but to risk the jump. He said: 'Very close consideration would be required to family relationships, as well.'

Stamfordham's face clouded and Mycroft at once feared that he had gone too far and lost everything, but the expression quickly lifted, although there was a stiffness in the man's voice when he spoke. 'The King's first allegiance is to his country, not to German cousins.'

The man *had* misunderstood! Hurriedly trying to recover, Mycroft said: 'I was reflecting more upon the Russian imperial family, not doubting the King's allegiance. Would the Romanovs not consider Great Britain their most likely refuge?'

Stamfordham's look now was of astonishment. 'You are surely not suggesting the possibility of the Romanovs being overthrown – forced into exile?'

'I do not consider it beyond the realms of possibility . . .' Remembering how the conversation had been contrived, and the other man's apparent admiration, Mycroft quickly added: 'That's most definitely the view of Sherlock.'

'This conversation has given me much to think upon,' said the King's secretary.

He hadn't got his guidance! Mycroft thought, desperately. Risking another abyss, he said: 'In your opinion, would the King be receptive to the Russian royal family seeking sanctuary here?'

Stamfordham lapsed into contemplative silence for several moments, so long that Mycroft again feared he had overstepped propriety. But then the man said: 'It is difficult to imagine that

185

he would not. There is a friendship between the King and Tsar Nicholas: they've even sailed together, here in Cowes. I cannot believe the Romanovs would be abandoned. But the view of the government would obviously need to be considered.'

That was as much as he was going to get, Mycroft accepted. It would have been facile to expect more. Emboldened nevertheless by what he had achieved, Mycroft said: 'I have enjoyed our exchanges. Perhaps we might meet again upon our respective returns to London.'

'I think that would be extremely worthwhile,' agreed the other man.

It was Sherlock Holmes who abandoned their pursuit of the man who had been identified after the American spy arrests as financial division diplomat Otto von Hagel at the German embassy, but who, as Otto Meyer, had tried to lure Sebastian to his death on the New York waterfront. As they'd walked deeper and deeper into the increasingly deserted and disreputable suburbs of Geneva, Sherlock Holmes had declared their situation too dangerous, and, to Watson's immediate assurance that he as always carried his now unholstered service revolver, explained that he feared for their detection, not their lives.

'We'll let Hagel come to us,' he declared.

At Holmes's insistence, they were about early the following day, seeking out a cheap clothing shop and buying ready-made suits, topcoats and hats, careless of the ill fit of any of it.

'The secret of disguise is to become invisible,' said the detective.

'As you've frequently advised,' acknowledged Watson, surveying his regalia in his bedroom mirror back at the hotel. 'Who or what am I supposed to be, apart from invisible?'

'A struggling clerk, perhaps? But a local man, wearing badly made Swiss clothes, not an affluent visitor, as Hagel is a visitor, and one who might become suspicious were he to isolate you more than once, which as a well trained spy there is risk of his doing.'

'And you?'

Sherlock Holmes slumped, as a marionette would collapse upon having its strings cut, remarkably reducing his commanding height. 'An artisan whose indeterminate craft has badly affected his health.'

'And where do we go to become invisible, unaware as we are of Hagel's lodgings?'

'The Gare de Cornavin and its adjoining streets, most specifically the Rue Massat where the good Chief Superintendent Kuranda told us Lenin has rooms. The convenience of a railway station, with its constant passage of people, is greatly to our advantage, Watson: we'll be inconspicuous minnows in a swirling sea of other human minnows.'

'Larger fish eat minnows,' protested Watson, trying cynically to match the analogy.

'Not us, Watson,' insisted Sherlock Holmes. 'We're inedible.'

'That leaves no doubt in my mind,' said Winston Churchill. 'There could not be a higher, more guaranteed source.'

'It was an opinion, not a positive assurance,' tempered Mycroft.

'There can be no doubt,' insisted the First Lord of the Admiralty. 'And what a source you've cultivated, with his agreement to further meetings.'

'There seems an appetite for unofficial conversation.'

'To both your advantages,' judged Churchill. 'I convalesced on the Isle of Wight after an indisposition. I found it depressingly insular, the people most unfriendly. Couldn't wait to quit the damned place.'

Mycroft couldn't imagine an abundance of Pol Roger or claret stocks. 'I found it charming.'

'And Carnarvon?'

'He's convinced, from Howard Carter's dispatches, that they will uncover something at Thebes, and I hope he's right. He's expended a modern king's fortune in his quest: Carter's been digging in the Valley of the Kings for four years and found little.'

'It's about time he did!' judged an uninterested Churchill.

'I'll telegraph Sebastian tonight,' decided Mycroft, moving on. 'Advise him he can give the assurance the Grand Duke seeks.'

The Notions telegram to Sebastian read: AGREE FIELD HEBE IF BROCK.

187

# Seventeen

Sebastian was responding to the Grand Duke's summons, actually crossing the hotel foyer in expectation of the promised coach, when Captain Black thrust through the doors from the opposite direction, immediately smiling at the coincidence.

'Lucky to have caught you, it seems,' greeted the attaché.

The carriage wouldn't have arrived yet, Sebastian guessed. 'You didn't telephone to tell me you were coming.'

'It's been a fallow couple of days. I didn't think you'd want me to waste time,' said the immaculately pressed and polished man. He remained, expectant, blocking Sebastian's path.

He had to get rid of the man, Sebastian decided. Get him as far away as possible from the hotel before the arrival of Orlov's identifiable coach. 'What is it?'

'A telegram from London,' said the soldier diplomat, offering Sebastian the envelope.

How hard had Black tried to decipher the latest baffling words? Sebastian wondered, gazing down at the single-line communiqué, briefly surprised that Mycroft had used two non-Notions words – 'agree' and 'if' – although acknowledging at the same time it was to guarantee the paramount clarity of something so important. He accepted, too, that their inclusion would further confuse rather than help the attaché if Black were attempting the translation that Sebastian suspected. 'Field' was a Notions word meaning 'to help'. Sebastian was momentarily baffled by Hebe until he realized he was expected to read the word literally, not as Notions at all, although it featured in the language: Hebe in Greek mythology was the cup holder to the Gods, which was appropriate indication of the Tsar, who traditionally was considered a near deity by many pious Russians. And one of the definitions of 'brock' was an 'injustice'. King George V had agreed to help the Tsar if he suffered the injustice of a revolution that forced he and his family into exile.

Anticipating the military attaché, before the man could ask the inevitable question, and anxious to end the encounter as quickly as possible, Sebastian said: 'It's an acknowledgement of the last shipment. Nothing of the German matter.'

'I believed the last shipment already acknowledged,' frowned the other man.

'So did I,' said Sebastian, feigning ingenuousness. 'An unnecessary duplication. I apologize for your waste of time.

Black stood regarding Sebastian curiously. 'You have an appointment?'

'Making my way to you. As you've reminded me, it's been a quiet few days.' Black would immediately recognize the too easily identifiable monogrammed coach, which Orlov had assured him was already on its way. By now it had to be waiting outside.

'Without telephoning?' challenged Black.

'Neither of us showed sufficient forethought,' said Sebastian, embarrassed by his own inadequacy in the exchanges. It would be wrong to try to bustle the attaché out. The strategy had to be to keep Black inside the hotel until he could create an excuse for himself to leave momentarily and gesture the transport out of sight. Indicating their usual lounge enclave, Sebastian said: 'Let me at least compensate by offering some refreshment.'

'Briefly,' accepted Black, consulting with his regimental pocket watch. 'My time hasn't been wasted. My coming here was a minor detour. Our photographs have arrived at last. Jefferson is carrying out the first embassy watch. I'm to relieve him shortly.'

Sebastian led the way further into the hotel, gathering his thoughts as they walked. Orlov had not explained his summons on the telephone, but Sebastian hopefully inferred it to be the result of the Okhrana surveillance upon the German embassy, which they'd had three days – and nights – to conduct ahead of the British. How long would it be before he received something from the military attaché to show which, if either, of the two were honestly offering their promised co-operation? As he

189

ordered tea from the prepared samovar in the middle of the hotel lounge, Sebastian said: 'I would have expected your receiving the photographs to be the first thing you would have told me?'

'I thought your message might have contributed.'

'It doesn't,' repeated Sebastian, searching for a way to carry the conversation on. 'Ludmilla Berringer is an unusual woman.' He and Black had not physically met since the night at the opera.

There was a fleeting smile from the other man. 'She remarked the same about you. She identified whose son you were, which is hardly difficult, either in features or stature.'

Damn upon damnation, thought Sebastian. 'Did you confirm it?'

'I haven't yet been asked.'

'She will tell others at the embassy.'

'Undoubtedly. If she hasn't done so already.'

It was something about which immediately to warn London, Sebastian recognized. Objectively he had been lucky to escape identification – as far as he knew – until now. 'So you are professionally compromised. My use of embassy facilities must cease. I'll advise London at once.' Sebastian was glad he'd already considered the likelihood, and wondered how long it would take for his coded use of the hotel telegraph to arouse Orlov's interest. It would be a cumbersome, time-consuming business.

'Ludmilla made her recognition on the night of the opera, which means there's been three days for the identification to circulate,' said Black. 'I have not been challenged upon anything so far.'

'The concern is not my identification. It's that Churchill should become known to be involved.' Within the space of thirty minutes, potential problems were becoming as entangled as a ball of wool in a kitten's basket. It was not just Churchill's position that was endangered. Of equal if not more importance was the catastrophe that could engulf his uncle.

'I understand that,' said the soldier, although Sebastian detected the doubt in the other man's voice and was not convinced that he did.

'You will not forget our agreement, the last I'll call upon, to exchange the results of your German embassy observation?' pressed Sebastian. He not only had to make his brief escape

190

from the hotel. He had to warn London before keeping the now much delayed appointment with the Grand Duke.

'Of course not.'

'And I wish to be kept fully informed of what arises about my identification at the embassy. I will do everything within reason that you might require to protect your position.' The chances of his ever achieving the slightest hint of an Okhrana spy within the legation were gone now, even if it had existed in the first place.

'I see no reason to change our arrangements until I am formally asked about our association,' protested Black. 'Maybe not even then.'

Sebastian felt a surge of exasperation. Had Ludmilla Berringer genuinely identified him? Or was Black playing his threadbare game in the hope of learning more of the exchanges with London, one of which appeared greatly to have enhanced the man's reputation? Forcefully, Sebastian said: 'It ends, now! We have danced around this problem before and now is the time to resolve it. I am in your debt and will recommend you to Churchill for all you have done.' There was an escape for Churchill in what amounted virtually to the truth, he realized. It was his uncle's involvement that lacked a satisfactory explanation.

'Let us at least remain in social contact,' urged Black, urgently.

It would at least give him a tenuous link to the embassy, accepted Sebastian, although he had realistically to accept his spy search was over before it had begun. There was, still, the arrangement again to contact Kerensky, but, realistically once more, he had to accept there was no possibility of the Russian politician volunteering anything. Abruptly starting up, Sebastian said: 'You must briefly excuse me. Something I need to request at reception.'

Black came up as quickly with him. 'I've stayed longer than I intended. I'll walk with you.'

He was trapped, Sebastian accepted. Trapped without an escape; conceivably, even, about to be suspected of being an Okhrana spy himself! But why? Why did it naturally follow that if Black isolated the waiting carriage it was there for him? They halted once more in the foyer. Sebastian said: 'I'll

191

telephone tomorrow, to learn of any success from our embassy watch. But I'll not approach you again directly.'

'I've every hope of knowing something by then,' said Black.

His earlier explanations now clear in his mind, Sebastian said: 'If you are challenged about my identification and our association, persist with the story of my being a journalist, introduced to you by your school acquaintance. Which would only leave you to explain my use of the embassy's communication facilities.'

'The path I'd already chosen,' smiled Black, with the slightest trace of the familiar condescension.

To emerge too closely behind the attaché, in search of the coach, would betray his expectation of it being there, Sebastian decided. He needed to advise London of his being recognized: warn Churchill and, even more importantly, Mycroft. He couldn't immediately call to mind appropriate Notions phrases or words and, in his hurry, decided upon ziphs, an alternative method of student communication at Winchester, in which vowels were doubled and into each word was inserted a medial *g*. Upon a telegraph form he wrote:

IIDEENTGIIEED HEEGREE AABAAGNDOON EEMBGAASY
ROOUGUTEE FOGOR HOOGTEEL DIIRGEECT

As he wrote, Sebastian occasionally looked up, half-expecting the hurried re-entry of Captain Black, but the man did not appear. Sebastian finally but hesitantly emerged out into the street, initially more intently seeking the attaché than the carriage. And saw neither. He felt the touch, though, from behind, and turned to his earlier Tsarskoye Selo escort, no longer liveried but in the dark suit he had worn guarding Princess Olga at the British Embassy garden party. The man gestured for Sebastian to follow. The coach, completely unmarked, was in a side alley off the road that bordered the hotel.

Unadjusted to the contrast of the inner, curtained darkness with the outside daylight, Sebastian was unaware of anyone else being in the coach until the Grand Duke Alexei Orlov said: 'There's no cause to apologize for your lateness. We saw you were delayed by Captain Black.'

192

'With a message of great import,' picked up Sebastian, recovering in the facing seat as the coach jolted into motion. 'The King will offer sanctuary to the Tsar and his family.'

Orlov sighed, releasing the satisfaction. 'Black – the ambassador even – is aware of this?'

Sebastian shook his head. 'This is unofficial, as you know. It will require to be formally introduced if the necessity arises.'

'Black receives your telegrams: they are there in front of him!'

'It's an unusual code.' But it would not be difficult for a codebreaker to decipher ziphs, Sebastian thought. He added: 'I have been identified at the British embassy. I have just warned London in a different cipher, far more easily broken, that I can no longer use our embassy facilities.'

'I have your word that the Tsar and his family will be under British protection and welcomed into England in the event of another, more successful revolution?' pressed the Grand Duke.

'Yes,' confirmed Sebastian, uncomfortably. It had nothing whatsoever to do with his word, but everything to do with the integrity of whomever Churchill or Mycroft or his father had obtained the assurance from. From no conscious reflection, a remark of the Grand Duke's – *We saw you were delayed by Captain Black* – thrust into Sebastian's mind. How could the British military attaché be so easily known to the head of the Okhrana unless the man were the Russian secret police informant? It slotted so very easily into all the other suspicious inconsistencies, adding to the mosaic.

'A positive plan needs to be established, in the event of what we fear may become reality!' insisted Orlov. 'Emergency code words decided upon and understood by the Tsar, his family, and trusted courtiers. Your suggestion, of bringing the Royal family from Tsarskoye Selo closer to the British embassy here in St Petersburg, is a good one. I'll prepare a plan for that. Most important is their safe passage out of the country. It cannot be by train, through a country as vast as Russia: it would be too vulnerable to interception. St Petersburg is ideally placed for a sea escape. Great Britain will have to provide a cruiser, with frigate protection perhaps . . .' There was a pointed hesitation. 'And a cruiser would have accommodation for others who would be murdered if they remained . . .'

193

Sebastian swayed with the turn of the carriage. Needing time to digest the babbled demands from the bearded man opposite, Sebastian said: 'Where are we going?'

'Nowhere!' dismissed Orlov, impatiently. 'We are going, in complete anonymity, around the city at the driver's whim, the only purpose to have the conversation we're having now.'

'You could not have known of the King's agreement when you arranged this meeting!' Unless Black had broken the code sufficient to understand every nuance – and was the Okhrana spy! If he were, Black would have made copies of everything for the Russian. Sebastian believed Notions, which had no mathematical formula, would have defeated the Okhrana codebreakers, although ziphs most certainly wouldn't.

'I did not arrange this meeting in the expectation of what you've told me,' said Orlov. 'I have some results of our observation of the German embassy.' He offered three separate prints across the carriage.

One was of the already identified Hans Vogel. The first of the other two was of a small man with pointed features whom Sebastian was sure had been among the would-be assassination group, first at Lafayette Park in Washington DC, and without question among the intended killers in the New York harbour warehouse. The second was of a saturnine, sleekly dark-haired man whom Sebastian most positively recalled firing twice at him in the waterside confrontation which he had survived only by the fortunate entry of the New York police. Vogel was now identified as Wolfgang Brecht, although he was still listed as being attached to the embassy's legal department. The name on the German diplomatic list for the rat-faced man was Fritz Langer, whose position was given as a security officer, as was that of the third man, Konrad Blum.

Orlov said: 'We haven't completed the check.'

There was another lurched turn. Sebastian said: 'What are you going to do?'

'Discover what they're doing here, to begin with. And then decide how best to use the information. They're not committing any crime under the Russian criminal code, merely being attached to their country's embassy.'

'Is that a consideration?'

'Only if I decide it to be.'

Sebastian wondered what part of the city lay beyond the enclosing curtains: there'd been no baying guttersnipe pursuit, but perhaps they recognized the carriage for what it was, despite its absence of any official markings and Orlov's insistence upon anonymity. 'I saw Rasputin – and Prince Yusupov – at the Meriinsky theatre. The Wagner opera.'

'I know,' said Orlov, unhesitatingly. 'Rasputin goes nowhere without my knowledge.' He added: 'Olga is looking forward to the ball.'

'As I am. Is there a likelihood of the Tsar and Tsarina attending?'

Orlov shrugged. 'It remains uncertain. The child is still suffering and the Tsarina needs little excuse to avoid St Petersburg and its social scene, despite this being in their honour.'

'But Rasputin could leave the Tsarevich, to attend an opera?'

'It's an indication, if any more were needed, of the man's confidence in what he can do in the court.'

'His presence at the theatre caused a sensation.'

'It invariably does, in such circumstances. In which he delights. The stories are gaining credence that, so deeply is the Tsarina under his influence – and the Tsar in turn under hers – that Rasputin is dictating some government decisions.'

'Do you believe it?'

'He's been responsible for the replacement of some people with choices of his own. The Church are treating him cautiously: with some deference even.' The Grand Duke took a heavy hunter from his waistcoat pocket, snapping open the cover of the timepiece. 'I am late for Tsarskoye Selo. Your message from London puts me further in your debt.' He rapped upon the carriage roof with his cane.

'It was our arrangement,' reminded Sebastian.

'You are determined against communicating through your embassy any further?'

'Definitely,' insisted Sebastian.

'Which will greatly delay the exchange of material too lengthy to be telegraphed.'

'That is unavoidable.' Where was this conversation going?

195

'If treaty obligations are invoked, through conflict in the Balkans, Russia and Great Britain will be allies.'

'Yes?' agreed Sebastian, guardedly.

'I can authorize the same diplomatic courier arrangement through the Russian embassy in London,' offered Orlov.

And by so doing learn Mycroft to be the recipient, thought Sebastian at once. But just as quickly corrected himself. Orlov knew of his father. It would be a simple matter to substitute one addressee for another, to protect his uncle. 'I'll give it serious thought.'

The carriage slowed, made its final swaying turn and then stopped. 'Enjoy the ball,' said the Russian.

When Sebastian stepped out of the carriage he saw he was back in the secluded alley beside the Grand Hotel. Only then did he remember Orlov's earlier guarantee of discreet transport arrangements and realize there had been no need for concern at Captain Black's unexpected arrival. It still didn't explain Orlov's identification of the man.

Their first day of observation upon Lenin's lodgings on the Rue Massat had passed without any sighting of either the Russian or of Otto von Hagel, causing Watson to complain that so many Swiss cream confections in so many cafés in which they established vantage points ruined his appetite for dinner, and Sherlock Holmes to become concerned that there was another access at the lodging house, through which Lenin and any visitors could come and go unobserved.

Both their concerns evaporated the following morning with the arrival, shortly after ten, of von Hagel. The blonde, militarily upright German strode confidently, familiarly, along the Rue Massat in the direction of the railway station, but abruptly paused at an enclave into the terrace of houses in which Lenin lodged.

'Who knows, Watson,' suggested Sherlock Holmes, looking accusingly at the breakfast array before the doctor in the Konditori most directly opposite, 'this could be your opportunity to shed yesterday's indulgence in so many cream cakes and pastries.'

It was scarcely exercise. Lenin, von Hagel and another man who had been on the stage at the rally emerged after just fifteen

196

minutes, setting off in head-bent conversation in the direction of the lake. Sherlock Holmes and Watson allowed their customary and well-rehearsed delay of three minutes, which Watson counted with moving lips despite their having engaged in such timed pursuits innumerable times before. They divided, on either side of the Rue du Mont-Blanc, first Holmes, then Watson, breaking off into side roads to conceal their purpose by hurrying through the three-sided road diversion to bring them back on their original route. It terminated, as they'd anticipated, at the river Rhône. Already waiting at a water-bordering café close to the Pont des Bergues were three other men, who rose to effusive handshakes at Lenin's arrival.

'Well, Watson?' demanded Sherlock Holmes, as they seated themselves at another café just a hundred metres further on.

'All, with the exception of von Hagel, were upon the stage at the political rally three nights ago,' replied Watson, at once.

'Well identified,' agreed Sherlock Holmes. 'We're looking at a veritable revolutionary cabal.'

'What now?' questioned the doctor.

Sherlock Holmes nodded back inside the café. 'You contact Chief Superintendent Kuranda by telephone and ask him to meet us at the Cornavin railway station. And advise him to alert his counterpart at Bern to await our arrival. If I am not here upon your return, you know where to find me.'

Watson opened his mouth to question but thought better of it, hurrying inside. Sherlock Holmes was still at their table, a second coffee before him, when the doctor returned. Watson said: 'He promises to be awaiting us.'

It was another thirty minutes and another coffee before the group rose, to backslapping farewells as effusive as their arrival. They followed the same route as their approach, and Sherlock Holmes, having brought Watson from his opposite, covering side of the road, impatiently passed the three men to arrive at the rail terminal ahead of them.

Hugo Kuranda was there, as promised. The portly Swiss detective said: 'As Bern was mentioned, I purchased our tickets in readiness.'

The Bern express was five minutes from departure when Otto von Hagel hurried on to the platform, found his carriage and settled into it. Kuranda used his police authority to secure seats three divisions away, within the same carriage.

Watson said: 'Tell me, Holmes, how did you know he would be catching a train to this specific destination?'

'Where – and how – else would he go, his business so obviously over. Bern is the Swiss capital, where the embassies are.'

'Do you always think ahead?' smiled Kuranda.

'Forethought is always better than afterthought,' said Sherlock Holmes.

There were three detectives and a waiting, unmarked car at Bern station. Which they needed. Von Hagel strode directly to a waiting vehicle, also unmarked, and was driven directly to the German embassy close to the river.

'A proven German spy is treating with Russian revolutionaries,' announced Sherlock Holmes, satisfied.

'Not a criminal offence,' reminded Kuranda.

'But good cause to heighten your interest in Vladimir Lenin. Both men, in fact.'

'Very good reason,' agreed the Geneva detective chief.


'What's this matter, Stamfordham?'

'Something that was included in the London box that I thought important to bring to your notice, sir.'

'I think I remember the American business.'

'There was quite a furore.'

'And these are the same scoundrels?'

'That's the indication from St Petersburg.'

'How's it fit into the scheme of things?'

'There's a lot of nationalist unrest in the Balkans. And there was the 1905 episode in Russia.'

The King was silent for several moments. 'Charge Asquith with providing a full picture.'

'Of course, sir.'

'I'm going to win again tomorrow, Stamfordham! Nothing in the class to beat me!'

'The best of luck, sir.'

'Don't need luck. Just good wind.'

# Eighteen

Princess Olga Orlov looked exquisite and knew it, taking her time slowly to descend the circular marble staircase to where Sebastian waited in the black and white checker-floored entrance hall. She wore a sheer, figure-hugging, black, high-collared gown that seemed her favourite design, the perfectly matched diamond necklace extending in graded sizes to five strings. The earrings were a further perfect match, as was the diamond-surmounted comb that held the chignon cleat in tight control. There was a solitaire diamond sparkling from the ring on her right hand and there was occasional further lustre from the infrequent glimpses of her shoe buckles beneath the floor-sweeping skirts.

She extended her hand as she reached him, and Sebastian bent to kiss it. He said: 'I shall be the envy of every man in the room tonight.'

She said: 'You are very gallant. And gracious, to endure the determination with which my father is forcing us together. It embarrasses me.'

'It delights me,' said Sebastian, meaning it. His only embarrassment was conducting the greeting and the conversation in the presence of three statued footmen. At least, he thought on reflection, they would not be able to understand the conversation. Or would they?

'Gallant again!'

'I do not consider us forced together. I meant what I said.'

'Tonight is the first opportunity for us properly to talk. Which I wish to do.'

'Then we shall.' About what? he wondered.

Her taking his offered arm was the signal for two of the footmen to open the palace doors with faultless precision, the prompt for another to open the door to the waiting carriage.

There was one carriage escort ahead and another two behind. Sebastian was curious how many guards there were in the three. Remembering Orlov's insistence, he had not carried the swordstick; the cumbersome revolver would have been unthinkable. Olga seated herself in a corner but Sebastian declined the clearly invited space, sitting opposite.

She said: 'So why is he doing this? And please don't continue the gallantry by denying that you understand my question.'

'What has your father told you of my reasons for being here in St Petersburg?'

'That you are gathering information on the political situation here . . .' She laughed. 'Which I suppose makes you a spy. How dashing.'

It was a better opening than he could have hoped. 'What do you consider the political situation to be?'

'Uncertain,' the princess responded, without hesitation. 'But it will be dispelled – everything stabilized – by my father.'

'What if it isn't?'

'That's a hypothetical question that doesn't need answering. I just told you that my father will stamp out the unrest; restore the affection of the people for their Tsar.'

'There are many people who don't share your confidence.'

'You among them!'

It would be wrong to disclose her own father's doubt. 'Possibly.'

'Then you are wrong! Forming impressions after too little time here based on rumour without substance!'

It was not, after all, proceeding well, Sebastian accepted. 'Do you disagree as strongly with your father?'

'Ah!' the princess exclaimed, in apparent understanding.

Sebastian said nothing. They surely had to be close to the Yusupov Palace on the Moika Canal!

'Why did my father believe you would be any more successful than he in persuading me to move to Paris?'

He had to lie, Sebastian supposed; exaggerate at least. 'There is an opinion among certain people in England, people with insight and awareness, that the unrest here in Russia is not containable.'

'What did my father say to that?'

Not the question he'd wanted to prompt, thought Sebastian. 'He did not dismiss it as readily as you.'

'Perhaps he is more polite than me.'

'Perhaps he is more realistic than you.' He had to be careful that this did not degenerate into an outright argument.

'So people like me, privileged people of the ruling class, are supposed to scuttle abroad, abandoning the country we love to a rabble with no concept of government or law, letting it go back into the dark ages!'

'People like you, privileged people of the ruling class, were massacred over a ten-year period in France, from 1789. France – where you have property and resources – still successfully exists as a republic, not as an example of the dark ages . . .' Sebastian hesitated, unsure if he should risk being so gauche, but anxious to lessen the tension. 'You look literally breath-taking: is your dress from a Russian or French couturier?'

Olga fought against the smile that finally came. 'I appreciate the compliment but not the argument. I will flee the revolutionaries alongside my father, not without him. Only then will I accept that my country has gone the disastrous way of too many others.'

He'd taken things as far as he could, Sebastian acknowledged. And lost. So far. He said: 'This isn't how I envisaged this evening.'

'Nor I, although it is of my doing.' She smiled again.

Sebastian was relieved at the noticeable slowing of the coach. 'Shall we start again?'

'I think we should. And I will stop being so rude.'

'And I meant what I said. You look breathtaking.'


Everything about the palace was grandly opulent and huge, a dwelling for giants or people who considered themselves to be giants. The forecourt beyond the initial gate was ablaze with fire torches marking the route to the enormous double doors now opened on to the shimmering, chandeliered interior. Countless black-liveried servants and ostlers darted between coaches and cars and disembarkations, ensuring a continuous if unavoidably delayed arrival. There were even more, accepting cloaks and stoles directly inside. Beyond which, through a reception room, the cavernous ballroom dominated the ground floor, dozens more fire torches flickering on surrounding verandahs to reflect off the flaccid waters of the bordering canal, upon which two orchestras played on boats for those venturing outside through the ceiling-to-floor French windows. A larger orchestra performed within the ballroom itself.

Prince Felix Felixovich Yusupov, Princess Irina attentively beside him, stood slightly in from the entrance, receiving their guests. Olga announced their names, in Russian, to the major domo and spoke again as they approached their hosts. Prepared, Yusupov said in French as he took Sebastian's hand: 'Welcome to my home. Please enjoy the evening.'

Sebastian was aware of a rapid exchange in Russian between the two princesses before he and Olga moved further into the ballroom. Olga said: 'The Tsar and the Tsarina are not attending. But the Grand Duchess Olga is expected.'

There were not as many people actually dancing as Sebastian had expected. In Olga's wake, Sebastian passed from the main ballroom into a minor antechamber and, as they did so, Sebastian recognized, surprised, that he was following the woman's lead. He took two champagne flutes from a passing attendant and said, stopping her: 'Where are we going?'

'Looking,' she said, pausing reluctantly.

'At what? For what?' How many of Orlov's people – protectors, spies, informants – were there all around them? wondered Sebastian.

'Looking,' repeated Olga, awkwardly.

She occasionally acknowledged people with a head movement or a smile, but did not accept any of at least three obvious invitations to engage in conversation. She made as if to move but, abandoning formality, Sebastian said: 'Olga! I won't dance like a puppet to your string-pulling without knowing the tune.'

She halted properly this time, frowning towards him, a woman never opposed genuinely, if only briefly, astonished at being so openly confronted. 'I appear to have forgotten my promise not to be rude.'

'As I have just been.'

Looking very directly at Sebastian, she said: 'I am very happy to be addressed as you've just addressed me. Princess is a title acquired by a quirk of birth: it is not the name of an infectious disease . . .' There was the vaguest hint of a smile. 'Which I thought you might already have discovered from acquaintances with princesses.'

It was her first, but a very obvious reference to his near-disastrous relationship aboard the *Lusitania* with Princess Anna Boinburg-Langesfeld. 'I escaped contagion.'

'And death, by a whisker. My father told me of it all: of her being one of the German agents you specifically went to America to identify.'

Yet again Sebastian was surprised at the degree to which Orlov shared the secrets of his position with his daughter. 'It would not be fitting to discuss someone to whom we both know we're referring.'

'Even though she exposed you to possible assassination! Your gallantry has no limits!'

'Neither has my curiosity and refusal to be deflected,' seized Sebastian. 'Looking for what, at what?'

'I am aware of the guest list,' she replied shortly. 'There are many who should be here who are not.'

'It is still early,' shrugged Sebastian.

'It was not known whether the Tsar and Tsarina were attending. Which therefore required people to be here ahead of them, to avoid an unacceptable social offence which would still be created by arriving after the Grand Duchess.'

How to interpret what he was being told? thought Sebastian. 'Risking even greater offence to the imperial family, in whose name the ball is being held, by not attending at all?'

'Perhaps the most offensive demonstration imaginable. One I never believed would be made.'

Sebastian still didn't understand, but couldn't risk showing his ignorance by a wrongly phrased question. He was still seeking the appropriate ambivalent remark to move Olga on, hopefully to some clarity, when she said, with suppressed anger: 'How can a dynasty demean itself and ostracize itself from people upon whose loyalty they so much depend?'

Olga was looking beyond him, over his shoulder, and Sebastian turned and believed he understood most of the so far inexplicable conversation. Through the separating door there was a perfect view of Gregory Efimovich Rasputin entering the grand ballroom to a handclasped greeting from Prince Yusupov. A smiling Princess Irina offered her hand to be kissed, which the bearded, long-haired monk was overly long in doing. Having eventually done so, he turned, looking out almost challengingly into a huge room and its watching occupants. He wore the floor-length cassock of the Mariinsky Theatre, the same cross on its long chain.

'Look at such arrogance!' said the unsteady-voiced Olga, beside Sebastian. 'It is as if he were the Tsar. The Grand Duchess should not be exposed to such humiliation.'

'Perhaps not everyone will interpret it as you have done?'

'There's not a guest in this palace who has not interpreted everything exactly as I have,' dismissed Olga, curtly. 'And even more so those who have declined to attend. Without a word being uttered, it's being made clear to the Tsar and Tsarina that affairs of the country can not any longer be dictated by a drunken, depraved mystic who disgraces the cloth he chooses to wear and hide beneath.'

There was a discernible stir that spread from the ballroom into the antechamber, and Olga said: 'The Grand Duchess is arriving. This really should not have been allowed!'

They reached the larger room as the Grand Duchess Olga Nikolaievna Romanov entered, chaperoned by two older women and an even older man. A respectful avenue formed automatically and, as the Grand Duchess proceeded along it, accompanied now by Prince Yusupov and his wife, the women curtsied and the men bowed, as did Sebastian, aware, as he showed his respect, that Rasputin remained nonchalantly upright and unbending. As the royal group passed them, on their way to a raised area upon which seats were already arranged, Olga said: 'The man is Grand Duke Michael Alexandrovich, the Tsar's younger brother. The woman in green is Grand Duchess Olga Nikolaievna, the Tsar's youngest sister. I do not recognize the other chaperone.'

Knowing as he did the closeness of their ages, Sebastian found himself instinctively comparing the princess by his side and the Grand Duchess only a few yards away. Although their colouring was very similar, the difference between them was remarkable. The Grand Duchess looked much younger than her 19 years, and almost visibly insecure, her hair coiffeured girlishly, her insufficient make-up too light. She was using Prince Yusupov's arm for necessary support as much as for social etiquette. The black and white patterned dress was that of a young, not mature teenager, unhelped by the emerald choker and bracelet. She walked with a fixed half-smile, looking neither left nor right, and when she sat, pointedly concentrated upon those around her rather than looking out into the room. The woman beside him was by contrast the very epitome of assured and poised sophistication, already the obvious object of several admiring looks from men around them. Sebastian even had the impression of Rasputin's attention: certainly it was in the monk's direction that she responded with a look of utter contempt.

Coming back to Sebastian, she said: 'I should go to talk to her. There'll be an approved list.'

'I understand,' said Sebastian. 'I shall wait in the anteroom. Or here.' He'd seen Rasputin walk that way after Olga's dismissal.

He did not however go immediately back to the smaller refreshment room. He remained instead where he was, watching Olga pick her way through the crowded room with the confidence – and perhaps some recognition – that had paths opening before her, and he again felt a twinge of pity for the isolated girl on the far edge of the room. The discreet protective shield – so discreet Sebastian had not until that moment isolated it – withdrew at Olga's approach. So intent was the Grand Duchess to avoid looking out into the room that she was only aware of the princess at the last moment. Her face opened, in obvious relief and delight, and she stretched forward with both arms in greeting, uncaring of the embrace in front of such an audience, of whom Olga was equally dismissive. A chair was instantly provided and the two women, so close in age and friendship, yet so far apart in every other way, fell into animated conversation.

Sebastian finally withdrew into the anteroom, plucking a fresh glass from an attendant's tray. There was a guffaw of laughter and Sebastian saw it came from a group huddled sycophantically around Rasputin, who appeared literally to be holding court at the far end of the room, close to a long table of canapés and one of the doors opening on to the torch-lit verandah. Sebastian sidled along the table gradually, unobtrusively, to get as close as he could to the noisy group, realizing when he got nearer there were almost as many attentive women as there were men. His stronger awareness was of the separation – a positive, visible gap, a moat – between Rasputin's surrounding acolytes and others in the room, a confirmation of Olga's judgement. Sebastian halted at its isolating edge, his back to them, irritated at not having the language to eavesdrop, although not needing to understand to be sure the conversation was inconsequential. Sebastian snatched his observation between his apparent interest in the refreshment table and the passing champagne waiters, not expecting what he discovered close-up. The traditional straggled beard of a holy man was not just unkempt but deeply flecked with careless food debris, and the teeth exposed by his frequent laughing were dirty and unwashed, maybe even green or black at their roots. The full-length cassock, so seemingly immaculate from afar, was visibly pockmarked by stains which were being added to by the manner in which he was eating now, thrusting canapés whole into his mouth as he talked and sniggered, uncaring of stray pieces that fell as he chewed, as a lizard was careless of what fell from its mouth from a half-trapped insect.

So quickly did Rasputin catch Sebastian's surreptitious examination that the abrupt and loud challenge startled him almost into a physical reaction. He had been turning away but accepted at once that he could not pretend to have failed to hear the shout. He looked back at the man at the shouted repetition, extended his hands in a helpless gesture and in German said: 'I am sorry. I do not speak Russian.'

In the same language, one of the group said: 'He's inviting you to join us.'

'That is kind but I have become separated from my companion.' Fully confronting the monk, Sebastian was conscious of the intense, unblinking, deeply black eyes boring into his. It was the briefest of images but Sebastian had a sensation of Rasputin's face distorting until the man's eyes dominated the bearded face to become its entire, inescapable focus.

The impression broke with another burst of Russian, immediately translated. 'He invited you to bring your companion in the black dress with you.'

'I will convey that invitation.'

The next translation was: 'He will not accept a refusal. He never does.'

There was a burst of shared laughter at a double entendre. 'Then he must hope against a rare disappointment.'

The remark was greeted with silence.

Sebastian made his way back along the table, more curious than dismayed at the recognition. It positively confirmed that the cleric had been looking at Olga in what was clearly a lascivious way, which also explained the double entendre that had amused the group. It certainly wouldn't amuse Olga. It was, in fact, a clearly obscene sexual reference. Was it fitting for him to tell her? Normally the easy answer would have been no, but Sebastian did not regard the situation or Rasputin's attention to the princess as normal. It could even represent danger.

He re-entered the ballroom and found the spot where he'd stood when Olga left him. Across the other side of the room she was still engrossed in conversation with her namesake, but as Sebastian looked, Yusupov leaned across to interrupt and almost at once the Grand Duchess rose and took the prince's arm on to the dancefloor. Olga turned to the others on the raised section, spoke briefly and then rose herself, picking Sebastian out at once. As she came towards him she acknowledged and spoke to several people, pausing at something said to her by an elaborately uniformed and decorated officer, smiling but shaking her head.

'I am sorry I was so long,' Olga apologized, finally reaching him.

'I had much to occupy me.'

'Olga is hating it. As soon as she's fulfilled what she considers her duty she intends to leave. She is furious at Yusupov for allowing Rasputin here.'

'He was with Yusupov at the opera. Your father knew.'

'My father didn't know the man was to be included tonight!' protested the princess. 'I don't wish to extend my presence here . . .' She stopped. 'I seem to be making a practice of being rude. Forgive me.'

'We will leave whenever you wish,' promised Sebastian, at once. He should tell her about the Rasputin episode, Sebastian decided: tell Olga as well as her father. 'It's a ball and we haven't danced. Or would you prefer the supper room?'

Olga appeared to consider the alternatives. 'Supper room. Dancing is for when people are happy.'

The supper room was also set out as a buffet with tables and chairs, with an expansive view of the canal and the river. Olga chose sparingly, as did Sebastian. There were wine waiters in immediate attendance when they sat, at a table set for two. Olga accepted champagne. Sebastian preferred a flat white wine which was sweeter than he would have liked.

'So what was there to occupy you?' demanded Olga.

Sebastian hesitated. 'I am undecided upon the propriety of telling you, although I believe you should know, as should your father.'

She stopped eating. 'My father and I have few secrets. What you tell him of this evening, he will tell me.'

Sebastian didn't believe for a moment that Olga shared as many secrets as she boasted with a man in Orlov's position, but thought again how the man included his daughter in ways that had already surprised him. Even quoting some of the remarks, Sebastian described his encounter with Rasputin, although he held back from the blatant sexual reference. Olga begun to colour practically from the beginning of the account, but Sebastian decided the flush was anger, not embarrassment.

'He looked at me in a disgusting way!'

'I was aware of it.'

'Were you close enough to smell him?'

'Smell him?' questioned Sebastian, confused.

'Olga told me that he smells; that he never bathes.'

'Only close enough to see how filthy he was outwardly. Have you heard of hypnotism?'

'Don't patronize me, Sebastian!' she said, although unoffended.

'I suspect that is how he treats the Tsarevich. Not through any divine power, as the Tsar and Tsarina are convinced, but by an ability to put the child into some sort of trance in which his pain is minimized.'

'You told him it was unlikely we'd accept his invitation?'

'Yes?' questioned Sebastian.

'I'm minded to confront him!'

'I don't think that is a good idea; or that your father would consider I was offering the proper protection by allowing you to do so.'

'I don't consider my protection your responsibility!' rejected Olga, with a hint of outrage. 'Nor that you are in any position to dictate my behaviour!'

'I do,' insisted Sebastian, forcefully. 'You made clear to me this very evening the attitude of the majority of people towards the man, and his influence over the imperial family. There is a visible divide between Rasputin and his group, and others, others who would not know why you approached the man. And would misunderstand. The risk to your reputation – and that of your father – is greater than any small, personal satisfaction you'd achieve by showing your contempt face to face. You've already done that, by the way you returned his improper look. To go into his presence would only give him the opportunity to humiliate you, and by inference the Grand Duchess, in whose presence you have so very publicly been.'

Olga began picking at her food again. 'You make a convincing argument. Thank you, for preventing my making such a mistake . . . And a fool of myself . . .' She smiled. 'But we will dance after all, not slink off as if we have been driven away by the man!'

Their return to the ballroom coincided with the departure of the Grand Duchess, just in time for the two Olgas to exchange smiles. Sebastian and the princess came together as perfect partners, to whirling waltzes and choreographed gavottes. Olga became aware of renewed attention and played up to it, laughing and acknowledging people she knew, the more so at the noisy emergence into the bigger room of the monk and his attendants, insisting that Sebastian lead her past the group to make her disdain obvious to everyone. After an hour she announced: 'And after our performance, I think it is time for us to depart.'

Which they did, and which Olga again staged, taking them directly in front of Rasputin and his coterie as if none of them existed. As they donned their cloaks, Olga said: 'One of the great advantages of a royal upbringing is the training in rendering unwanted people invisible.'

But she hadn't been invisible to Rasputin, Sebastian thought.

Olga had gained her corner of the coach seat by the time Sebastian followed. She patted that much which remained beside her and said: 'I wish you to sit beside me.'

Sebastian hesitated and then sat, putting himself in the opposite corner to ensure there was no contact between them, so much so that she was able to half-turn towards him.

She did so smiling. 'My father places great trust in you by not insisting upon a chaperone within the coach.'

'It will not be misplaced.'

'He would not have permitted such a liberty had he doubted that.' She continued to smile, a confident expression, across the half-darkened interior. 'It would be unthinkable for me to invite you into the palace when we reach it.'

'Unthinkable,' Sebastian agreed.

'There are disadvantages of being a princess.'

'I can understand that there are,' said Sebastian, believing he understood the exchange but remaining cautious.

'The most common belief is that they are inclined to break when touched.'

Sebastian's momentary hesitation was not at the obviousness of the remark, but at the abrupt recollection of a similar remark from Princess Anna Boinburg-Langesfeld before their ship-board affair. 'I have heard something very similar said before.'

'I'm sure you have.' She reached out to him, accepting his hand. 'You see? Every finger intact.'

He raised her gloved hand to his lips. 'I think I much prefer coaches to motor vehicles.'

'Don't have me make myself clearer.'

Olga came eagerly to him, responding to the tentative kiss, pulling his head towards her and exploring his face with her lips and tongue, and he explored back, bringing her into him so that her legs came over his to sit more comfortably.

When they parted, breathlessly, she said: 'Are you shocked?'

'No.'

'I am. At myself.'

'Don't be.'

'But happy. More happy than shocked at myself.'

He was happy, too, Sebastian accepted. Uncertain, as well, but curious at what was going to happen. She was holding herself very close to him, as he was to her, the long skirt of the black dress covering both of them. 'You didn't break.'

'I promised I wouldn't.'

Entangled as they were, Sebastian's left leg began to cramp. 'For what horse-drawn coaches gain in discretion they lack in comfort. In this situation, that is.'

'Then we must seek another place.'

The coach juddered into a rut and her weight, light though it was, numbed his leg further. 'Not an easy task.'

'But not insurmountable. My father will be home from Tsarskoye Selo tomorrow. Shall you call?'

'Of course.'

'I will have put some mind to our problem by then.'

'As I will.'

The coach perceptibly slowed and Olga said: 'We're nearing the palace.' She kissed him, once more, before pulling herself away from him and smoothing her skirts. Coquettishly she said: 'I think you should regain your proper seat, sir!'

'I think so, too,' Sebastian smiled back.

'Do I look like someone who has misbehaved in an enclosed coach?'

'You look the model of decorum.'

The coach trundled through the initial entrance and then even more noisily over the drawbridge to the inner enclosure. Sebastian disembarked ahead of Olga, to hand her down, and retained her hand politely to bend over to kiss it. Too softly for the attendant footmen to hear, Olga said: 'I prefer the more direct approach.'

'So do I,' said Sebastian, bringing himself up.

Whispering still, she said: 'Do you think of me as a harlot?'

'I think of you as exquisite.'

'Don't forget, I won't break.'

Where was this adventure going to lead, wondered Sebastian, back in the coach still redolent of Olga's perfume. But then his mind went back to the encounter with Rasputin and he began isolating what he had to report to London.

\* \* \*

'I don't like it!' declared Churchill.

'I like it even less,' said Mycroft Holmes. 'It's me to whom the communications have been identifiably addressed, using a diplomatic route.'

They were alone in Churchill's eyrie in Admiralty Arch. Churchill indicated on the desk between them Sebastian's warning that he had been recognized, and said: 'Sebastian's abandoned the embassy route, as of yesterday. We've already received his last shipment. There's nothing that's traceable to you.'

'Black put the packages in the diplomatic pouch. He can identify me as the addressee.'

'If the offence is the improper use of diplomatic facilities, then it is Captain Lionel Black who has committed it, which I doubt he'll readily confess.'

'We can't be sure of that,' argued Mycroft.

'We don't know that Sebastian's recognition will automatically lead to any question of his using the facility,' insisted the politician, building his argument. 'Sebastian presented my letter of introduction to an acquaintance. Sebastian is registered at the embassy and has enjoyed social introductions. There's nothing reprehensible in that.'

Mycroft wondered which of them Churchill was trying to reassure the most. 'Black is our weakness. And we know Sebastian doesn't trust the man.'

'It was through Sebastian that Black learned of the German spy presence and was able to warn London,' reminded Churchill, smiling at his own recollection. 'That overwhelmingly mitigates any improper use of the pouch.'

'We have a serious uncertainty,' insisted Mycroft.

'I think I might write again to Captain Black. Openly ask about the recognition of which Sebastian has advised us.'

'Which will disclose our concern.'

'Not at all,' disputed Churchill. 'It will prompt a response and bind Black into any wrong-doing, if indeed there is ever such an accusation. Sebastian innocently asked for a favour, which Black was in error for granting. Any explanation required from us will be irritating, nothing more.'

'I hope you are right,' said Mycroft, doubtfully.

# Nineteen

The Grand Duke was white-faced with fury, the colour – or lack of it – accentuated by the deep blackness of his beard. He went jerkily, without direction, around the trophy-stuffed study, needing movement in his rage. Sebastian, in his accustomed chair, was unsure now at the wiseness of telling the man of Rasputin's blatant sexual reference to his daughter.

Orlov stopped near his desk, his hands fidgeting. 'Olga did not tell me that; everything else, but not that.'

'I did not tell her,' said Sebastian.

'You are a true gentleman,' said Orlov, some of the tension going from him.

Sebastian thought of the previous night's return in the enclosed coach, and felt a twinge of hypocrisy, at the same time wondering when she would make her promised appearance. 'There was no purpose.'

'She also told me how you prevented her exposing herself to further ridicule by confronting the man, creating a spectacle. I thank you for that, too.'

'She was very angry, responding instinctively. It would have had the reverse effect from what she intended.'

'Rasputin knows of me, obviously,' said Orlov, finally coming to sit across from Sebastian. 'So, his remarks were a direct challenge, setting himself against me!'

'He did not refer to Olga by name, only by the colour of her dress,' said Sebastian.

Orlov appeared not to hear the qualification. 'He knows his strength; and of my contempt for him. And he knows I cannot move against him as I would against any other man, priest or otherwise, who exposed Olga to such humiliation.'

'If he had such confidence, he would have surely talked of

213

Olga by name?' persisted Sebastian. 'As it transpired, the humiliation was more Rasputin's, by the contempt with which Olga publicly disdained him in front of his followers.'

'What's Yusupov's game?' demanded Orlov, a question more to himself than Sebastian. 'Until these most recent weeks, I held him as a man of honour. Why does he choose even to acknowledge the man?'

'You knew the guest list in advance,' said Sebastian, in sudden, curious recollection. 'Olga remarked upon the number of people who did not attend, presumably because of prior knowledge of Rasputin's presence. Yet she also told me that you didn't know he would be there?'

Orlov nodded. 'All of which I've already considered, and which fuels my anger. Yusupov knows well enough the court had to approve the list, and that it had to be complete.'

'Could it have been that Yusupov believes, like many others believe, that Rasputin is beyond court restrictions?' suggested Sebastian.

'He's to be reminded to the contrary this very day!' declared Orlov, the quietness of the threat heightening the determination. 'Prince Felix Yusupov has become someone of great interest to me. Rasputin always has been. Now Rasputin will not have a waking or sleeping moment when I am unaware of with whom or where he is. If he has divine perception, I trust it will guard him against misadventure; absolute though my attention will be, neither I nor my people can be expected totally to protect him.'

'He was largely ostracized at the ball,' said Sebastian. 'There was only a small coterie around him. I do not know their names, of course.'

'I do,' declared Orlov. 'Olga recalled them all. As well as those who showed their disapproval by failing to attend. Each and every one of the acolytes who fawned around the man and thought his references to Olga so amusing have made themselves of special interest to me . . .' The older man lapsed into reflective silence, which Sebastian did not break, caught by the cold, whispered anger of the Okhrana commander.

'Was there any contact between Yusupov and Rasputin?' abruptly demanded the Russian.

'Not that I saw, at the ball, apart from the arrival courtesies. Yusupov attended the Grand Duchess. You remember, of course, that they were together at the Mariinsky.'

There was another prolonged silence, so long that Sebastian became uncomfortable, unable to quit the room, in which he began to feel unwelcome, tensed for the hoped for, relieving arrival of Olga. Then, as if awakening, Orlov straightened in the facing chair and said: 'Enough of this! We have other things to discuss: a definite evacuation proposal has to be established, understood by everyone.'

Sebastian felt another stir of unease. 'I hope to have established the outline of agreement, but anything further is beyond my capability. We are talking of arrangements of the highest delicacy that have to be established between London, its embassy here, and whomever else in the imperial court is to be included in the matter.'

'I am not imposing beyond what I know you can provide,' assured Orlov. 'What I want is to lay out a plan that can, through those you represent, be laid before your government and the King. That can be the point at which it leaves your hands, when it is discussed and refined and presented as an official decision to your embassy here.'

Orlov made it sound very straightforward: easy, almost, thought Sebastian. 'I infer you've got a detailed proposal already in mind?'

Orlov smiled, nodding. 'It has to be a sea-borne rescue, my initial idea. A British warship, with escorts. Sufficient provision for the Tsar and his family and as many of the court as possible.'

'That number to include Olga?' questioned Sebastian, openly for the first time.

'Unless she is persuaded to leave earlier.'

'She won't be,' said Sebastian, positively. 'I kept my undertaking. Tried to convince her. Her rejection was that she would only abandon Russia at your side.'

Orlov's smile now was sadly resigned. 'And I will not abandon Russia even as I put the imperial family within the safety of a British flotilla.

'Then you face a serious impasse,' judged Sebastian.

'Which I always expected,' agreed Orlov. 'But my personal difficulties cannot impede the major objective. There would possibly need to be an armed response, aboard the flotilla, although I seriously doubt any physical harm to the imperial family; not even an attempt, not in the immediate aftermath. The essential thing would be to get the family *out* of such potential risk as quickly as possible. My proposal includes your suggestion, to bring them in from Tsarskoye Selo to a city palace from which they could easily transfer to the sanctuary of the embassy, pending the arrival of the rescue fleet. Which will provide the opportunity for safe passage to be discussed and agreed.'

Altogether too straightforward and easy, Sebastian thought again, as the doubts and objections crowded in upon him. Confident enough now of his relationship with the Grand Duke openly to argue, Sebastian said: 'There are surely too many assumptions! The most obvious is that your plan predicates any overthrow, were it to come, to be in the ice-free summer when any ship or ships would be able to reach St Petersburg at all! The first revolution was triggered, literally, by the navy. What guarantee is there that the Russian navy will *allow* a British flotilla to enter Russian waters, with armed men aboard! Rather than accept it to be an evacuation mission, isn't the stronger likelihood that it would be seen as an invasion force to keep the Tsar in power! That's an objection I can foresee occupying British consideration . . .'

'I take your points, particularly that of winter,' broke in Orlov. 'My wish – what I see as my responsibility – is to establish an official commitment, beyond your unofficial assurance. Once that has been reached, alternatives can be devised and refined. I only look upon what we're discussing as a basis from which to work.'

'Without the authority of the Tsar? Or the knowledge of the Duma?'

'I need a strategy if the time ever comes to implement one!' said Orlov, betraying his desperation.

'I will report this conversation, setting out what you seek, without any observations of my own,' promised Sebastian. They'd hardly be necessary, he thought: Orlov had to be very

216

anxious indeed to press the idea. The need to avoid the slightest misunderstanding would make using Notions impossible. 'Do I have your guarantee of security, communicating through your London embassy?'

'Absolutely,' confirmed Orlov, without hesitation.

'Then I accept your offer of its use,' said Sebastian. He still had much material of his own to relay to London, he remembered.

'Olga asked me to apologize for her absence,' abruptly announced Orlov. 'There was an invitation to Tsarskoye Selo, after her meeting with the Grand Duchess last night. She asks if you would call upon her tomorrow. She is promising an outing.'

'With your permission,' said Sebastian, uncomfortably.

'I think you've well earned my trust,' said Orlov.

He didn't, thought Sebastian.

'There's unquestionably a conspiracy of the highest importance afoot,' declared Sherlock Holmes.

'Unquestionably,' agreed Churchill, at his palace-view window in Admiralty Arch. 'What's the Swiss intention?'

'To do nothing, unless Lenin breaks any local law. Which he remains careful to avoid doing,' answered Sherlock Holmes. 'Their hope is that Lenin and his group will soon choose another European location for their plotting.'

'What of von Hagel?' asked Mycroft.

'He's a diplomatically accredited diplomat to Switzerland,' replied Sherlock Holmes. 'In view of the publicity that Lenin is attracting, I suggested a discreet newspaper leak of his association with a man expelled from America for spying, but got a very cold response. The Swiss are not seeking any sensations.'

'How are we going to get this discovery into the official domain here, so that it can be fitted into the mosaic?' questioned Churchill. 'Yet again we're hamstrung by our own knowledge.'

'And what of the uncertain Captain Black?' said Mycroft, posing a question to a question.

'I've had no reply to my letter,' said Churchill.

217

'Why don't we further his career even more?' suggested Mycroft. 'We know he's charged with officially investigating the German presence in St Petersburg. Sebastian could pass on Sherlock's Swiss findings to have Black officially advise London as if they were his, gained through his own sources.' Aware of his brother's face clouding at the prospect of losing the credit, Mycroft said: 'Expediency, Sherlock! It's the means to an end.'

'Black's end, as far as his career is concerned, if the damned recognition endangers Sebastian in any way,' threatened the detective.

Sebastian's announcement – coded in a combination of Notions and ziphs – of his new method of communication, with the packages addressed to his father, was waiting upon his telegraph when Mycroft returned to the Diogenes Club.

Sebastian wrote in open script, his mind shifting between thoughts as he moved from his own impressions and conclusions of the previous evening to the virtually verbatim account of his meeting with Grand Duke Alexei Orlov. He decided that Rasputin had to have known Olga for who she was. The priest had full access to the royal palace at Tsarskoye Selo, as Olga appeared to have; she was even there now! No matter how vast the palace or how separated its apartments, it was inconceivable they would not have encountered each other, at some time or another. So last night's episode was the challenge Orlov was taking it to be. Had Orlov meant that Rasputin was aware of his being the head of the Okhrana when he'd said the priest knew who he was? Or just that the awareness was of his being a senior, royal member of the court? It was a vital distinction. If Rasputin knew Orlov to be head of the Tsar's secret police, then it was a staggering indication of how secure – and royally protected – the mystic considered himself to be. And of how inwardly decayed the Romanov dynasty had become.

Sebastian worked late into the afternoon, rewriting and refining his reports, curious, when he finished, as to London's reaction to how his material would be reaching them in the future, one reflection prompting another. His accounts – certainly this package – would be totally secure, although he had to accept that Orlov would intercept and copy everything for his own translation and information. But Orlov would ensure himself to be the only one; the very revolution the man was trying to anticipate could be precipitated if anyone else gained sight of what he was sending to London. Sebastian was unsure what sort of reassurance that was; if, in fact, it was any reassurance at all.

There scarcely seemed to be a ring from the other end before Captain Black snatched up the receiver with his customary curt self-identification. When Sebastian identified himself in return, the military attaché said: 'I was just about to call you.'

'You've established some spy links from the photographs!' anticipated Sebastian.

'I'm afraid not. Only Vogel thus far.'

The man was lying, accepted Sebastian. The circumstances hadn't been right earlier that day, to ask Orlov if his organization's observers had made any further identifications. 'I'm disappointed.'

'So am I.'

'You've compared every one?'

'No. We're matching against the published diplomatic list. There's still seven to be excluded.'

Sebastian supposed he should give the other man the benefit of the doubt but didn't. 'How much longer do you think it will take?'

'Another day. Two at the most,' said Black, irritatingly dismissive. Then: 'I had a letter from Winston, asking if there were any difficulties with the transmission facilities. I've told him no.'

'I've made alternative arrangements,' reminded Sebastian. 'I'll stick with them now.'

'There's no reason!' protested Black, at once. 'Nothing whatsoever's been said. The Berringers are even talking of another outing: making up a bigger party to introduce you to more people. The son of the famous Sherlock Holmes is quite a catch!'

An invitation he supposed he'd have to accept, thought

219

Sebastian, despite knowing it wouldn't lead him any closer to solving the uncertainty of a spy within the British embassy. An uncertainty created by Alexander Kerensky, with whom he still had a scheduled meeting, Sebastian reminded himself. 'It's been established now. I'll look forward to more socializing, though.'

'Whatever your alternative, it can't be as secure as the diplomatic bag!' persisted the attaché.

'Safe enough,' countered Sebastian. There was a perversely juvenile enjoyment in denying a man whom he believed to be denying him.

'I'm sorry there's been this misunderstanding,' capitulated the attaché.

'I don't consider it to be that.'

'I'll be in touch about the Berringer party.'

'What about the German embassy observation?' seized Sebastian.

'That too,' hurried the other man. 'Of course, I'll speak to you in the next day or two about that.'

Sebastian was sure he could predict the conversation.

# Twenty

'Congratulations, sir, upon your success at the Cowes Regatta,' flattered Herbert Asquith, judging his weekly audience with King George V to be nearing its end without his being challenged on anything he'd recounted from the cabinet.

'It was capital sailing,' said the King, leaning forward over his Buckingham Palace desk, at which he preferred to conduct his regular meetings with the Liberal Prime Minister. 'I studied everything that was sent in the box, though.'

'I am sure you did, sir,' said the politician.

'You got my message about this German business, in St Petersburg?'

'It's a positive identification at the German embassy there of one of their diplomats expelled from the United States for unacceptable behaviour: conspiring to obtain weaponry and suspicion of espionage,' replied Asquith, glad he hadn't ignored Stamfordham's memorandum, which it had been his first irritated intention to do.

'What's our embassy there make of that?'

'We haven't received any assessment, yet,' said the broad-featured, fair-haired politician. 'Grey's asked for more information and an opinion.'

'Why is it so important for Wilhelm to equal our fleet, practically ship for ship?'

'The feeling is that the Kaiser sees it as a matter of pride, matching Great Britain as an imperial power.'

'Do you think there's any likelihood of aggression?'

'Not directly. That's unthinkable.'

'What about contributory events?'

'I can't foresee any at the moment.'

'It was a bold move from Mr Churchill, bringing the

221

Mediterranean fleet home for North Sea exercises, don't you think?'

Asquith stifled any hint of the irritation which he persistently felt with the First Lord. 'He felt a public display of our sea power was justified.'

'But you don't?' demanded the King, perceptively.

'I think it might have been interpreted as provocative.' Taking advantage of the opportunity, Asquith went on: 'Mr Churchill proposed directing the returning fleet to the north of the Isle of Wight, during the Cowes Regatta, for a royal sail past in your honour, sir. I did not consider advising you after being advised by our admirals at Portsmouth that the depth of water going through the Solent into Spithead and then back out into the Channel was insufficient for dreadnoughts.'

The King erupted into laughter. 'Dreadnoughts among sailing yachts! It would have been chaos, Asquith! Carnage even.'

'Quite so, sir. Mr Churchill sometimes acts ahead of necessary thought.'

'It would have been a spectacle, though, wouldn't it!'

'And possible carnage, as you rightly point out.'

'What's the guidance from our embassy in St Petersburg on the political situation there?' demanded the bearded monarch, abruptly serious. 'Have things settled down after 1905?'

'I've received no information to the contrary,' said Asquith, frowning. 'Would you allow me the impertinence to ask if there has been any private correspondence that has prompted this conversation?'

'From Nicky to me?' questioned the King, shaking his head. 'No. Had a conversation with Stamfordham, after that embassy message, that's all. What would the government's view be upon sanctuary, if the question ever arose?'

'For the Romanovs?' queried Asquith, making no attempt to conceal his astonishment at the question.

'Yes.'

It was not the first time that the King's private secretary had intruded into things that did not concern him, thought Asquith. 'I assure you, sir, that I am mindful of the relationships as well as friendships that exist between your two families. But to receive the Russian imperial family in exile would need serious and detailed consideration. There is unrest in Europe, although I do not believe it will erupt into conflict. If it did, it could result in the upheaval of several royal households, the Hapsburgs the most obvious. If there were conflict, we would be bound by treaty obligations, some of which link us to Russia, whose support as an ally we would need. As we would need continued good relations with any succeeding government in the event of the Tsar's overthrow, which might not be forthcoming if we accepted the imperial family in exile. And there would perhaps be an additional question of other royal households who might look to us for sanctuary.'

'That's a forceful observation,' said the King.

'But a very necessary one, sir,' said Asquith, with unaccustomed boldness. 'We face the prospect of civil war in Ireland. And there is great unrest throughout the country, as I continue to report to you, at the activities of the women's suffrage movement.'

'I find it difficult to include the suffragettes in this discussion,' objected the King. 'I'm not totally convinced we should be continuing to deny women their franchise.'

'In the opinion of your government, it would be unwise,' insisted the Prime Minister, who was the foremost opponent of female emancipation, and was coming under increased pressure, from both inside as well as outside his party, at the publicity-attracting demonstrations that were gaining public support for their cause.

'Put some thought to the Russian situation,' demanded the King. 'I don't want us to be found wanting, if a situation arises.'

'I must stress, sir, that there is not the slightest indication of that occurring.'

'And I do not doubt for a moment that your judgement is sound, Prime Minister. But I would like to discuss it further, when you have had the opportunity for some cabinet consideration upon what comes from St Petersburg.'

'Of course, sir.'

'Imagine!' chuckled the King, the discussion over. 'Dreadnoughts competing for space against twelve-metre

223

yachts! I'd have risked overthrow myself from the Royal Yacht Squadron.'

'Got a cold response from Asquith,' disclosed the King. 'Dismissed out of hand the thought of any danger to Nicky or the Russian throne.'

'Had there been previous discussion, sir?' asked Lord Stamfordham.

'Nothing.'

'I'm surprised the Prime Minister was able to be so positive without receiving guidance from St Petersburg.'

'Surely a mark of a competent Prime Minister?'

'If such instant judgement is accurate,' heavily qualified the private secretary.

King George gave no reaction at the easily interpreted innuendo. 'I've asked for a more considered opinion.'

'Second thoughts are always wise.'

'What of you, Stamfordham? What are your feelings?'

'I would imagine the Tsar would expect to be received here hospitably, if a disaster befell him.'

'You move in appropriate places. Have you picked up word of instability on the scale that we're discussing?'

'No, sir. An occasional suggestion,' allowed the secretary, guardedly.

'Ask around. See if there is any talk of it.'

'You would surely require more than club gossip.'

'Not to stir Asquith. There are times I feel the man patronizes me.'

'I'm sure that suspicion is unfounded, sir,' said Stamfordham, who knew it was not.

'Ask around,' repeated the King.

'There are some to whom I might address the question.'

'Have you heard of a proposal by Mr Churchill to stage a royal sail past of the Mediterranean fleet in my honour during the Cowes Regatta?'

'A what?' exclaimed the incredulous secretary.

'Up the Solent and back out through Spithead.'

'Good God!' Immediately embarrassed at the outburst, Stamfordham hurriedly added: 'No, sir. I had not heard.'

'Asquith's spreading the story. He's not an admirer of Mr Churchill. Nor, do I understand, is Mr Churchill an admirer of Mr Asquith.'

'It'll gain in the telling,' predicted Stamfordham. 'Willingly or otherwise, Mr Churchill attracts attention.'

'Schedule it for cabinet discussion, Holmes. Grey's sent a full brief to the embassy.'

'Yes, sir,' said Mycroft. He was surprised at the lack of any inner turmoil, even though he accepted that he was the direct cause of Asquith's flurried activity since his return from the palace.

'There's something underhand afoot,' insisted the Prime Minister. 'I'll wager it's that confounded man Stamfordham, who exceeds his position whenever there's an opportunity.'

'I understood him to be a very competent secretary to the King,' ventured Mycroft.

'The man's a meddler! We've got far too much to occupy us domestically to worry about events and situations that will never arise in Europe or Russia.'

'It will be interesting when the opinions come in from the embassies,' suggested Mycroft. 'I presume Grey is canvassing the Balkans? Vienna even?'

Asquith frowned. 'I haven't asked him to.'

'The Balkans is the tinderbox.'

'Memo Grey. Ask him to extend the remit beyond what I've already requested.'

'I'll do so immediately,' promised the Cabinet Secretary. 'Were you inconvenienced, returning from the palace, by the women who've chained themselves to the railings outside?'

'Of course I was!' said the Prime Minister, irritably.

'The Home Secretary called, while you were with the King. One of the suffragettes has gone on hunger strike. He pointed out that there would be great public disquiet if she were to die.'

'Get him for me on the telephone. We've got to ensure at all costs that that doesn't happen.'

# Twenty-One

The comparison was unavoidable, which Sebastian at once guessed to be Olga's intention, although the river steamer fell far short in every way from any similarity with the *Lusitania*, upon which they had first met. It was stubby-prowed, with only three funnels, although there was a brave if discordant attempt at a departure band, and a few dispirited, limp bunting flags.

'You have your own steam yacht!' protested Sebastian.

'With a too attentive crew.'

'You choose to embarrass me,' lightly complained Sebastian, playing to Olga's mood.

'It could be a dangerous strategy if there's another princess on board.'

'I won't make the same mistake again,' said Sebastian, meaning it. Olga wore a shimmering blue, tight-bodiced dress with a full skirt that swished and sighed with every movement, her hat held by a lighter blue gauze over-scarf that perfectly matched the colour of her parasol.

They moved from the shadow of the carriage, in which they'd initially stood watching the embarkation pier, and joined the shuffle to board, Sebastian alert to everyone and everything around them, glad that he'd decided upon impulse to carry the swordstick for the first time in several days, weeks even.

As they climbed the gangway, Sebastian said: 'What's our ship called?'

Olga looked towards the Cyrillic on the lifeboat. 'The best translation is *Flight of Fancy*.'

'I wonder if it will be.'

'So do I.'

Aboard, Olga led confidently through a restricted divide on the port side of the vessel, where their tickets were closely examined, announcing when they reached the rail that that was the best side from which to view the centre of St Petersburg from the river vantage point. 'All the way along the river there are romantic bridges – drawbridges sometimes, to let us pass – before we get to the Fontanka River itself.'

'This clearly is not your first excursion.'

'Always before with a governess or chaperone; unlike most people in court, my father has never believed in keeping me apart from the people.'

Sebastian gestured back to the guarded entrance through which they'd passed. 'First-class people.'

'You're mocking me again!'

'The mockery is much more yours today.'

'Are you angry?'

'You know I'm not.'

'It's not possible to make a luncheon reservation until boarding,' prompted Olga.

'I'll do so immediately, if you'll excuse me.'

'On this side.'

'Of course.'

'And a day cabin,' she said.

Sebastian remained looking at her, both serious-faced for the first time since their meeting that morning, after Sebastian had handed over to the Grand Duke his sealed package for delivery to London. 'Day cabins can only be reserved by people who have boarded?'

'That's right,' said Olga.

'Do you believe we're alone, even though there is no governess or chaperone?'

'Trust me.'

'Or that I would for a moment compromise you?'

'I always rest in the afternoon.'

'I regret my lapse in the coach.'

'I don't believe you do, any more than I do. And stop spoiling the outing with your irritating gallantry!'

The thought avalanched in upon Sebastian, so completely that it briefly obliterated everything else from his mind. He still didn't know Olga Orlov well enough to be sure – doubted that he ever would – but he was seized by the idea that she was as free-thinking and as uninhibited and as careless of the opinion of others as his unknown mother had been.

The concept must have shown upon Sebastian's face because Olga frowned and said: 'What is it?'

'Nothing,' denied Sebastian, hurriedly. 'An impression . . . something that fleetingly crossed my mind . . . it was nothing.'

'Are you sure?' She was still frowning.

'Quite sure. I should make the reservations.'

'Yes, you should.'

The first-class dining salon was far more luxurious than Sebastian had anticipated, chandeliered and with crisp linen and glittering cristal. Sebastian secured a table on the recommended side, next to a substantial porthole, and had champagne put on ice. He hesitated, in the purser's square, before thrusting forward to get a day cabin, again on the port side.

Olga was waiting where he had left her, gazing beyond the rail at the grandeur that was the outward face of St Petersburg. She turned at his arrival. 'Is everything arranged?'

'Yes.'

'*Everything?*'

'Yes.'

There was a sudden siren shriek and a surge of the engines, and the river boat cast off, its course taking it directly before the Winter Palace and its enormous fronting square. Olga played the tourist guide, identifying the bridges beneath which they passed – some of which, as promised, parted at their approach – and the legends of some of the more prominent and historic houses. When they were in distant view of the passage to the Gulf of Finland, Sebastian tried and failed to imagine a waiting British rescue flotilla, curious as to London's reaction to what he had dispatched that morning. They were among the first in the dining salon, lingering over their champagne to choose their caviar and fish.

'I didn't see Rasputin at Tsarskoye Selo,' Olga unexpectedly announced. 'The palace is enormous. The Grand Duchess has her own apartment suite.'

'Your father believes Rasputin knew who you were.'

'He told me.'

'What do you believe?'

She shrugged. 'I'm not sure. I do know that he's made a formidable enemy in my father.'

'It's difficult to imagine someone like Rasputin possessing the power and authority he seems to command.'

'The Tsar and Tsarina are in total thrall to the man. The Grand Duchesses Olga and Tatiana are terrified in his presence, making any excuse to avoid him.'

He scarcely needed any more confirmation of the weakness of the Romanov rule, Sebastian decided. It would be interesting to explore in greater depth the British embassy feeling if he were invited to any more social events, as Black was promising. Was it something he might even introduce during his next meeting with Alexander Kerensky, whose second, hoped-for invitation had that morning been forcefully slipped beneath his door, as before, to not be visible from the outside corridor.

Their conversation slowed as their meal came to an end.

Olga said: 'There is little to see along this part of the river. And sometimes it is very windy.'

'Aren't you concerned at the hidden eyes?'

'No.'

'I think . . .'

'Stop!'

He was endangering more than Olga's reputation and his own integrity, Sebastian recognized. He was risking the wrath – family banishment – of a father upon whom he'd allowed himself to become increasingly dependent. 'Do you wish to go ahead of me?'

'That would be best.'

Sebastian kept the key completely concealed as he pushed it along the banquette towards her. Olga accepted it just as discreetly, managing at the same time to slightly caress his fingers with hers. Sebastian rose politely at her departure, signalling for the bill but lingering before paying it, accusing himself of each and every despicable foolishness, all the time knowing that he was going to keep the assignation. He paused immediately upon attaining the open deck, attentive for anyone who followed from the dining salon and who might keep in step when he climbed to the higher deck, but isolated no one. Nor did he when he descended, not stopping until he reached the covered section, continuing on until he gained the cabin level, grateful that the alleyway was deserted in both directions and stayed so as he quickly entered the cabin.

Olga had removed the hat and loosened her hair for it to fall to her shoulders, but was fully dressed, standing close to the curtained porthole. She said: 'You were a long time.'

'I went on deck. You're right. It's windy.'

'You won't have seen them,' guessed Olga, presciently. 'You only see them if they want you to see them, so that you know. I told you, I don't care.'

Sebastian didn't either, not any more. He reached out for her and she stretched forward for him and he pulled her to him and it was better than the side-by-side awkwardness in the coach, both searching, mouthing, hands feeling, touching.

Pulling very slightly away, Olga said: 'Undress me. I want you to undress me and then I want to undress you. But slowly. Very slowly.'

Sebastian did, hindered anyway by so many buttons and hooks and straps, letting her clothes puddle where they fell, enjoying the hesitation of something silk that caught on her breasts, and something else that needed tugging over her hips, until she was unashamedly, proudly naked, holding herself to be looked at and admired and wanted.

Thick-voiced Sebastian said: 'You are truly, wonderfully breathtaking.'

'Now you,' she insisted, heavy-voiced as well. 'Now it's your turn.'

She took her time too, unfastening every button, holding his eyes, smiling, putting her hands inside his clothes to ease them from him, wincing at the scar from the attempted American assassination, but quickly leaning forward to kiss it, trailing her tongue along it. When he was totally naked, she said: 'And you are truly, wonderfully, breathtaking.'

Sebastian knelt, bringing her to his face and his tongue, and she mewed and slightly parted her legs, cupping his head tightly against her, holding it there, until she began to shake, unable to remain upright any longer, lowering herself and more widely splaying herself upon the sheeted chaise longue. She relaxed her grip slightly but not enough to release his head from where it was, twitching and arcing and groaning more loudly now at the sensation.

'Me!' she demanded at last. 'I want to taste you, too,' and swivelled and enclosed him with her lips and murmured with the pleasure of it, and then in brief, sharp disappointment when he withdrew to turn to face her, for a moment keeping himself suspended over her. She still had him cupped between both hands, guiding him, eyes wide at the first nuzzling touch, her lower lip between her teeth at his proper entry, hands behind him now, forcing him hard into her, giving a tiny scream at the fullness of it. Almost at once they found their perfect, easy, unhurried rhythm and Olga said: 'Oh that's good: so very, very good.'

'And for me.'

She said: 'I don't want it ever to end . . . I want it to go on forever.'

He said: 'Yes, it must go on forever,' and it did, longer than he thought he would be able, so excited was he.

It was Olga who quickened, bucking beneath him, and he matched her urgency again and their climax was a simultaneous explosion, and she cried out again, louder, raking his back with her nails, and they desperately clung together, wanting to keep every shuddering moment. They remained like that, wetly glued to each other, for a long time, neither willing to break.

At last Sebastian said: 'We have to get dressed.'

'I don't want to.'

'We must.' He carefully eased himself away, despite her clamping legs, kissing her breasts and trailing downward, but was abruptly stopped by a swirl of confusion. He knew she'd broken the skin of his back with her raking nails, and began to think, before blocking the thought, that the blood was his, and was overwhelmed by knowing it wasn't. 'You should—'

'What?'

'I didn't know.'

'Why should you have known?'

231

'Did I hurt you?'

'Exquisitely. More exquisitely than I'd ever imagined.'

'I'm—'

'Don't say you're sorry,' she halted him, with yet another of her quick interventions.

'I wasn't going to. I was going to thank you, for it being me.'

'It was a fantasy, from the voyage . . . why I planned it to happen on another, limited though it was.'

'Can I do anything?'

Olga tested herself against an unmarked part of the covering sheet. 'It's stopped.'

'You're sure you're not hurt?'

'Just pleasantly reminded.' She smiled at him. 'There are lots of buttons and hooks. You'd better start helping me.'

Lord Stamfordham was waiting for Mycroft Holmes just beyond the porter's lodge of the Travellers Club in Pall Mall, coming forward in immediate greeting.

'Though this would be mutually convenient,' said the King's secretary. 'About the same walking distance for both of us.'

'Well chosen,' agreed Mycroft, following the other man into the library. Their discreet table was clearly held for them, although until that moment Mycroft hadn't believed it was possible to reserve such places. Both ordered whisky.

With a directness that surprised Mycroft, Stamfordham said: 'How was the King's request received?'

'Unwelcomed,' replied Mycroft, matching the directness.

'But acted upon?'

'Of course. And expanded, to bring in reactions from our Balkan legations. And Austria.'

'That's wise,' nodded the other man.

'Was the King receptive?'

'His words were that he did not want to be caught wanting.'

'I need your assessment of that remark,' said Mycroft.

'The King prefers measured responses, after as much and as wide a guidance as is available.'

That was more guarded than he'd judged the man to be on the Isle of Wight, decided Mycroft. 'His guidance will surely be restricted to that of the Prime Minister?'

'There are a selected, well-trusted number from the Privy Council.'

'From whom it will be opinion, without the benefit of ambassadorial response?'

'Which is largely the purpose of the Privy Council,' reminded the secretary. 'What do you think of Churchill's proposal?'

'What proposal?' demanded Mycroft, apprehensively.

Sniggering in advance of his anecdote, Stamfordham recounted the suggested Isle of Wight sail past of the Mediterranean fleet, intent upon the Cabinet Secretary's response. Mycroft laughed, dutifully, but said: 'I hadn't heard it proposed.' Which he was sure he would have done, either from the man himself or during cabinet discussion.

'It's the story of the week in every club,' insisted Stamfordham.

'I'm sure it is,' said Mycroft.

Stamfordham rose, bringing Mycroft up with him. 'Tuesday's special is steak and kidney pie, topped with an oyster. I recommend it.'

Would it be possible to pursuade the man to recommend something more positive in Russia? wondered Mycroft.

'No doubt whatsoever?' demanded the ambassador.

'Absolutely none, sir,' said Lionel Black, offering the photographs of the three expelled Germans identified from the American photographs.

'I've personally double-checked all three,' assured Roger Jefferson. The two attachés were side by side in Sir Nigel Pearlman's study.

'Any evidence of their engaging in anything subversive?'

'We don't have the facilities to mount that sort of surveillance,' said the military attaché.'

'We couldn't risk our interest becoming obvious,' said the naval attaché, supportively.

'Of course not,' quickly agreed the ambassador. 'These are hard facts, though. Something very positive to give to London.' He looked directly at Black. 'What about your source who alerted you?'

'Nothing more, I'm afraid,' said the younger man.

'Don't let up on this,' instructed Pearlman. 'This has the very highest priority. Our response has got to be one hundred per cent accurate.'

To provide the ambassador with his homecoming sinecure in the Foreign Office, thought Black. And mine in the War Office, he mentally added.

They'd remained in the day cabin until the river steamer was actually tied up against its pier, reluctant to surrender the intimacy, their last act each to examine the other to ensure they were as immaculately dressed as when they'd entered, and for Sebastian to leave a fifty-rouble note on top of the laundry basket in which they'd bundled the stained sheet.

So late were they leaving, that the outside corridor was again deserted, but they still left separately, Sebastian joining Olga in the purser's square for them to approach the gangway together. At its top, Sebastian hesitated, gesturing for Olga to precede him, looking down at the quayside as he did so. He saw someone at the bottom and at once held Olga back for other stragglers to go ahead of them.

'What is it?' demanded Olga.

'Someone I don't want to encounter,' said Sebastian, from the concealment of a lifeboat, from behind which he was still able perfectly to see a disembarking Ludmilla Berringer in animated, gesticulating conversation with the man with the upright bantam-cock hair to whom he'd been forced to apologize in an Okhrana prison cell.

'She was at the garden party,' recognized Olga, beside him. 'A diplomat's wife. But that isn't her husband.'

'No,' said Sebastian. 'It's not.'

# Twenty-Two

Because he feared the warning message about the Okhrana informant within the British embassy could too easily be deciphered simply from Notions, Sebastian additionally encoded it into ziphs. The transmission, through the Grand Hotel telegraph, read: AANGTII COOLLGEEGEE OOAGATH CHIISEGELLEER IIDEENTGIIFIIEED. As he watched it being tapped out by the resigned telegraphist, Sebastian remained uneasy at how simply it might be broken by a trained cipher analyst, until he reassured himself at the lack of a formula for what amounted to not one but two codes. Its translation was *Anti College Oath chiseller identified*, College Oath being, he hoped, an obvious reference to embassy allegiance, and chiseller, although with an obvious definition, a Notions word for a cheat or deceiver.

Back in his suite after the transmission, Sebastian hunched over the paper-strewn bureau, re-examining what he had concluded. And he satisfied himself there could be no doubt. Ludmilla Berringer had to be the Okhrana spy whom Kerensky had hinted at: certainly the most important, if there were more than one. Because of her husband's position, Ludmilla would have access to virtually everything of importance passing to and from London. Which Grand Duke Alexei Orlov would know full well. Didn't it follow that the *chef du protocol*'s wife was equally well informed in return? Of course not, Sebastian contradicted himself at once. Orlov's trade was obtaining information, from each and every quarter, and from it creating his own pictures, not offering any exchange other than what it suited him to plant. For money if necessary. Was Ludmilla Berringer motivated by financial reward? Sebastian found that difficult to paint into his own picture, particularly if the woman expected

235

to be the next ambassador's first lady. Which answered an uncertainty, Sebastian at once acknowledged. How well established would a fervently opinionated husband-and-wife ambassadorial duo believe themselves to be, albeit naively, in a country in which one of them had an open conduit to the head of the Tsar's security service? Very securely, Sebastian answered himself. It had to be the Berringers prompting the feeling within the embassy – and being passed on to London – that no threat existed against the Romanovs. Which went against everything he was telling Churchill and his father and uncle. So who would be believed? The embassy, unquestionably: theirs was the assessment that had to be believed. Something else that Orlov would know well enough. As he would know how to manipulate and utilize that to his benefit. So what was Orlov's intention, feeding such total contradictions? Back to back insurances, guaranteeing influence within the British embassy if he were successful in keeping the Tsar in power, but with an escape route if he failed? In the mindset of secret police and covert intelligence, that had a convoluted rationale, but fell at the first hurdle of logic: Sebastian decided, objectively, that whatever he was supplying to London would be dismissed – diminished at least – by official embassy judgement. So that couldn't be Orlov's intention. What then? He was relying too much and too closely upon guesswork and surmise, Sebastian recognized. How could he even half reach a conclusion based upon what little dependable information he had to work upon! He actually regretted, now, sending to London the message that he had, unquestionably accurate though it basically was. He should have waited; given himself more time for this limited reflection, inconclusive though it remained.

There was much else to reflect upon, what had happened between himself and Olga the most intrusive, persistently nagging distraction. The affair aboard the *Lusitania* with Princess Anna Boinburg-Langesfeld had been an adventure, regarded as nothing more than that by either of them, quite apart from her later emergence as a German agent. He didn't in any shape or form look upon what had happened that day between himself and Olga as an uncomplicated adventure. What then? he asked himself again. He didn't have an answer for that either. Olga had given herself to him – openly confessed her fantasy – but not wantonly or carelessly, despite her total lack of inhibition: surrendered herself in each and every ultimate way, as someone would who was in love. As someone would, he thought, once more, who shared the unconventional attitude and thinking of his unknown mother. Whom his father had loved, totally, in return. Did he love Olga? Another unanswerable question. He'd never known love from anyone – nothing that he'd understood or recognized as love – so he didn't have any signs, any criteria. Didn't imagine that it was possible to decide – to fall in love or be in love – after just one intimacy, exquisite though that intimacy had been. How long did it take to realize or decide? To be sure? That was, he supposed, the purpose of courtship, the period of growing familiarity. What more did he need to know – could he know – about Olga Orlov? Nothing; nothing that came to mind.

In a rush, like the sudden opening of a sobering sluice of ice-chilled water, reality descended upon Sebastian. What was he thinking – allowing himself to imagine or contemplate? Olga was a princess, of a bloodline going back possibly centuries, judging from the ancestral portraits at the Orlov palace. And he was a legally illegitimate commoner. They had been brought together by bizarre circumstances, and Olga had fulfilled her fantasy, and for him to try to speculate beyond that was a fantasy on his part, a totally unrealistic, unfulfillable, penny fiction fantasy.

The shrill of the telephone startled Sebastian, physically bringing him back to actuality. Captain Black said: 'This is my third attempt. Thank God I've got you at last. I need to see you at once.'

The military attaché was waiting with visible impatience at the gatehouse to hurry Sebastian through, announcing the identification of the three German spies as they crossed the inner courtyard to the man's office. Directly inside, Black at once locked the door, something he had never done before.

'Three!' he repeated, excitedly. 'What do you think about that?'

'Something you should certainly advise London about,' said Sebastian, calmly. The three – Hans Vogel, now Wolfgang Brecht – Fritz Langer and Konrad Blum – were those whom Orlov had identified days before and whose photographs were now laid out like exhibits on the attaché's desk. How long would it be before Black disclosed the reason for this belated, originally unintended offering?

'I have,' said Black.

Had it been entirely Black's discovery, without any assistance from the naval attaché? Pointedly Sebastian said: 'Surprising that all three should have remained unidentified until the last seven.'

Momentarily Black appeared confused, before remembering their last conversation. 'Incredible! It's caused a total uproar at the embassy . . .' The man separated his forefingers one above the other, to create at least a two-inch gap. 'We've got personally authorized demands and questions and instructions from Sir Edward Grey at least that thick!' There was a pause. 'As well as some from the Prime Minister himself!'

The most obvious reason for the hurried telephone call and the German identification, judged Sebastian. 'What's caused such a furore?'

'That's obvious, surely! There's something going on.'

It was almost an impossibly fortuitous opportunity, so close behind his earlier sighting of Ludmilla Berringer. 'How's it being judged at the embassy?'

'We need more!' insisted the overly eager soldier. 'Let's be honest with each other, Holmes. Ours hasn't been the easiest of relationships. Maybe I've tried too hard to intrude into your remit, and if I've offended you – put you at a distance because of it – then I apologize. I'm asking for your help now; not for myself but for our country. That's the level at which it's being treated at the embassy.'

'*How* is it being treated?' insisted Sebastian. This was another potential gold seam that had to be sifted and sieved for every conceivable grain.

Black frowned. 'I've just told you.'

'What's the considered conclusion?' persisted Sebastian.

'I thought I'd told you that, too,' protested Black, just failing to suppress the obvious impatience. 'I've got to prepare a report on the significance of the German sightings. That's what I need, to be able to suggest the importance of three proven · German spies here in St Petersburg.'

It was difficult for Sebastian, who thought they'd verged on such a conversation before, not openly to wince. Doggedly continuing upon his chosen path, Sebastian said: 'There must be an opinion already reached?'

'The obvious, certainly. But there's conflicting opinion.'

A diplomatic answer, words without meaning, thought Sebastian. 'Surely the significance is self-evident?' suggested Sebastian.

'Not to some,' complained Black.

'What are the Berringers saying?' asked Sebastian.

'That it's being blown up out of proportion,' disclosed Black, indiscreetly, but showing no surprise at Sebastian's directness.

He most definitely didn't need any further confirmation of what Ludmilla Berringer had been doing aboard the river ferry with an Okhrana official: he'd been provided, if it were necessary, with the final proof. And with it came the final, staggering realization – he surely had to be right! – of the web in which he had been entangled. And with it the gouging awareness of how so very close he had been to missing the Machiavellian manoeuvrings of the Grand Duke Alexei Orlov. Ludmilla Berringer had been sacrificed that day, whatever use she'd been in the past fulfilled. He had been *meant* to encounter her – confront her even – with someone he would recognize, precisely and intentionally to undermine all the assurances and guidance London had been receiving – and were still in danger of receiving – in which Orlov no longer believed.

'You've grown quiet, sir!' accused Black.

'With good reason,' said Sebastian. The military attaché's position within the embassy hierarchy was too low for him to initiate any open confrontation.

'I very much hope it suits my purpose.'

Sebastian sat in Black's regimentally decorated and picture-lined office, silently regarding the man across his regimentally ordered desk, hesitating as the intention – and its unpredictable repercussions – formed in his mind, at the same time remembering his suspicions about Black himself, which might even provide a second test. 'I need your assurance that you did not identify me as the original source identifying Hans Vogel.'

'I have already given you that.'

'Your reassurance then.'

'You have it.'

'Do you report direct to London? Or do your communications go through a chain, to be considered – vetted even – by a superior?'

'I report direct, but duplicate everything for the ambassador's eventual attention,' said Black, attentively forward over his desk. 'I understand that isn't the normal procedure. It's a personal innovation of Sir Nigel's. It makes people responsible for their own information and judgements, absolving him but giving him the opportunity to comment. He's very determined nothing will impede his Foreign Office reassignment.'

Sebastian hesitated for a second time before announcing. 'There's an Okhrana informant within your embassy, being fed misinformation, upon which the opinions of the embassy are being formed, and – unchallenged, I would assume, by the ambassador – are being conveyed to London.'

Black's mouth physically dropped, his throat working but no words forming. When they did, they were stuttered, utterances but not sentences. 'I . . . no . . . that's not . . . I couldn't . . . that's . . . no . . .'

'I've already alerted Churchill,' declared Sebastian.

'Who?' demanded Black, recovering. 'I can't make such an outrageous accusation without knowing who . . . having evidence to substantiate it. Incontrovertible evidence to substantiate it . . .'

'I'm making the accusation!' reminded Sebastian. 'I'm not proposing your being so positive, not initially. I'm proposing you *suggest* it.'

'The effect will be the same. There will be an absolute insistence that I provide everything upon which I am basing my assertion. And if I can't provide it, I shall be discredited and dismissed from the embassy, and sent back to London. I could even lose my commission.'

More the justifiable protest of an ambitious career soldier than that of a second spy, gauged Sebastian. 'You've conveyed the impression of having access to an informant?'

Now it was Black who hesitated before finally admitting: 'Yes.'

'Meet the demands by insisting your informant holds the evidence.'

'But you're my source!'

'Prepared to come forward to admit to so being to cleanse the embassy.' The Grand Duke had manipulated him like the marionette he'd suspected himself to be, accepted Sebastian. How successfully would he be manipulating the Grand Duke in return? It was a contest to anticipate, he decided. And an excuse, if one were needed, for him to once more visit the palace where Olga would be.

'Tell me now!' insisted the attaché. 'I won't make any move until I'm assured there's substance to the accusation. To do otherwise would be to commit professional suicide.'

An additional possibility abruptly occurred to Sebastian. 'The arresting Okhrana officer, to whom I had to make that absurd apology? Did you have his name?'

'How is he involved?'

'His name?' insisted Sebastian. As a suspicious afterthought he said: 'At least the name by which he identified himself to you. It's essential.'

Black did not respond immediately. Then he said: 'Krazin. Viktor Andreevich Krazin. I doubt it's genuine.'

'It's what he called himself?'

'Yes.'

'It will be enough.'

'Not for me. Not unless I know his importance in whatever mystery you're talking about.'

'You asked for my help,' shrugged Sebastian. 'I've given you what I've already told London. If you don't choose to make use of it, then so be it.'

'You'll come forward?'

'I've told you I will.'

'Why the change of heart? You impressed upon me in the beginning not to talk of your arrest or purpose here.'

'Many things have changed since my arrival here, perhaps the most important being what I've disclosed to you today. And what's more understandable than a journalist innocently trying to gain sight of Tsarskoye Selo being caught up by the Tsar's police?'

'There is much – too much – for me to consider,' protested Black.

'No there's not,' refused Sebastian.

'I need time.'

'I've already told London,' repeated Sebastian.

'You don't know what you're asking me to do!'

'I'm not asking you to do anything, I've told you what I've done and given you the opportunity to match the information; to comply with the requests coming from London.'

'It's more than that!'

It was, conceded Sebastian. He should have consulted at much greater length with London before embarking on this course, no matter how sure he was. 'I cannot offer you any more than this.' A distant, indistinct clock strike reminded him of his summons to meet Kerensky late that afternoon, and Sebastian quickly consulted his pocket watch, relieved he still had more than an hour. Despite which, he said: 'I have another appointment. There's nothing further for us to discuss; nothing more I can say.'

'You are sure?' persisted Black.

'I would not have told London had I not been. Nor you,' reiterated Sebastian, rising. 'Let me know your decision.'

'You're very much involved in it,' reminded Black. '*Every* part of it.'

Sebastian remained in good enough time to dismiss his carriage some way from the Duma, to complete his journey on foot and use the intervening opportunity to prepare for the encounter. And almost at once decided it was impossible to do, without the slightest awareness of the politician's reason for proposing this second meeting, eager though he had been to maintain the contact. There were, though, guesses that he could make, the most likely and obvious that it would be a continuation of their first encounter, and however Kerensky had used him to bait his own spy trap. In which case, Sebastian decided that he was in a much stronger – certainly more informed – position than he had been that first time, no longer stumbling in disbelief that there could also be a spy within his own embassy. But was there only one? Sebastian could not shake the needling irritation that Ludmilla Berringer might not be the only traitorous source. Was there a way he could use his knowledge of one to discover another? He couldn't imagine how, but it was a thought – a possibility – to keep in the forefront of his mind if an opening presented itself. He was also confusing situations, he recognized. Kerensky's ploy was to discover the informant within their own ranks, within the Duma, not in foreign legations. It was even possible that Kerensky's remark had been nothing more than an intriguing ruse that had proved correct by coincidence.

In the midst of a pavement throng as he was, Sebastian saw the waiting Alexander Kerensky before the politician isolated him. And at once identified the person to whom Kerensky was talking as Josef Stalin, despite the man's hunched, head-lowered stance of concentration, which shielded much of his face. Sebastian came close to delaying until they parted, but then continued on and was glad he had, keeping the politician and the *Pravda* columnist together for his arrival. Kerensky saw Sebastian first, his face opening in recognition. There was a brief, unheard exchange before Sebastian reached them, turning Stalin to face him. Unlike Kerensky there was no recognition, from which Sebastian took his guide, remaining blank-faced himself at Kerensky's introduction – 'a fellow journalist of some influence here in St Petersburg' – and necessarily repeating on his part that he was researching a series of articles on the social situation in the Russian capital. Neither attempted their German-language bridge, accepting Kerensky as their interpreter, and almost at once Stalin excused himself, shuffling into the Duma building ahead of them.

'A man to be reckoned with,' further qualified Kerensky, as they followed. 'Like us all, once the Tsar's Siberian guest.'

'How influential is he?'

'Considerably. He is acquainted, friends even, with most of

243

the leading socialists, both here and in exile. And reflects their opinions as well as his own in what he writes. It's even suggested that he is their chosen avenue for their views.'

'Which must make him someone of interest to the Tsar's people?'

'Everyone is of interest to the Tsar's people.'

Kerensky's cell-like office appeared as unused and as uncomfortable as before, the legal textbooks atrophying on their solitary shelves.

At once, although keeping the demand general, Sebastian said: 'Did it work?'

Kerensky smiled, bleakly. 'I think so.'

'I believe I'm entitled to know my part in it.'

'Only three people, apart from myself, knew of our meeting; who you were. The Okhrana knew of our encounter the same day.'

How could he press for more? Choosing the obvious, Sebastian said: 'And you knew from your own source within the organization?'

'You didn't tell me you were associated with the Okhrana,' challenged the heavily featured man.

Sebastian's stomach dipped, uncertainties crowding in upon him. 'I was over-impetuous, I confess, in trying to see Tsarskoye Selo. And I underestimated their efficiency.' How well placed was Kerensky's informant? Surely no one within the organization would know – could know – of his personal association with Orlov?

For several moments, Kerensky remained expressionless. 'So you've experienced their hospitality, too?'

'Something I've no wish ever to have repeated.' Sebastian's apprehension eased, very slightly. 'Why did you pick upon me as your bait?'

'You're a foreigner and available, from your eagerness at the garden party. My meeting with you would have been considered particularly interesting.'

'More so, for instance, than one in the Duma courtyard with the influential Josef Stalin?'

Kerensky allowed one of his rare smiles. 'An unnecessary confirmation.'

Believing he saw his opportunity, Sebastian said: 'Your source is well placed.'

'Sufficiently,' said Kerensky.

'Sufficiently to identify embassy sources?' Sebastian further risked.

Kerensky stayed silent, regarding Sebastian across the bare table. Finally he said: 'I do not have a name. Just an indication. It would be something dealt with at a higher level – a different department even – than that of the person upon whom we are relying.'

Whether or not that were true, it very definitely closed the door against his discovering anything further, accepted Sebastian. Still reluctant to give up, he said: 'Is this, my second summons, a further confirmation?'

'It was to tell you that we have established that the Okhrana have penetrated the Duma. Which I would have thought would have been of interest to a journalist.'

He should not have forgotten his supposed role, Sebastian accepted. 'What are you going to do with your knowledge?'

'Protest it, from the floor of the Duma. Let the Okhrana know they can't any longer rely upon what their informants supply. We're sure of one. If I can stimulate a sufficient debate, we can perhaps smoke out more; I'm sure there are more.'

It was his opportunity! Sebastian realized. 'You used me?'

'Which you knew, very quickly, at our first interview.'

'You'll appreciate that, beyond my being a journalist, I have, as an Englishman, concern at the thought of the Tsar's police having a source within the British embassy?'

'*Yes?*' agreed Kerensky, stressing the doubt.

'Include it, in whatever you say publicly in the Duma,' urged Sebastian. 'Add your suspicion that foreign legations have also been infiltrated.' Should he disclose the German presence? No, decided Sebastian. It would confuse the situation.

'It would indicate the extent of the attempted Tsarist control,' allowed Kerensky, although still doubtfully.

'And surely ensure a much greater, international impact for your claims?' encouraged Sebastian, remembering his belief that Kerensky sought a reputation outside Russia.

'Now you seek to use me,' accused Kerensky.

'Levelling the balance,' qualified Sebastian. At Winchester and again at Cambridge they'd talked of levelling the playing field, but he didn't believe that anything in which he was involved was being played on any sort of level field.

Because of what he considered the urgency of the moment – as well as the hopelessness of very much longer concealing his participation in what was going to end his career – Mycroft had for the first time agreed to come to Winston Churchill's rooms at the House of Commons, inevitable though his recognition would be by so many ministers; he'd considered himself lucky to have been curiously acknowledged by only five on his way through the inner labyrinth of MPs' quarters and committee rooms.

Churchill, forewarned by telephone, was impatiently waiting, the outer room cleared, at Mycroft's request, of any secretarial or support staff. The impatience seeped away at Mycroft's translation of Sebastian's spy alert, and for several moments Churchill actually appeared slumped over his desk, as if burdened by the information. At last he said: 'Things have escalated far beyond our expectations. We're in dangerous waters now.'

I have been for a long time, thought Mycroft; although Churchill was speaking in the plural, he was, as always, thinking in the singular. 'This has to be brought out.'

'Sebastian has to be right!' insisted the politician.

'He would not have sent the message if he had not been sure beyond any question or caveat,' replied Mycroft, just as insistent.

'Sebastian must come home,' decided Churchill. 'He has to tell us everything in detail, rather than go on as we are, particularly risking everything through this new-found Russian conduit. He's achieved enough . . .' There was a pause. 'Maybe even more than enough.'

'It has to be brought out,' repeated Mycroft.

'Once we're sure!' echoed Churchill, in return. '*We're* sure, not just Sebastian.'

'There's Stamfordham,' said Mycroft.

'He couldn't agree to any complicity,' protested the politician.

'I wasn't proposing to make him complicit,' said Mycroft, irritated at Churchill's concentrated self-preservation. 'I'm suggesting a conduit through which to make available the information to those who should receive it.'

'Through which everything would be exposed!'

'The most important thing being what Sebastian has discovered within the St Petersburg embassy. Which has to be rectified as soon as possible.'

'This is not the moment for hasty decisions,' argued the politician. 'It needs to be discussed with the benefit of reflection; and it requires Sherlock Holmes and Watson to be included. And for Sebastian to be part of it, too.'

'I'll not let this be stretched out, Winston. It has to be dealt with, urgently.'

'I'm cognisant of that. Have you considered your own position in all of this?'

'From every aspect, to only one conclusion,' said Mycroft. But still not, he was sure, as comprehensively as the other man.

'I demand proper consideration!' said Churchill.

'I'll arrange the meeting with Sherlock,' undertook Mycroft.

'When should Sebastian receive his father's discoveries about Lenin, in Geneva?'

Mycroft made an uncertain gesture. 'Tomorrow, perhaps.'

'I wonder if there's a connection?'

'Everything has a connection!' declared Mycroft, irritably.

Sebastian's telephone was ringing as he entered his suite, and he ran to pick it up, not wanting to lose the connection.

Captain Lionel Black announced: 'I've done it. Sent the message to London, with a copy to the ambassador.'

Which the man would not have done if he were involved in anything underhand, thought Sebastian. Or would he? Wouldn't the exposure of one spy protect another? He said: 'To what reaction?'

'I'm waiting,' said the attaché.

It wouldn't be for long, guessed Sebastian.

# Twenty-Three

It was, however, sufficiently long to benefit Sebastian, who guessed, before the military attaché openly told him so, that the delay in contacting him, until past noon the following day, was because of Alexander Kerensky's overnight bombshell parliamentary accusation, not just of Okhrana infiltration within the Duma, but also into St Petersburg-based foreign embassies.

'Did you know Kerensky was going to say that?' demanded Black, sounding breathless on the telephone.

'No,' said Sebastian. Hoping was not knowing, he consoled himself.

'The embassy is in uproar. London is, as well.'

'You told me that yesterday.'

'Nothing like this. I've openly been told that my future is in jeopardy.'

'By whom?' Sebastian was curious if it might have been Berringer.

'I've lost count of how many people.'

'It isn't. And won't be.' Shouldn't Black have also been concerned about King and country?

'I shouldn't have gone along with you,' bemoaned Black, his voice jagged.

'There's more on Germany.' Orlov hadn't referred to Kerensky's claim during their earlier telephone conversation, merely advising Sebastian that a package from London was on its way to the hotel, and inviting him to dine at the palace that night. Sebastian was curious at the prescience that had led to his father's discovery in Geneva.

'What?' asked the attaché.

'Why have you called?' said Sebastian, disregarding Black's urgency.

'I did what you suggested: told Sir Nigel you were my source,' said Black. 'He wants to see you as soon as possible. Hear your explanation. What shall I tell him?'

'Of course I'll see the ambassador.'

'What about Germany?'

'It can wait until I come to the embassy,' refused Sebastian, despite the suggestion from his uncle that Black should be the person through whom the information about Vladimir Lenin's Geneva companion should officially be communicated to London. Mycroft had proposed that in the note that accompanied his father's account, unaware of how things had moved on in St Petersburg. Sebastian decided he might need all the varied evidence he could muster.

'I need to know!'

'You don't,' said Sebastian.

'Why are you refusing me?'

'We've been through this too many times; you're close to being distraught.'

'How can I be otherwise?'

'By leaving everything to me.'

'Sir Nigel suggests three o'clock.'

'Tell him that I'll be there. Is the meeting to be confined just to the ambassador and myself?'

'I don't know. He's beside himself. This is the last thing he wanted to happen.'

'I'm sure having a secret-police informant within their embassy is the last thing the British government wanted.' Sebastian was sure that Pearlman, anxious as he was to spread responsibility for everything, wouldn't be alone. Which made John Berringer's presence virtually inevitable. Which Sebastian hadn't wanted. Would it be possible to gauge from the *chef du protocol*'s reaction if the man were party to what his wife was doing? It would, Sebastian decided, provide another test. For which of them, he wondered, soberly.

'I'll come to get you,' offered the attaché.

'That's not necessary.'

'It'll get me out of the embassy.'

With time to spare, Sebastian returned to the package that had come through the Russian embassy route, re-examining it for any indication of tampering, which he'd already failed to find after it had been couriered to him that morning. There was no telltale resealing, as there had been with Black's clumsy intrusion, nor was there any looseness in the glued edging of the manila package to suggest it had been steamed open. Sebastian was not reassured. He expected the Okhrana to be far more adept at opening and closing correspondence than the British military attaché. If it had been breached, he had to suppose cryptologists would already be poring over the Notions code. He wondered if they would succeed in breaking it before his openly telling Orlov that night. Sebastian hoped he would be first. It would be another indication of his intended good faith, which was intended only as long as it suited him, for as much as he could gain or benefit.

Sebastian was waiting in the foyer for Black's arrival, surprised at the man's appearance. For the first time ever, the attaché was no longer immaculate. The suit was unpressed, worn for too long – slept in, perhaps – the shirt crumpled for maybe the same reason, and the usually burnished shoes were scuffed and unpolished. He said at once: 'There's talk of Sir Nigel being recalled to London.'

'That doesn't surprise me.'

'It's the end of me. I'm done for.'

Sebastian wondered if that would be such a serious loss to the diplomatic service or the army. 'Why don't we see what happens?'

'I know what's going to happen.'

They sat opposite each other in the official embassy coach. Black appeared for the first time to become aware of his unkempt appearance, plucking and pulling at the creases in his trousers and jacket and straightening his regimental tie. He said: 'There's been a lot more traffic from London. Kerensky's claim was reported in *The Times* and a lot of other newspapers. Both the Bolsheviks and the Mensheviks in the Duma are demanding fuller explanations . . . names . . .'

'I'm sure they are,' said Sebastian. Would Kerensky meet any of them? Or become a victim of the Okhrana before he could? The man had embarked upon a perilous course, possibly more physically than professionally dangerous.

'I'm not to be included in the meeting,' revealed Black.

Sebastian hadn't considered whether or not the man would be. 'You won't be victimized by the exclusion.'

'I have . . . ?'

'Yes!' Sebastian stopped him, impatiently. 'You have my word. You'll be told everything that transpires.'

Sebastian was immediately conscious of the special attention, even from the lowly clerk at the gatehouse with the ambition to visit the Grand Hotel before his recall, and the more so from virtually everyone within the main embassy building. The attaché led him through a more opulent part of the building, to which he had never before been, not even on their way through to the garden party. Secretaries and clerks were standing in groups that went silent as he passed; Sebastian was conscious that Black, in front of him, was walking with his head bowed, as if in some embarrassment. John Berringer was waiting in what had to be the immediate outer office to the ambassador's suite, flanked by two other men and a woman, notebook in hand. The *chef du protocol* dismissed the attaché with a jerk of the head, regarding Sebastian expressionlessly, with no offered hand.

The man said: 'I very much hope you have a complete explanation for what you've brought about.'

'That will be for you particularly to judge,' said Sebastian, intent upon the other man's reaction.

There was a curious frown but no indication of uncertainty or apprehension. 'What do *you*, particularly, mean by that remark?'

'I've come to see the ambassador,' said Sebastian. 'My appointment is for three, which it now is.'

'I asked you a question, sir!'

'Are you attending the meeting?'

'Of course.'

'Then you will have it answered. No purpose is served by repetition.'

'It is not for you to decide purpose or otherwise!'

'Shall we go in?'

There were discomfited movements from the people surrounding Berringer. Sebastian hadn't set out so obviously to antagonize the man – not this soon at least – but decided he couldn't retreat now. For several moments they remained staring at each other, Berringer's face colouring from rage at the dismissal. At last he moved, turning to lead the way into the ambassador's office.

Sir Nigel Pearlman sat rigidly behind his protective desk, leaning forward with both hands upon it, as if preparing himself. There was a semicircle of chairs already arranged to the left, beneath a portrait of King George V, and an isolated seat directly in front, which Sebastian assumed to be his before being gestured curtly to it.

'Allegations have been made concerning this embassy, which we require you to explain!'

It was Berringer, not the ambassador, who spoke with quasi-legal stiffness. The seated woman wrote a rapid note, as did one of the men beside her whom Sebastian took to be an embassy lawyer. Speaking to the ambassador, not the *chef du protocol*, Sebastian said: 'Can I have the benefit of full introductions?'

Berringer, still red-faced, this time at so obviously being ignored, said: 'A full note is naturally being taken of everything. Peter Johnson –' the scribbling man looked up and nodded – 'is attached to the embassy's legal division . . .'

'My name is Henry Smallwood,' broke in the other man, in a strong north-country accent. 'I am in charge of security.'

Sebastian nodded: 'I don't imagine you want a formal introduction on my part.'

'I asked you a question,' said Berringer.

'What has Black told you, Your Excellency?' asked Sebastian, still addressing the ambassador.

Berringer said: 'That you were the source for his reporting a German diplomat as a spy at the celebratory garden party here at the embassy. And suggesting how three more at the German embassy could be identified, as they subsequently were, from newspaper photographs. None of which is why you've been brought here today.'

'Agreed to come here today, because of my very justifiable concern,' modified Sebastian. Was Berringer a bully? Or was the attitude for another purpose?

252

'You've told Black, who in turn has told London, that there is a Russian police informant within this embassy!' declared Berringer, his voice uneven. 'That would appear to be linked to a statement made last night in the Duma by Alexander Kerensky, who attended the garden party here and whom we know you briefly met – because of which, collusion between the two of you is easy to understand. We want your evidence for your assertion! And to know of your complicity with Kerensky!'

'Why is this meeting being conducted in such a hostile manner?' demanded Sebastian, watching the secretary and the lawyer hurriedly jot the question down on their pads.

Berringer appeared aware as well. Slightly less aggressively – but curtly – he said: 'We were not informed of your claims before we understand you to have alerted London. We also require to know who it was to whom you communicated!'

'Your military attaché was told within an hour of my advising London,' insisted Sebastian. 'That was the earliest possible opportunity.' He hesitated. 'My father was the recipient of my information.' He'd wait for the direct challenge before saying more.

'Black was not told of your evidence,' said Berringer, in continued poor recovery.

'Mr Holmes,' said the white-haired ambassador, speaking – calmly – for the first time. 'I have been made aware of who you are – who your father is – and for that reason take you as a man of integrity and honour. I very much regret your believing you are being treated hostilely. You must surely appreciate the concern that your suggestion has caused London, as well as me – all of us – within this embassy. To get to the bottom of it, we need evidence to support your claims and try to fit in with what was said in the Russian parliament . . .'

'Irrefutable evidence,' insisted Berringer.

Sebastian decided that he'd insufficiently prepared himself for such active participation by John Berringer, predictable though the man's presence had been. Directly addressing the man for the first time, he said: 'I think it would be fitting for your wife to be brought into this discussion.'

'My wife!' exploded Berringer.

'She features in what I have to say.'

'I will not allow this!' insisted Berringer. 'This is outrageous!'

'What is?' said Sebastian.

'Your associating my wife with your preposterous allegations,' said the diplomat, although less stridently.

'I haven't yet made any allegations concerning your wife.' Berringer indicated the embassy lawyer beside the note-taking secretary. They'd both momentarily stopped writing. 'Nor should you, sir! You are treading a very dangerous legal path!'

Was this outrage genuine or a desperate bluff? 'Which I am prepared to follow to a court of law if necessary.'

'I refuse to subject my wife to any of this!' declared Berringer. 'It is an affront.'

'London are demanding a complete and full explanation,' reminded Sir Nigel, addressing his *chef du protocol.*

'This man is inferring that my wife is treating with the Okhrand! You surely don't expect me to respond to such a claim!'

Berringer was complicit, Sebastian decided. 'You've responded most forcefully. The suggestion was for your wife to be invited into this meeting.'

'I want her here, John,' insisted the ambassador, with unexpected firmness. 'Of course any suggestion against Ludmilla is ridiculous, so let's get it over and done with: clear everything up and reassure London it is all nonsense.'

Berringer hesitated, about to protest further, but instead abruptly turned and left the room.

To Sebastian the ambassador said: 'This is a sorry business.'

'Very sorry indeed, sir,' agreed Sebastian.

'I was referring to the disgrace to your very honourable family name,' said Pearlman, stiffly.

The ambassador had already made up his mind and imagined his clearing the way towards his Foreign Office sinecure was at hand, decided Sebastian. 'I fully understand your anxiety and am prepared to overlook that remark at the present time, Your Excellency. But as you've invoked the name of my father, I'd welcome a later apology.'

'You are arrogant, Holmes!'

'It is not my intention to be, sir. My only intention is to acquaint you with a dangerous and totally unacceptable situation within your embassy.'

Now it was Sir Nigel Pearlman who was obviously angry, his fingers drumming against his desktop. 'Is your father part of this enterprise?'

'My father and I are in communication,' said Sebastian, cautiously. Suddenly believing he saw an avenue, he added: 'From whom did you hear the identity of my father?'

Sebastian was unsure if the older man's pause was for recollection or an indecision about replying.

'Berringer,' the ambassador said, finally. 'Berringer said—'

'That his wife had recognized me?' hurriedly completed Sabastian.

There was another pause. 'Yes. I believe—'

The ambassador was interrupted for the second time by the return of the Berringers, entering unannounced and without warning. It was Sebastian who was the first of the men politely to rise at the woman's arrival. Before she or they had time to sit again, a flush-faced Ludmilla Berringer said: 'What are these accusations you are making against me? I demand to know . . .' She swivelled, still standing, to the lawyer and said: 'I want you to record everything! I intend to sue and will need a record of every false charge.'

'How many do you expect there to be?' asked Sebastian, mildly.

The ridicule dented if not actually punctured some of the woman's clear predetermination to overwhelm him with threats. Ludmilla Berringer finally sat in the extra seat her husband added to the existing semicircle. Trying to maintain the belligerence, she announced: 'I'm waiting!'

'So am I,' said Sebastian, his course decided by her attitude. 'How many imputations are you expecting me to make?'

'None that are not completely unfounded, slanderous fabrications for which you are going to pay most heavily.'

'You know my father is Sherlock Holmes?'

'Am I supposed to be impressed – frightened – by that? Or are you seeking to hide behind his coat-tails?'

'Neither,' said Sebastian, looking between husband and wife.

'Sir Nigel's told me it was you, one of you, who recognized me.'

'It was me,' insisted Ludmilla, without hesitation.

'How?' asked Sebastian. It was essential to keep the Berringers unbalanced, stoking their arrogance.

For the first time, the positive aggression faltered. Berringer began but then halted, throwing a look towards his wife, who said: 'The name, of course!'

'Holmes is not an uncommon name.'

'And the physical resemblance,' she added. 'It's very close.'

'You've met my father?'

'I've seen photographs. Sketches.'

'Sufficient to mark the similarity?'

'What's this got to do with your charges against my wife?' intruded Berringer.

'No accusations have been made against your wife,' reminded Sebastian. To the lawyer and note-taking secretary he said: 'You are maintaining a verbatim record of everything that is being said, aren't you?'

Both looked up from their respective pads, nodding, and Sebastian repeated: 'Sufficient to mark the similarity.'

'Yes,' said the woman, defiantly.

'Wasn't I identified to you by Viktor Andreevich Krazin?' It was his biggest and potentially most disastrous bluff, the greatest risk that the Okhrana interrogator had dealt with the woman under a different alias. Sebastian's gamble was in believing that Orlov was sacrificing Ludmilla Berringer and that she would know the man by that name. The hesitation, too long by just a few bare seconds, was enough to convince Sebastian that he was right.

The rejection came from Berringer, not Ludmilla. 'Who in God's name is Viktor Andreevich Krazin?'

'Mrs Berringer?' pressed Sebastian, hoping his tension wasn't discernible.

'I have not the slightest idea of what or about whom you are talking,' said the woman.

'I do not speak Russian,' said Sebastian. 'Would you tell me in Russian, Mrs Berringer, the nearest approximation to *Flight of Fancy*?'

256

The shock briefly but very obviously registered on the woman's face before she could straighten her features.

'This absurdity has got to stop!' insisted Berringer, loudly, trying hurriedly to come to his wife's aid.

'Did you enjoy your river cruise yesterday with Viktor Andreevich Krazin, Mrs Berringer?' persisted Sebastian. He was later to reflect that, had the Berringers held their nerve, they still might have out-bluffed him, because, essential though it was to rid the embassy of them, he was unsure if, confronted with their continued denials, he would have involved Princess Olga Orlov as his supporting witness.

But Ludmilla Berringer panicked, badly and unthinkingly, forgetting even her disavowal of Viktor Krazin of only seconds before. Forcing the indignation, she said: 'There is nothing reprehensible in encountering an acquaintance, a local businessman whom I understand to be in shipping, an export agent, I believe.'

'Not moments ago you told us you did not know the man. As did your husband.'

'I did not associate him with what you are alleging,' improvised Berringer. 'So inconsequential was the chance meeting that my wife did not see fit to mention it to me.'

'Then how do you know such a meeting occurred?' pounced the ambassador.

'I'm assuming . . . from what Ludmilla just said . . .' stumbled the diplomat.

'So you do know Viktor Andreevich Krazin?' He'd done it! thought Sebastian. Completely outwitted them by trading on their arrogance, which had for so long been an unchallenged, motivating source within an embassy controlled by a weak ambassador.

'Insufficiently to call him immediately to mind, as is the case with several of Ludmilla's Russian friends,' Berringer tried to recover.

Was the man trying to distance himself from his wife? wondered Sebastian. From her quick sideways frown, he guessed the same thought had occurred to the woman, too. Sebastian said: 'On my initial arrival here, I quite wrongly and foolishly attempted to approach Tsarskoye Selo, unaware of the security surrounding it. I was arrested by the Tsar's secret police and interrogated. My interrogator was Viktor Andreevich Krazin, who was clearly a man of rank within the service, in command of a squad of men. My release was secured by Captain Black, to whom I had presented a letter of introduction. Quite obviously, to achieve that release, Captain Black also encountered Krazin and is aware of the man's position within the Okhrana.' Sebastian considered every word before uttering it, sure he had so far endangered no one – certainly no one in England – with anything he'd said, but remained apprehensive about closer questioning.

'I was most definitely unaware of the man's position, as I am sure my wife was,' said Berringer. 'As she has told you, we believed him to be an export agent.'

'Trading in what?' The question came from the ambassador, hard-voiced.

Berringer laughed in attempted dismissal. 'It was a casual acquaintanceship. It was never discussed.'

'But the stability of the Tsar's position was very much discussed, wasn't it?' demanded Sebastian. 'Krazin was the person who assured you, enabling you in turn to assure London, that the Romanov throne was secure against overthrow. Great, if misleading, perspicacity for a shipping or export official.'

'To imagine I would draw political opinion from someone I barely knew, in the position I believed him to occupy, is a ridiculous suggestion,' blustered Berringer. Beside him, Ludmilla was fidgeting, leaning towards her husband as if seeking physical protection.

'It's upon your opinion – and that of your wife, because she is Russian – that our advice to London has been based,' said the ambassador. 'Who are your reliable sources for the opinions I have been following?'

'Are you doubting me, sir?' said Berringer. 'Against the word of this man whom I now charge to be the true spy, communicating as he has been, through this very embassy, on matters concerning revolutionaries and their London congresses, and clandestine meetings with such people here in St Petersburg!'

'Is that so?' Sir Nigel demanded of Sebastian.

He had to turn the attack back upon the man as quickly and as convincingly as possible, Sebastian knew. 'And by my so doing, discovering a far more accurate picture of the political uncertainly here than has been provided by this embassy . . .' Sebastian stopped, halted by a sudden, full awareness of Berringer's remark. 'Although the information on revolutionaries and their London conferences came *to* me from my father. Clearly the interception of which in transit was another spying activity of your *chef du protocol*, doubtless passed on to his secret-police associates – although it would seem not to you, Sir Nigel. And on the matter of discoveries, revolutionaries and spying, my father has further advised me in a communication I received today that, only a few days past in Geneva, he observed the exiled revolutionary Vladimir Lenin and some of his associates in close contact with an Otto von Hagel, a fourth German spy expelled from the United States with those already identified here.'

'I can explain . . .' started Berringer, to be instantly stopped by Sir Nigel Pearlman.

'Which I will have you do, in a far more satisfactory manner than you have so far,' insisted the ambassador. 'But in a manner restricted to this embassy. I think we need detain you no longer, Mr Holmes. I would, however, welcome a further meeting at a later date. And I do apologize for my earlier remarks concerning your family.'

'I accept that apology and await your summons, sir,' said Sebastian. There was still the summons from Grand Duke Alexei Orlov, Sebastian reflected. He wondered if he could control it as successfully as he had this one.

'You've individually told the cabinet to hold themselves in readiness for immediate recall the moment we hear further from St Petersburg of this infiltration?' demanded Asquith.

'I have a means of contact for everyone,' assured Mycroft. 'Sir Edward Grey is remaining at the Foreign Office for some time yet.'

'It's a damnable situation if it's true, the Tsar spying on us!'

'His people, sir,' qualified Mycroft. 'It might not be with

the Tsar's personal knowledge.' He remained curious why Sebastian had alerted the military attaché ahead of the expected arrival of the suggestion that the man should be the obvious conduit.

'Still profoundly disturbing if it proves to be true.'

'And possibly connected with the enquiries initiated on the King's behalf,' hopefully exaggerated Mycroft.

'I fail to see the connection. And I'm unconvinced there's anything to exercise us there,' declared Asquith.

'Most of the embassy replies are equivocal,' Mycroft argued.

'I don't agree,' refused the Prime Minister. 'Vienna says Serb nationalism is not a new problem, and the ambassadorial consensus from the Balkan countries as a whole is that it's always volatile but that there's little risk of escalation. Grey thinks that the King has got a bee in his bonnet, probably stemming from Churchill unnecessarily bringing the fleet home from the Mediterranean as he did. The man's a confounded nuisance!'

'Do you wish me to schedule a discussion in cabinet?'

'No,' decided Asquith, positively. 'The concentration has to be upon this spying allegation.'

'What shall you tell the King?'

'About there being a Tsarist spy within the embassy, nothing until I know everything there is to know. About the possibility of war in Europe, I shall acquaint him with the opinions of the embassies whose guidance we sought, upon which we have to rely. Which leads to the conclusion that no war is likely, let alone conceivably imminent. And that there is no indication from St Petersburg of the Tsar's political instability.'

Mycroft's secretary saw him enter his Downing Street suite and raised the hand holding the telephone to gesture the importance of the call. As she passed the receiver to him, her free hand cupped over the mouthpiece, she said: 'It's the Foreign Secretary. Sir Edward says it's personal.'

260

# Twenty-Four

For the first time ever Winston Churchill arrived on time, hurrying into 221b Baker Street, discarding his coat as he did so, and demanding, before any of the three already waiting men could offer a greeting: 'What's come from St Petersburg about Sebastian?'

'About *Sebastian*,' insisted Mycroft, more forcefully than the politician. 'Your name has not been invoked.'

'What is it?' persisted Churchill.

'Grey contacted me as a personal favour, believing Sebastian to be my adopted son, not Sherlock's progeny, which has apparently been discovered,' said the Cabinet Secretary. 'All the St Petersburg telegram said was that Sebastian had been identified and summoned to explain a claim that there was an Okhrana source within our embassy there. I had no alternative but to admit who Sebastian's true father is.'

'Are you going to be questioned about it by Asquith?'

'I would imagine it's inevitable. I'm seeing Sir Edward tomorrow.'

Churchill finally accepted the whisky that Dr Watson offered, sitting but not relaxing in the prepared chair. 'There's got to be a connection with the Duma statement reported in *The Times*!'

'We've no information about that,' said Mycroft. 'We know, of course, that Sebastian had contact with Kerensky.'

'This wasn't what Sebastian was told to do: he was supposed to supply the information through Black!' said Churchill.

'He was not!' refused Sherlock Holmes, instantly. 'That advice concerned the expedition of myself and Watson to Switzerland. Quite clearly a change of circumstances has occurred, to which Sebastian had to react without the benefit of consultation with us. I trust my son to have made the proper decision.'

'Things are getting out of hand!' protested the First Lord of the Admiralty.

'There's no justification whatsoever for that judgement,' again refused Sherlock Holmes. 'Matters upon which we're embarked do not have a formula that can be followed. Our need was to gain information upon which the government could make a fitting response. Perhaps Sebastian is providing that . . .' The detective indicated a sheaf of papers lying on the table between them. 'As he has provided other material, which I collected from the Russian embassy today.'

Churchill made no attempt to pick up the dispatch. 'What does it contain?'

'Proposals of the Grand Duke Alexei Orlov to rescue the Russian imperial family from St Petersburg in the event of their overthrow,' identified Sherlock Holmes. 'Written in open hand; there was clearly no purpose in encoding what Orlov himself was initiating.'

Churchill snorted a disbelieving laugh. 'Orlov seeks British assistance but at the same time cultivates an informant within our St Petersburg embassy?'

'Orlov's business is a confusing one,' suggested Watson.

'Too confusing for me,' protested Churchill. 'I fear Sebastian has been taken for a fool!'

'As I fear you may be, sir, forming opinions without evidence to base them upon!' said Sherlock Holmes. 'Contrary to that opinion, there's every indication that my son is discharging himself far beyond any expectation, most certainly yours!'

'There's certainly insufficient for this ill humour,' interceded Mycroft. To Churchill he said: 'You might benefit from reading Sebastian's latest communication.'

The politician hesitated at the rebuke, gesturing to Watson with his empty glass, but then took up the ignored papers. He read without comment, several times referring back to preceding passages, before looking up. Tasting his replenished drink, he said: 'There's little doubt here that the man entrusted with their safety believes the Romanovs will be deposed.'

'Or that he sees his function as preparing for every eventuality,' argued Sherlock Holmes.

'Either way it's too extravagant,' dismissed Churchill. 'Orlov's not just thinking of rescuing the imperial family. He's including an indeterminate number from the court. I'm certainly not minded to order British warships up the Neva river to an uncertain reception in the event of a political overthrow.'

What about through a regatta of sailing yachts? wondered Mycroft. But Churchill was right: Orlov's request was far too extravagant even to suggest to Stamfordham. 'The family – but no more – could be offered the protection of the embassy while safe passage was negotiated.'

Sherlock Holmes nodded towards the dispatch which Churchill had replaced on the table between them. 'Orlov doubts such safe passage overland could be guaranteed. And Sebastian's impression from Stalin was that, if revolution comes, it will be bloody. We've the French as a precedent for that.'

'And proof enough of German machinations in Russian unrest,' pointed out Watson. 'The Tsarina is German. Would it be too much to expect that Berlin would intercede on the family's behalf?'

'It would be high – and difficult – diplomacy in time of war,' said Churchill.

'Which is being persistently doubted by our relevant embassies, which you well know from the most recent cabinet meeting,' reminded Mycroft.

'Then there's an impasse,' said Churchill.

'In which Sebastian is now very much caught up,' said Sherlock Holmes. 'We've indicated certain possibilities concerning the Tsar's safety.'

'Which Orlov appears to have put in jeopardy if he has indeed infiltrated the embassy,' said Churchill.

'By being *caught* infiltrating the embassy, if indeed he has,' said Sherlock Holmes.

'We should recall Sebastian, as I've already demanded,' insisted Churchill. 'There's no more he can usefully do in Russia.'

'I concur,' said Sherlock Holmes, in rare agreement.

'Can we decide that without knowing more about his summons to the embassy?' asked Mycroft, fearful that the unrestrained animosity between Churchill and his brother could cloud their judgement, and in little doubt that Churchill was anxious to conclude something in which he personally felt increasingly endangered.

'I don't see why not,' said Churchill, belligerently.

'We can at least tell him to prepare his return, once he's fulfilled whatever obligations remain there,' said the detective. Sebastian appeared greatly to have expanded his remit, and Sherlock Holmes wanted his son safely back from the unpredictability in which he appeared to have become enmeshed.

Sebastian's uncertainty grew the closer his arrival at the Orlov palace became, the various reasons not difficult to isolate. The predominant one, obviously, amounted to a continuation of the nervous excitement of the embassy confrontation, in which he believed he had acquitted himself satisfactorily, but with the consciousness of the encounter with the Grand Duke still to come. Would it be wise to make that a positive confrontation too, announcing his steamboat identification of Ludmilla Berringer and his denunciation of her, and directly charge the Russian with her abandonment, in order for Sebastian to maintain the determination always to deal with the man as an equal? Or was it wiser to take his lead from Orlov, in the hope of learning – inferring at least – some further manipulation the man might be contemplating. As it might be possible to learn other things, Sebastian reminded himself. There was still a reaction to gauge on the disclosure of his father's sighting in Switzerland, seeking telltale foreknowledge from Orlov, despite there having been no indication of the Russian-couriered package having been interfered with. Better – more sensible – to avoid a face-to-face challenge, Sebastian decided. Which immediately brought another question. Was that entirely professional reasoning? Or was there interwoven into it the intrusive personal distraction of seeing Olga for the first time since their river cruise? A ridiculous and unfounded doubt. The personal situation between himself and Olga was entirely and totally that, personal. To be kept at that distance and not allowed to overlap into any other part of his thinking.

Thoughts of Olga, of seeing her and of being in her presence, were still the foremost in Sebastian's mind when his carriage delivered him at the palace gates.

There was no longer any need for identification. The usual attendants were in readiness, one actually smiling, for the walk across the spiked and bayonet-embedded moat from the outer to the inner courtyard. Footmen were at the palace door and Olga was alone, already dressed for dinner in indigo blue, in a smaller salon, into which Sebastian hadn't been before. An unrecognized butler was on station behind a drinks trolley.

Sebastian bowed, formally, and said: 'Good evening, Princess,' to which Olga giggled and said: 'He doesn't speak French.'

'How can you be sure?'

'I am.'

'Quite sure?'

'Quite sure. But thank you for your caution.'

'You look—'

'Breathtaking,' she finished. 'You must find a new word.'

'None other fits.'

'Shall I order you a drink?'

'No.'

'You haven't looked away from me since you entered, and I haven't looked away from you. If you don't sit down and behave like a guest, it won't matter whether he can understand what we're saying or not. He'll understand.'

The customary Cristal champagne nestled in its cooler but Sebastian said: 'Perhaps vodka.'

Olga ordered in Russian, without looking at the butler. Sebastian took a seat at what he judged to be required distance.

He said: 'Where is your father?'

'Delayed. He apologizes. I don't.'

'For what?'

'Anything.'

'Should I?'

'For what?'

'Nothing.'

'You're not drinking,' she accused.

'I want to touch you.'

'Tomorrow I intend to visit our dacha, our summer house, in the country. Have you ever visited a dacha?'

'No.'

'It's beautiful at this time of the year: the daffodils particularly, like a yellow carpet.'

'I'd very much like to see that.'

'I'd hoped you would. I thought we'd set out in time for lunch.'

'There are staff?'

'Of course. But I am proposing a picnic. The weather is warm enough; more than warm enough, in fact. Sufficient even to swim.'

'There is a river?'

'A lake. Amid daffodils. Don't say exquisite.'

'Never again.' It was light, playful, uncommitting. As everything should be. Except . . . Sebastian refused the correction, forcing another thought. Wasn't he expected to hold himself in readiness for a second summons from the ambassador? There'd been no suggestion it would come as soon as tomorrow. Or the day after tomorrow.

Olga moved to speak but stopped at the opening of the door by a waiting footman to admit the hurrying Grand Duke with repeated apologies for his lateness, further delayed by his changing into his evening clothes before joining them. The bearded man's arrival initiated the opening of the special champagne and Orlov's vague reference to his being held at Tsarskoye Selo, and Olga's announcement, to the Grand Duke's immediate agreement, of the intended following day's outing to the Orlov dacha. They dined off wild boar and afterwards, as she had on Sebastian's first visit, Olga set out upon a piano recital, but unlike that first occasion played so badly that she stopped short and blamed her difficulty on a Rachmaninov prelude she'd attempted with insufficient practice. And upon Olga's retirement the two men retreated to the familiarity of the trophy-roomed study, brandy and the Grand Duke's choice of cigars.

The moment they settled, Orlov said: 'What word from London?'

'Nothing yet on the evacuation plan. But more of German intrigue.'

Orlov studied the glowing end of his cigar as Sebastian recounted his father's visit to Geneva. When Sebastian finished, the Russian said: 'Intrigue indeed!'

'Here, too, according to Kerensky's claim in the Duma,' embarked Sebastian.

Orlov sipped his cognac, unhurriedly. 'The Duma is a nest of revolutionaries. Isn't it obvious we would need to know of their activities?'

'Kerensky referred to foreign embassies.'

'It's important to know who are our friends.'

A virtual confirmation, accepted Sebastian. 'It's caused consternation in London. And at the embassy here.'

'It needn't.'

He'd risk the demand, Sebastian decided: he was ill suited to the role of marionette. 'Are you assuring me that there is no Okhrana source within the British embassy?'

Orlov frowned, looking very directly at Sebastian for several moments. 'Would it not endanger the understanding I am attempting to reach with London, through you?'

'Completely,' agreed Sebastian, urgently. 'Which was the entire point and purpose of my question!'

'You are exercised, Mr Holmes!'

He was committed now, despite his earlier decision against such directness. 'I am, sir! I understand full well that there is much that we cannot share . . . admit equally fully that I sought you out for my advantage, not initially for your benefit . . . but since your approach concerning the imperial family's safety, I have, between the two of us, conducted myself in good faith!'

'As I am, for my part, but for my already admitted advantage, ensuring an escape route for the Tsar I represent and whom I am sworn to protect to the utmost.'

Sebastian was totally, bewilderingly confused. Without a flicker of discomfort, the other man was fixing him with an unblinking stare and blatantly lying! Yet Ludmilla Berringer and Viktor Krazin had been aboard the river ferry upon which he and Olga were known by the Grand Duke to be sailing! Lying himself, Sebastian said: 'I am reassured.'

'As I am, to have removed a doubt you appeared to be harbouring.'

Sebastian welcomed the brief interruption of the attentive butler adding to both their brandy goblets, snatching for a way forward. 'What of the German embassy?'

'I am in your debt for the protection of my daughter at the Yusupov incident,' said Orlov.

'Which you've already made abundantly clear,' frowned Sebastian. 'I fail to understand—'

'And you identified the German spies. Two debts I seek to repay.'

'How so?'

'I have him!' declared the Grand Duke, extending an open hand and then closing it in a crushing movement.

'Rasputin!'

'He is an habitué of a brothel on Sadovaya Ulitsa. So, in recent days, has been Konrad Blum, one of the Germans you encountered in New York.'

'They have definitely met?' pressed Sebastian.

'Brothels operate by my permission and for my advantage. I have sworn statements of encounters and of identification, of them both.'

'Is it sufficient to undermine Rasputin's influence with the Tsar? Or perhaps more importantly with the Tsarina?'

'Not as a direct accusation, too easily denied. And Rasputin's reputation as a lecher is no secret to either of them, just something they choose to ignore.'

'How then?'

'It will reach them not from me but from those in court whose opinion they respect . . .' He smiled. 'Maybe, even, from public remarks in the Duma. Mine will be the confirmation when asked for, when it becomes a scandal too big to ignore.'

'The statements you have . . . do they contain accounts of their conversations?'

The Grand Duke shook his head, understanding the question. 'They are careful, allowing no one close to them.'

'You could move immediately against Blum,' suggested Sebastian.

'Rasputin is the greater danger to Russia. Blum's place would be taken by others.'

'Does the Tsar really share affairs of state with such a man?'

'The Tsar discusses in great detail affairs of state with the Tsarina, who, as I have already made clear to you, is totally under the influence of Rasputin. Berlin could have no better or more important source.'

'The course you intend against Rasputin will take time,' Sebastian pointed out. 'Is it yours to spare?'

'It has to be spared. Rasputin has to hang himself.'

Yet more to advise London of, Sebastian recognized. But what about what he had earlier supplied through the embassy?

That same uncertainty was in Mycroft Holmes's mind when he returned, past midnight, to his rooms at the Diogenes Club. Awaiting him was a handwritten and hand-delivered letter from 10 Downing Street, summoning him for a meeting with Herbert Asquith at nine the following morning.

# Twenty-Five

Sir Edward Grey was already in Herbert Asquith's private office overlooking Horseguards Parade when Mycroft entered. Both looked up from what Mycroft immediately recognized to be a sheaf of Foreign Office cables, and Asquith said: 'I'd like an understanding of what's happened here, Holmes.'

'So would I, sir,' said Mycroft, cautiously. In the reflective light of his brisk walk across St James's Park to Downing Street, the strategy agreed with his brother and Winston Churchill seemed less convincing than it had the previous night. It was Sherlock's insistence that he try to discover as much as possible before volunteering anything in return.

'The Russian wife of John Berringer, our *chef du protocol* in St Petersburg, has confessed to being an informant for the Tsar's secret police,' declared Grey, succinctly. 'Berringer has admitted being complicit.'

'Upon the accusation of a Sebastian Holmes, who acknowledges being the son of your famous brother!' added the Prime Minister. 'A relationship that has confused us as much as the man's curious presence in Russia and involvement in matters of diplomacy.'

Mycroft's hesitation was to assemble his thoughts but, before he could speak, Grey said: 'Could the fellow be an impostor?'

'No, sir,' denied Mycroft. 'He is, in fact, legally my ward.'

'Which confuses us further,' complained Asquith.

Mycroft observed his brother's familiar dictum to keep the explanation as truthful as possible. Mycroft referred to the circumstances of Sebastian's birth and of his acceptance of wardship as an intimate family matter, until Sebastian's attainment of manhood and belated but now proud acceptance by his father. Sebastian was tempted by a career in journalism,

270

to which end he had obtained accreditation to the *Morning Post* and travelled to Russia to research the political situation there. Honestly, Mycroft concluded: 'I have no knowledge of how he came to be in a position to identify the Berringers as you tell me he did, although I am aware of his registering his presence in Russia at the embassy.'

Mycroft's strictly limited account was initially greeted with silence from both men. It was the Foreign Secretary who spoke first. 'How were you aware?'

Mycroft felt a small knot of apprehension. 'I have a telegraph at my lodgings.'

'Through which there has been regular communication?' persisted Grey.

Should he risk the opportunity? wondered Mycroft. 'Some of which has surprised me. My understanding of the guidance from our embassy in St Petersburg has been that there is little unrest among the population and that the Tsar's position is secure. That has not been Sebastian's impression.'

Asquith moved a hand among the discarded cables. 'We asked the ambassador for an assessment of the Berringers' treachery. Theirs was the opinion that was reflected: great dependence was put upon Mrs Berringer's views because of her birth.'

The two ministers *were* having difficulty assimilating what had happened, Mycroft recognized. Which was to his advantage. 'What is going to happen to them?'

'They're being repatriated at once, accompanied by the embassy security officer,' disclosed Grey.

'Whose own position will be considered, upon his arrival,' threatened Asquith.

'It's essential to prevent a scandal,' said the Foreign Secretary.

'How's that to be achieved?' persisted Mycroft, surprised at the latitude he was being allowed despite his awareness of their uncertainly. It was, he guessed, a recognition of his experience as a civil servant who had served successive governments as Cabinet Secretary for so long; no doubt their openness was aided by the reputation of his brother.

'Berringer is to be allowed to resign, on the grounds of ill

271

health,' announced Asquith. 'It would be disastrous, politically as well as internationally, if what's happened ever became public.'

'Surely what *has* happened requires a complete re-evaluation of the situation in Russia?' suggested Mycroft. Could it be that he had not after all been called in upon suspicion, but as someone of long experience trusted to provide unbiased advice?

'You believe there is a real possibility of a conflagration in Europe that will engulf us all?' dramatically and unexpectedly challenged the Foreign Secretary.

The abruptness once more made Mycroft hesitate. 'I believe there to be such a possibility.'

'A view which none of our Balkan embassies supports,' reminded Asquith.

'As neither did St Petersburg,' reminded Mycroft in turn. He might have relaxed too soon, he realized.

'Good heavens, man, you're surely not suggesting that every British embassy in Europe is infiltrated to supply us with misleading guidance!' demanded the Prime Minister, exasperated.

'No, sir!' refuted Mycroft, strongly. 'I am, though, suggesting that more consideration be given to the potential of such an outbreak of hostilities. A provision for which Berlin appears to be preparing, from our identification of known German provocateurs in the Russian capital and elsewhere.'

'The *Morning Post*!' exclaimed Sir Edward Grey, as if in sudden recollection.

Mycroft's apprehension grew. Asquith said: 'What about it?'

'The journal that in the past has provided Churchill with much needed income,' completed the Foreign Secretary.

'Churchill facilitated an introduction,' offered Mycroft.

'As he introduces dire warnings of war at every opportunity,' sneered Asquith.

'An opinion in which he is not alone, although greatly in the minority,' fought back Mycroft. He was lost, he decided: certainly teetering on the very edge of the feared abyss.

But instead of the anticipated demand that integrity would

have prevented Mycroft denying, Asquith said: 'When is your ward returning to this country?'

'Soon,' promised Mycroft, quickly. 'It has already been proposed to him. I would expect within days.'

'There could be benefit in our meeting,' proposed the prime minister.

'To which I know Sebastian would be most willing,' assured Mycroft. 'As would my brother.'

'Arrange it, immediately upon his return,' ordered the prime minister. 'I am sure you need no reminder of your oath that nothing of which we have spoken should be repeated outside this room!'

'No, sir,' said Mycroft, hurriedly rising. 'Sebastian will be at your convenience upon the very day of his return.'

'I thought we had prepared him for the ultimate demand,' said Sir Edward Grey, the moment Mycroft left the office.

'There's sufficient, for the moment, with the Berringer treachery,' said the Prime Minister. 'I do not believe Holmes a traitor to his country. The contrary. I see him as someone overly influenced by Churchill's machinations. And there really could be benefit from my meeting this unknown progeny. As Holmes himself quite rightly suggested, there's need for an accurate presentation of the true state of affairs in Russia.'

'Which would be unlikely, however, to affect the opinions of the other embassies.'

'Not the point, Grey. Not the point at all. We will be seen by those in the cabinet we need to carry with us over the Berringer debacle to have moved instantly to recover: acted, indeed, with the entrepreneurialism befitting Churchill himself. And let's not overlook the personal interest of the king in the Tsar's safety.'

'Well thought out, sir!' congratulated the Foreign Secretary.

'I thought so,' smiled Asquith.

It was the perfect day that Olga had forecast, the early warmth promising perhaps sultry heat later. The recall message from his uncle had awaited Sebastian when he returned to the hotel the previous night, but there had been no expected embassy summons. Neither had there been before he left the hotel that morning, nor any contact from Captain Black or Alexander Kerensky. Mycroft's message had talked of his returning to London when he considered his task finished, which Sebastian objectively supposed it was, once he kept his undertaking to Sir Nigel Pearlman and received a response – an indication at least – on Orlov's sanctuary proposal. It meant, he calculated, that he could extend his time in the Russian capital by at least another three or four days, longer if he managed another meeting with Kerensky or Stalin. A week, estimated Sebastian. He'd suggest a week and spend as much of it as was practicable with Olga, who sat opposite him in the jolting coach, bewitching – his chosen alternative to breathtaking – in summer white, smiling at the shared secret of their tryst, her familiarly tightly pinned hair still stirred by the wind through the open carriage window. They'd left the city an hour ago and were travelling through what Sebastian guessed to be flood plains, increasingly dotted with Olga's promised daffodils.

'There is a swimming lodge by the lake,' she said. 'Word has been sent ahead for it to be made ready. And the picnic prepared.'

'For our escorts as well?' asked Sebastian, gesturing behind. In the bends in the road, their following guarding coach was keeping a measured distance.

'They're to ensure our road safety, nothing more. Their orders come from me, which will be that they occupy their day with the servants at the dacha.'

'I've been asked for a return date to London,' announced Sebastian.

Olga's smile went instantly, her face clouding. 'What have you replied?'

'I haven't, not yet.'

'Let's not spoil the day by talk of it, or thought of it,' Olga insisted.

'Paris is not a day's travel from London.'

Olga frowned once more. 'An echo from my father!'

'My own remark,' insisted Sebastian.

Olga's smile returned. 'Maybe I should consider a holiday in Paris very soon?'

'Maybe I should, too.'

The carriage discernibly slowed for its turn off the main highway, and was at once enshrouded by a thick forest of trees on either side of the track, some so close their outer branches actually brushed and rattled against the cabin's side. After about fifty yards, the vehicle stopped completely at a command post, the deference immediate from the rifle-carrying guards when they saw the princess. As it was respectfully gestured on, Sebastian said: 'Is there a perimeter wall?'

'Patrols,' said Olga. 'But not too close to our destination.'

There must have been some forewarning system because servants in the same livery as at the St Petersburg palace were assembled in a greeting formation when they pulled up outside the dacha. The building was, predictably, impressively large – larger, Sebastian guessed, than the entire Diogenes Club. It was predominantly constructed of massive baulks, upon stilts which Sebastian assumed to be a precaution against the thickness of the winter snows, and entirely surrounded by an equally raised verandah. A lot of the windows were now thrown open, but all were bordered by heavy wooden shutters, which Sebastian again guessed to be a winter protection. The building was set amid expansive lawns, all of which were yellowed by the promised daffodils, which continued on uninterrupted into the surrounding woods.

Sebastian stood, impressed by Olga's natural command as she greeted everyone, aware at one point of the shifted attention of the butler and some of the assembled staff, curious at how she had obviously referred to him. The inside corridor and the room into which Olga led was, predictably again, a veritable Noah's Ark of hunting trophies.

Conscious of his examination, Olga said: 'I was assured that beaters have been out for the past two hours, clearing any animals from around the lake or the bathing lodge.'

'Are you serious?' frowned Sebastian.

'Bear and wild boar, mostly, and deer of course,' replied Olga, dismissively. 'I told them I don't want armed huntsmen on guard. My protection from wild animals is entirely your responsibility.'

'You *are* serious!'

'Are you frightened?' she goaded.

'I will be, if we're attacked!'

'If we are, we will have to lock ourselves inside the lodge until we're rescued!'

The butler appeared at the door and Olga announced: 'They're ready.'

There was a retinue of five, in addition to the butler, carrying hampers and linen and containers. They lined up behind Sebastian and Olga outside the dacha as Olga struck off familiarly along a path that Sebastian had not identified upon their arrival, despite its wideness sufficient for them to remain side by side. As they walked, Olga said: 'I introduced you as a very important European friend of my father's.'

'I suppose I have become one.' It depended, Sebastian supposed, upon London's response to the sanctuary request. Which might well have made his acceptance premature.

Sebastian tried – but quickly abandoned – superlatives for the scene that opened before them. The placid, unruffled lake was in a sudden cupped depression, hung like a sun-sparkled jewel between the supporting diamond strands of its supply and exit streams, threaded through competing yellow-gold banks. The lodge was its tiger's eye or onyx clasp, midway between both tributaries. The analogy was broken by the yellow dappled clearing all around, a jetty thrusting out its finger into the water, a sleeping but obviously polished and prepared launch slumbering alongside a sail-rigged skiff.

'I've never seen – imagined – anything like it,' managed Sebastian. 'It's spectacular.'

'Isn't it, though,' said Olga, pleased with his reaction.

Only when they reached the lodge did the wagon train surge ahead, to meet others already there, who'd set up tables and chairs and gazebo canvas, beneath which they now spread cloths on tables and blankets and cushions on lawns, and pole-suspended hammocks. While the picnic was being assembled under the militarily precise command of the butler, Olga led Sebastian out upon the jetty to inspect the waiting craft.

Olga said: 'You have a choice.'

'I'm not a sailor,' apologized Sebastian.

'I am,' she boasted.

'Are you to prove it?'

'I am inappropriately dressed to do so.'

'I have a confession,' teased Sebastian. 'I am equally ill equipped to swim, not having brought bathing apparel.'

'Neither have I,' said Olga.

'I did not imagine it necessary.'

'Neither did I,' she repeated.

They picnicked off chilled caviar and sturgeon, and cold grouse and pigeon breasts, and drank crisply cold white wine and scarcely talked, without need, so enclosed were they in each other and with each other.

When they'd finished, Olga said: 'To swim naked with you is another fantasy.'

'How many more do you have?'

'Do you want me to stop creating them?'

'No.'

The lake water was breathtakingly cold and they held each other more than swam, touching each other and supporting each other, and she cupped him between both hands and said: 'I hope this injury isn't permanent,' and he said: 'It could easily become so,' and she said: 'We should get out of such withering coldness at once, to prevent it happening.' They tantalized each other, lying naked on separate hammocks for the sun to dry them before Sebastian lifted her easily on to the cushioned rugs and they explored each other again and made discoveries that they hadn't before, and after she climaxed for the second time, Olga said: 'I'm so glad I nursed your injury back to full health and well-being.'

They lay entwined, exhausted, for a long time, careless even of the humming things that swarmed and occasionally pitched around them. Sebastian said: 'I cannot believe we are unobserved, any more than I believe we were upon the riverboat.'

Olga, nestled in the crook of his arm, shrugged and mumbled: 'It's of no matter to me.'

The recollection of his sighting of Ludmilla Berringer in his mind, Sebastian said: 'Your father knew which steamer we were upon, didn't he?'

Olga giggled, pulling very slightly back. 'No! I told him another from a different pier at a different, earlier time. When

277

he asked later, I said we had arrived too late and had to take another.'

'The deceit of it!' exclaimed an affronted King George V.

'There is no indication that the Tsar had personal knowledge of it,' said Herbert Asquith.

'Do we attempt to infiltrate their embassy here?'

'No, sir!'

'Exactly!' said the King, as if a point had been proved. 'It's damnable. I'm minded to write personally to Nicky; let him know of my offence.'

'The matter is being resolved with the greatest of discretion,' reminded the Prime Minister.

'I'm not sure about that, either. The damned couple should be publicly exposed.'

'With respect, Your Majesty, your government believes the matter should be dealt with in the manner that I have proposed.'

'Don't like it! Don't like it at all!'

'It's for the best,' assured Asquith. 'Both here and abroad.'

'Still don't like it.'

'Touching upon a possibly connected subject, in the light of your personally expressed concern, your government has carried out an exhaustive enquiry into the likelihood of serious unrest initiated by the Serb nationalism,' said Asquith. 'The virtually unanimous opinion from all your embassies in the Balkans is that, while there is evidence of local skirmishing, it is unlikely to result in escalating international conflict.'

'So, Nicky's not endangered, if ever he were in the first place?'

'No, sir. Your government do not believe that the Romanov family is at any risk from a repetition of 1905.'

'Just as well!' said the king. 'It was deceitful, Asquith. No matter what you say, it was deceitful.'

Mycroft remained bemused by the encounter with Asquith and the Foreign Secretary, expecting, literally at any moment throughout the nerve-gnawed day, a denunciating recall which never came. So extended was he that he only relaxed, and then just slightly, when he realized the day to be that of the Prime

Minister's scheduled audience with the King, and he at once risked contact with Lord Stamfordham, relieved at the easy acceptance by the man of his invitation to dinner that very evening. Too often reminded by his brother of the limitations of the Diogenes kitchens, Mycroft proposed Rules as the venue and was apprehensively there a full thirty minutes before the arrival of the King's secretary.

'Capital choice, Holmes!' declared the man, as he sat. 'Close to being my favourite. The brown Windsor soup at the Travellers pales, noticeably, after too much experience,' and, as if proof were necessary, he ordered a dozen Colchester oysters to begin his meal.

Anxious though he was, Mycroft allowed the initial conversation to continue in generalities, although seeking an opening, which in the event he didn't need, as Stamfordham abruptly declared: 'Nasty business in St Petersburg, don't you think?'

'Asquith told the King?'

'Who is most exercised. Can't bring himself to believe the Tsar would behave in such a manner.'

'There could be many explanations that we don't yet have,' lured Mycroft. 'It surely won't affect the King's underlying concern for the Romanov family?'

'The King has asked my advice, as well as that of Asquith,' disclosed Stamfordham. 'He's hardened against Nicholas: dismisses the idea of there being any risk to the Romanov throne.'

'What would be his response to a sanctuary request if one were to arise?' openly demanded Mycroft, close to exhaustion after the extremes of the day.

Stamfordham stopped eating, looking across the table in surprise. 'If there isn't going to be such a request, it's a baseless question. But he certainly wouldn't contemplate it if he thought his own throne was endangered, which he seriously thinks to be a risk if there is a religious civil war in Ireland.'

'That's unthinkable!' protested Mycroft.

'That was exactly the King's remark at leaning that the Tsar has suborned people within our embassy in St Petersburg.'

\* \* \*

Sebastian strained outwardly to maintain the perfection of their day, but inwardly his mind was put in turmoil by Olga's casual admission of her simple deception. Orlov had *not* intentionally sacrificed Ludmilla Berringer, and through her exposed her husband! Sebastian had not the slightest regret nor doubt that, in having identified the woman with Viktor Krazin, he had behaved in the only possible manner open to him, but, with the benefit of examination, he recognized that he had created a conflict with the rest of his remit. Or had he? That remit had been to assess the political stability in Russia, as reflected in its capital, and within that context judge the personal safety of the Tsar and his family, both of which he had fulfilled. The unexpected detection of a German espionage presence was an additional and unquestionable success. As with the discovery of the Berringers' liaison with the Okhrana. Whatever endangerment that constituted to Orlov's escape plan, if indeed it was endangered, was of Orlov's creation, not his. The rationalization did nothing to resolve Sebastian's personal disquiet, and he knew readily enough its cause. Sebastian had no doubt whatsoever that there would be another attempt to overthrow the Tsar, nor that the second would be better planned and less spontaneous than the first, substantially improving its chances of success, and the need for royal evacuation. Which, according to Orlov's proposal, would include the evacuation of his daughter, about whose safety Sebastian believed himself as closely concerned as her father.

'You grew quiet,' accused Olga, as they dressed each other, for the first time in the concealment of the lodge. 'Of what were you thinking?'

'Not of what. Of whom. You.'

'What about me?' Olga invited, flirtatiously.

'How much I want to protect you . . . keep you from harm.'

Caught by his seriousness, Olga said: 'Aware as you are of the precautions my father has in place, you can surely have no cause for concern on that score?'

'Circumstances all too frequently exceed expectations.'

'My father anticipates everything,' she insisted, proudly.

Except, perhaps, subterfuge on river boats, thought Sebastian. 'Move to Paris, where we can be often together!'

he urged. 'Again it's me asking you, nothing of your father's interference.'

'There is nothing I could wish for more than for us to be often together,' said Olga, totally serious now. 'But you already have my answer to why I will not leave Russia.'

'At least spend more time there than here!'

'I have promised vacations.'

'Promise more.'

'I cannot. Will not.'

He had openly and fully to warn Orlov how he might have put at risk any sanctuary agreement from England, Sebastian decided: press the Grand Duke to initiate alternatives, difficult though that would doubtless be, because of the man's undisclosed, non-political role within the imperial court.

The lightness had gone from their day. Unspeaking, they made their way back to the dacha through the flower-perfumed woodland bower, beyond which the carriages were drawn up in readiness, the butler and three other permanent staff assembled. The princess briefly addressed them before letting Sebastian hand her into their lead coach, the windows still lowered against the late-afternoon heat. They sat as before, opposite each other.

As they jerked into motion, Olga said: 'I told them it was a magnificent picnic and that we might visit again, very shortly.'

'I would like that,' said Sebastian. Would he be allowed, after his admission to the Grand Duke?

'Shall it be a definite arrangement?'

'Yes, a definite arrangement.'

'With no more talk of Paris, beyond vacation visits?'

'With no more talk of Paris,' Sebastian accepted, emptily.

The return to St Petersburg was busier than their outward journey, the road heavier, with cars as well as with coaches, and noisy with impatient, anxious drivers sounding their horns to pass, and shying the horses, further unsettled by the galloping coach teams whipped past.

'Would you have me raise the windows?' offered Sebastian.

'I prefer the breeze. We're almost into the city now.'

Sebastian had his back to the driver and became aware of the disappearing flood plain. With his backward view of the curves and twists in the road, he was relieved that there was no immediate sight of cars or coaches preparing to overtake.

'Shall you dine with us tonight?'

'I'm expecting things to be awaiting me when I get back,' said Sebastian. Would one be a reaction to Orlov's proposal? It would be cause for him to accept the invitation and, at the same time as conveying the response to the Grand Duke, to make his full admission. Having reached the decision he'd decided integrity demanded, Sebastian was anxious to complete it.

Houses and buildings came into Sebastian's sideways view as they entered St Petersburg, but he was attracted back towards the rear as a carriage that had for several miles remained behind their escort coach suddenly pulled out, to overtake, the coachman busy with his whip, the horses strained by the demand. Although the highway was sufficiently wide, Sebastian was surprised at the realization that the driver intended not just to overtake their escort behind, but to continue on to go by theirs as well. He was first conscious of the lathered horses drawing abreast of their open window, and then of movement at the window of the passing coach, and of an indistinct object being hurled. It struck his leg and bounced further along his seat and Sebastian's recognition was instant, like his movement. He snatched up the bomb, feeling its grooved metal casing, twisting with the same movement to toss it back out. There was a kaleidoscope of seconds in which everything appeared slow, unmoving. Sebastian had the vision of a face he knew, eyes wide in startled recognition, of the bomb bouncing along the road behind, an ear-shattering roar of an explosion that lifted him bodily, and then he was engulfed in total black oblivion.

# Twenty-Six

Sebastian was embalmed in pain, his skull feeling as if it were being crushed by unrelenting bands tightening and tightening around his head. He tried to speak but couldn't hear himself, couldn't hear anything but a throbbing, echoing, tuneless hum. He could not see, either, not properly, his eyes filmed as if he were in the thickest of a thick London fog, only able vaguely to make out movement but no real shape. But he could feel hands on him, pressing him down, and he tried to fight against them but was too weak, and then there was a lighter, smoothing touch against his face and he thought there was a voice, a mouth, close to his ear, but the words wouldn't come through the meaningless buzz. He was lying down, Sebastian guessed: held down, but not roughly, not to hurt him. To quieten him then, for him to realize that he was not being attacked, not a prisoner. The hand was still soft, soothing, against his cheek, and he heard the voice at last, Olga's voice, he thought, but he wasn't sure. He thought the word was 'still', which he didn't understand. He tried to say it back, but wasn't sure that he did, although the sound in his ears changed every time he tried, the buzzing becoming a drone. Then he made out, or thought he did, another word and it did make sense. He was being told to lie still, and he said, 'Yes,' and heard the drone of the word and relaxed against the restraining hands. Sebastian tried to see, squeezing his eyes tightly shut and opening them wide, tightly shut and open wide, and gradually the fog began to clear, although the outlines of those around him were still hazily indistinct.

He was sure of Olga, though; that it was her gentle, comforting hand on his face.

Sebastian tried to say: 'Where are we?' but only managed,

'Where . . .' to a droning resonance. Olga said: 'Home. We're home. Safe. Don't talk, not yet,' and so he didn't, but continued to open and close his eyes and swallow against the diminishing hum. His hearing cleared and his eyes cleared and the torturing bands stopped tightening around his head and as the pain subsided he remembered everything – the face he had recognized the most starkly of all – and isolated the Grand Duke and a frock-coated man at the foot of his bed, in unnecessarily head-bent, hushed conversation.

Sebastian's recovery was neither complete nor immediate. He drifted in and out of consciousness, encouraged each time that he could hear and see and speak more easily and that the pain in his head was lessening, although, as it did, he became aware of other aches in other parts of his body, but when he managed to touch those that he could, he did not detect any bandages.

It was dark when Sebastian fully awoke, the room dimly lit by candles, not overhead light. Olga, the white summer dress stained and dirty and torn at one arm, her hair straggled, slept in a chair drawn close to the right of his bed. Her face was smudged with dirt, too. A hand he guessed had been holding his had fallen away, but still rested a few inches away on the bed covering. A nurse, crisply uniformed, slumbered on the other side in another chair. Otherwise the room was empty and totally quiet. His head didn't hurt any more but his body ached, particularly his back and right shoulder, the pain knifing through him if he tried the slightest movement, which he stopped attempting, apart from, very gently and gradually, feeling again for bandaging which he still couldn't find.

The nurse roused herself with a snuffled cough, hurriedly straightening in her chair, her eyes widening when she saw Sebastian was looking at her. Her blurted question was unthinkingly loud, instantly waking Olga.

She came anxiously forward, reaching out again for his hand. 'Is it bad?'

'No,' Sebastian said, hoarsely. He coughed and said: 'No, not bad. Not bad at all.'

'You were in such pain!'

'It's better now. My head scarcely hurts at all.'

'You mustn't move. The doctor says you must stay still.'

The nurse said something, to Olga's quick reply, and hurried from the room. Olga said: 'She's gone to get him, the doctor. My father had him stay.'

'Tell me.'

'Later.'

'You weren't hurt?'

Olga looked down at herself, tugging at her torn sleeve. 'They say I would have been if you hadn't acted so quickly. And then totally taken what blast from the explosion reached our coach.'

'Who died?'

'Everyone in the carriage behind. The driver, of course. Even the horses.' She shook her head, impatient. 'I *am* telling you, aren't I?'

'What about the other coach, the one from which the bomb was thrown?'

'They all escaped. No one knows who they were . . . revolutionaries, obviously.'

He knew, thought Sebastian. 'How long was I unconscious?'

'All last night. It's early morning now, three, maybe four. I haven't heard a strike.'

The bedroom door thrust open, the Grand Duke close behind the frock-coated doctor, the nurse at the rear now accompanied by two more. Olga replied to a curt remark clearly addressed to Sebastian, and said: 'I've told him you don't speak Russian and that I shall interpret.'

It was a protracted, careful examination. The doctor shone various intensities of light into Sebastian's eyes before having him count fingers displayed in quick, conjuring succession. After the checks with his eyes open, responding to relayed instructions, Sebastian performed a series of tests bringing the forefingers of each hand to various parts of his face and body with his eyes closed. Two of the nurses busily intruded themselves between Olga and the bed, holding up its covering between them as a shielding screen, when the physician extended the examination to Sebastian's body, which included a selection of reflex-response tests to Sebastian's wrists, elbows, knees and feet, which he struck or irritated with a rubber-headed hammer. Through Olga, he also identified where discomfort or pain existed – repeatedly denying that any remained in his head – as he followed instructions to carry out exercises with his arms, legs, shoulders and back. It was only when he was actually twisting and bending that Sebastian properly realized he was naked, and saw the extent of the bruising by which his body was discoloured. There were grazes and cuts, too, although none was deep or any longer bleeding. Sebastian was grateful finally to lie back in bed, to be covered again, sure he kept any grimace from his face.

'He says the comparatively new scar to your chest appears to be a wound.'

Sebastian had forgotten the result of his attempted assassination in Lafayette Park, in Washington DC. 'A riding accident,' he improvized.

'Is it painful?'

'Not at all.'

'He wants to be assured you have no head pain,' insisted Olga.

'I have no pain there whatsoever.'

'What about your neck?'

'None.'

'How is it when you breath?'

'It aches.'

'When you breath, do you get any sensation in your ribs, a grating or a rubbing together, as if any bones might be broken?'

'No. It's just a general ache of a bruise.'

'There's no blurred or double vision, the outlines of things superimposed, one slightly apart from the other.'

'No. I can now see quite clearly.'

The conversation expanded beyond Olga, to include her father, and briefly the nurse who had been in the room when Sebastian awoke. Olga said: 'He thinks you're remarkably fortunate. He believed that you had broken your head but there's no indication of your having done so from his examination of your eyes or your reflexes.'

'How did I get so bruised?'

'You were thrown backwards into the coach by the blast.

Your head and a lot of your back hit the frame of the opposite door. If you'd hit the door itself, you'd have probably been thrown out completely and caught more of the explosion.'

'So I am lucky,' agreed Sebastian.

'He's prescribing laudanum, to make you sleep for the rest of the night. And he'll see you in the morning.'

'Thank him. And the nurses.'

'The nurses are staying.'

'You saved my daughter's life by what you did,' said the Grand Duke, speaking for the first time.

'And my own,' Sebastian pointed out. 'It's bad that others had to die.'

'I want to speak tomorrow about what you can remember,' said the man. 'You can remember something about it, can't you?'

Everything about it, with cristal clarity, thought Sebastian. 'I'm sure I can.'

Sebastian tried to argue against the sleeping draught, but the doctor, with Olga's added insistence, prevailed, and he lapsed almost at once into a heavy, uninterrupted sleep until the sudden bright daylight the following morning. He must have lain virtually unmoving, because his bruised body had stiffened and initially hurt more than when he'd recovered in the middle of the night. He was relieved, though, that his head remained clear. Two of the nurses, using hand signals, insisted upon bodily washing him, and it was only when he saw the colour of the twice-changed water that Sebastian realized he had been put to bed still filthy from the explosion. Olga arrived just as they were finishing, bathed and coiffured and immaculate as ever. There was an exchange in Russian and both nurses left.

Olga said: 'You have a black eye that wasn't there last night.'

'And a very black body.'

She smiled. 'Which I was not allowed to see last night. Although I don't think I would have liked it so hurt. How's your head?'

'No pain.'

'Father has sent people to the hotel, for fresh clothes and

linen. Those you wore are ruined.' She smiled again. 'The nurses actually had to cut them away from you. I was jealous!'

A further drain on his wardrobe, thought Sebastian. 'What about you? Weren't you hurt at all?'

'You really did take the whole force, concentrated through the open window. I was shocked, more by thinking that you were dead than by the explosion itself. And a little deaf, although not for long.'

'How did we get back here?'

'In the coach. One of the rear wheels was buckled but not fully broken, and the horses weren't injured, just panicked. The coachman got them under control and continued on, even though it was in the same direction as those who attacked us. He did not see them again.'

'The driver behaved well.'

There was an unannounced flurry of arrivals, the hurrying doctor trailed by the Grand Duke and the nurses. The examination was a repetition of the first, again with the instructions and questions coming through Olga. On this occasion, when told to, she retreated further into the room, while Sebastian, once more shielded by sheets, was bundled into a newly provided robe. Once covered, he was told to stand fully and unaided – which he managed after the briefest moment of dizziness – before being ordered to walk in a straight line and after that complete a circle of the room.

Sebastian did not get back into bed during the ensuing discussion in Russian, but sat in an easy chair, overwhelmed by the robe, which he guessed to belong to the Grand Duke. Olga did not translate the exchanges simultaneously but waited until they finished.

She said: 'The doctor was most worried about your head. He's satisfied now it isn't cracked, but wants you to rest for a day or two. The nurses will stay, of course.'

'I don't want them to,' refused Sebastian. 'The bruising is going to restrict my doing anything strenuous . . .' To the Grand Duke he said: 'With your permission I will stay here today. There is much for us to discuss.'

'Of course,' said Orlov. 'There is a communication from London.'

Perhaps he would not be welcomed to remain after all, thought Sebastian.

Sebastian was not aware by how much the contusions and cuts were adding to his general discomfort until he bathed again, properly this time, in a bath, but thought the water, as hot as he was able to bear, helped reduce the stiffness of the bruising. It was still difficult for him to dress in the replacement clothes that arrived within fifteen minutes of the doctor's departure, and it took him three times longer than normal to complete. Olga, on his emergence from the bedroom, insisted that he eat, despite his protests that he was not hungry, waiting until Sebastian had with difficulty finished a fish preparation that reminded him of kedgeree to announce that her father was waiting for him in the familiar study.

The Grand Duke Alexei Orlov was at his desk when Sebastian entered, the recognizable secured package on a side table. The older man rose at once, coming forward with arms outstretched, but stopped short of the body-hugging embrace several feet away. 'I fear you are still too fragile to accept my physical gratitude.'

'I fear so too,' said Sebastian, gratefully, as he slowly lowered himself into his accustomed fireplace-bordering chair. Despite the care with which he held himself, a dull ache was returning in his head, although nothing like the earlier tightening band.

'I want everything of what you recollect of the attack,' demanded the Okhrana chief. 'I want those who did it!'

'It was planned, premeditated, and specifically against you,' declared Sebastian at once. 'The princess and I were in an enclosed coach which we'd boarded out of sight within the palace grounds. Nor were we visible from the highway leaving the dacha. Your would-be assassins would have been unaware that it was not you.'

Orlov slumped into the opposing chair, momentarily silenced. 'How can you be sure of that?'

'I did not notice our being followed, on our way to the dacha from St Petersburg, despite the lightness of the traffic. But we must have been. It was heavier, for our return, but again I was unaware of the carriage closely behind that of our protecting coach; several others, as well as cars, were anxious to overtake and did so.'

'Those supposed to guard you should have been aware,' broke in the Russian.

'And by failing to do so suffered the ultimate consequences,' said Sebastian. 'It was the fact that it made no attempt to pass until we entered the city, before which there had been many easier opportunities, that caught my attention, but only then out of curiosity, which increased when I realized the driver intended to overtake not just our guards but us as well in the same manoeuvre. Which was why, although I was not conscious of it at the time, I was looking when the missile came through our open window, and was able to react so instantly . . .'

'Thank God that you did,' interrupted the Grand Duke again.

'To eject it, as I did, I went automatically to the window through which it entered. Which put me momentarily face to face with your intended killer.'

'You saw the man!' exclaimed Orlov.

'One of those expelled from the United States and now attached to the German embassy here, as Fritz Langer,' identified Sebastian.

Orlov greeted the identification in disbelieving silence, initially even shaking his head in refusal. 'That cannot be . . . could not be. There is no possibility of Langer, anyone else at the embassy, being able to know where you were going . . . how you were going . . . knowing that the coach in which you would be travelling . . . belonged to me. I am reluctant to challenge you, Holmes, but you must be mistaken. This has to be an attack chosen by chance, for no other reason than that it's clearly a conveyance of someone of stature.'

'No, sir,' refused Sebastian in return. 'The only chance of which they took advantage, or tried to, was of our travelling with the windows lowered, because of the heat. It was Langer who inflicted the wound about which the doctor questioned me last night . . . the same man who later, having failed once, levelled a pistol at me in a New York harbour warehouse and missed, again by the grace of God, less than a year ago.'

'Who could have guided them here, clearly prepared as they were, to pick up a trail?'

'The same man who frequents a particular brothel on Sadovaya Ulitsa to engage with another known German, as well as with the women of the establishment,' set out Sebastian. 'The same man whom I no longer doubt knows your true function within the Tsar's court and supplied that information to his German friends, who would see your demise as a positive advantage to their interests here. The same man who attempted to humiliate the Princess Olga at the Yusupov celebrations . . .'

'Rasputin!' stopped the Grand Duke, his voice barely above a whisper.

'Rasputin,' agreed Sebastian.

There was the briefest incoherent fury before the Grand Duke, with visible effort, regained control with an expression of chilling, revengeful calculation. One of the first things they discussed and agreed, following Sebastian's lead, was that it would be pointless seizing Langer with any hope of a criminal trial: quite apart from Langer's certain denial of Sebastian's uncorroborated sighting, the man would anyway invoke the diplomatic immunity through which the entire cell had escaped prosecution in America. Another of their equally quick realizations was that the coach-to-coach recognition would have been mutual, putting Sebastian's life at as much risk as that of the Grand Duke appeared to be.

'Which makes the course obvious,' insisted Orlov, quite calmly. 'They will be sought out and disposed of. It's a simple matter of necessary removal.'

'To be replaced by others,' argued Sebastian, curious at his own lack of revulsion at knowingly discussing murder.

'To be replaced by others,' agreed the Grand Duke, eyes unfocused in his obsession. 'Whose identity I will establish by comparing the new arrivals against those already attached to the embassy. And who will be removed as those who preceded them.'

'You can't sustain a campaign of murder against a foreign legation,' argued Sebastian. 'You'll achieve nothing by a bloodbath.'

'Sufficient deterrent,' insisted Orlov.

'These are not people to be deterred,' rejected Sebastian.

291

'They're not gangsters; not revolutionaries even, not in the normally accepted definition of the word. They're working, acting, for their country. They believe they have a justification.'

'As I am working for my country, for my Tsar,' said Orlov.

He'd been out-argued by an unacceptable, obscene logic, accepted Sebastian. 'Olga must be removed as a target, whether an intentional one or otherwise.'

'Yes,' agreed Orlov, at once. 'Olga must be protected; must never be allowed to become a victim, like her mother.'

'It should be explained to her . . . Fully, properly explained,' suggested Sebastian. The headache he'd feared would get worse was lessening, as it had during the night.

'And now there can be no argument against Paris,' insisted Orlov.

Olga still tried, after being summoned to the study, talking of arrests and public exposure, for a long time refusing their counter-arguments that nothing could be confronted or dealt with publicly. The Grand Duke obviously did not tell Olga how he did intend responding, and Sebastian was impressed by the man's compromise to get Olga safely out of the country. He promised her move to the French capital was only temporary, until he succeeded in removing the unacceptable Germans from their embassy by what he called unofficial diplomacy.

Sebastian expected Olga to demand what that vague phrase meant, but she didn't. Instead she said: 'How long?'

'Six months,' said Orlov.

'What if you have not succeeded in that time?'

'I will have done,' assured Orlov.

'No longer than six months,' Olga tried to bargain.

'You will leave, as I have asked you to,' said Orlov, the insistence turning the request into an order.

'And I will escort you,' said Sebastian.

Lunch was an uneasy interruption, a break none of them enjoyed, the London delivery still unopened and the potential difficulties of Sebastian's admission of having exposed the Berringers hanging over him. The meal, little of it eaten, was occupied with talk of Olga's move to Paris, with Orlov announcing the staff there would be warned by telegram that very afternoon of her intended arrival, and Sebastian estimating that he would be ready to leave St Petersburg to escort her there within forty-eight hours, possibly even sooner. Infected, at last, by the urgency, Olga met her father's announcement that he and Sebastian still had matters to discuss with an assurance that she had much packing to organize.

Back in the study, under Orlov's unbroken gaze, Sebastian finally opened the latest to arrive from London, surprised – although not by the content itself – but that it even included an initial reaction to the Okhrana infiltration of the embassy. He wasn't, however, surprised at Churchill's complete rejection of the idea of sailing a squadron of British warships into the Gulf of Finland amidst the uncertainty of a revolutionary government.

Having thought about it – anticipated it – for so long, the words weren't difficult for Sebastian. He remembered Olga's excuse for catching a different river steamer, and did not talk of only seeing Ludmilla Berringer with Viktor Krazin at the very last moment of disembarkation. Despite the closeness with which he and Orlov had allied themselves, and the personal friendship extended towards him, he'd considered, as he still considered, he'd had no alternative but to disclose their deception to the embassy. It had subsequently transpired that they had consistently misled the embassy – and through it, London – about the stability of the Tsar's throne, and by so doing directly and positively contradicted the dangers to the dynasty that he had relayed. London – possibly the King himself, from the inference of what he had just received – believed itself doubly deceived. Orlov's rescue proposal was considered totally impracticable: quite apart from what had arisen over the previous twenty-four hours, Sebastian felt it necessary to return to London as soon as possible, hopefully to correct as much misconception as possible. He still hoped to achieve some promise of protection in the event of the Tsar's overthrow.

Orlov did not respond at once. He remained head forward, his beard overflowing on to his chest. At last he roused himself and said, quiet-voiced: 'Defeated by my own attempted cleverness.'

'Badly served by it,' judged Sebastian.

'The Berringers were cultivated before the opportunity of your totally unexpected arrival.'

'Why did you have them misinform, as they so blatantly did?' demanded Sebastian, allowing the exasperation.

'That was a mistake too; of a time when I did not believe the situation as fragile as I now see it is. Is there to be a public exposure?'

'I don't know. I've yet to see the ambassador again. It's in the expectation of doing so that I am delaying my return for forty-eight hours.'

'Not knowing that they have already been discovered – but aware of it now, as they are of an association between us – the Germans will doubtless try to seek you out. Your safety would be better assured by your remaining within these walls.'

Sebastian shook his head. 'I cannot deal with the embassy from here.'

'You won't be unattended, throughout the rest of your time in the city. But do not any longer risk moving around unarmed.'

'I don't intend to.'

'I'm entrusting Olga to your care.'

'I'll not be found wanting,' promised Sebastian. *I hope*, he thought. His head had begun to hurt again.

# Twenty-Seven

Sebastian insisted upon leaving the Orlov palace that evening, admitting to himself within minutes of passing through the gates, accompanied both in front and behind by guard carriages, that the departure was premature. Every pothole and road hump jarred through him, setting his bruises on fire, and bringing back the threatening headache. Messages from the previous day awaited him from both Captain Black and the ambassador, but Sebastian responded to neither, returning at once to bed. He slept fitfully, always half-aware of where he was, awakened by spurts of pain whenever he shifted position. He came fully awake before dawn but remained where he was, extending the rest as long as he could in the hope it would further restore him, using the time to reflect upon where he found himself on his mission. A second meeting with Stalin had always depended upon the man's whim, but Sebastian had held out more hope of another approach from Kerensky, still undecided – and wanting to know – precisely how the man had used him. But he supposed Kerensky's Duma claim had been repayment enough, and that there was little of benefit to expect from another encounter. Extending his time had in any case been more for personal than professional reasons, and they no longer existed now that Olga had agreed to move to France. Sebastian could not imagine – didn't want to imagine – how their relationship would develop, if it would develop at all, or instead remain at the level of Olga's choosing, as an adventure. He'd accompany her to Paris, as he'd promised her father, but continue directly to London, to discharge whatever duty remained unresolved from this assignment. Only when his duty was completely fulfilled would he go back to France and whatever awaited him there. There was a large aristocratic émigré presence in Paris. It was even conceivable that, by the time he returned, Olga would be involved in another, different adventure, ungallant though that objective thought might be.

Remembering how long his preparations had taken the previous day, Sebastian still arose early, lingering in the bath to relieve the overnight stiffness, which it perceptibly did, so that dressing was easier. There was no trace at all of a headache. He breakfasted in his room, to be there if the military attaché called, but made the approach himself when it passed nine.

'Where have you been, Holmes?' demanded Black, sounding unusually excited.

'Incapacitated. Another accident. I want to meet now, today. And during the same visit to see the ambassador. He's summoned me.'

'You clearly haven't heard the news.'

'What news?'

'There was an assassination last night!'

'Of Sir Nigel?' blurted Sebastian.

'No! One of the German spies, Fritz Langer. Shot dead in the street, practically outside the embassy. Isn't that incredible?'

'Incredible,' agreed Sebastian.

Which it was, decided Sebastian, swordstick by his side, revolver uncomfortable against one of his worst bruises, as he waited in the foyer for Black's promised collection. Sebastian hadn't doubted Orlov's determination, but equally hadn't imagined that the Grand Duke would carry out the retribution so immediately. Nor be so unthinkingly reckless; stupid even. Langer would have reported their bomb-throwing mutual recognition to Hans Vogel and other agents – known and unknown – at the German embassy. So, Sebastian accepted, his would be the name most obviously connected with Langer's murder, and the person against whom the first retaliation was most likely to be attempted. Double and eager retaliation, in fact, for the damage he had earlier inflicted upon them in America. Sebastian's concern was not, however, for himself. It was for Olga, whom he was escorting to Paris, and who now quite literally risked getting caught in the crossfire if their

296

departure were detected and they were pursued. Sebastian's reasoning confirmed, if confirmation had been necessary, his decision to abandon any further encounters with either Stalin or Kerensky, conclude whatever business remained at the embassy, and conceal himself against discovery until his very moment of boarding the European express. Abruptly Sebastian emerged from his total inner concentration to realize that he was sitting, openly visible, in the busiest public place in St Petersburg's foremost hotel. He thrust up, painfully, to return to his suite, but changed direction at the sight of the attaché entering through the main door, hurrying him back out at once.

'Good heavens, Holmes! You're bruised! Battered!'

'A misadventure with a coach.'

'You're remarkably accident-prone.'

'A problem I'm trying strenuously to avoid,' said Sebastian, settling gratefully within the concealment of the embassy carriage: the sort of marked conveyance to which the Germans might pay particular attention, he thought.

Unprompted, Black recounted the decision immediately to repatriate the Berringers, enforce the man's premature retirement on health grounds, and conceal the debacle from any public awareness.

'Sir Nigel fears it'll ruin his hopes of a Foreign Office posting, too,' disclosed Black.

'What of you?'

'Personal praise from Sir Edward Grey, early recall to discuss my future in the War Office,' smiled Black. 'That's why I called you. To thank you, for everything. And return the material I've been holding for you, in my safe. I'm starting to pack, to go back to London.'

Sebastian hesitated, deciding against telling the other man of his own intention to return. Instead he said: 'Tell me something about the Berringers. Did either of them have access to your safe?'

'Absolutely not!' insisted the attaché, indignantly. 'No one had a key except me.'

So Black had been the one who'd spied upon him. It was of little consequence now. 'What's known of the German business?'

'Very little. Langer was apparently seen to leave the embassy alone last night a little after eight, late for a dinner appointment with some others from the embassy. He never arrived. The others found his body in an alley, about fifty yards from the legation, on their way back. He'd been shot once, in the back of the head. No one saw anything, heard anything. It's caused a hell of a furore among the diplomatic community.'

That was obvious from the flustered greeting from Sir Nigel Pearlman. The man was physically disarrayed and at first had difficulty completing full sentences. He called Berringer and his wife despicable and asked for the undertaking, which Sebastian gave, not to disclose to anyone how the matter had been so discreetly settled. By the time he began questioning Sebastian upon the discoveries he'd made and the opinions he'd formed in St Petersburg, the ambassador had become more composed. It was Sebastian who began hesitantly before realizing that he was most probably providing the man with what he saw as his attempted rehabilitation in London's eyes, and expanded at length about all that he felt able, stressing his belief in the decay within the Romanov court and in the dangerous influence of Gregory Rasputin. He stopped short of the liaison between the monk and the known German agent, not able to provide a source for the knowledge, but insisted the presence of the German spies was a positive indication of their support of the revolutionaries, either Bolshevik or Menshevik or both.

'Do you seriously believe there's the likelihood of the Tsar being overthrown?' pressed the diplomat.

'I have not the slightest doubt of it happening,' said Sebastian, seeing his opportunity. 'If you intend sharing anything of this conversation with London, I would also suggest you remind them of the family connections between the Romanovs and our own royal family and ask for official guidance if there were ever to be a request for sanctuary.'

'You've heard from Black of the appalling attack upon the Germans?'

He could utilize it, Sebastian decided. 'Surely proof of how strong the revolutionaries consider themselves to be.'

'My interpretation exactly,' seized the ineffectual ambassador.

For much of the return journey, Sebastian sat with his revolver held in readiness, holstering it out of sight only when he reached the hotel, alert to everyone and everything around him as he hurried directly to his suite. The Grand Duke came at once to the telephone, initially silent to Sebastian's accusation as to the risk to which he'd put his daughter by the assassination of Fritz Langer.

'We are forewarned,' insisted Orlov. 'It would take nothing short of an army to penetrate the protection that will be around you and Olga during your journey to Paris.'

'And once there?'

'It will remain around her,' said the man. 'You accepted your mission well aware of its potential dangers.'

'Indeed I did,' agreed Sebastian. 'My concern is not for myself but of my endangering Olga by association.' Were those dangers – to which it was unthinkable to expose Olga – going to form an impassable barrier to their continuing relationship? As is so often the case, one uncertainty compounded another. Surely the Grand Duke Alexei Orlov didn't believe he could cordon Olga from harm while at the same time offering him up as bait for German revenge! Sebastian wanted very much to believe that to be overly conspiratorial nonsense. But couldn't bring himself to do so, certainly not after Olov's reply.

The Russian said: 'That association will end upon her arrival in Paris, won't it?'

It remained difficult for Sebastian the day of his advanced departure, of which he telegraphed London at the last moment, while his luggage was actually being assembled. Orlov had insisted upon organizing their journey. There were two guard carriages, with an additional baggage wagon, accompanying the coach that collected him from the Grand Hotel to take him to a completely closed-off section of the rail terminal. The carriage exclusively assigned to him and Olga was between two other reserved coaches for their guards and Olga's travelling staff. Sebastian's allocated section consisted of a sitting room, separate bathroom equipped with a full-sized bath, and an adjoining bedroom. It was gas-lamped and heavily over-stuffed Victorian; the comparison with the personalized carriages in which he'd travelled on his American venture was more favourable than it had been on his journey out, and Sebastian decided he preferred it. Most particularly of all, he liked the internal connecting door to that part of the carriage in which Olga would be travelling.

He had no sight of her during his bustling, steam-enveloped arrival, nor after he established himself in his quarters to unpack his travelling trunks before returning to the outside corridor overlooking the platform. There was, though, a lot of activity upon it, an ant-like procession of servants laden with every size and type and shape of luggage.

Orlov emerged, seemingly alone, like an ephemeral mirage through the swirling steam, a protective phalanx of secondary ghosts materializing behind to form a physical barrier in front of the door through which Orlov entered Sebastian's section.

Sebastian led their way back into his sitting room. Orlov shook his head against Sebastian's invitation from the already open, decanter-filled cabinet.

Sebastian said: 'I was looking for the princess.'

'The train will not leave without her. Are you reassured by the security?'

'Assault would be difficult,' conceded Sebastian. 'But it surely resembles a royal departure, certain to attract attention and gossip.'

'About which nothing can be done.'

'Does Olga know of Langer?'

'There was no reason for her to,' dismissed Orlov. 'Is all your business completed here?'

'I urged the ambassador yesterday to raise with London possible sanctuary for the Tsar and his family.'

'You leave much indebtedness behind you.'

'There has been mutual benefit.'

'What of the unfortunate Berringers?'

'A settled matter.'

Orlov nodded, accepting the refusal. 'We have been well met, Holmes.'

'Perhaps again, in the future?'

'Who of us knows our fate?' The train rocked back and forth, to further effusions of steam. Orlov said: 'It is almost time. I put my daughter in your care.'

'Aided by sufficient others, I trust.'

'You'll not be taken by surprise.' Orlov rose, extending his hand. 'Travel safely and well.'

'Which is what I hope to do,' said Sebastian, taking the offered hand.

Unthinkingly Sebastian had expected the Grand Duke to go out into the corridor but instead the man opened the connecting door, without knocking, to enter Olga's quarters. Sitting again, Sebastian gazed out of the window opposite their platform, easily able to pick out across the bordering tracks guards on the next platform on that side, too, conscious for the first time that there were no intervening, overlooking trains. They were, he supposed, as secure as it was possible to be.

Sebastian estimated it to be another fifteen minutes before there were further, final shunting movements, accompanied by official shouts and whistles from the outside platform. He decided against going out into the corridor again for the actual departure, leaving the moment, if she so chose, for Olga's farewell to her father. He remained looking in that direction, though, but did not see Orlov disembark. Nor was the man visibly standing there for a waved goodbye when the train finally lurched into movement and pulled out of the station. Sebastian allowed a few moments, almost until the train lost the mansions and houses to the open marsh plains, before knocking lightly on the connecting door.

Olga opened it at once, framed in the doorway. 'You took a long time!'

'I thought some of your people might be with you. I almost waited for your approach.'

'Yours is the only company I seek during this adventure.'

Another adventure, noted Sebastian. They sat comfortably, familiarly entwined in his carriage, abandoning it only for it to be set for lunch, prepared by the Grand Duke's travelling chef and staff. During the interruption, Olga remarked that she always rested in the afternoon, to be reminded by Sebastian that she'd told him that on a previous occasion. Olga kissed and caressed his bruises and promised to be gentle, which she was, although several times Sebastian had to bury his face into her shoulder to disguise the pain their love-making caused him.

There was even the cristal-bottled champagne for their pre-dinner aperitif, and while they were drinking it, Olga said: 'How long will you remain in Paris?'

'Not at all,' said Sebastian. 'I shall at once continue to finish my business in London.'

'But then return?'

'If that's your wish.'

'You know it is!' said Olga, petulantly. 'Don't tease me.'

How easy it was, cocooned as they were, secure as they were, to forget the dangers. 'You do properly accept how careful you are going to have to be, even in Paris? This might be an adventure, but it could easily change, as far away from St Petersburg as you might be.'

'Do you really expect me to forget so quickly what happened?'

'I want you to go on remembering it and not expose yourself to any risks.'

'I made a promise to my father and now I am making a promise to you. I will avoid every risk. But neither will I remain in permanent exile. I will stay in Paris for the six months and then I will return to Russia. That's my agreement.'

Their journey across Europe was a languorous idyll, enclosed in themselves, wanting no one but themselves. The only time Sebastian gave any attention to the countryside through which they passed was when he estimated they were near where he'd seen the begging waifs, ready in the corridor with coin with which he could possibly reach them, but on this home-ward journey the train did not slow and they flashed by the outstretched hands before he could properly lower the sash. He still tossed out everything he had ready in his hand, but they were gone too quickly to be sure it landed anywhere near them. Sebastian was satisfied he'd identified the halt at which the naked child had been tethered for sale, but she was no longer there. He thought he saw the strip of securing cloth still attached to the post against which she had been tied. Sebastian shook his head to Olga's question, denying that he had been specifically looking for something beside the track.

Their idyll evaporated, the adventure over, early the third day, with their obviously crossing the border into France. The previous night Olga had refused to release him after their love-making, increasingly difficult though it was to attempt to stay together, until finally he'd pleaded discomfort from his remaining bruises.

In the morning Olga said: 'Must you continue on so quickly?'

'I am expected. Arrangements will have been made.'

'They could be changed.'

'I'll return to Paris at the earliest opportunity.'

'Make me a promise?'

'Of course.'

'Stop worrying about me. Take every care yourself. You are already too much scarred.'

'Too scarred indeed,' Sebastian agreed, with forced lightness. 'It has to stop.'

Olga didn't smile. 'Yes. It has to stop. Make it stop.'

I hope I can, thought Sebastian.

Their Paris arrival was chaotic, without the Grand Duke's authority to seal off their section of the platform. They were almost at once, unexpectedly, separated, Olga encircled by bodyguards and bustled away to a waiting, protected carriage, with staff remaining to follow with her luggage, Sebastian abandoned to arrange his own porterage and onward transfer to the waiting London packet train. The bustled, abrupt change from the immediately preceding days was like awakening from a long hibernation. The opportunities for physical attack, despite the full daylight, were too numerous to contemplate or guard against; the best Sebastian could manage was to keep people at a distance. He carelessly waved money to assemble his baggage retinue, and doubled the price of the ticket from the reservations steward to secure his own exclusive compartment. He was, of course, still exposed from the outside public corridor, alert to every sound, his revolver again in readiness across his lap.

Sebastian began to question his caution by the time they reached Calais, although he remained tensed during the transfer to the cross-Channel ferry. He obtained a cabin but this time didn't incarcerate himself in it, emerging to walk on deck, failing to isolate anyone or any group paying attention to him. Reassured, he took lunch in the open dining room, although choosing a table with a bulkhead at his back, and by his Dover arrival he was sure that, despite the attention-attracting pomp of the St Petersburg departure, he and Olga had escaped unnoticed.

His father and uncle awaited Sebastian's early evening arrival at the Diogenes Club.

'There's much for us to discuss and fully understand,' greeted Mycroft.

'But it's already clear that you've acquitted yourself well,' praised Sherlock Holmes.

# Twenty-Eight

Sebastian had not fully anticipated the activity in which he would be caught up from the very moment of his arrival at the Pall Mall club. Winston Churchill joined them within the hour, leaving only Dr Watson absent, and during the long evening Sebastian judged the concentrated examination to which he was subjected by all three men to be more of an interrogation than questioning to answer doubts or misunderstandings from his communications from St Petersburg. He was called upon for what he considered a lot of repetition about the Tsar's instability and the position within the court of Gregory Rasputin. The longest exchange was over the apparent dichotomy between the co-operation extended to him by the Grand Duke Orlov and the man maintaining a misleading informant within the British embassy, which Sebastian found difficulty explaining simply as Orlov switching between changing political circumstances and convictions, which the man's role required. Churchill queried whether Orlov's newly disclosed information about Rasputin's dealings with a German espionage cell could be believed, which Sebastian answered by a full account of the attempted carriage bombing, expecting a questioning – which never came – of his being with the princess.

'There's no doubt Orlov had Langer killed?' demanded Churchill.

'None,' replied Sebastian, at once. No one in the room was showing any surprise at the almost casual enquiry about premeditated murder.

'Or that Langer recognized you and would have already passed news of your presence on to his cohorts?' asked Sherlock Holmes.

'None,' replied Sebastian, again. 'Those I exposed in New

305

York know full well of my presence in St Petersburg and with whom I was dealing.'

'Unfortunate,' remarked his father, with surprising mildness.

'I believe I successfully quit St Petersburg undetected.'

'Let us sincerely hope that you did,' said Sherlock Holmes.

'Is it your belief that Orlov will move further against the Germans identified as spies in St Petersburg?' pressed Churchill.

'My positive conviction,' confirmed Sebastian.

'The most likely outcome will be to exacerbate rather than subdue the danger to the throne,' insisted Churchill.

'An argument I lost to Orlov,' admitted Sebastian. 'What of his approach for sanctuary?'

'Badly undermined by the Berringer business,' said Churchill.

'I proposed it to the ambassador,' admitted Sebastian.

'Who set out the proposal as if it were his own,' disclosed the First Lord.

'To what reaction?'

'None, so far,' said Mycroft. 'The Prime Minister has expressed the wish to speak with you. You have an appointment at ten tomorrow morning.'

'Before which there needs to be much rehearsal,' insisted Churchill. 'But in advance of that let us charge our glasses.'

Mycroft escorted Sebastian across the park to Downing Street the following morning, agreeing with Sebastian as they walked that Churchill's insistence upon preparation the previous evening was prompted by political self-preservation.

'What of your position?' asked Sebastian. 'Haven't you been compromised?'

'I've expected far more challenge than I've received,' admitted Mycroft. 'I suspect at the moment I'm benefiting from Asquith's uncertainty.' The Cabinet Secretary hesitated, slowing their pace, and disclosed his approach to the King's secretary.

'But Asquith doesn't know your part in the King raising the matter with him?' suggested Sebastian.

'I'm reliant upon Stamfordham's discretion, which I believe I can trust, but still fear myself to be endangered.'

'As we all have been,' said Sebastian. But which he was no longer, he thought.

Sebastian's interview with Herbert Asquith extended unexpectedly for almost an hour, and Sebastian was again reminded of an interrogation. He had believed himself prepared, even before the previous night's positive rehearsal, but very quickly acknowledged its benefit, particularly when pressed in the detail he was by the Prime Minister upon his relationship and connection with Winston Churchill, steadfastly insisting it to have been limited to an introduction to the *Morning Post*, to the military attaché at the embassy, and to possible professional guidance on the presentation of articles he was still undecided upon offering to the newspaper. Sebastian had entered the meeting hoping to be able to ask – infer at least – if a sanctuary offer might be favourably considered, but Asquith's brusqueness brooked no direct question, nor offered the slightest hint. Neither was there any indication of the Prime Minister accepting that Churchill's connection had been limited.

'There are occasions when governments are sometimes grateful for the unofficial involvement of their citizens where official participation could be diplomatically difficult,' said Asquith, as the meeting finally drew towards its close. 'I think, Mr Holmes – as has occurred in the past with your father – that this might be one such occasion. I thank you and in so doing impress upon you that everything that has passed between us is in the utmost confidence.'

'I am honoured to have been of service,' said Sebastian. 'And to have been admitted to such confidence.'

'It is not, however, a practice to be considered lightly or indulged in at whim.'

'I fully understand that, sir.'

'It's best you do. From his reputation I know your father always to have remained his own man. I would recommend you follow his example.'

'I will endeavour to do that,' undertook Sebastian.

'I do not seek, of course, to influence any career choice

upon which you might have set your course. But I do not think the situation about which you have been most forthcoming would benefit by its publication in a newspaper.'

At lunch Mycroft agreed that the Prime Minister's parting remarks were a very clear warning against Sebastian becoming any further involved with Winston Churchill, and that the request not to publish anything in the *Morning Post* was part of that admonition.

'I don't consider journalism to be my calling anyway,' dismissed Sebastian.

'What plans do you have?' asked Mycroft.

'A weekend, with my father. And then perhaps a visit to Paris.'

Dr Watson accompanied them to West Sussex and, after Sebastian answered with total honesty his father's questions about the obvious although fading bruises and the still-new scar upon his cheek, insisted upon a full medical examination, despite Sebastian's insistence that he had already been subjected to a stringent one in St Petersburg. It required Sebastian to remove his shirt, which revealed the knife scar inflicted in Washington DC, which Sebastian had not disclosed even to his father.

'Good God, man!' exclaimed the doctor. 'You resemble a battle-scarred veteran. I'm relieved as well as surprised not to find a lasting, debilitating condition.'

'I have been unfortunate,' conceded Sebastian.

'Or fortunate not to have suffered more seriously, from half of what you've recounted,' contradicted Watson.

'Which is what I would like,' said Sherlock Holmes. 'The remaining half of the story.'

Which Sebastian provided over after-dinner port, the two older men contented with their cigars. It lapsed almost into a reverie, Sebastian not setting out to talk at all about Olga, but finding himself doing so and then making no attempt to stop. His only hesitation came at the very end, but then he plunged on: 'I have come to believe Olga very similar to the independently minded free spirit that you have described my mother to have been.'

308

Sherlock Holmes reflected over his glowing cigar for several moments. 'Don't you think you've set your cap a little high, sir?'

'She refers to our situation as an adventure, nothing more.'

'What do you regard it to be?' asked his father.

'That will suffice. And I did pledge myself to be her protector.'

'From what you have told us, she is protected by an army; her father's very words, according to you.'

'I've promised to visit her.'

'Don't expose the princess to danger from your identification by your enemies in St Petersburg,' cautioned Sherlock Holmes.

'We left undetected,' insisted Sebastian, confidently.

'Then we must hope that you remain so,' said his father.

Sebastian very quickly came to regard the Sussex weekend as a very necessary recuperation. Apart from the night of their arrival, he retired early and slept late and dutifully obeyed Mrs Hudson's demands that he eat everything she put before him, as well as extra portions. He embarked upon the exercise of walking, wandering without intended direction across the undulating Downs, a stark contrast to what little he'd seen of the St Petersburg hinterland. Dr Watson occasionally accompanied him while his father tended his preferred rose gardens, and on their first outing Sebastian said: 'How is the wretched problem that concerns us both?'

'A problem no longer,' insisted Watson. 'I'll admit to concern – some initial suspicion even – during the visit to Geneva, Switzerland being such a place of distressing memories. But my apprehension was unfounded and there has been no indication since the time of which you were aware, before you went to Russia.'

'I am relieved.'

'As are we all.'

They'd walked in silence for some time before the doctor said: 'And I believe he has come to accept you as a worthy successor.'

'Which could be a heavy responsibility.'

'Too heavy a weight?'

'One I welcome,' said Sebastian.

Sebastian returned to London alone upon his father's decision to remain longer, impatient to make his travelling arrangements and alert Olga to his arrival, uncertain of the propriety of his staying at the Orlov mansion, which had been one of her parting insistences.

An envelope awaited him in his pigeonhole at the Diogenes Club, and Sebastian accepted it eagerly, expecting it to bear a Paris postal mark but instead saw it had been hand-delivered, addressed only with his name, although in the formal script of a foreign hand.

The envelope contained a tourist postcard, the lithograph of the Winter Palace instantly recognizable, as was the perspective from which it had been drawn to show the highway upon which he and Olga had been travelling when their coach had been attacked.

From his Heidelburg education, Sebastian recognized just as instantly, in the same formal hand, the inscription accredited to Johann von Goethe, Germany's most famous writer – *Ohne Hast, aber ohne Rast*. Aloud, numbed, Sebastian translated: 'Without haste, but without rest.'

His father had known – been able physically to recognize – Professor Moriarty as his nemesis. He had no way, no possibility, of recognizing his, Sebastian accepted. At that moment there was only one recognition, one awareness, his father's words echoing in his mind. *Don't expose the Princess to danger from your identification by your enemies in St Petersburg.*

From which came another recognition. He had no travel plans to make.

310

# Postscript

According to historical records, events that led to the outbreak of the First World War, which Great Britain declared against Germany on August 4, 1914, came as a surprise to the Liberal government of Herbert Asquith. The catalyst was the assassination in Sarajevo by Serbian student Gavrilo Princip of the heir to the Austrian throne, Archduke Francis Ferdinand, on June 28. Austria-Hungary declared war on Serbia, claiming it instigated the plot, on July 28. Russia mobilized along the German and Austrian borders on July 29 and Germany declared war on Russia on August 1 and on France on August 3, invading Belgium the same day.

In his diary of July 31, King George V recorded being awoken at twelve fifty-five a.m. in Buckingham Palace to be told Asquith sought an immediate audience. The King wrote: 'He (Asquith) showed me a draft of a telegram he wanted me to send to Nicky as a last resort to try to prevent war, which of course I did.'

By then Russian mobilization was too far advanced to halt.

Tsar Nicholas II was dominated by the Tsarina Alexandra, a granddaughter of Queen Victoria, through whom he met Gregory Rasputin. After the outbreak of the war, the Tsar assumed supreme command of the Russian army, leading it to several defeats. It was at his headquarters in Pskov that the Tsar was forced to abdicate on March 15, 1917. He and the Romanov family were held by Bolshevik revolutionaries in various locations throughout Russia, confidently expecting rescue by the combined White Russian and Czech army, to understood sanctuary in England. On July 16, 1918, the Tsar,

311

the Tsarina, the haemophiliac Tsarevich Alexei and the four Grand Duchesses were shot by Bolsheviks in the basement of Ipatiev House in the Urals city of Ekaterinburg.

By that time Vladimir Lenin headed the Bolshevik government in St Petersburg, which had been renamed Petrograd. He was carried there from his Swiss exile in March, 1917, in a sealed train provided by the German General Staff, to foment disaffection among Russian soldiers. Briefly exiled to Finland after an abortive Bolshevik coup d'etat, he returned finally, to succeed in overthrowing the provisional government of Alexander Kerensky in the October Revolution. Lenin masterminded the end of the war with Germany in 1918 with the Treaty of Brest-Litovsk, negotiated by Lev Trotsky.

Alexander Kerensky served in the Duma from 1912 until he was overthrown in 1917. Throughout his time in the Russian parliament, Kerensky worked tirelessly to expose Okhrana spies. He was the chief accuser of Roman Malinovsky, who was cleared by a Bolskevik enquiry. After gaining power, the Bolsheviks discovered from Okhrana files that Malinovsky had been a Tsarist agent for seven years. He went before a firing squad with the words: 'I know what is in store for me. I deserve it.'

The previously accepted legend of Gregory Rasputin's murder is that in March, 1916, he was invited to the palace of Prince Felix Felixovich Yusupov, who served the monk cakes poisoned with cyanide. When they failed to kill the man, Yusupov shot him in the heart, but again he did not die, but attacked the prince so violently that another conspirator, Duma member Vladimir Mitrofanovich Purishkevich, had to shoot him again, before dumping Rasputin's body in the frozen Neva.

But a BBC *Timewatch* documentary in October, 2004, suggested surviving photographs of Rasputin's body showed two different bullet holes and one coup de grace to the forehead. It was further suggested in the documentary by Richard Cullen, a retired Scotland Yard commander who examined records of the assassination with intelligence historian Andrew Cook, that the fatal head shot was fired by Oswald Rayner, a schoolfriend of Yusupov's and a member of the British Secret

312

Intelligence Bureau who was known to be attached to the British embassy in March, 1916. *Timewatch* claimed that Rasputin was killed to prevent his negotiating a peace between Russia and Germany that would have released 350,000 German troops to fight on the Western Front.

Quoted on the programme was a surviving memorandum between Rayner's two superiors at the St Petersburg embassy, John Scales and Stephen Alley. It read: 'Although matters have not proceeded entirely to plan, our objective has clearly been achieved. Reaction to the demise of 'Dark Forces' (the code-name by which Rasputin was known) has been well received by all, although a few awkward questions have already been asked about wider involvement. Rayner is attending to loose ends and will no doubt brief you on your return.'